"The Xanth books constitute Anthony's longest and most successful series. . . . They are intended to be kind-spirited, fun reading, a series of wondrous beasts and beings, and most of all, an endless succession of outrageous puns."
—Lee Killough, *The Wichita Eagle*

"Newcomers and old-timers alike will enjoy Anthony's latest collection of truly mind-boggling puns. Every so often, most readers get a craving for a book like this; be grateful to Anthony for continuing to satisfy it."
—*Booklist* on *Swell Foop*

"In *Up in a Heaval*, the twenty-eighth chronicle in Piers Anthony's best-known series, the puns for which the Xanthian corpus is famous are as numerous and outrageous as ever."
—*Booklist*

"This fantasy confection is full of puns, clever mathematical and grammatical lessons. Xanth fans will rejoice at this fast-paced romp."
—*Publishers Weekly* on *Swell Foop*

TOR BOOKS BY PIERS ANTHONY

PIERS ANTHONY

STORK
NAKED

TOR®
fantasy

A TOM DOHERTY ASSOCIATES BOOK
NEW YORK

STORK NAKED

Copyright © 2006 by Piers Anthony Jacob

A Tor Book
Published by Tom Doherty Associates, LLC
175 Fifth Avenue
New York, NY 10010

www.tor.com

Tor® is a registered trademark of Tom Doherty Associates, LLC.

ISBN-13: 978-0-7653-4312-3
ISBN-10: 0-7653-4312-6

First Edition: October 2006
First Mass Market Edition: October 2007

Printed in the United States of America

0 9 8 7 6 5 4 3 2 1

CONTENTS

PARADISE LOST

H ow come that stupid bird is green?" Ted asked. "Is it sick?"

"No, it's just too small to manage a better color," Monica said.

"Children!" Surprise exclaimed. "Don't tease the pet peeve."

"Aw, why not?" Ted asked. "It's just a dumb cluck."

"It can't understand a thing we say," Monica agreed.

Surprise Golem was babysitting the half-demon children, Demon Ted and DeMonica. Her husband and parents were away, scouting for a suitable home for the new family. With her magic talents she could handle the children, but they were trying to set off the peeve. That was mischief.

The peeve eyed Ted. "Your father can't get out of bed. Want to know why?" It spoke in Ted's voice.

Ted swelled up indignantly, but the peeve was already eyeing Monica. "Your mother slithers on her belly," it said with her voice.

Monica opened her mouth angrily.

"Because it may tease you back," Surprise said. "And nothing teases worse than the peeve."

But the battle was fairly started. "I know why he can't get out of bed," Ted said. "It's because Mom keeps him there, blissed out, so he won't be in the way."

"And how does she do that, you ignorant juvenile cross-breed?" the peeve demanded insolently.

"Don't try to answer that!" Surprise said.

"Why not?" Ted asked.

"Because of the Adult Conspiracy, dummy," Monica informed him. "You're only ten years old."

"Well so are you, double dummy!"

"Children, don't fight," Surprise said. "It's no shame to be ten. I was ten once."

"But you outgrew it," Monica said.

"And so will you, in a few more years." It was tricky keeping a lid on it, because both children knew more of the dread Conspiracy than they admitted, because of their half-demon heritage and suspiciously tolerant parents. Surprise didn't want to get blamed for a violation. She was babysitting them because their parents were busy elsewhere and few others could handle them. The two children were not related, but were like mischievous siblings with special powers. They were indeed ten years old, but often acted half that age, reveling in their childishness.

"Yeah, I guess so," Ted agreed, grudgingly satisfied.

But the peeve wasn't satisfied. "That leaves your mother, who can't stand on her own two feet," it said in Monica's voice. That was one of its annoying properties: it borrowed the voice of the one it was with, or whoever it was addressing, so that it seemed to third parties that the victimized person was talking. That could be distinctly awkward at times.

"That's because she's a naga," Monica said. "Nagas don't have feet in their natural forms."

The peeve opened its beak, ready to set the children off again. It lived to insult people, and the angrier it made them, the more satisfied it was. It had finally found a home here because Surprise's father was Grundy Golem, the only one who could match the irascible bird insult for insult. The two got along well. But the last thing she wanted was to have the two half-demons getting into a contest with the bird. The Adult Conspiracy was bound to get tweaked if not outright abused.

"Let's tell a story," Surprise said. Children always liked stories. "About the Adult Conspiracy." Oops; she had meant to name some safe minor adventure, but her nervousness about the Conspiracy had made her misspeak. "I mean—"

"Yes, let's!" both children exclaimed, picking up on it instantly. "With every dirty detail," Ted concluded.

"No, I meant *not* about it," Surprise said desperately.

"You said, you said!" Monica chimed. "Now we have to have it. Exactly how does it work?"

They were really trying to get her in trouble, and knew how to do it. How could she handle this?

"It's not as if it is any mystery," the peeve said with a superior tone that was also Surprise's voice. "All that is required is for the man to take the woman and—"

"Don't you dare!" Surprise said, conjuring a black hood that dropped over the bird's head and muffled it.

"____!" the peeve swore, the badness stifled by the hood. It flapped its wings, lifted into the air, did a loop, and dropped the hood to the floor, where it faded out. It opened its beak again.

"If you say one bad word, I'll lock you in a soundproof birdcage," Surprise warned it.

"You wouldn't dare, you uppity wench!"

A birdcage appeared next to the bird. It had thick sound-absorbent curtains.

The peeve reconsidered. It had brushed with Surprise before, and learned that she could do just about anything once. If she abolished the birdcage, she would not be able to conjure it again. But she could conjure a very similar one, or a bandanna knotted about its beak, or a cloud of sneeze powder that would prevent its talking for several moments and some instants left over. Her magical ability was limited only by her imagination. She was in fact uncomfortably close to being Sorceress level, and might one day be recognized as such when she perfected her ability. That was why she was able to handle the demon children, and they too knew it.

"No bad words, harridan," the bird agreed, disgruntled.

"Idea!" Ted exclaimed, a bulb flashing brightly over his head. "Have the peeve tell about the Adult Conspiracy."

Oh, no—they were back on that. No amount of magic could handle that violation if it happened. She had to change the subject in a hurry. But for the moment her mind was distressingly blank.

Monica clapped her hands. "I thought you were out of ideas, Ted, but that's a good one."

"It is *not* a good idea," Surprise said. "The peeve can't speak a sentence without insulting someone."

But the children knew they were onto something. "Is that true, birdbrain?" Ted asked.

"No, poop head. I just don't care to waste opportunity. I can cover every detail of the Adult Conspiracy without uttering a bad word."

"Wonderful!" Monica said.

"No you don't!" Surprise said. "I'll make a laryngitis spell."

"Awww," the children said together.

"I can tell about it without violating it," the peeve insisted.

"See—the bird's reformed," Ted said eagerly.

"Under a pig's tail," the peeve said. "I'll never reform."

"But you can really annoy Surprise if you make good on your pledge," Monica said with a canny glance. "No bad words, no violation, but you cover the subject and she can't stop you."

The peeve received her glance and sent it back. "You're not half as stupid as I took you for, Harmonica."

"That's DE-Monica, greenface. As in Demon-ica."

"Ick," the bird agreed.

"So it's decided," Ted said. "The bird sings."

Surprise hesitated. The three were ganging up on her, but she was curious how the peeve could do what it said, and maybe it would help get them through until some more innocent distraction turned up. "Very well. But the rules will be strictly enforced."

"Absolutely, honey-pie," the bird agreed with her voice. But there was a shiftiness about its wings that suggested it was going to try to get away with something.

The children sat on the floor facing the peeve's perch. Surprise set about making a snack for them all, but she kept a close ear on the bird. Nothing daunted it except a direct enforceable threat.

"Long ago and far away," the peeve said, "there was no such thing as the Adult Conspiracy. People summoned storks freely and no one cared. Children knew all about it, and watched when they wanted to. That was how they learned how to do it. But then confounded civilization arrived and messed up the natural order. Adults started concealing it, and setting other ridiculous rules such as not letting children hear the most effective words. It seems the adults were jealous of the carefree life of children, so decided to keep interesting things away from them."

"Hear hear," Ted agreed.

Surprise did not see it quite the same way, but as long as the bird stayed clear of key words and concepts she couldn't protest.

"There are also stories that the adults grew fearful of a revolution by the children, so acted to prevent it. After all, suppose children started summoning babies on their own? What further need would there be for adults? They might discover themselves superfluous, and be on track for elimination. They didn't like that, so decided to stop it before the children made their move."

"That's interesting," Monica said thoughtfully. "Something should be done about it."

"Tyrants never yield their power voluntarily," the peeve said. "Power is addictive; they do everything they can to hang on to it."

Now both children were thoughtful. Surprise was disgusted. It wasn't like that at all. She had not been party to the Conspiracy long—only a year or so—but in that time had summoned the stork with her husband Umlaut, and was expecting delivery of her baby at any moment. Babies needed adults to take care of them; children were too irresponsible. So there was good, sensible reason to prevent children from summoning storks. But of course children didn't see it that way. The confounded bird was succeeding in really annoying her, without breaking any rules. In seemingly good language it was insulting the entire adult species.

"It crystallized with little Princess Ivy in the year 1071, thirty-five years ago," the peeve continued. "Adults had been preaching the gospel of secrecy, but it hadn't been very effective; most children saw through it soon, and used bad words, and could have signaled storks if they had really wanted to. They told Ivy she had been found under a cabbage leaf; only later did she learn that babies didn't just materialize under leaves, they were brought there by storks. Her talent was Enhancement, and she Enhanced the story until it became a wider reality. Later she told her twin sister Ida, whose talent is to make real what others who don't know her power believe. Thus the Conspiracy became thoroughly established, extending well into the future and half a smidgen into the past. It has been almost inviolate ever since, and most folk believe it always existed. But it didn't; it was mostly myth until Ivy and Ida made it literal."

Surprise was astonished. Could this be true? It didn't really matter, because certainly the Conspiracy existed now, but the idea of it not existing at some time in the past was subtly disturbing.

"That's really something," Ted said, impressed. "How did you learn about this, peeve?"

"I made it up, crazy boy."

Both children burst out laughing. "You're lying, bird beak," Monica said. "We can tell. You weren't lying before, but now you are."

"Just testing," the bird said, annoyed.

"Say," Ted said. "I heard about a man with a spot on the wall talent with a difference: he could summon them from elsewhere. Some spun, making folk nauseous. More fun."

"And the relevance is . . . ?" Monica inquired snidely.

"If he summoned one from where the Adult Conspiracy first got started, and took it to Princess Eve to analyze it, we could learn exactly how it happened."

The peeve looked at him. "You do have some good ideas, lunatic lad."

"No you don't," Surprise called. "That man is adult; he would never cooperate."

"Awww," both children said together.

Surprise smiled to herself. Not for nothing was it called the Adult Conspiracy. All adults participated, to the eternal frustration of children.

There was a sound outside. Surprise glanced out the window and saw a heavy bird coming to a landing. It looked like a stork.

"The stork!" she cried. "It's making the delivery!"

"Another brat on the scene," the peeve said peevishly.

"Great!" Ted said.

"We never saw a delivery before," Monica said.

Surprise wasn't sure they were supposed to, but there was no way to stop them following her to the door. She opened it, her heart pounding.

There stood the stork, a bundle before him. "Surprise Golem?" he inquired.

"That's me!" Surprise said. "I've been expecting you."

"I am Stymy Stork, with a bundle of joy. Let me handle the formalities, and the baby is yours." The stork used his beak to draw a piece of paper from his vest pocket. That was odd, as he wore no clothing, only feathers. He donned glasses so he could read the note. That was odder. "You ordered a baby, gender unspecified, nine months ago?"

"Yes!" Surprise was so excited she felt faint.

"You are duly married to one Umlaut?"

"Yes. Give me my baby."

"Not so fast," Stymy said. "I'm on probation; I have to follow every rule exactly or I'll get my flight feathers pulled. You are of appropriate age to receive a baby?"

"Yes, I'm eighteen."

The bird perused the paper. "You were delivered in the year 1093. Let's see, that would make you—I'm not good at math—thirteen years old." He did a double take. "That's too young."

"I was five years old when delivered," Surprise said. "That's why I was named as I was: Grundy and Rapunzel had almost given up waiting for me in five years, and then suddenly there I was, late but whole. I really am eighteen."

"I'm not sure of that," the stork said. "According to the rule, age is counted from the moment of delivery forward. I can't complete this delivery."

Surprise was stunned. "But that's my baby! I must have it. You can't let some idiotic confusion deny me my motherhood."

"Take your complaint to headquarters," Stymy said. He put away the paper and glasses, poked his beak into the loop of material tying the bundle together, and lifted it.

"No!" Surprise cried. "Don't take my baby!"

The stork turned, ran down the path, spread his wings, and took off, bearing the bundle away. Surprise was so amazed and chagrined that she just stood there and watched it happen.

Even the peeve seemed taken aback. "Why didn't you scorch his tail and ground him before he got away?"

"That sort of thing is not done to storks," Surprise answered automatically. Yet she might have done it, had she thought of it in time.

"Better go see the Good Magician," Ted suggested. "He always knows what to do."

"Or Clio, the Muse of History, to fix the records," Monica said. "Before that stupid bird delivers your baby to someone else."

Surprise's flustered awareness fought to return to control. She knew she had to do something immediately; it just wasn't clear what. So she grasped at the most reasonable straw. "Good Magician Humfrey. I'll try him. Thank you, Demon Ted."

The boy turned bright pink, including his hair and clothing. The appreciation had caught him entirely off guard.

"Leave us here and go," Monica said. "I'll tell the folk when they return."

That alerted Surprise to practical aspects. "I can't leave you! I'm responsible."

"No problem," Ted said. "Take us along."

Had she not been under such pressure, Surprise would have known better. As it was she made a dreadful decision. "Of course."

She took a moment to formulate a suitable spell, then formed an invisible permanent basket and had the children join her in it. She conjured the basket to the edge of the moat around the Good Magician's castle.

There was the moat monster guarding the drawbridge, which was down. "Hi, Sesame," Monica called.

It was Sesame Serpent, Souffle's girlfriend, emulating a moat monster. She was good at emulations.

"I have to see the Good Magician," Surprise said. "It's urgent."

Sesame shook her head.

"You mean I have to go through Challenges?" Surprise asked, appalled. "I don't have time. I have to get my baby from the stork."

But the serpent was adamant. There was no free passage here. She had her orders.

"You're as bad as the stork," Ted said. "Always got to go by the book, no matter how stupid it is."

"Isn't that a rancid kettle of fish," Surprise's voice said. "Must give you quite an appetite, snake-eyes."

Oh, no! The peeve had come along too.

Sesame frowned at the bird, then coiled like a giant rattlesnake and made ready to strike. It was an excellent emulation, and she clearly knew it was the bird who had spoken. Moat monsters were hard to fool. The peeve fluttered its wings as if ready to fly, but it was obvious that it could not get away fast enough to get beyond the range of the serpent's jaws. "Not that that's necessarily bad," it said hastily. "I've eaten some very nice rancid fish in my day."

Sesame considered, then uncoiled. She had made her point, forcing the bird to back off.

A woman crossed the drawbridge, leaving the castle. Sesame did not challenge her; obviously her business with the Good Magician was done. "Hello," she said brightly. "My name's Susan. I just learned my talent. Now I have to inform my family that I'll be away a year serving my Service for the Good Magician. It's worth it."

"What's your talent?" Ted asked boldly.

"I'm so glad you asked," Susan said. "I can't wait to try it out. I'm supposed to be able to turn spoken words into tangible shapes and colors, which I can then use to make sculptures or paintings. I always wanted to be an artist, but lacked the wherewithal." She concentrated, then spoke: "Red shoes." The red shoes appeared. "Blue trousers." They appeared, dropping on the shoes. "Yellow shirt." It was there on top of the trousers. "White hat." It landed on the pile. "Black gloves." They were there. Then she arranged the items on the ground to form the image of a man. "It's crude, I know, but it's my first effort."

"You're right about it's being—" the peeve started.

"A nice first effort," Surprise said loudly, overriding the bird's insult.

"Thank you," Susan said, pleased. She gathered up the items and walked away.

Unfortunately Surprise was still stuck with the need to run the Challenges, if she wanted to see Magician Humfrey. It was an awful nuisance, but she couldn't afford to waste time arguing. She would simply have to navigate them. There would be three, and her magic would not avail her.

"Sesame, I am babysitting the demon children, Ted and Monica. I won't be able to keep a proper eye on them while handling the first Challenge. Please, would you keep an eye on them and the peeve while I'm busy? I know you're a good person, and this shouldn't conflict with your moatly duties."

The serpent nodded. She would do it.

"What do you know about babysitting?" Ted demanded. "You're just a big snake."

Sesame oriented on him, assuming the aspect of a horrendously strict schoolmarm. Forbidding authority fairly radiated from her.

The demon child quailed. "Not that there's anything wrong with snakes."

There were things to like about Sesame. But now Surprise focused on the first Challenge. The obvious way across the moat was the drawbridge, which remained down across it. But there was now a small lighthouse at its outer landing, blocking the way. There might be a path around it, but when she tried to make it out, the lighthouse flashed so brightly that she was blinded for the moment. That was no good; she had to see where she was going, or she would fall into the moat instead of setting foot on the bridge, and surely wash out.

She walked around the lighthouse to check the far side. It was no better; there was hardly room to skirt it to reach the drawbridge. Acute vision was important. But the lighthouse wasn't flashing now, so she took a step toward it.

The second flash was worse than the first. She had to cover her eyes and wait for her vision to return. This was definitely the Challenge.

Just in case, she tried her magic, invoking a spell of darkness to cloud around the lighthouse. Sure enough, it didn't work; her magic was null during this exercise. She had to get through by her body and wit alone.

Could she manage it by feel? If she squinched her eyes tight shut and shuffled forward with her hands before her, she should be able to feel the path and the wall of the lighthouse, and nudge her way around it to the end of the bridge. Then she saw that in places the moat lapped right up against the house, and the stones looked irregular and wobbly. She was likely to misstep and fall, she couldn't afford that.

She paused to ponder, sure there was some way. There was always a way, in a Challenge. She had missed it so far because she was just blundering through; she needed to use her mind. But how could her mind save her eyes from the flash? She wasn't used to using her mind; her magic talents had solved most of her problems so far.

There must be something special about the lighthouse, some key to getting by it. A key—was there a key to its door, so she could get in and turn off the light? Where would it be?

She looked, but saw no key. Too bad. Now if only there could be some pun key instead. Xanth was mostly made of puns; she had stepped on one more than once, getting disgusting smears of it stuck on the bottom of her shoe. Ugh!

Pun. Her mind circled around that. This was a lighthouse. Could it also be a light house?

With abrupt resolve she shut her eyes and advanced on the structure. She felt the light come on, but she didn't need to see for this. She advanced until her hand touched the curving wall. Then she squatted and reached as far around the tower as she could, her fingers catching in crannies. She heaved.

The house came up. It was feather-light. She carried it away from the moat a suitable distance and set it down. Then she faced away from it and opened her eyes.

The bridge was open. She had cleared the light house.

She went to fetch the children, who were watching a story being acted by the serpent. Sesame emulated one character after another, most effectively. As Surprise approached, she emulated the grumpy Good Magician, and they burst out laughing. Who needed words, with ability like that?

But by the time she got there, they had started another game. Children's lives moved so swiftly! Had she ever been like that, Surprise wondered? She paused more than a moment, to let them finish before taking them away. They were pretending to have special talents, with Sesame as the judge of the best one.

"Summoning flying rugs," Ted said, sitting down on the ground as if riding a rug. "Zooom!"

"Conjuring useful elixirs," Monica said, gesturing as if holding up a vial. "Only I can't control which." She pantomimed sipping. "Beauty cream, I think."

"You turned into an ogress!" Ted said. "That was ugly cream."

Sesame angled her head toward Ted. He had won the exchange, mostly because of his rebuttal of Monica's talent.

"Now I'm making a whole gram," Ted said, shaping a form in the air with his hands.

"That's hologram," Monica said with a superior tone.

"Whatever. It shows what's happening to one person, or animal, or thing. Like maybe a nymph showing her panties."

"Nymphs don't wear panties, dummy."

"Oh, yeah. Well, then, the nymph herself, running around, bobbling. That's almost as good."

"Talent of confusion," Monica said, making spell-casting motions. "So she's there but you can't think to look."

"Oh, mice!" Ted swore.

Sesame angled her head toward Monica. She had won that one.

This seemed to be the best moment to break it off, before the children got tired of it and started something else. "Time to cross the bridge," Surprise said. "Thank, you Sesame."

The serpent nodded, then sank under the water of the moat. Surprise liked her; Sesame had once traveled with Umlaut, helping him deliver letters, in the process bringing him to meet Surprise. That was not a favor to be forgotten. Surprise had liked Umlaut, so naturally married him when she came of age. And signaled the stork, and—

"Darn!" she swore under her breath. The horror of her loss had sneaked up on her.

"Oooo, what you said!" Ted said, scraping one forefinger against the other.

"Mustn't swear in the presence of children," Monica informed her imperiously. But she couldn't hold her severe expression long, and dissolved into giggles.

"She misspoke," the peeve said. "That word is not a full cuss. What she really meant was—"

"On," Surprise said sharply, cutting off the bird while herding them to the drawbridge. Probably it had not really been about to violate the Conspiracy, but she couldn't take the risk.

A man was crossing the bridge, going the other way. His nose was bright blue. "Hey, pinkeye," the peeve called. "Whatcha poke your nose into?"

But the man was not annoyed. "I came to see the Good Magician to learn how to nullify my blue nose. But the Gorgon knew the answer and gave it to me free: I have only to drink the liquid of the beer barrel tree. So now I don't have to serve a year for my answer."

"Well bully for you, beer belly!" the peeve said. But the man was so pleased with his free answer that he still wasn't annoyed. The peeve was, though; it hated to have insults fall flat.

"Maybe you'll get your Answer free, too," Ted said.

"I doubt it," Surprise said. "But it really doesn't matter. I'll pay whatever I need to, to get my baby back."

"I guess that answer stunk your britches," Monica told Ted, putting him in his place as usual. Then she turned momentarily thoughtful. "You know, a nice talent would be the ability to grant wishes, but only for those who have wishes for others and don't know they'll be granted."

"Princess Ida's already got that, dodo," Ted said witheringly.

Monica refused to wither. "It's not the same. If I had that talent, and you wished for Surprise to get her baby back, I could grant it, if you didn't know my talent."

"What dope would grant a wish for someone else?"

"Enough, children," Surprise said. "I think we're somewhere, and I want to concentrate."

The bridge debouched at a garden outside the main castle gate. It was filled with trees of different types. They grew so close together and branched so thickly that it was impossible to pass them to get to the castle gate. So this was the second Challenge.

"Aw, who cares about stupid trees," Ted said snidely. "They have wood for brains."

A branch lifted, sprouting big sharp thorns. "Stay out of this," Surprise said. "It's my Challenge. I may be disqualified if you participate."

"Awww."

"Why do you have to see the old gnome anyway?" Monica demanded. "This is dull."

"If you brats don't shut up, she'll change her mind and

take you home before seeing the grumpy gnome," the peeve warned. "She knows she should have done that before coming here."

Both children went seriously silent. They did not want to miss the action. "Thank you peeve," Surprise said. That shut the bird up too; it wasn't used to being appreciated, and wasn't sure how to handle it.

Now she addressed the crowded copse. It was clear she couldn't simply pick up any of the trees to clear her way, but there had to be a way to nullify their opposition. What could it be? They were all different types, no two the same. Was that a hint? But it hardly seemed to matter whether the species matched; they were all too solid, and as the thorny branch had shown, capable of opposing any effort to pass them.

She pondered, cogitated, considered, contemplated, and finally thought about it. Again she was reminded of how little actual thinking she had done in the past. Her magic had taken care of most things, and her parents Grundy and Rapunzel had handled the rest. But now she had no choice.

She couldn't think of a sensible idea, so she tried a nonsensical one. "Who are you?" she asked the trees. Of course she got no answer. But that gave her a better idea. Maybe she was supposed to identify them. She wasn't sure how that would help, but at least it was an effort.

The nearest tree in the center had leaves with what looked like printing on them. She knew that type. "You're a Poet Tree," she said, laughing.

The tree disappeared.

Surprise stared. She hadn't been expecting anything, but that was something she still hadn't expected. She had named it, and it was gone. Was that a good or bad sign? Then she realized that it had to be the key to the Challenge: she had to name the trees to clear a path through this tight little forest. Good enough.

She looked at the next tree straight ahead. It was a vast ugly thing whose whole aspect was arrogant and negative. She hated it on sight, and wanted to spit on it. In fact she wanted to spit on anything handy; she didn't much like anything that was the least bit unfamiliar or different. That was odd, because she was normally a tolerant person. Why should she instinctively hate a tree? Was there some magic aura making her react that way?

That was it! "A Bigot Tree," she said. Sure enough, the tree vanished. Its wood was notorious, making people get stiff-necked and condemnatory without good reason. It was like reverse wood, only it instilled bad attitudes. Nobody liked the wood of the bigot tree. She hoped never to encounter anything like it again.

The third tree was a considerable contrast. It had a nice ambiance, with many pretty flowers and a sweet smell. She liked it immediately. That was a clue to its nature: what was this nice one?

"Sweet gum?" she asked. The tree did not move.

She hadn't really thought it was that anyway. This tree was amiable throughout. What would perfectly describe that?

Then she had it. "Pleasant Tree!" It vanished. She was almost sorry to see it go; she had really liked its company.

The next tree was another contrast. It seemed to have been burned. Its trunk and leaves were gray and flaky, as if the fire had been so sudden it had consumed all the living substance without affecting the form. All that was left was ashes.

A bulb flashed. "Ash Tree." And it departed.

She was developing a channel through the thick forest. The trees were tight on either side, but she had eliminated four in the center. She was getting the hang of this.

The next tree had normal bark and leaves, but its fruit consisted of an assortment of what seemed to be caged propellers, all of different design, and colorful oblongs. She had never seen anything like this, and had no idea what it was.

"Propeller tree?" But she knew as she spoke that that could not be it; there was no pun. Things without puns had only dubious legitimacy in Xanth. Anyway, many of the fruits had no propellers; they were more boxlike. The tree did not fade.

She reached out very carefully and touched the rim of the nearest fruit. It whirred, dropped to the ground, and buzzed in circles around her before returning to its branch. She touched another, one of the oblongs. This one spread out like the tail of a peacock to display a group of dancing hippopotami whose skirts flared to allow fleeting glimpses of their panties. It was a good thing she wasn't a man; she might have freaked. A third one whirled its blade and produced a series of vile-sounding bleeps. It was cursing!

Surprise paused to ponder further. What were these things? What did they have in common? Only the breeze of their activities, she thought wryly.

Then she got it. They were fans, in the tree. A rotary fan going around her, a fan-tasia showing an ungainly dance, and pro-fan-ity cursing. "In-Fan Tree," she exclaimed, and it vanished.

But her identification seemed to have set up the next tree, because this one bore fruit that was actually tough little babies in helmets and armored diapers. She recognized it immediately as an Infant Tree, but hesitated to say so lest there be some trick. It was too obvious, and too similar to the last one in name if not nature. "Hello, babies," she said tentatively.

"Hello yourself, wench," the nearest baby said. "Don't give us none of that shift."

That startled her. "You talk."

"Small talk," the baby agreed. "Now if you'll get the bleep out of our way, sweetheart, we'll prepare for the march." He turned his head and bawled "Companee—ten-SHUN!" All the other ten hanging babies snapped to attention.

This was ridiculous as well as annoying. She was looking for a baby, but nothing like these military brats. "Infant Tree," she said, and it vanished. Maybe the similarity of names had been intended to make her suspect a ruse.

The next tree bore full-grown men and women in scanty costumes that showed too much of their bodies. They hung in pairs of male and female, but were not paying attention to their immediate companions. They were constantly turning in place and eying others of the opposite gender. In fact they were flirting, exchanging secretive smiles and glimpses of flesh. It seemed they preferred any partners but their own. Surprise was disgusted. Where did these folk think they were, Mundania? Xanth wasn't like this.

But her Challenge was not to be judgmental but to name the tree. It seemed to be the last one, and vanishing it would clear the way through. So what could it be? A Grownup Tree? A Cheater Tree? Those weren't suitable puns.

The people started swinging on their branches, the couples going in opposite directions. The swings became larger, so that they were almost touching their closest neighbors. In a moment, certainly no more than a moment and a half, they would start connecting. Then they were all too likely to do things the children shouldn't see.

A guy reached out and caught the hand of a gal. They drew each other together. She kissed his face while he grabbed her bottom. Surprise heard the children behind her giggling naughtily. The situation was desperate.

Then it came to her with an ugly flash. "Adult Tree." It wasn't a perfect pun, but it worked, and the tree faded out. The way into the castle was clear.

"Come on, children," Surprise called. "We're going in."

"Aww," Ted said, "I wanted to see what those swingers did when they got together."

"After they kissed and groped," Monica agreed.

"And tore off their clothes," the peeve added helpfully.

Exactly. She had acted just in time.

They were now at the entrance to a comfortable room. A woman stood there. Did she represent the third Challenge?

"Hello," Surprise said, uncertain what else to do. Politeness always seemed best when in doubt. "I am Surprise Golem, and these are my charges, Ted, Monica, and the pet peeve."

"I am Ann Serr," the woman said. "I have answers; what are the questions? All of you must respond."

"All? But this is my Challenge, isn't it?"

"If they are to enter the castle too," Ann said firmly.

Surprise sighed. Things just kept complicating. "I suppose," she agreed reluctantly.

Ann looked at Ted. "Ida Moons."

That baffled Surprise. How could Demon Ted ever figure it out?

"Aw, that's easy," the boy said. "What does Princess Ida do when out of sorts?"

He had gotten it! Surprise masked her relief, knowing more was coming.

Ann looked at DeMonica. "Comes the Dawn."

"What does Princess Eve say when her traveling twin sister returns?" Monica asked immediately.

Ann looked at the peeve. "Gross Prophet."

"Who is that huge fat guy dispensing ugly driblets of the future?" the bird asked without hesitation.

Ann looked at Surprise. "Thesaurus."

She knew what a thesaurus was, she thought: a big book of words. But it surely wouldn't do to ask what was the name of such a tome; there needed to be a pun. She couldn't think of any. What an irony: the others all got their questions readily, while she was stuck.

Suppose she failed to find the question? What would she do then? She would have to take the children back, of course, delivering Monica to Nada Naga and Ted to the demoness Metria. But she would lose her baby. That was too horrible to contemplate.

Something nagged at a loose corner of her mind. Metria—what was there about her? Her constant mischievous curiosity about human events, her messed-up words—

A bulb flashed. She had it! "What ancient reptile gives Demoness Metria her many wrong words?" she asked aloud. And of course the answer was the thesaurus.

Ann Serr was gone. Surprise had handled the third Challenge and was free to enter the Good Magician's castle. "Come along, children," she said briskly, as if this were routine.

2

STORK WORKS

Wira appeared. She was Humfrey's daughter-in-law and was the chief castle guide though she was blind. "Hello, Surprise," she said. "I am so sorry for your loss."

So she knew. "Thank you, Wira. I do not intend to lose my baby. That's why I'm here."

There was a look almost of pity in the woman's blank eyes. "Please come this way. The Gorgon has cheese and cookies for the children, along with tsoda pop."

"The Gorgon?" Surprise knew of her, of course, but had never actually met her.

"She is the Designated Wife this month. She likes children."

Oh, right: the man with the blue nose had mentioned her, so of course she was here. The woman with the devastating countenance but nice nature.

They entered the guest room. Assorted pastries and cheeses were already laid out, with pitchers of pop. There was even a perch for the bird, with a variety of colorful seeds. They had evidently been expected.

"Half a greeting, stoneface," the peeve said. "When did you get your burgeoning butt out of Hell?"

"The same time you got your tainted tail out, pigeon poop," the Gorgon replied. "How's your fowl-mouthed beak these days?"

The children tittered. It was clear that the bird and woman liked each other. They had indeed known each other in Hell, and the Gorgon had rescued the bird and brought it back to Xanth.

"I will notify the Good Magician," Wira murmured as Ted and Monica dashed for the goodies and the peeve flew to the perch.

The Gorgon was a tall, stately matron with myriad little snakes in lieu of hair and a veil over her face. This was to stop her from stoning all those who gazed on her visage. Surprise remembered that at one time the Good Magician had made her face invisible, but it seemed that folk found that more disquieting than the veil. "So good of you to come, dear," she said to Surprise.

"It's not a social visit," Surprise said tersely. "I have to recover my baby."

The Gorgon did not comment. "Have some cheese. This is Gorgonzola; I stoned it lightly myself."

"Thank you." Then things abruptly caught up with her, in this moment of relaxation, and Surprise burst into tears.

"I would comfort you if I could," the Gorgon said. "But I fear there is worse to come. Humfrey tried to discourage you from coming. I'm sorry."

Surprise stared at her. Worse than losing her baby? The Gorgon had been to Hell and back; she surely knew. But the shock stiffened her resolve. "I will handle it."

"Meanwhile, which binding do you think looks better for this volume?" The Gorgon indicated a fat but coverless book on a separate table, beside a pile of colored covers. "It's a dyslexicon."

"A what?"

"A dictionary of words spelled backwards. Some of our visitors are backwards, so I use this to translate. It unclutters Humfrey's library a bit. But I want a tasteful cover on it."

Surprise looked at a sample page that was open. NOGROG–Gorgon. The woman had been checking her own entry, understandably. "Maybe a confusing shade of gray?"

"Very good," the Gorgon agreed, and stared hard through her veil at a black wrapper. Daunted, it faded into a confusing shade of gray, and she put it on the book. "A confusing cover for a confusing book. Thank you."

"She was just lucky guessing," the peeve said.

"You're almost as grumpy as Humfrey," the Gorgon said, amused. "Maybe that's why I like you, Sickly Green." To Surprise she added: "The peeve does have a redeeming quality, though it would rather be roasted on a spit than admit it."

Wira reappeared. "The Good Magician will see you now."

Surprise followed Wira up the curving narrow stone stairway to the dark crowded chamber that was Humfrey's office. The gnomelike man was sitting at his desk, poring over a huge tome. That would be his fabled Book of Answers.

"Surprise Golem is here, Magician," Wira murmured, and faded back.

Humfrey looked up. "Give over, girl. This is not for you."

"You haven't even heard my Question!"

"I am not answering your Question. I am giving you apt advice. You have no idea how ugly the situation is. Go now, without pursuing this matter further."

She glared at him, her astonishment shifting toward outrage. "The bleep I will! I want my baby. How do I recover it? That's my Question. I'll perform your year's Service. Give me your Answer."

The Magician shook his head. "You will not be sensibly dissuaded?"

"I will not be," she agreed grimly.

"There will be no Service as such. The mission is more than sufficient."

"I don't understand."

"You will, in time. You are quite certain?"

"Yes."

"Then go to the Stork Works. Che Centaur will accompany you. He knows the way, and has a pass to enter."

"As soon as I return the children and peeve to their homes," she agreed eagerly.

"No. They must go with you." Ted and Monica appeared, evidently done with the Gorgon's refreshments.

"They can't! If there is danger—"

"Their parents have already agreed, knowing the stakes."

"That's impossible! They don't even know their children are here."

Humfrey snapped his withered fingers. "Parents, show yourselves."

The demons Vore and Metria appeared. "We learned while you were tackling the Challenges," Vore said. "My wife Nada knows and reluctantly approves."

"My husband Veleno says it's up to me," Metria said. "My referee."

"Your what?" Surprise asked.

"Reference, judge, arbiter, umpire, determination—"

"Decision?" Surprise asked.

"Whatever," the demoness agreed crossly. "It has to be done. But I insist on coming along."

"No," Humfrey said.

"Listen, gnome-butt, that's my son going into dreadful danger. You can't deny me my protective bent."

"Your what?" Humfrey asked tiredly.

"Talent, faculty, genius, flair, gift, inclination, aptitude, knack—"

"Instinct?"

"Whatever, grump-face. I insist. After all, it's my turn; I never got to see the unclear missives of the Howl of Oinks."

"That's the nuclear missiles of Cuba, Mundania," Humfrey said. "And they weren't in the Bay of Pigs."

"Whatever," she agreed crossly.

"Demoness, only two adults can go on this mission, and they are already accounted for. The rest must be children, animals, mixed-breeds, or other. You do not qualify. Physically, if not mentally or emotionally, you are single-species adult."

Metria considered half a moment. Then she vanished, replaced by a soulful big-eyed little girl in a tattered patch-work dress. "I am Woe Betide," she said. "A pitiful five-year-old orphan waif."

Ted and Monica sniggered. They had seen this coming.

Humfrey glowered down at Woe. "Are you sure you want to invoke this loophole, demoness?"

"O, yes, your Awesome Grumpiness. I am just a poor brave little match girl with matches that give folk their hearts' desires." She produced a box of matches. "Shall I strike one for you, to make you less grumpy?"

He ignored that. "And you won't revert and renege the moment I am out of sight?"

"Never, O Auspicious Ancient." A little halo appeared.

The children's sniggers became stifled snorts. They loved seeing the auspicious grump get teased in his own lair. Metria was pun-intended matchless at annoying folk in any of her guises.

The Good Magician uncorked a small vial and let its swirling candy-colored vapor waft out. "So be it. Remain as you are, for the duration, match child."

All sniggers and snorts were abruptly stifled.

Woe looked alarmed. "Oops! I smell a stasis spell."

"That will keep you as you are for the duration, as agreed," Humfrey said with grim satisfaction. "You weren't going to renege anyway, so it makes no difference, does it, waif?"

"No difference," the tyke agreed woefully.

"There remains the peeve," Surprise said. "It may be ob-noxious, but shouldn't be thrust into danger." As she spoke, the disreputable bird appeared.

"Keep your yap shut, woman," the peeve said politely. "It can't be as dull as Hell."

"The centaur awaits you," Humfrey said, returning his tired gaze to the tome. They had been dismissed.

Sure enough, Che Centaur was appreciating the Gorgon's half-stoned cheese. He was a handsome winged stallion. "I did not realize that I was to have Companions on this dan-gerous quest," he was saying as they entered the room.

"A nice young woman, three naughty children, and an irascible bird," the Gorgon agreed.

"But that's ridiculous! This is not a mission for innocents."

"Who are you calling innocent, hoof-nose?" the peeve demanded. "I have served in Hell."

"And soon wore out your welcome there," the Gorgon said fondly.

The centaur turned and saw them, recognizing them all instantly. "Oh, my. Surprise, you do not belong with this motley crowd."

"The stork took away my baby," Surprise replied evenly.

Che nodded. "Now I understand."

"Well, I don't. What is so dangerous about going to the Stork Works to demand that they correct their mistake and give me my baby?"

"Your baby has probably gone to the same place the Simurgh has. Otherwise the Good Magician would not have put us together. He demanded no Service?"

"No Service," she agreed. "How did you know?"

"Because the mission *is* the Service, and it is extremely disproportionate to the Answer." He frowned. "Surprise, you are such a nice girl, this is hardly fair to you. You must decline."

"Never!"

"I feel guilty, but I can certainly benefit from the support of your myriad talents. Yet your chances of recovering your baby may be unconscionably slim."

"Why? Why is everyone so negative? What is it I don't know?"

"Let's get on our way to the Stork Works, and I will explain," Che said with regret.

They assembled outside the castle. Che had saddlebags full of the Gorgon's cheese and cookies, guaranteed to keep the children and bird occupied so that the two adults could talk on the way. Surprise transformed into a bare-breasted centaur mare and carried Monica and Woe Betide on her back, while Che carried Ted and the peeve. She pretended that she felt perfectly at ease, as centaurs had no shame in being natural, as they put it, but she did feel awkward without clothing. Suppose someone stared at her front? In fact Ted was already doing so, the nasty boy.

They flicked their tails to make themselves and their riders light, spread their wings, and took off. In two and a half moments they were flying high above the forests and fields of Xanth. This was fun, actually, though Surprise knew she would not be able to become the same kind of centaur again unless she fathomed a different spell to accomplish it. She was glad she was flying beside Che, who knew the way, because she would probably have gotten lost at the outset. She was not used to flying, having saved her abilities for future need. Now that future had arrived.

Che wasted no time in incidental discourse. "As you know, I tutor Sim Bird, the Simurgh's chick. Thus I am privy to aspects of the Simurgh's existence that may not be generally known."

"I know Sim is guarded by Roxanne Roc, so is quite safe," Surprise said. "His destiny is to learn everything in the universe. He is a very smart bird."

"True. But now he has a task for which he is as yet unprepared. He has to watch over the universe."

"But that's the Simurgh's job. It will be centuries or millennia before Sim takes her place."

"The Simurgh has disappeared."

Surprise flew several wingbeats before that registered. "She deserted her post? She wouldn't do that."

"Not voluntarily. But she is gone. It is my task to locate and rescue her."

That was daunting indeed. "Do you know where she is?"

"In a general way, yes. And that, I fear, is where your baby went. The Good Magician knows. I asked for his help, knowing that I could not manage it on my own, and he said I would have capable if unusual Companions. I never suspected they would be you and the children. I suppose Metria could help if she chooses."

"No. She is locked into her Woe Betide aspect. I'm not sure how much demon magic the waif can do."

"I have matchsticks," Woe called helpfully.

"Small magic," Che agreed as the waif lost interest. "Ted and Monica will be more capable. As for the peeve—unless we require the aggravation of assorted monsters, that's a serious liability."

"The Good Magician must have reason."

"He always has reason," Che agreed. "But this seems even more deviously obscure than his usual."

"Just where is the Simurge, in general terms?"

"In an alternate universe. An unfamiliar one."

Surprise's mind balked. "An alternate what?"

"There are perhaps an infinite number of realities," Che explained. He was very good at explaining, being a tutor. "Each is much like the realm we know, but not identical. One may be the same as the familiar Xanth, but have one different character. There might be a Surplus Golem instead of a Surprise Golem, for example, able to do half the available talents, each one twice. Yet it seems that little differences can rapidly become big ones. A difference of a single grain of sand might in a thousand years lead to a remarkably different Xanth. There may also be convergent evolution."

"You just lost me."

"I apologize. I explained the concept some time ago to Sim, and forget that it isn't generally known. Suppose that ancestral horses and humans interbreed and in time produce centaurs. Suppose that ogres and unicorns interbreed, and in time evolve to become very similar to centaurs, so that it is hard to tell the two species apart."

"They're converging," Surprise said, getting it.

"Evolving and converging," he agreed. "They are not the same, but seem very similar. So some of the alternate Xanths may be less similar to ours than they appear. It may be a devious situation."

"And the Simurgh is in one of those similar-seeming Xanths?"

"Yes. That much we know. It is a small subset of a very large picture. Unfortunately we don't know exactly which one."

"Why not check them all? How many are there, half a dozen?"

"Half a million dozen, perhaps. The prospect is daunting."

"But you said it's a very small subset."

"A small section of infinity is still infinity."

"Now that I really don't understand!"

Che explained it more carefully, and with time and some straining of her brain she came to realize it was true. Infinity was like a huge cake: no matter how small the slice, it was always possible to divide it further. All one needed was a sharp enough knife, or an apt enough mind.

"And you think my baby is in that same alternate Xanth? Why?"

"Because normally there is no known connection between realities. They are entirely separate, not even knowing of each other. I know of them only because the Simurgh knows everything. She told Sim where she was going, and when she did not return, he told me. It seems that a fissure opened up between realities, allowing folk to pass from one to the other. The Simurgh went to investigate, as this was a thing she did not know about. Then the fissure closed, trapping her. This must have happened at the same time as your stork sought an alternate couple to deliver your baby to. Only the stork returned just before the fissure closed. So it must have been the same Xanth."

"The fissure closed," Surprise said slowly. "How then do we go there, to rescue either the Simurgh or my baby?"

"That is where it gets complicated. It seems that there is a way to travel between realities, but it has not been used before, because there is no control over which realities connect. Now we must use it. The storks have the secret; the Stork Works connect to all realities, so they can deliver anywhere. The problem will be locating the right reality."

"Out of a small infinity," she said. "That sounds difficult."

"Difficult and dangerous," he agreed. "We run the risk of getting lost ourselves, and being similarly trapped away from our own Xanth. We also run the risk of encountering something lethal. There is a smell of something ugly here, but we don't know what it is. That is why the Good Magician tried to discourage you. He knows you could lose much more than your baby."

Surprise fastened on something else. "An alternate couple for my baby. I thought the storks were exceedingly choosy. Mine was; it balked on a mistake about my age. How could he just deliver my baby to just any other couple?"

"He couldn't," Che agreed. "He would have to find the next closest couple, in a hurry, because storks have tight schedules. That must have been one beyond the fissure."

"What, an ogre and unicorn?" she demanded bitterly.

Che laughed, briefly. "By no means. It would have to be an alternate Surprise and Umlaut couple who lacked a baby."

"Another *us*?" Somehow that aspect hadn't sunk in before.

"Yes. The fissure must have made that possible just when the stork needed to place the baby, so he didn't need to return it to the Stork Works and trigger an investigation. A remarkable coincidence."

"A remarkable foul-up!" she said. "He didn't even wait for me to get the record corrected." Then she realized there was something else. "When you say 'remarkable coincidence,' that's not exactly what you mean, is it?"

"True. I tend to question remarkable coincidences."

"Please, I'm not nearly as smart as you are. Tell me in plain language."

He sighed. "I dislike being unkind. But the unusual nature of the coincidence, and the seriousness with which the Good Magician is taking it, suggests to me that this was not sheer chance. I suspect someone deliberately stole your baby. That is why it is apt to be difficult to recover it. You will not be able simply to clarify the error and get it back. You may encounter opposition. Someone might try to do you harm, rather than yield your baby."

Surprise felt a chill. Indeed, Humfrey's attitude was making ugly sense. Steal a baby, and if the mother was bothersome, get rid of her. She might indeed lose more than her baby.

Still, she persisted. "If my baby went to an alternate Surprise and Umaut, how could they hurt me? They would have to be like us, and we wouldn't hurt them."

"And of course they wouldn't try to steal your baby," he agreed. "That is why I suspect some malign influence."

"What could there be? We're just an ordinary couple. Who would care about us?"

Che glanced sidelong at her. "You are hardly ordinary, Surprise. You were delivered five years late, with a truly remarkable talent barely shy of Sorceress caliber. Umlaut did not even exist; he was a temporary construct made to facilitate a Demon wager. You with remarkable bravery put your very soul on the line to enable him to become real. Now he has half your soul, on loan from the Demon Jupiter, and you have the other half, parked in you by the Demoness Fornax for convenience. Things were all up in a heaval before the Demons decided on that compromise."

"Well, since then we've been pretty ordinary."

"Still, this perhaps provides a clue. There are foreign Demons in your background. They are of course forbidden to interfere in the Demon Xanth's dominion, but since Demons have no souls of their own, they lack conscience and will cheat if they discover opportunity. They could legitimately take your two half-souls if they chose."

"Actually, we have whole souls now," she said. "Souls regenerate in living creatures of human derivation."

"True." He thought for most of a moment. "So if they took back their half-shares now, it would not really affect you and your husband. But suppose the Surprise and Umlaut in the other reality did not get those half-souls?"

"Making them just like us, except for no consciences or decency," she said.

"They might not have cared to go to the trouble of signaling the stork themselves, but found it easier to steal your baby."

Surprise stared at him. "A couple—just like us—but completely unscrupulous."

"Who fooled the stork into delivering to them."

Surprise was appalled. "I find that hard to believe." But it was getting easier the more she considered it.

"Of course this is far-fetched," Che said. "It would be an amazingly complicated way to get a baby, when I understand most couples don't really mind signaling the stork. So probably that isn't the explanation."

"Probably not," she agreed. But the chill was taking root in her bones. Magician Humfrey had urged her not to undertake this quest; his reasons might be starting to show. "But about these many realities—are there Demons associated with each too, as with ours?"

"My understanding is that Demons are infinite too, so that there is a thin slice of each in each reality. Thus a Demon has only to focus on a particular slice to be there, when it chooses. But it is probably best not to invoke any Demons if we can avoid it."

"I agree," Surprise said, shuddering. The Demons had virtually infinite powers, and considered the residents of Xanth as little better than inconsequential bugs, as a general rule. The Demon Xanth had married one such bug, as it were, but that was probably more like a game for him.

"We are approaching the Stork Works," Che said. "This is strictly off-limits territory; only the fact that the Good Magician arranged for passes for us makes it possible for us to visit. They surely won't let us know any of their secrets. Fortunately we don't need their secrets; we simply need the stork who misdelivered your baby."

Surprise gazed down at the complex. It looked like a giant clump of mushrooms with tops of many pastel colors. As they drew closer she realized that each mushroom was the size of a house. In fact they were buildings, with storks flying busily between them. There were no sharp edges or corners; everything was rounded and looked soft enough not to hurt a baby. The largest was in the center, with a line of storks entering one side and emerging the other side, carrying bundles. That had to be where the babies originated.

They came to a landing at an outbuilding labeled INFOR-

MATION OFFICE. A stork with an officious hat emerged immediately to challenge them. "I am Stifle Stork, Officer of the Day. What are you doing here? No visitors are allowed. Especially not children. Go away."

Ted, Monica, Woe, and the peeve opened their mouths. "Silence!" Surprise snapped warningly before they could get them all kicked out. She retained her centaur form because once she reverted to her human form, she would not be able to make that particular transformation again. She would have to become something else that was capable of carrying the children. It was better this way.

Che showed their passes. The stork eyed them. "Well, it seems you are entitled to information, but you can't go beyond this spot," he said grudgingly. "What do you want here, before you go away? Remember, we will not vouchsafe the secret of the origin of our babies."

"We need to talk with the stork who didn't deliver Surprise Golem's baby," Che said.

"That is hard to believe. We always deliver."

"He balked on a technicality," Surprise said angrily.

The stork produced a tablet with a long list. "Name?"

"Stymy Stork," Surprise said.

The stork sighed. "Naturally it would be him."

"He makes a habit of not delivering babies?" she asked sharply.

"A habit of fouling up. He is on probation. I wish he would go away too."

"So he said. He refused to deliver my baby because he thought I was too young. He followed a stupid rule."

The stork eyed her. "You look like a mature filly or young mare to me."

"I am. But there is a confusion in the records."

"And you are?"

"Surprise Golem. I am presently in another form."

The stork checked pages. "Surprise Golem," he read. "Age thirteen, according to date of delivery."

"That's the error. I was delivered five years late. I am eighteen."

"Five years late? That is highly irregular. This will have to be reviewed by headquarters. Supervisor Stork will decide. Then you can go away."

"Meanwhile please bring Stymy Stork to us," Che said.

The stork nodded. "That I can do." He flipped more pages, found the name, and tapped on it with a feather. A small pattern of dots flew out and disappeared. "There will be a brief delay. In the interim I must identify the other members of your party for our records."

"I am Che Centaur," Che said.

"Of course; you are generally known. But who are the children? Kindly name them with their ages for ready verification." He had his list poised.

Surprise established an adult Glare to keep the children from making smart-bottom remarks as she identified them. "Demon Ted, age ten." She paused as the stork checked the list, which was evidently comprehensive. "DeMonica, age ten." Pause. "Woe Betide, age five."

Stifle's feathers stiffened. "Who?"

"Woe Betide. She is—"

"We have no record of ever delivering that child."

"That's because I was never delivered, your Storkship," Woe piped up. "I am the child aspect of the demoness Metria."

"The perpetual word-tangling mischief maker! We don't want your kind here."

"She is locked into the child mode," Che said quickly. "Woe Betide is sweet and innocent."

"I find that hard to believe."

"So do we," Che said with a smile. "But it seems to be so."

"Very well, I suppose. I will make a special note." Then the stork did a double take. "Demon Ted: there is an asterisk by that name."

"What did you call me, feather-head?" Ted demanded.

"Asterisk is not a bad word," Che said. "It simply means there is an additional note about you."

"And what a note," Stifle said. "You are notorious. In one of the alternate realms you discovered a stork resting after a delivery and slipped a sliver of reverse wood in among its feathers. Thereafter that stork delivered several babies to the wrong parents. It became a huge mess. When we tried to correct it, some parents were attached to their wrong babies and refused to give them up. Finally the demon Xanth had to intervene, and the Stork Works got a black mark." He paused, for Ted and Monica were rolling on the floor laughing.

"But that wasn't in this reality," Surprise said quickly. "He wouldn't do that here."

"Sure I would," Ted said gleefully. "What a great joke."

"He didn't do that here," Surprise said, wasting another glare on the unpenitent boy. "It was surely a fluke."

"Hardly that," Stifle said grimly. "In another alternate he participated in a hostile takeover of the Stork Works. That truly smells."

"But not *this* reality," Surprise repeated.

"Perhaps true," Stifle agreed dubiously. "But he is banned from those realities where he committed those crimes."

"Aw, who cares?" Ted asked.

"*We* do," Che said severely. "If the reality we need turns out to be one of the banned ones."

"Hey, you forgot me," the peeve said.

"A talking bird!" the stork said, startled.

"*You* talk, baby-brain!"

"We don't deliver birds, so you are not listed."

"Then how do you get baby storks, pinhead?"

"We summon the Man who brings the incipient egg, of course."

Then another stork flew to the office. This was Stymy; Surprise recognized him by the marks of the spectacles he wore when reading. "You summoned me?"

"Talk with these folk," the office stork said. "So they will go away."

"Where did you take my baby?" Surprise demanded.

Stymy blinked. "I don't deliver centaurs."

"I am Surprise Golem, transformed for now to centaur form. It's my talent. The supervisor will review my case and verify that I am really eighteen years old. Meanwhile, we have to recover my baby. Where did you take it?"

"I'm not sure I am allowed to divulge such information."

Surprise glanced at the office stork. "Tell him to cooperate with us."

A fluorescent bulb flashed over the office stork's head, the kind that denoted a quirky but effective notion. "I will do better than that. I will assign him to your mission so you will all go away."

"All we need is the information," Che said.

"I can't tell you," Stymy said. "I will have to show you."

"Why can't you tell me?"

"Because the fissure closed up and there is no longer a direct route there. But I will know it when I see it."

"Good enough," Stifle Stork said. "Go away with them. Don't come back until they are satisfied, if then."

"But it's in another reality."

"They will doubtless get there," Stifle said. "Stay with them until they are satisfied."

"I'm not sure about this," Surprise said. "How can we go there if the fissure closed?"

"The storks have access to all realities," Che said. "I believe it is a particular spell they do not share with others. They even have access to parts of Mundania, to deliver to conservative families."

"Then why hasn't the Simurgh gone to the Stork Works in that reality to return herself?"

"That remains a mystery I mean to solve." Che looked around. "But first we need to obtain the Mask."

"Mask?"

"The Reality Mask. It sifts and sorts realities according to parameters we can select, so that we can reduce the number of Xanths to check. With Stymy Stork along, we should be able to zero in on the right one fairly efficiently, then go to where he delivered your baby." He paused. "However, it may not be easy to obtain the Mask."

"Nothing is ever easy," Surprise muttered. "Let's get on it. Where is the Mask?"

"A fiery nymph has charge of it, on Lion Mountain. It is a fair flight there from here."

"Then by all means get started." She looked at Stymy. "Follow us, wherever we may go."

Stymy nodded glumly.

The children mounted the centaurs, who spread their wings and took off. The peeve and Stymy followed.

As they achieved cruising altitude, Surprise tried to befriend the stork flying beside her, knowing that they would be dependent on him to locate her baby. "I realize that you were just doing your job as you saw it," she said carefully. "I can see that the Stork Authority is very strict. Do you care to tell us how you got put on probation?"

"It's no secret," Stymy said glumly. "I am cursed by bad luck, whether I'm working the Gold Coast, the Silver Coast, the Copper Coast, or the extinct Ivory Coast. I do the best I can, but things go wrong."

"I know the feeling," Surprise said sympathetically. She really did feel it, now that she was coming to know the stork. He had evidently been around, but was obviously very low in the stork hierarchy.

"First I flew through an invisible forget whorl that wasn't on the chart. I suffered only a glancing blow, but it was enough to lose the baby's name. I delivered the little girl safely, but she never knew her name until she grew up and quested for it. I got a reprimand for that, but I don't see how anyone could have known that whorl was there."

"Forget whorls are always mischief," Che said, flying close enough to join the dialogue.

"And there was the time a boy kissed a girl so ardently it half-summoned the stork. I got struck by the signal, and almost put in the order before realizing that it was incomplete. That was a close call."

"Just how are stork signals handled?" Che asked. He glanced back at the children, who were listening intently. "I don't mean how the signals are made, but once they are on their way. There must be a great deal of information encoded in those three dots of the ellipsis."

"There is," Stymy agreed. "One dot identifies the parents, their species, ages, state of marriage, and such; you'd be surprised how some try to send illicit signals when they don't qualify."

"Not necessarily," Surprise said grimly. "Remember, I was balked on an age error."

"Yes. Some thirteen-year-old girls—well, never mind. The second dot describes the baby in general terms: species, gender, appearance, potential, preference. The third dot powers the connection, locating the nearest stork and identifying the spot where the signal was made, which serves as a reference for delivery. It is all very efficient."

"Efficient?" Surprise repeated. "A nine-month delay is efficient?"

"It takes forever to catch up on the paperwork. Even so, there can be problems. Once the address dot was incomplete and I had to leave the baby in the flowers."

"You left a baby by itself?" Surprise asked, shocked.

"I had no choice. The parents met at a love spring, had a brief but intense session, then separated and never returned. Nine months later I brought little Azalea to the designated coordinates, but had no information where either parent had gone. I couldn't take her back to the Stork Works; they have a no-return policy. There was nothing to do but leave her in the flowers and hope for the best. As it turned out, local flower fairies discovered her and raised her. She had a talent of conversing with flowers. That was fifteen years ago; as far as I know, she's fine. I check on her every so often, just to be sure."

"I should hope so," Surprise said severely. "I thought it was bad when I was delivered five years late, but to leave a baby like that—" She broke off, lest she say something unkind. She was not an unkind person.

"Then I ran afoul of the stork-eating monster," Stymy continued. "I had to make a wide detour around it, and that made me late delivering. In fact there was a backlog, and another black mark."

"Don't they do something about that sort of thing?" Surprise asked. "Or at least post warning signs?"

"No, it's up to the individual storks to find safe routes. The authorities are not sympathetic about excuses. They say deliveries must be made on schedule and that's that." He glanced warily at her. "That's why I had to find another couple for your baby, in a hurry. Another black mark would put me in the soup."

"Stork soup!" the peeve said, and all three children giggled. But Surprise noticed that Stymy did not seem half a whit amused. Instead he shuddered.

"That's literal," Che said, catching on.

"His goose is cooked," the peeve said, and there was another chorus of giggles. "Maybe someone should drop an F-Bomb on him."

"What's an F-Bomb?" Ted asked.

"When it explodes, it makes everyone in the vicinity explode with proFanity."

That set off the children again. They loved the concept, even though they knew no proFane words.

Che's bow appeared in his hands, a wickedly long arrow nocked. "I wonder if I can still score on a distant flying bird?" he murmured musingly. "If an obnoxious one should happen to appear in my vicinity."

The peeve's beak snapped shut. So, curiously, did the mouths of the children.

Surprise changed the subject. "Perhaps you can answer something I have wondered about. We know that some talents attach to the souls, and some to the bodies. Is there a reason for that?"

"Not a good one," Stymy said. "The delivery storks are supposed to pick up the assigned talents at the same time as the babies, and fasten the talents securely to the souls. Usually the talents are already anchored, but when they aren't, then the storks have to patch them up. But some are lazy and hook them to the bodies instead. They get away with it because it generally goes unnoticed, and it saves them time on the deliveries."

"It's a wonder you remain in a largely thankless job," Che said.

"Oh, it's a good job," Stymy said. "I love babies, and it is wonderful to see how happy their families are to have them. It's just the stork authorities that are a pain in the tail feathers. Sometimes I wish I could transfer to Mundania."

"Mundania!" Surprise said, appalled. "But there's no magic there."

"Not much that's recognizable," the stork agreed. "They do have rainbows, mirages, and things called cars that cause it to rain when they are washed. But some Mundane families still prefer to have their babies delivered the old fashioned way, storked, as Che noted, instead of the messy newfangled inconvenient do-it-all-yourself fad that others attempt. So there is business, and I understand that there are stork nests in cathedrals in Iberia, Mundania. I would like to operate out of a cathedral. That would have a lot of class."

"Perhaps you will, some day," Surprise said. "That might be for the best." She was satisfied to let the dialogue lapse.

3

MOUNTAIN LION

We are approaching Lion Mountain," Che announced. "Now it may become problematical."

Surprise did not like the sound of this. "Don't we just need to approach the fiery nymph you mentioned?"

"We do, but the problem is the mountain. It doesn't necessarily appreciate visitors."

"Can't we simply fly over it until we come to the nymph's residence?"

"Hardly. It would snap us out of the air and consume us in a fraction of one bite."

"Lion Mountain," she said carefully. "Would that be literal?"

"It would be," he agreed. "Depending on its mood. If it is Lion Mountain, we should be able to pass. But if it is Mountain Lion, we would be foolish to risk it."

"How do we know which mood it is in?"

"By whether it snaps us up, or doesn't."

Was he being difficult? "I may be mistaken," she said

even more carefully, "but I am not at all certain I care to gamble on its mood."

"I thought you might feel that way. So we'll have to land and see if we can walk up it without its noticing."

"Why wouldn't it notice?"

"Well, an animal generally doesn't notice fleas until they bite, and we should try to avoid biting it."

"We walk," she agreed, relieved. Her centaur form could readily do that as well as fly.

"There is something you may not know about Lion Mountain," Stymy said. "I have not made deliveries here, so can't be sure, but I have heard a rumor that it may be dangerous in other ways than leonine."

"What ways?" Che inquired.

"I don't know, but my source was credible."

"A credible nonspecific rumor?"

"Yes." The stork seemed unconscious of any irony, perhaps because there were no ironwood trees growing nearby.

"So how do you propose we investigate this rumor?" Che asked. It occurred to Surprise that his patience might be thinning, though that was just an impression.

"We should land and inquire of a local resident. My stork sense tells me that one of my clients is in this vicinity." He paused, startled. "In fact it is Azalea, the girl I told you about."

"A fifteen-year-old flower fairy?" Surprise asked dubiously.

"She is not a fairy. She was raised by the fairies, but she is physically human."

"And she would know of this vague rumor of danger?"

"She might. Her talent is conversing with flowers, and flowers can know special things. At any rate, she is a responsible creature, though I'm not sure what she would be doing in a place like this."

"Smelling flowers," Surprise muttered. She thought she was inaudible, until she heard the children tittering.

The stork guided them to a landing place beside, sure enough, a field of flowers. A startled nymph with flower-colored hair gazed at them as they landed, ready to flee.

"Azalea!" the stork called.

"Stymy!" she responded gladly. "I haven't seen you in two years."

So this was Azalea, not a nymph but a girl with a nymphly shape. Some girls could manage that when they were young enough.

"I have been busy getting into trouble," he said. "As usual. Now maybe you can help my associates."

Azalea flounced her hair, and a few petals wafted out. "Flying centaurs can fly and think much better than I can. Are they looking for some special flower?"

Che approached her as the children jumped off and frol-icked among the flowers of the field. "Allow me to introduce myself. I am Che Centaur, on an urgent mission for the Simurgh. We need to see Pyra up on the mountain, but fear nebulous danger. Do you know anything of this?"

Azalea gazed up at him appraisingly, and Surprise real-ized that Che was in fact a handsome stallion. Nymphs no-ticed such things. "What does that hothead have that I don't?" she demanded, inhaling. It seemed that the girl did not regard age or species as much of a barrier. Some of them knew more of the Adult Conspiracy than they were sup-posed to, and heedlessly exploited its dangerous aspects.

"The Reality Mask."

The nymphly bosom deflated. "Oh, that. Well, I have bad news for you. You can't readily get there."

"Because of the supposed danger?"

"That depends how you see it. The mountain is sur-rounded by love springs. Just being near that lake of elixir gives a girl wild notions."

That explained the girl's attitude, Surprise thought.

"That's it!" Stymy said. "I remember now. That forget whorl must have faded it. You have to wade or swim through love water."

This did indeed give Che pause. "This is standard love elixir? Male loves nearest female, and vice versa?"

"Yes," Azalea said. "I have seen creatures there. I couldn't make out exactly what they were doing, but always male and female. It's not safe to touch or drink that water unless you have someone you want to be very friendly with." She smiled a trifle sadly. "I wish I had someone to be friendly with."

"Not at your age," Che said.

"Of course," Azalea agreed reluctantly.

"We can't take the children through that," Surprise said.

"We can't take *ourselves* through it," Che said. "Not without compromising our situations."

"Actually, you look like a nice centaur couple," Azalea said. "You might make it through if you kept wading, betweentimes."

"That is out of the question," Surprise snapped. "We are not a couple."

Azalea shrugged. "Too bad."

"Then I am afraid we shall have to fly across after all," Che said with regret.

"No!" Surprise was horrified. "The risk is too great."

"We must be practical. We can't complete our mission without the Mask, and even then it may be a considerable challenge. Unless we want to give up now, we shall have to take a risk."

Surprise cudgeled her reluctant mind. "Suppose I revert to my natural form, thus recovering my ability to do other magic? I could ride your back as you fly across, and fend off any threats."

"The Mountain Lion strikes too rapidly and massively to resist unless you are savagely prepared," Che said. "We would still be severely risking our lives by flying."

"Then I could ride you as you wade across, and try to counter the elixir."

"A whole lake full of it? Unless you achieve quite strong immunity for both of us, that too is a considerable risk."

Surprise knew it was. Their choice of risks seemed to be between death and illicit love. She made an uncomfortable decision. "I think Umlaut would understand. Would Cynthia?" Cynthia Centaur was Che's mate.

"Yes. She is very rational, of course."

"I think that once clear of the lake and free of contact with any of its elixir, I could make a spell to nullify its effect. Does this seem to be a reasonable compromise?"

"Yes, more rational than emotional. But it does not account for the children."

"I can babysit them," Azalea said. "I'm old enough for that. Maybe we can make a deal."

"No wading," Che said.

She laughed. "I didn't mean that. I am traveling, seeking my fortune. I want to visit strange places and see weird things, if I can safely discover them. Then when I come of age I'll bring some nice young man here and take a swim, and settle down with him."

"You are asking to accompany us?" Che asked.

"Yes. You are going on a great dangerous adventure; I can tell. I'll be safer traveling with you than by myself, especially with Uncle Stymy along. Already I have encountered males who—well, I don't know what they wanted, but I was pretty sure it would have violated the Adult Conspiracy."

"It would have," the stork agreed grimly.

Che remained dubious. "I am not at all sure you would be safer with us than on your own."

"But I'll surely see weirder things with you than on my own. That counts."

"You surely will," he agreed. "But you may also be risking your welfare or even your life. We are going where few if any Xanthians have gone before."

Azalea clapped her hands with nymphly glee. "Wonderful!"

Che looked at Surprise. "We do need separate care for the children, if we face what we fear we face." But she could see that he was looking for an excuse to turn down the girl. He probably had not been thrilled to have to travel with Surprise, and a younger girl would be that much more trouble. She agreed, so it seemed it was up to her to nix the notion.

"We do," Surprise agreed emphatically, thinking as fast as she could manage on short notice. "But the last thing we need along is an adventurous girl. Let's make some other deal."

"She is correct," Che told Azalea. "Is there any other exchange we might fairly make?"

Azalea frowned. "I see I must be more candid. I have another reason to travel. I have a twin sister, Lotus, who talks to water flowers, just as I talk to land flowers. She disappeared a month ago, and I fear for her welfare and want to find her."

"You have a twin?" Stymy asked, astonished. "How could I not know this?"

Azalea seemed very faintly amused. "You delivered a single bundle. I guess you didn't open it."

"I didn't," the stork agreed. "But when I checked on it another day, you were all I saw."

"I guess Lotus was napping at that moment. So you thought there was only me, and didn't notice her. It really didn't matter; the flower fairies took good care of us both, and helped us to develop our talents."

The stork shook his head. "I fouled up more than I thought."

Azalea returned her attention to Che and Surprise. "Since I have no idea where she is, I must travel widely, hoping for the best. All I know is that she was in this region, because I found one of her lotus petals, and then must have gone somewhere else, as there's no sign of her here now."

That put a different face on it. Surprise felt guilty. "Maybe we could help you find her. Using what we get from Pyra."

"That might be feasible," Che agreed.

"It's a deal," Azalea said quickly.

Surprise was relieved. "You and Stymy remain here with the children until we return, which we hope won't be long. Then we'll do our best to locate your sister."

"Great," Azalea said. "I miss her so much." She looked across the field of flowers at the children. "Kids! Get out of those poppies."

"Poppies!" Surprise exclaimed. "Aren't they the kind that—?"

"Yes, but the effect isn't very strong," Azalea said. "I told the poppies to turn it down."

Surprise decided not to question that further. The girl's talent was useful. "Then let's go." She kept her centaur form, as it was easier to keep his pace.

"What about me?" the peeve demanded peevishly.

Che smiled. "Now if we thought of it, we might say that we don't want a loud-beaked bird accompanying us and insulting the mountain lion and causing it to become dangerously aware of our intrusion. But since we lack the wit to think of that, we'll just say that there may be need to divert some stray monster that threatens the children, and we know of only one creature capable of insulting a monster to death. So for the good of the children, and incidentally the chance to have verbally at some really thin-skinned monster, we believe you should remain here."

The peeve considered. "You are dangerously smart, centaur."

"Thank you."

"That wasn't a compliment!"

"And my suggestion wasn't a compliment either."

The peeve was plainly disgruntled, but shut up. It did recognize when it was overmatched.

Without further ado they forged into the marsh that bordered the lake. By mutual consent they moved as rapidly as was feasible, to get beyond the sight of the children before the water had much effect.

Surprise felt that effect almost immediately. She became acutely aware of the stallion beside her, handsome, very smart, and age twenty-one. Meanwhile she was reasonably fetching, having selected a good centaur shape, but not remotely in his intellectual league. That made a difference.

"How are you holding up?" he inquired without looking at her.

"I am quite aware of you, and my admiration is intense, but I believe we have no future together, regardless of the effect on other people we associate with."

"How so?"

"There is a good deal more to a relationship than reproduction. Practical considerations make that awkward. I pre-

fer an intellectual appreciation, to the extent that is feasible."
She realized that she was talking like a centaur. Well, she
was one, for now.

"How is it of limited feasibility?"

Why was he questioning her like this? "I am not nearly as
smart as you are. For example, I could never have handled
the pet peeve the way you did. Therefore I have little to offer
you, regardless of what you may offer me. I recognize that."

"You are thinking like a centaur."

"I am trying to, yes."

"There is something you may not have fully appreciated
about centaurs. We are rational rather than emotional. We do
have emotions, but they are separate from and subservient to
our higher intellects. We lack the attitudes about modesty
and sexuality that human beings possess. We honor significant aspects of the Adult Conspiracy when in the presence
of humans so as not to embarrass them unduly, but they are
largely meaningless in centaur society."

"I am not sure I understand your thrust." Then she wished
she had not used that particular word.

"We are capable of loving without attempting to repro-
duce. You have just expressed a centaur attitude."

"You are saying that we may be knee-deep in love elixir,
but we don't have to react like—animals or humans?"

"I was concerned that you, as a transformed human being,
would retain your human attitudes. Instead you have
adopted the centaur mind-set. That makes the centaur approach feasible."

"Centaurs are proof against the love elixir!" she exclaimed, amazed.

"By no means. It has caused me to love you. Fortunately
this does not require me to do anything with you that would
embarrass you at such time as you return to your human
form."

"But I'm not—in fact I am stupid compared to you."

"That is an unfortunate human concept. Each species pos-
sesses the mind it requires to function optimally. Humans
are less rational and more emotional than centaurs, but have

their points. You have phenomenal magic together with courage, common sense, and compassion. I love those things in you, literally. I know this is the immediate effect of the elixir, but it would have occurred in the course of our association regardless. You are worthy as a person."

Surprise found herself almost overwhelmed by his kind words. That, too, was an effect of the elixir. At the same time she was immensely relieved that the particular effect she had anticipated had not occurred. "Thank you."

"Now that we have felt the impact and expressed ourselves, there is no need to address this subject further. We must proceed to accomplish our mission."

"Agreed." But she remained transported by the wonder of it. Love that was not possessive or guilty. That would not interfere with their other commitments.

They came to the inner verge of the lake and trotted along through the forest there. They were on Lion Mountain, and had not gotten snapped up. They moved on up the slope, their centaur bodies handling the effort well. Now was the time to see if she could work a spell to nullify the effect of the elixir, but maybe it wasn't necessary.

The ground was solid, but moved somewhat, as might the body of a monstrous animal as it breathed. Which aspect was dominant?

In due course they reached the summit. Now Surprise could see that it was in the shape of a huge lion's head. At its top, between two peaks in the shape of ears, stood a castle. She realized that the castle was rather like an elaborate hat, or a crown.

There was no forest surrounding the castle. Instead the area seemed to have been burned. That signaled the nature of its occupant.

"Something maybe you should know," Woe Betide piped up. "Here there be monsters."

Che halted at the edge of the scorched plain. "You are a child, but of course possess the knowledge of your adult form, excluding matters restricted by the Adult Conspiracy. Your two adult forms have gotten widely around, naturally, in the course of their mischievous quests. What do you know about Lion Mountain?"

"That there is a deal between Pyra, Mistress of the Mask, and a number of male and female brutes." Woe spoke with solid vocabulary and syntax, another legacy of her wide background. "Whoever comes through the love lake will fall in love with the first creature of opposite gender seen. Pyra doesn't want that to be her, because for all she knows it could be a three-eyed troll, so she lets assorted monsters surround the castle, and any visitors will encounter one of them first, and fall in love. Then the monster gets to depart with its love-slave."

"But doesn't that tend to isolate Pyra?" Surprise asked.

"Sure. D. Vore once passed her way on other business, and she almost kissed him to death with fiery passion. She was so mad to learn he was already married to Xanth's most beautiful naga princess that she scorched all the furniture."

The other children tittered, and the peeve let out a loud caw-caw-caw. Startled, Surprise looked at them, and there were none. They had been left beyond the lake, and she had imagined their likely reaction. She would have to tame her half-guilty imagination.

"Warning taken, thank you," Che said. "With respect to both monsters and mistress." He glanced at Surprise. "Fortunately we shall be able to explain to both that we crossed the lake together, so our love is already taken despite the pre-emptive effect of the elixir."

That did seem to be a viable story, Surprise thought. But she suffered a twinge. She had thought that her love for Che was largely intellectual, in the centaur manner, but now realized that it wasn't limited to that. She wanted to hug him and kiss him and—

She stifled that thought. It was not Centaurly. She would suppress it and not say anything to him.

Then Che did a double take. "Woe! Why aren't you with the children?"

Surprise realized with a shock that she had checked on the two real children, and overlooked the illicit presence of the fake child. The distraction of the love elixir was really getting to her. Of course the demon could pop across, neither flying nor wading.

The child frowned cutely. "What, when the interesting stuff is occurring here? Not that anything really naughty has happened, yet."

Surprise pointed back the way they had come. "Back to the babysitter. *Now*." She put the last word into bold italics, making it irrefutable.

Woe popped off, leaving behind only a disgusted fading "Awww."

Che looked thoughtful. "Could she have been along, invisibly, during our lake dialogue?"

"It's possible. Fortunately we didn't say anything naughty, as she put it."

"Surely a severe disappointment," he agreed. "Now we must disappoint some monsters."

They resumed motion, trotting across the plain. Before long the monsters manifested, fanning out from the castle to intercept them. Soon two detached themselves and came forward, while the others hung back. Evidently they had a system to determine whose turn it was for love.

The two were a motley four-footed female griffin and a grotesque warty male winged dragon. Winged monsters— that made sense, since technically two winged monsters were approaching the castle.

"Sorry, folk," Che said. "We crossed together. We're not interested in any of you."

"Not at all," Surprise agreed.

The monsters sighed and gave way, as it was obviously true. Had the visitors been love-smitten, they would have immediately clasped their opposite numbers and proceeded to actions that would have freaked out Woe Betide, for all that her adult selves were thoroughly familiar with them. As it was, the only creature Surprise wanted to clasp was—

She damped that down to a smoldering remnant and made her way through the clustered monsters toward the crown-shaped castle. Che walked beside her.

A young woman appeared at the front gate. "Centaurs!" she exclaimed.

"I am Che, and my companion is Surprise," Che said. "We are effectively immune to the love elixir for obvious reasons. We have come for the Mask."

"I am Pyra, as you must know." A patina of flames danced about the woman's skin, thicker across her bosom and hips. That seemed to be her only clothing. Her hair was auburn, turning red at the ends. "You can't have the Mask."

"Perhaps we shall be able to persuade you that we have legitimate need of it," Che said smoothly.

"You couldn't use it even if you stole it."

"We wouldn't do that," Surprise protested.

Pyra considered, frowning. She did not seem at all friendly. "Come in and talk." She turned and walked into the castle, her body moving like flickering flame. It was a shapely effect, Surprise thought, for those who might like that type. Che did seem to be taking it in.

The center of the castle was a huge covered dome, with a pleasant garden growing inside. Nothing looked scorched. Evidently Pyra could control her temper when she had reason.

"This is very nice," Surprise said, looking around.

The woman thawed, for all that she had hardly been frozen. "Are you hungry?"

Surprise exchanged a surprised glance with Che. "We are," he said.

"The elixir does it. New love consumes energy. Wait here." Pyra went to a side chamber.

"Love consuming energy," Che remarked. "That is not something I anticipated, but there does seem to be a rationale."

"I, neither," Surprise agreed. But probably her energy was being expended trying to suppress the awkward feelings that were burgeoning. It wasn't that she didn't love her husband Umlaut, but that Che was here and fascinating. Knowing that the elixir was responsible helped only intellectually.

Che looked around. "This is a veritable garden of rarities. I recognize a number of obscure plants."

"It must be her hobby. She has time to give it full attention."

Pyra returned with a tray. "I do. Plants make excellent companions, demanding little, providing sweet flowers and tasty fruits." She set the tray on a stone table. "Baked apples, toasted buns, baked potatoes, roasted chestnuts, burned beans, boiling beverage—I'm afraid I'm not good with cold refreshments."

"These will certainly do," Che said, as the two of them attacked the meal with ferocious appetites.

"One man passed by here some time ago with the talent of growing plants on animals. He offered to grow some on the monsters, but I declined. So we don't have any plants here that rare."

"Surely just as well," Surprise agreed, suppressing a shudder. She didn't care even to visualize such a plant.

"It is not that I am possessive of the Mask," Pyra said as they ate. "Indeed, I wouldn't mind giving it up in exchange for a decent life with a worthwhile companion. It's that I am responsible for it, and until I find a successor, I must meet my responsibility. Someone who won't mind the isolation."

"That is understandable and worthy," Che said around a mouthful. "It is a potent device that could cause much mischief if wrongly used."

"It certainly could. That is why it is here. The isolation is to protect it, not me. But apart from that, you would have difficulty using it without considerable training. Like other powerful tools, it seems simple but is not simple to control."

Surprise noted that the woman was not at all as the demoness had described her, eagerly grabbing any available man. She was reasonable and lucid. That was an incidental warning: don't be too quick to trust what demons said. However, the news about the monsters surrounding the castle had been accurate. So it wasn't smart to be too quick to disbelieve, either.

They caught up on their meal enough to abate their sudden hunger and discuss the matter with better attention. "Thank you for the excellent repast," Che said.

"That was very kind of you," Surprise said.

Pyra thawed further. "You're welcome. Do you wish to see the Mask now?"

Che elevated an eyebrow in an appealing way he had. "You do not hide it?"

"There is no need. No one else could use it, as I said, and few reach the castle unscathed. Here is the Mask." She lifted a square frame from the table beside the food tray.

"It was under our noses!" Surprise exclaimed.

Prya shrugged, causing waves of fire to radiate from her shoulders. "As you see, this is a blank screen. That is deceptive. It is always active, but reverts to an everything state when not in use. What are you looking for?"

"My baby," Surprise said. "My human baby. I'm not really a centaur."

"I wondered. You did seem a bit emotional for that species, but of course centaurs vary, and the love elixir would stir up whatever passions you possess. But if you have a baby, how is it that you do not have it with you?"

"That is my frustration. The stork brought it, then concluded that I was not old enough, and took it away undelivered. Now I mean to find it and get it back, though I confess I don't see how some mask can help me."

"It is a Reality Mask. It should be easier to understand once I demonstrate it."

"Please do," Che said.

Pyra held the frame up before her so that her face was hidden behind its pane. "When and where did this occur?"

"This morning, at my home," Surprise said, bemused. "Where my parents Grundy Golem and Surprise Elf live."

"Golem residence, morning," Pyra murmured.

The panel glowed and became a picture of the Golem house. The peeve perched on a tree branch outside it, watching for passing strangers. "That's it!" Surprise cried.

"Fast forward," Pyra said.

The picture quivered. The bird zipped into the house. A monk chip scurried by at blinding velocity. Then a big bird plummeted down to the ground. It was the stork, with a bundle suspended from its beak.

"Normal time," Pyra said.

The stork slowed to regular motion, approaching the house. The door opened and Surprise stood there. There was a brief dialogue they couldn't hear, as the screen was soundless. Then the stork turned, spread its wings, and flew away, bearing its bundle.

"That was it," Surprise said, tears in her eyes. It seemed like an age since she lost her baby, but had been only a few hours. "But how can this—this mask—make such accurate pictures?"

"This is only part of its functioning," Pyra said. "It selects specified pictures, masking irrelevant ones. In this case I confined it to this reality." The image of the stork returned, this time unmoving, like a painted picture.

"This reality," Surprise echoed, remembering the discussion she had had with Che.

"Here is the same scene without masking." The screen became blank again."

"But it shows nothing!"

"No, it shows everything. All the realities. Now I shall mask out a number." Pyra paused, then spoke to the frame. "Mask all without storks."

The screen flickered, but remained opaque.

"Mask all without balks."

The screen became filled with tiny images of still storks. Surprise gazed at them, amazed anew.

"Mask all female storks."

Now half the number of pictures appeared, each twice the prior size.

"We can reduce it to a single picture, in a single reality," Pyra said. "But it will be the wrong picture, or the wrong reality, if the masking is not proper. Do you care to try it?"

Surprise knew better, but gambled. "Yes."

Pyra put the frame in her hands. "Try zeroing in on the same scene," she suggested.

The picture had reverted to blank. Now Surprise understood that this was actually a display of so many tiny pictures that each was the size of a dot. She had to reduce their number by masking out the irrelevant ones.

"Mask all storks," she said.

Nothing happened.

"What you have now is all the scenes that don't contain storks," Pyra explained. "An infinite number."

Oh. "Mask all without storks," Surprise said.

There seemed to be no change. There were too many with storks. "Mask all where the stork doesn't balk."

Now she got the myriad tiny pictures. But it wasn't the same; the house was gone. "What happened?"

"You allowed the scene to drift. You have to keep it steady with your hands, as it is responsive to motion of the frame."

Surprise realized that even copying what she had just seen, she was fouling up. How would she have done entirely on her own? "You're right; I'm not good at this," she said, handing the Mask back.

"It requires years of practice," Pyra said, laying it back down on the table. "I still don't have it perfectly."

"I don't have years! I have to do this in hours!" Surprise realized she was verging on hysteria, a human failing.

"I doubt I would do any better," Che said. "Pyra, what is your purpose?"

"Take me with you. I will operate the Mask." She picked up the frame and folded it so that it became a mere stick, and tucked it into her belt.

Surprise quailed. They had barely avoided having Azalea accompany them, and here was another. "The Good Magician said that only two adults could go on this mission. The rest had to be children, animals, or crossbreeds."

"You have only one adult human," Pyra said. "The centaur is a crossbreed."

"We're an established species!" Che protested.

"An established crossbreed species. But I suppose I could use the Mask to seek the man with the Numbers Validity talent."

"I don't understand," Surprise said, nettled.

"He works with numbers. He can make a limit of n work for n+1. If we consult him I'm sure he will validate the mission for three adults."

Surprise was blank, but Che, being a centaur, understood about n and n+1. It seemed it was indeed possible to make numbers perform. They would have to find some other way to dissuade the fire woman.

"But we expect to be going into unspecified danger," Che said. "The Good Magician indicated that aspects could be extremely ugly. Why would you want to face that?"

"Because I am tired of being cooped up here alone except for monsters," Pyra flared. They had to step back from her heat. "I want to get out and see Xanth, live life, find a good man to be with, and become a family woman. I don't know in what reality there may be someone for me, but I may find out if I visit several."

"Oh, I understand," Surprise said. "You're a woman."

"I'm a woman," Pyra agreed. "I need to act while I remain young enough."

"Can you not use the Mask to orient on suitable prospects?" Che asked.

"I can and have, often. But they are far away, and don't know I exist, and have girlfriends of their own. Most are in other realities, which I can see with the Mask but can't go to in person. You folk, I gather, have the means to cross realities."

"We do," Che said.

"That makes a difference, obviously. In any event, how can I know a man is right just by looking at him? His personality counts a lot. And even an ideal one may be turned off by my talent. What man desires a woman as hot as I am when aroused?" Now her whole body glowed with fire.

"Personal interaction counts considerably," Che agreed. "I believe you have made your case. Surprise?"

He was asking her agreement to bring Pyra along. The fiery one's plea was reasonable, and they did need her, but Surprise had trouble responding. This was a talented, shapely, mature woman. The last thing Surprise wanted was such a creature constantly near Che. She had turned Azalea down; Pyra was worse.

That brought her up short. Was she jealous of Pyra's possible influence on Che? As if they were rivals for his attention? He was married elsewhere and not interested in any such dalliances. She was letting the love elixir influence her unrealistically.

They were waiting for her answer. What else could she do? "Yes, she should come with us," she agreed.

"You agree," Pyra said, amazed.

Surprise did not care to elaborate on the reason for her hesitation. "It does make sense."

"But you are in love with Che, because of the elixir."

"In the centaur manner," Che said. "Which differs from the human manner. In addition, you are not seeking a centaur."

"I am seeking a suitable male. If that turned out to be a centaur, I would take him and find an accommodation spell."

"But not one who is married elsewhere."

"No, of course not," Pyra agreed. But it seemed to Surprise that there was an element of doubt. This could become complicated.

"What about your garden?" Che asked.

"The monsters will care for it. They like pretty things. They are ugly only to others; inside they can be beautiful. Those who have come and married some of them have fared better than others expected. The grounds and garden will be all right until my return."

"Return?" Surprise asked. "I thought you wanted to get away from here."

"Not exactly. I want to have a full life. I can do that here, with the right man. I simply need to go out and find him."

Che nodded. "Then you can ride one of us across the marsh so as not to touch the elixir. Thereafter we will repair to the Stork Works, where they have the ability to transfer across realities. We can use the Mask there to locate the one we require, then enter it personally. But I must warn you again that there may be danger. There are elements of this situation we do not understand."

"In short, you expect to have an adventure," Pyra said. "I think I will enjoy that."

"Perhaps." But he was grave. What did he know that he wasn't saying?

Before long they were on their way back across the lake. Surprise carried Pyra, who kept her feet well up clear of the water. They waded carefully so as not to splash.

"I confess I am impressed by the way you handle the elixir," Pyra said. "All others have been besotted by it."

"We must be your first centaur visitors," Che said.

"As a matter of fact, you are. That surely explains it."

Surprise kept silent.

They reached the outer bank. Pyra carefully jumped off so as not to touch any wet skin, and stood well clear as the two centaurs shook themselves off.

Surprise looked around. "Where are the children?"

They checked the area with increasing misgiving. Azalea, Stymy, the three children, and the peeve were inexplicably gone.

"They wouldn't have gone voluntarily," Surprise said. "They knew they were supposed to stay here."

"I wonder," Che said. "First Azalea's sister Lotus disappeared in this area. Now Azalea herself and the children have done so. Another remarkable coincidence."

"And we don't trust coincidences," Surprise said grimly. "I think we need to use the Mask already."

"Of course," Pyra agreed. She drew out the stick and unfolded it into the frame. "I shall focus on the recent past of this area. We'll surely run it down."

They watched anxiously as the picture formed.

4

PUNDERGROUND

A zalea kept a careful eye on the children, especially the smallest one, the waif. She wanted to be the best possible babysitter, not just to uphold her part of the bargain but to prove that she was on the very verge of social maturity, fit to join the Adult Conspiracy. Fit to take care of children of her own, soon. Once she learned how to order them from the storks.

"I don't suppose you would care to enlighten me about—" she said to Stymy Stork.

"Certainly not. You have to be at least sixteen, preferably seventeen or eighteen, maybe even older."

The little obnoxious green bird flew across to perch on the stork's head. "For shame, you prying twit," it admonished her, using the stork's voice.

She wasn't really surprised. Storks were bound to enforce the cruel code. "If you don't mind telling me, then, how is it that you got stuck with this group, instead of delivering babies?"

"I followed the rules. That turned out to be a mistake.

Now I am required to—" He paused, his birdly eye glancing past her.

"Well, now," the pet peeve said enthusiastically. That was a sign of trouble; she had already learned that it never did anyone any verbal favors.

Someone must be in trouble. Again. These children were distressingly naughty, obviously possessing demon parentage. She turned to look. And stared.

A portion of the flower garden was rising, carrying the flowers with it. The three demon children were watching, interested. Was this dangerous?

Azalea did what came naturally: she asked the flowers. "What is this?"

"It's the door to the Punderground," they chorused. She was the only one who could hear them, but there was no doubt of their dialogue.

"Is it safe for children?"

"We don't know," the flowers replied. "But we don't think so. Folk who go down never came back up."

Azalea hurried toward the forming mound. "Children! Get away from there! It's not safe." Unfortunately they were slow to obey, interested in the phenomenon.

A door opened in the mound, shedding hapless flowers. A goblin garbed in a clown suit appeared. "Welcome, children! Come into my parlor."

"Who are you?" Azalea demanded as she arrived on the scene.

"I am the Hobgoblin of Little Minds," he answered grandly. "I am very consistent. And lo, here are several little minds to usher into my realm." He smiled at the children, who smiled back.

"Oh no you don't Hobgoblin! These are my charges. They're not going anywhere."

The goblin gazed at her with a certain muted contempt. "You are still technically a child yourself, nymph. You can come too. As can the birds. The Punderground welcomes all little minds."

"Not at all," she protested. "Ted, Monica, Woe—get away from him."

"Today we have fresh hot punapple pie," the Hobgoblin said. "Right this way, children."

The children stepped toward the door.

"Don't do it!" Azalea cried desperately.

But the Hobgoblin had their little minds mesmerized. They walked past him and started down the stairs that went down into the ground.

"This isn't right," Stymy Stork said.

"You bet your sorry tail it isn't," the peeve agreed. "What a dirt bag!"

The Hobgoblin glanced at them. "You odd birds become annoying. But you are children at heart, are you not?" He made a gesture. A sparkle of magic flung out and bathed the birds. They fell into line behind the children.

Azalea realized that she was up against a serious threat. She ran to intercept the children. In the process she passed through the dissipating cloud of magic. Her head seemed to spin and she lost control of her feet.

By the time the effect wore off, she found herself marching down the steps, following the children and birds. She turned to try to block the door open so she could help the children escape, but the Hobgoblin was already drawing it down behind them. She heard the click of a solid lock. They had all been taken prisoner.

She thought of charging the Hobgoblin, trying to make him let them go. But she realized that he would simply sprinkle her with more sparkle magic, nullifying her will. So she decided to play along, waiting her chance. There had to be some way out of this trap. She had to believe that.

They came to a large cavern with many colored stalactites. The Hobgoblin reached up to break off a point. "Candy canes," he said, handing it to Ted. "Eat your fill. And here is the pie." Indeed there was a table loaded with pies of all sizes. "All for you. Stuff yourselves."

Azalea wanted to protest, but knew that would be futile.

So she watched the children grab pies and bite happily into them. The stork followed suit, and the peeve jumped onto a small pie and pecked at it. Then, so as not to seem reticent, she took a pie herself and nibbled daintily on it. It was delicious. But she did not trust this at all.

"This is the thought screen," the Hobgoblin said, showing a large square screen behind the pie table. "If you have anything urgent inside you, you can squeeze it out here." He faced the screen. "For example, Stopwatch."

A group of people appeared on the screen, all watching a young woman who was just about to take off her clothes for a shower. Annoyed, she held up a small object. Immediately everyone stopped watching her.

It took only half a moment for the pie's effect to manifest. The children lined up eagerly before the screen. "Square Meal!" Ted yelled, and a pile of pies appeared, shaped into a square.

"Baby Shower," Monica said, and a cloud appeared, from which pelted hundreds of babies.

"Werehouse," Woe Betide cried, clapping her little hands with glee. The picture showed a den where several werewolves prowled.

"Ironies," Stymy said, and a huge set of metal legs appeared, focusing on the iron knees.

"Ire!" the peeve said, and an enormous angry eyeball appeared, looking at the woman who had used the stopwatch before. He was the eyer.

"Stop it!" Azalea cried. "This is horrible." But then, against her will, a pun erupted from her. "Hair Die." On the screen a huge woman's head appeared, with her hair wrinkling, turning gray, and falling out in clumps. Everyone laughed, but Azalea was mortified. How could she have emitted such a foul pun? She wished she had never nibbled the punapple pie.

Ted stepped up again. "Kidnapper," he said, and the screen showed a sinister figure approaching a roomful of children. The figure made a gesture as of casting a spell, and suddenly all the children fell asleep. The figure had made them nap.

It was Monica's turn. "Olive Yew," she said. The picture showed two trees, one roughly masculine, the other daintily feminine. The male wrapped several of his branches around the female, and little hearts surrounded them.

Azalea groaned. The words sounded like "I love you." An awful pun.

"Infantile," Woe Betide said. The picture showed a tiled floor. The tiles were very small, obviously not yet grown to full size. On each was a picture of a baby, and each baby was screaming. They were very noisy tiles.

"Pendants," Stymy said. The picture showed a young woman leaning over a small pen confining several colored ants. Penned ants, Azalea realized, stifling a groan. The girl picked up the ants one by one and set them on her ears, where they dangled prettily.

"Congenial Tea," the peeve said. The picture showed a friendly bar where special teas were being served.

"This nonsense must stop," Azalea said. But then the urge overwhelmed her, and she emitted another awful pun. "Juvenile." The screen showed a day care island filled with children, its name posted on a big sign: Juven Isle.

"No!" she cried despairingly, trying to push the screen aside. Instead she fell into the scene, scrambling it with the prior scenes, and her foot landed in a pot of tea. She tried to pull it off, but the pun fell apart, smearing both her foot and hand, smelling foul. She tried to throw the stuff away, but it stuck, and fragments landed all over her arms and legs. She had stepped in a pun, the last thing any self-respecting person would do, and now the messy pieces were all over her. It would take a shower and disinfectant to get it all off her. The children were laughing so hard they were literally rolling on the floor.

"Let me help you," the Hobgoblin said.

"Don't you dare!"

But she was too late, as he was already uttering the words.

"Age Spots." Suddenly the dirty splotches of puns sank into her skin, making it look old. In fact ner whole body was old; the spots had aged her.

She struggled to get out of the picture, but only blundered into the ant pen. Immediately several fetching female ants with exposed bellies started a seductive dance that hypnotized the males: they were bellied ants.

"Belly Dance," Azalea groaned helplessly.

But one male ant resisted the allure. "You can't snare me that way," he said gruffly. "I am Adam Ant."

Azalea groaned again: adamant.

This was so awful she couldn't stand it any more. She couldn't get out of the pun screen without making it worse. She fell to the floor and curled up, closing her eyes tightly as if asleep.

An insistent voice spoke near her. "Wake up, sleepyhead."

She tried to ignore it, but it persisted. "You can't sleep, lazybones. You have to get up, you fallen woman."

That did it. She opened her eyes. "I'm not a—" And broke off, surprised and disgusted.

There before her stood an ugly buzzard. The terrible pun smote her: a bird that annoyed her until she had to get up. She screamed.

The screen vibrated with the piercing sound, then shattered. Azalea was back in the regular Punderground, and the pun screen was gone.

But during her distraction the others had been swept up into another game. It was a set of circles of fauns and nymphs, the fauns on the inside, the nymphs outside. They seemed to be couples, with each faun gazing at a nymph. There was one extra nymph, who looked around, then winked at her choice of fauns. Catching her wink—it bounced off his forehead—he spied her and ran to join her. But his partner didn't like that, so ran to intercept him. She was too late; the faun had a new partner, and fell back into place exchanging gazes with her. The old partner was now "it," ready to wink at someone else's partner.

Azalea did not trust this half a whit. Fauns and nymphs

were notorious for their "celebrations" which were well into the Adult Conspiracy. Azalea did not know exactly what it was they did, but was sure that there would be the very mischief to pay if any of the children were to see it. She had to get them away from here. But how?

Ted and Monica had already joined the game. A nymph winked at Ted, and he ran gleefully to join her.

"No you don't!" Azalea cried, and ran to tackle him before he could reach the nymph. She collided with DeMonica, who was trying to hang on to her partner, and they both fell in a tangle on the floor.

Demon Ted, of course, made it safely to the nymph. She kissed him on the forehead, and he swayed visibly, spared the full impact of the kiss because of his age. Still, Azalea knew she had to get him and the others out of here in a hurry; there was no telling what would happen if they remained longer in this supposedly innocent game.

"Monica, you're a girl," Azalea said desperately. "You know we can't let the nymphs have Ted." She was gambling that there was at least half a smidgen of responsibility in the half-demon child.

Monica considered. "Yes, a nymph is more fun than he deserves."

That would have to do. "We have to haul him out of the game and out of here." She looked desperately around, and saw an open hole in the wall. "Through there."

They ran to Ted, each taking an arm. "Hey!" he protested. "I'm not through with my nymph."

"Yes you are," Azalea said, hauling him along. As they broke out of the circle she looked around. "Woe! Stymy! Peeve! This way!" She had to hope they would follow.

They did. In perhaps two and a half moments, certainly no more than three, they were in the next chamber.

But now the Hobgoblin was organizing the pursuit. "Don't let them escape," he cried. "They haven't eaten enough pie yet."

That was interesting. Pie prevented escape? Because of the puns? Maybe it was addictive.

"Can we kiss any we catch?" a faun asked.

"Yes! Kiss them, and feed them pie while they're stunned. Then they'll be ours forever."

Azalea felt a chill. The ugly side of the Punderground was being revealed. But that also suggested that they could escape, if they avoided capture and didn't eat any more punapple pie. But where could they go? In another three moments they would be overwhelmed by the fauns and nymphs.

The next cave had two men talking to each other. They weren't fauns or nymphs, so maybe they would help. "Please, is there any way out of here?" she asked them.

"Any way is way out," one man said. "Hello, pretty girl; I am Gent number One."

"Anyway, weigh out," the other man said. "I am Gent number Two."

"I don't understand." Neither man seemed to be properly addressing the question. Neither man smelled very good either; her nose was wrinkling.

"Then don't stand under," Gent One said.

"Stand over," Gent Two said.

"Pun Gents," Stymy remarked distastefully. "Naturally they reside in the Punderground and stink of puns."

Azalea tried again. "Are there any flowers here?" Because a flower would help her. "A rose, maybe?"

"A rose by any other name would smell," Gent One said.

"And the smell arose," Gent Two agreed.

Azalea gave up on the Pun Gents and not just because of the smell. For one thing, she saw fauns and nymphs coming. "This way, children," she said, hurrying them on through the next passage.

"What have we here?" Gent One said, grabbing a nymph, who screamed fetchingly and kicked up her feet as she swung her hair around, not at all dismayed.

"Hear, hear!" Gent Two said, catching a foot and sighting up a leg. "This swinging creature calls for a celebration."

"Move on!" Azalea urged the children, who were trying to hang back and watch.

The next chamber had several exits. Which one should

they take? Azalea had no idea, but was sure that if they took a wrong one, they would be doomed. She needed good advice. Maybe if she found the right flower it would have an escape root they could use.

Then she spied a small lonely flower blooming in a cranny. "Flower in the crannied wall!" she cried. "Which passage should we take?"

"The Ness way," the flower replied.

Azalea saw labels on the tunnels, saying things like TO HEAVEN, BEST ESCAPE, NETHER DELIGHT. One said AN-OTHER FINE NESS. "This way!" she cried, and led the party into the Fine Ness passage.

"Is this wise?" Stymy inquired as they funneled through the tunnel. "I mislike the sign."

"A little flower told me," she replied. "Flowers never lie to me."

"But did the flower tell you why this was best?"

"There wasn't time."

The peeve landed on her shoulder. "It's not the best, weed-brain," it said in her voice. "It's the least worst. It's the one tunnel where we won't be followed."

Azalea had learned that the peeve's natural mode was insult, and didn't take it personally. "What do you know of this, feather-head?"

"The Nesses are monsters. One found a key to the lock and escaped into Mundania, the Loch Ness Monster. Its siblings didn't make it, so are stuck here, and not pleased. No one wants to be gobbled by a Ness."

Azalea was not completely thrilled by that explanation, but it did make sense. "Thank you, peeve."

"Well, I don't want to be gobbled either, dimwit."

They came into another cavern. This one also had multiple exits, and each was labeled, but this time there were no flowers to ask.

First Azalea checked on the children. Ted, Monica, Woe Betide. They all seemed to be all right. That was a relief.

"Will we see the monsters?" Ted asked eagerly.

"Not if they see us first," Monica retorted. Both laughed.

Now Azalea read the signs. They were not encouraging. MAD NESS, GOOD NESS, SAD NESS, GREAT NESS, SLEEPY NESS, SICK NESS, UGLY NESS. It seemed they had to pick one. She didn't trust GOOD, as it might be an exclamation, here in the Punderground. Neither did she trust SLEEPY, as that could be a ruse to get them to try to sneak by. Any monster was dangerous.

The waif Woe Betide approached. "I can help," she piped.

"Of course you can," Azalea said reassuringly. But she knew the tyke was likely to be the first morsel gobbled by a monster. This was awful. How could she get the children out of here?

"I really can," Woe insisted.

"Of course, dear," Azalea repeated. She walked by the several tunnels, distracted. It seemed she had to make the decision, but the risk of disaster was formidable. There had to be a way through, because the flower wouldn't have sent them into doom, but she had no idea what it was.

"You don't believe me," Woe said, clouding over.

"Certainly I believe you," Azalea said insincerely.

"You better," Ted said. "Mom's a full demoness."

Suddenly he had her full attention. "Mom?"

"She's D. Metria, locked into her child aspect so she can't mangle words or know what secrets the Adult Conspiracy hides. But she's got her matches."

"Match Less," Monica said, and both tittered. "For Mad Ness."

This was a new wrinkle. Ted's mother would surely want to save her son from getting gobbled. "How can you help, Woe?"

"My matches give folk their Heart's Desire," the waif explained.

"Which we might trade for our safe passage," Azalea said, understanding. "If we can figure out what a monster wants more than tasty flesh." Then something else occurred. "If you are a full demon, can't you just pop off and summon help?"

"Not since we went down under," Woe said sadly.

Azalea realized that the Punderground must have some sort of barrier to prevent demons from escaping. That was not reassuring. But she had to be positive, for the sake of the children. "I will consider which Ness we can best use a match on. Assuming they have hearts or desires."

Ted and Monica chuckled, thinking she had made a funny. She smiled, letting them think that. But she was seriously concerned. She had not had a lot of experience with monsters, and wasn't sure what they had, apart from teeth and appetites.

She walked by the signs. What would be the heart's desire of a monster named Mad Ness? Sanity? What about Good Ness? Something naughty? Sad Ness—happiness? Ugly Ness—

She paused in mid-thought. She saw a lotus flower petal. *Her sister had been here.*

"This one," she said.

"Aww," Ted said. "I'd rather see Sexy Ness."

"OoOoo, what you said!" Monica said. "At your age, you naughty boy."

Azalea faced Woe Betide. "What kind of heart's desire would Ugly Ness have? Can you make a match for it?"

"The matches just do it, whatever it is," the waif said.

"They grant the heart's desire automatically? How do they know it?"

"Magic," Woe said wisely.

Azalea hoped that was the case. "How do you invoke them? I doubt the monster will strike a match."

"I strike it. If the monster wants."

Azalea was far from certain it could be that easy, but saw no point in expressing her doubt. Now that she knew her sister had come this way she was exhilarated despite her fears for herself and the children. "Good enough. You will strike a match for Ugly Ness, if the monster agrees to let us pass unmolested."

They went cautiously down the tunnel. Soon it came to a pool and skirted the edge. The moment their party approached, a fearsome reptilian head poked out of the water.

It had huge purple teeth, dangling green wattles, a giant slurpy tongue, and three black eyes. Overall it was breathtakingly ugly.

"Where'd you get that snoot?" the peeve asked. "Did you try to swallow a rotten tree, and the rancid roots got stuck in your maw?"

"Peeve!" Azalea reproved it as the children tittered. She hoped the creature hadn't heard the bird.

"Though it is a fair description," Stymy murmured.

Azalea nerved herself and took half a step toward the monster. "Ugly Ness," she said in a quavering voice. "We need to pass your pool. We—we want to make a deal."

Two of the eyes focused on her body. The tongue slurped across the teeth. Did the monster understand, or was it salivating at the prospect of crunching her tender body into juicy pulp?

"We offer you your heart's desire," she continued bravely. "In exchange for letting us pass."

The monster considered. Then, slowly, the huge head nodded. It was agreeing!

"Aw, it'll probably gobble us all anyway," Ted said.

"All but you," Monica retorted. "It'll spit you out, stinky."

"Thank you for that encouragement, children," Azalea said. "Woe Betide, we are ready for your match."

The waif stepped forward. "Watch the flame," she told the Ness. Then she struck the Match against the Box. It burst into bright flame.

The monster stared at the speck of fire. Then something wonderfully weird happened. Ugly Ness became beautiful. Not merely acceptable, not pretty-if-you-like-that-type, not merely handsome, but gloriously lovely through and through.

They all stared at the gorgeous creature, awed. Beauty fairly radiated from it, compelling their admiration. The Ness was simply stunning.

"Walk, dope," the peeve muttered at her ear. "Now."

Oh. Azalea gestured to the others, and walked forward along the path skirting the pool. They followed, still gazing raptly at the sheerly alluring creature. Its features had not changed, but now its aspect was rapturously pleasing. Beauty incarnate, and they were in their fashion worshipping it. They had no choice.

They completed their passage around the pool. They were safe! Then Azalea saw that Woe Betide had not joined them. She remained standing where she had lit the match, holding up its diminishing flame. What would happen when it went out?

"Wait here." Azalea dashed back to fetch the waif just as the match expired.

The monster blinked. Its ugliness returned. It gazed down at the two of them, precariously exposed.

After a long moment—really a moment and a half—Ugly Ness closed its eyes and sank slowly under the water. It had honored the deal. They had been spared.

Azalea led Woe around the pool to join the others. Her knees felt like bendy stalks. Had the monster had honor after all?

"If it gobbled you, there would be two fewer people who had recognized its luster," Stymy Stork explained. "Who else would believe it?"

Maybe that made sense.

"We must go on," Azalea said. "There has to be a way out."

Then her eye caught sight of another lotus petal. Her sister had passed this way, and made it safely past the monster. Now she knew what had happened: the Hobgoblin had lured or tricked Lotus into entering the Punderground, where she had been trapped. But she had had the wit to leave a trail of petals so she could be found. Only Azalea would have recognized that trail.

However, Lotus had not found the way out. So how could the rest of them?

The next cavern was filled with children and teens. They were not boisterous or happy; they were quiet and sullen. What was going on here?

"Stay together," Azalea cautioned the children. "We don't

know these people." They remained in a tight little group near the entrance tunnel. Now Azalea saw other entrances; evidently all the monster paths led to this same chamber. Her group could have chosen any route. What did it mean?

Two odd teens approached. Both had snow-white hair and ice-blue eyes. They looked like brother and sister. "You're new here," the boy said.

"We are new," Azalea said. "We don't plan to stay."

Both children laughed wearily. "None of us planned to stay," the girl said.

As she had feared. "I am Azalea; my talent is talking with flowers. These are my companions, also trapped. You must know something we don't."

"I am Kalt," the boy said. "My talent is shaping ice. This is my twin sister Frosteind; she freezes water."

"I also like to count steps between points," the girl said. "It passes the time."

"I don't understand why there are so many children here."

"It's ugly," Kalt said. "You sure you want to know?"

"We have to know," Azalea said grimly.

"They're leaching our souls," Frosteind said.

"They're what?"

"The longer we stay here, the more of our souls we lose," Kalt explained. "That's what happens in the Punderground. Near the surface some folk might escape, so they addict them to punapple pie. Down here there is no escape, so they don't care. They give us plenty of food and it doesn't hurt us. But we can't leave, and in time our souls will be gone."

"What do they do with your souls?" Azalea asked, appalled.

"We don't know," Kalt said. "We think they power their magic in some way—the pun screen."

"And the fauns and nymphs want them," Frosteind said. "It doesn't matter; we're doomed anyway."

"This is truly horrible," Azalea said. "We must escape."

"We know," Kalt said. "But we know of no way. Below this residential cave there is only the Death Pool."

"The what?" Azalea asked, startled.

"We call it that because that's where the kids go who can't

stand it any more. There's a whirlpool that sucks them down, and they're gone."

"The horror continues," Azalea murmured.

"We're thirsty," Ted said.

Azalea had to smile. "One thing these caves seem to have is plenty of water."

"Ugh!" both half-demon children protested.

"The kids here have many talents," Frosteind said. She peered across the cave. "Zach!"

A boy joined them. "I told you before, Frosty: no kissing."

"These new kids are thirsty and they don't much like water."

"Ah." Zach reoriented. "What drink would you like? My talent is to make any drink from any liquid."

"Purple milkshake," Ted said promptly.

"Green tsoda pop," Monica said.

"Do you have cups?"

Cups appeared in their two hands.

"Dip them in the water."

They went to the pool and dipped their cups. Then Zach touched the surface of the liquid in each cup, and it changed color. Ted's turned purple; Monica's turned green. They tasted them, and grinned with approval; the transformations were real.

"Thank you, Zach," Frosteind said. Then, suddenly, she kissed him.

"Ugh!" Zach exclaimed, fleeing.

"Fake," the peeve muttered. "He really liked it."

"He doesn't want to get razzed," Kalt confided.

"I wonder," Azalea said. "Is there a girl called Lotus here?"

"Sure," Frosteind said. "Why do you want her?"

"She's my twin sister."

"I thought you looked familiar! You have the same flowery features." Frosteind lifted her voice and called again. "Lotus! Your sister's here!"

And just like that, Lotus came forging through the throng. "Azalea!" she cried, hugging her almost as hard and tearfully as Azalea was hugging her.

"Ugh," Ted said. "Can't you cut out the mush?"

"Mush is fun," Monica said. "All you need is some nice girl to give you a big slobbery kiss."

"I do not!" But as with Zach, his protest lacked conviction.

"Like that Lotus," Monica continued teasingly. "A flower nymph. You'd float up to the ceiling."

"I would not!" he said, flustered.

The joy of their reunion soon faded into awareness of their predicament. "I came to rescue you," Azalea said. "But I got caught myself."

"That's the way it is," Lotus agreed.

"Ted wants you to kiss him," Monica said wickedly.

"Oh, really?" Lotus looked at Ted.

Ted opened his mouth to protest, but was too stunned by Monica's betrayal to get a word out. Lotus leaned down and kissed him. He floated toward the ceiling.

"Which reminds me," Lotus said to Azalea. "You must meet my boyfriend Wade. His talent is to wade through water knee-deep, no matter how deep the water really is. He helps me with my water flowers." She turned, lifting an eyebrow.

A handsome boy of about sixteen appeared. "You found your sister!" he exclaimed, seeing Azalea. His gaze was so sincere that for half an instant she was sorry Lotus had found him first.

"Yes. This is Azalea, who can talk to land flowers. Tell her about Ray."

"He's my brother," Wade said. "He can make a ray of sunshine, so flowers in shade can grow better. He must be out looking for me now. He'd really like you, as I like Lotus, if only for your nymphly fi—"

Lotus kicked his shin.

"Nymphly fire," he finished hastily. "That alert response. Those sparkling eyes. That wonderful talent."

Azalea liked Ray already, and it didn't really bother her that Wade had noticed her figure. "But he mustn't come down here."

"We've got to get out," Wade agreed. "Somehow."

Azalea cudgeled her brain, but nothing came out. "Can't anyone figure out a way to escape?"

"We've all been trying," Kalt said. "But we're stuck."

"But with all the talents the kids here have, there must be something."

"Maybe we just need someone smart enough to figure it out."

And obviously there had not been someone. It seemed that had become her responsibility, because she had to get the children out of this soul-destroying prison. Somehow.

She cudgeled her brain some more. Her brain didn't like that, and threatened to start a headache. *Then give me a good idea!* she told it.

Her brain capitulated. It focused and heated. Suddenly a light bulb flashed, illuminating her face. She had the idea!

"That was some flash," Wade remarked.

"Zach's talent," she said. "Making drinks from water."

"From any liquid," Frosteind said.

"I need to talk to him."

"He won't come again for me."

"I'll find him. Children, wait here." She plowed into the throng, looking for Zach.

Soon she found him. "No kissing," he said defensively.

"None," she agreed innocently. "Zach, how much water can you convert to a drink?"

"I'm not sure. Just about any amount, I guess, if I focus hard enough."

"How about a whole pool?"

"What pool?"

"The Death Pool."

He was taken aback. "That's big."

"But you could do it?"

"I guess. Depends on what I had to change it to. Tsoda pop is easy; Eye Scream shake is hard, because of the thickness. Anyway, there's no point; the kids would never drink all of that."

"I'm thinking of something breathable. With bubbles of air. Big bubbles all mixed in."

"I guess," he repeated. "But why bother? We have plenty of air to breathe. They want us healthy, because they lose our souls if we die too soon."

"Let's try it," she said urgently. "A small amount, to see how it works."

"But there's no point."

She caught him by the shoulders, held him in place, and kissed him. He tried to run, but she held on firmly. He didn't struggle very hard. "Do it, or I'll kiss you again." She had caught on to two secrets; nymphly kisses had power, and his no meant yes. That was probably true of most boys who claimed to hate mushy stuff. Was Ted still floating?

Daunted, he nodded agreement. She let him go and they went down to the Death Pool cave, which was next door. It was a sinister region, with dark water filling the lower portion, and a deadly whirlpool in the center.

They stopped at a recess that held a relatively small amount of water. "Try this," she said.

He touched the surface of the water. It became bubbly. She lay down, put her mouth to it, and tried to breathe. She sucked in some water, choking, but also some air. It was breathable, if she could just separate the air from the water.

"What are you trying to do?" Zach asked.

She caught hold of him. "Stop arguing."

"I'm not arguing! I'm trying to help."

She kissed him anyway. "Oops, too late. I apologize. I'll explain."

"That's all right," he said faintly.

"That whirlpool is going somewhere. If we can follow the water out, maybe we can escape. If you can change this whole pool to breathable liquid, we can go down in it without drowning. If we can find a better way to breathe it."

"To get just the bubbles," he agreed, seeing it. "There's a kid whose talent is to make little tubes. We thought it was useless, but if we put those in our mouths and poked the other ends into the bubbles—"

"Brilliant!" she exclaimed, leaning into him.

"You don't have to—"

She kissed him. "Too late. Sorry."

"Okay," he said as faintly as before. "Only—"

"I won't tell," she promised.

They returned to the main cave and Azalea explained her idea. "So if this works, we can all escape, maybe," she said.

There was half a hubbub. The kids were definitely interested. They put it to a vote, and decided to try it. "It can't be worse, long-term, than what we face here," Wade said.

They lined up by the bank of the Death Pool. Each person had several small tubes. Zach concentrated and slowly converted the entire pool to bubbly drink. They experimented, swimming in the water, ducking their heads, poking their tubes into bubbles and sifting the froth through their teeth. It was working.

Then Azalea led the way with her children. They were all in their clothing, because there was no other way to bring it along. She swam to the whirlpool and let it take her. This was the scary part, going down into the unknown, but she had to show no fear lest it spook the others. She was carried around and around, faster and faster, and sank below the surface. Ted, Monica, Woe Betide, and Stymy Stork with the peeve on his head followed in a line. They spiraled into the whirling maw.

Then she was being carried rapidly down to the bottom, and through a hole in the floor of the cave. The water plunged to a lower level. What if it smashed against a great rock? she wondered belatedly.

It didn't. She plopped into another large pool, surrounded by enough of the bubbly water to continue breathing. She swam for the surface and found a beach. She scrambled onto it, soaking wet but elated. The others followed.

"It worked!" Zach exclaimed, emerging from the water.

"Thanks to your talent," she said, and kissed him again. "Oops, too late."

"Don't—okay," he said weakly.

Frosteind appeared. "Did she kiss you?" she demanded severely of Zach. "I have half a mind to—"

"No, don't—" he protested.

"Kiss you myself." She did. "So there. Now behave."

"I will," he said. "Oh, darn. Who am I fooling?" He kissed her back.

"Ha!" Frosteind said. "You did it. Now you're my boyfriend."

"I guess so." He did not seem totally dismayed.

"It's a good thing our talents mesh. Now we can make iced tea together."

Azalea smiled to herself. It was nice to see things work out. She had done what she had to, to get the job done.

They all made it safely down. Now they assessed the situation. Four waterfalls dropped into this nether pool, including the one they had come on. One of them had daylight at its apex. That had to be the way out. But how could they get there? They couldn't swim up a waterfall!

She cudgeled her brain again. This time it didn't wait to be abused long; it gave her an idea almost immediately. "Kalt! Frosteind!" she called as the soggy bulb flashed over her head. "I think you can help."

"We want to," Kalt said. "What can we do?"

"Frosteind, you can freeze water," Azalea said. "Can you freeze that waterfall?"

The girl considered. "I think so."

"And you, Kalt—can you shape the frozen waterfall into steps? So we can all climb them to get out of here?"

"Yes!" he said, seeing it.

"Then do it, both of you. We all want to escape."

They got to work. Soon there was a winding stairway to the top, made of ice. This time Azalea let the others go first, so she could make sure no one was left behind. Kalt and Frosteind also stayed, to keep the steps frozen and shaped. "This is the fanciest job we've ever done," Kalt said ruefully. "And no one will see it, after this."

"But everyone will remember," Frosteind said.

At last everyone was up. They followed, letting the steps melt below them. It was scary, and their feet were cold, but they made it, as the others had.

Azalea was the last to step off the ice and onto warm dry land. And paused, amazed.

There stood all the children, applauding her for the rescue. With them was Che Centaur, Surprise Golem, and a fiery young woman.

"By the time we located you, you were well on your way," Che said. "So we let you finish. You're a hero."

"I was just trying to rescue the children," she said, abashed. "All of them."

"You succeeded," Surprise said. "Thanks to your initiative, determination, and sense. And you found your sister too."

"And a boyfriend, as soon as I tell my brother Ray about you," Wade said. "You're such a great girl."

But Azalea couldn't think about that at the moment. "It's not done yet. I have to get the other children back to their homes. We can't just leave them here."

"Of course," Che said. "We'll help, since we can't help you find your sister."

"And we'll warn Xanth about the Punderground and the Hobgoblin," Surprise said. "It's high time that awful scheme is stopped."

"Yes!" Azalea agreed. Then she sank to the ground in worn-out tears of relief. This was more than enough adventure to hold her for a long time.

5

FIRST PASS

Che Centaur watched Azalea, Lotus, and the last of the lost children go. Azalea, for all her youth, had turned out to be a redoubtable babysitter, and had risen to answer considerably more challenge than anticipated. Fortunately everyone had come out of it safely.

"We've got to do something about that Hobgoblin," Surprise said, looking darkly at the flower bed. "We can't have him taking any more children into the Punderground."

And there was another young woman with surprising (no pun) potential. Che was fighting against the realization that he was not after all effectively immune to the love elixir, despite his statements on the subject. Surprise, still in centaur form, was a lovely and motivated mare, and he wished he could—no, of course not. It was a good thing that she had accepted the proper centaur attitude; that made up for his own failure.

"Put up a sign, stupid," the peeve suggested.

"Good idea, peeve," Surprise said. Che admired that too:

the way she handled the obnoxious bird. "Who knows how to make a suitable warning sign?"

"We can," Ted and Monica chorused. The two half-demon children scrambled to find a flat piece of wood, and scraped it with a stone to form words. BEWAR THE HOBLIN. Well, perhaps that was close enough.

Now they were ready to return to the Stork Works. "It is time for you children and the peeve to return to your homes," Surprise said firmly. "This quest is not for you."

Immediately Ted and Monica fussed in protest, and the peeve let out a series of words that did not, quite, barely, violate the Adult Conspiracy. But it was Woe Betide who made the persuasive case: "If you don't let us come, we'll tell everyone how you and Che waded through the love elixir."

"We didn't do anything," Surprise said, taken aback.

"Who will believe that?"

"This is blackmail," Che said, disgusted.

"You bet it is, horse-head," the peeve said with satisfaction.

"This is outrageous," Surprise said angrily. Even her anger was appealing.

"You bet!" the two demon children said together.

Surprise looked appealingly at Che. Her appealing look was even more appealing. "Do we have to put up with this cheap threat?"

"By no means. Send them home and let them talk. Their folks will know they're just talking, and when Woe Betide reverts to being Ted's mother she'll know too."

She nodded. "Children—"

Seeing their ploy about to fail, both children burst into tears, and the waif looked painfully woebegone as she wailed. Even the peeve managed to force half a tear. Surprise looked stricken. She was way too softhearted. That was not really a liability.

"Don't let them get to you," Stymy said. "Do what's right."

"I can't help it," Surprise said. "I just can't let them cry." She made as if to tear her hair. She had nice hair.

Woe paused in mid-wail. "Does that mean we can come along?"

Surprise visibly gritted her teeth. She had nice teeth. "Yes. But if—"

Suddenly both children and the waif were all sunshine. "Thank you,————," the peeve said, evidently having stifled an insult and finding nothing to replace it.

"It's only because it would take too long to take you back now," Surprise said weakly. Even her feeble capitulation was attractive.

"At such time as I have children," Pyra muttered, "they'll never get away with that."

"In Mundania they would call that Famous Last Words," Che said with forty-five percent of a smile.

Things were organized remarkably efficiently thereafter. Surprise carried the three eager children on her back, the birds flew independently, and Che carried Pyra.

They flicked their riders to make them light, spread their wings, and took off. Soon they were flying across the Xanth landscape, following the birds.

"You're not immune," Pyra murmured.

Ouch. There was no point in trying to deny it, and it wouldn't have been honest. "I am married to Cynthia Centaur, and I love her," he said carefully. "Surprise is married to Umlaut, and she loves him. Wading through the elixir was a calculated risk we both understood. We do not wish to complicate our relationships."

"Of course you don't," Pyra agreed. "And I wish I had a relationship as good as either of yours. But the love elixir can not be denied. You are destined to suffer."

"Are there ways I show it?" he inquired. "I ask because I want to avoid them, and not put her under any strain."

"You are very good at concealing it. But when I mounted you, I felt the quickening in your body as you looked at or spoke to her. You can school the way you look and act, but you can't suppress the feeling in your body."

"Thank you, Pyra. Please don't speak of this elsewhere. I'm sure the effect of the elixir will pass."

"It normally passes when satisfied by desperately summoning the stork a few times."

"Centaurs don't summon storks. Baby centaurs are too heavy for them to carry, so we make our own foals."

"But you do go through similar motions, don't you? That should have similar effect."

"That is ironic," he said. "I can abate my passion for her only by mating with her—which is what I must not do."

"Why don't you talk with her about it? She seems pretty sensible. She might agree to let you do it. Then you would be free."

"When she does not share the passion? This would be unethical at best, and an unfair burden on her, quite apart from the larger background issues."

"I hope I find a boyfriend as ethical as you."

"You don't want a centaur."

"Perhaps."

The dialogue lapsed for a while, but Che remained disturbed. Logic suggested that Pyra was correct: his best course was to ameliorate his passion efficiently, so as not to be further distracted by it. Had Surprise succumbed similarly to the elixir, it would be the same with her. But she had not, and he would not be so selfish as to ask such a thing of her. So, as Pyra said, he was destined to suffer.

"I met an imp named Otence once," Pyra remarked. "His/her talent was to make males lose that sort of interest. I'm uncertain of the imp's gender. Maybe you should check with it."

Imp Otence. Che got it. "That would nullify my ability, rather than my desire. Or my passion but not my love. It would be similarly frustrating."

They reached the Stork Works in reasonable order and landed. "Che, I know your primary mission is to locate and rescue the Simurgh," Surprise said. "I don't want to be unbearably selfish, but can we rescue my baby first? I'm desperate."

She thought she was the selfish one. How little she knew! "I believe that is feasible," he agreed. "There is also the prospect that the Simurgh is in the same reality as your baby, so by locating one we also locate the other."

"Oh, thank you!" she said, taking a step toward him. Then she halted herself, visibly. Did she have an inkling how her touch might affect him? "Is it time for me to revert to my natural form, so I can have my other talents?"

Would her change of form defuse his passion? That would help. "Yes, you will need to be your own form to take your baby."

"Thank you." She shimmered, and became a human woman, fully clothed. "Oh, it feels good to be myself again."

Unfortunately Che discovered that the reversion made no difference. He still felt passionate about her. Neither had her change of form made it impossible. Wildly different species mated when caught in love springs, finding whatever way worked. But of course he uttered none of this. "Welcome."

The gate guard stork ushered them into a special chamber within the large central dome. One wall was shrouded by a heavy curtain. "This is the reality room," he said. "From here you can enter the reality you select. You have merely to let us know your choice."

"This is the dome where the babies come from," Surprise said, looking around.

"They are brought in from another reality, yes," the stork conceded grudgingly. "More than that we will never tell."

"Thank you," Che said quickly. "We will orient on the reality we want."

"I need specifics," Pyra said, opening the Mask.

Surprise got down to business. "This morning Stymy Stork here brought my baby, but took it away without delivery. He took it to another reality. We must go to that reality."

"You don't have a designation for that reality?"

"No," Stymy said. "A fissure opened between realities, and I passed through. It closed up again the moment I returned."

"I'll need a better description than that. There could be a million alternate choices."

"Logic should help," Che said. "The fissure opened between just two realities, we believe: ours and the other one. Can you orient on the specific one the fissure reached?"

"I can try." She set up the Mask. "Fissure between two realities."

Six pictures appeared. Each showed a stork with a bundle flying toward a slightly glowing rent in the sky.

"There should be just one," Che said.

"Evidently not."

"But there can't be more than one that Stymy Stork used between here and there."

"Maybe not, but there are evidently several connections between sets of realities. I don't know how to make the Mask specify particular realities. How do you define reality?"

That stumped him. "We'll just have to check them all," Che decided. "Six should be manageable."

"But in each a stork is delivering a bundle," Surprise said. "How do we know which one is Stymy? All storks look alike to me from a distance, and these ones may have glasses the same way Stymy does."

"Stymy surely knows," Che said. He turned to the stork. "Which of these six shows you?"

"I don't know."

"You can't recognize yourself?"

"I could by smell. Stork vision isn't that good."

"So we have to go and intercept you so you can smell yourself?"

"That won't work," Pyra said. "The Mask is showing the scene as defined, when there was the fissure. When we travel there, it will be in now-time. No storks remaining."

"Now what do we do?" Surprise asked despairingly. Even her despair was attractive. He wanted to hold her reassuringly, but knew better.

Amazingly it was little Woe Betide that had a useful suggestion. "Maybe some stork smell rubbed off on the baby."

"Could that have happened?" Che asked.

"Yes," Stymy said. "I can recognize the babies I deliver by the traces of my own smell on them."

"Victory!" Surprise said jubilantly. And of course her jubilation was alluring.

"Then we shall proceed," Che said, relieved. "We'll tackle them one by one until we find the baby with your smell." He looked at the children and peeve. "I trust you know that this is no occasion for foolish pranks."

"We'll behave perfectly," all three said, little halos appearing over their heads. Che didn't quite trust that, but had to assume that they would behave.

He addressed the guide stork. "This one," he said, indicating the upper left picture.

"Pass by the curtain," the stork said.

"Just like that?" Surprise asked.

"It is a very special curtain."

But Che had a caution. "If realities are so much alike, how can we be sure of returning to this one?"

"The mechanism locks the two together, for you," the stork explained. "Just return to the Stork Works, and it will automatically phase you back to this site."

"A permanent fissure," Pyra murmured. "Or at least a temporary one that exists as long as we are using it. That's a nice feature."

"Very nice," Che agreed dryly. It was in fact absolutely necessary, if they were not to be hopelessly lost among realities.

"This central site is of course neutral with respect to realities," the guide stork clarified. "It addresses all of them with equal ease."

Oops. They might already be lost. But it did not seem expedient to speak of that at this moment.

"Stay with me, children," Surprise said, leading the way. She drew aside the curtain and stepped by it. Che appreciated her unconscious courage.

The children trooped after her, followed by Stymy with the peeve on his head. Then Pyra, then Che.

It was a disappointment. The curtain way merged with the way they had come in, and they exited the central dome and walked on past the outlying station and back to familiar Xanth. Had the storks politely brushed them off? He decided not to voice his private misgivings.

"This looks the same," Ted said. "They tricked us."

So much for that. "We have to have faith," Che said. "One Xanth is surely much like another, with most of the same flora and fauna."

"The same what?" Ted demanded.

"Nymphs named Flora and fauns chasing them, dummy," Monica said with a superior tone.

Che wrestled with a smile, but five eighths of it got away from him. "Close enough. Plants and animals."

"Why didn'tcha say so?"

"No child of mine will ever be that insolent," Pyra murmured. Then she screeched as she leaped into the air. "Youch!"

She was the immediate center of attention. "What happened?" Surprise asked, concerned. Her concern was one of her fetching qualities.

"This—this *thing* whacked my, my—"

"Bottom, rear, end, tail, a—" Ted suggested.

"Fundament," Che said, cutting him off. "I recognize the genus. That's a Weed Whacker. It whacks girls."

"Whack her," Monica said, tittering.

"Well it better not do it again," Pyra flared. The heat made the weed lean away, wilting.

"Look," Ted said, pointing gleefully ahead. There was a whole patch of similar plants. That made Surprise, Monica, and even little Woe Betide quail.

"I can carry you across," Che said. He was trying to remember whether there had been such a patch on their way in, but couldn't be sure, because they had not been afoot. So it remained possible that this was the same Xanth.

But Pyra was grim. "I want to defeat these outrages on my own." She fished in her knapsack, found a pair of trousers and a rough man's shirt and boots. She quickly donned these, then tucked her luxuriant hair under the cap. She spat on the ground and scratched under an arm. "Let's get this bleeping show on the road," she said, and strode across the patch.

Not a single plant whacked her. They had been fooled into thinking she was a man.

Surprise and Monica, however, took advantage of Che's offer to carry them across. That left the waif. She simply lit a match and walked through, untouched.

Che gazed at the weeds. As Woe passed, holding her match aloft, they seemed to change, becoming rare, lovely, valuable flowers. The match granted them their heart's desires: to be precious plants instead of vicious weeds.

Once clear of the patch, Pyra reverted to her regular form, evidently preferring being a girl. But she had shown initiative and ability that impressed Che.

"That's a useful pack," Surprise said. "I should get one too."

"Over here, frump," the peeve called. It had found a pack rat carrying a number of packs.

Surprise took one and put it on. And started walking backward. "What?" she asked, perplexed. She looked nice, perplexed.

Then Che caught on. "I should have recognized it. It's a backpack. It makes the wearer go backward."

Surprise took off the pack and reversed it, turning it inside out. After that it encouraged her to go forward.

Meanwhile Ted had found another item of interest. It was a small disk he was throwing, that returned to him for more. "I got a diskette," he said.

"You're too young to play with females," Monica said jealously. "You should have a discus."

"Why should I have a discussion?"

"Let's move on," Che said. "We have a distance to go before nightfall."

But as it turned out, traveling by foot was much slower than flying, and they did not reach the Golem house that day. They had to camp out. Fortunately they had found an enchanted path, so didn't have to worry about bad monsters.

"Goody!" Ted cried. He and Monica dashed off to harvest fresh pies from a pie tree.

"Oh, I'm really glad for the chance to bathe and rest," Surprise said. She headed for the warm pond the campsite provided. Pyra went with her.

"Ted, let's explore the area by air," Che said. "In case there are any dangers nearby."

The boy was always glad to fly. As a half-demon he could do it himself, but it clearly wasn't the same as riding a winged centaur.

Stymy joined them as they circled upward into the dusky sky. "That was a diplomatic way to give the women privacy," the stork said.

"Aw, who wants to peek anyway," Ted said, disappointed.

Che did not comment. He was trying to let them bathe in peace, but that wasn't all of it. He had not wanted to let himself look at Surprise's bare body, lest he lose control. His desire for her was not fading, it was increasing. When she had ridden him across the patch of whackers he had feared his very fur was burning where her legs touched.

They explored the area, and found no lurking monsters. In due course they returned to the camp, and found that the women had not only completed their bath, they had harvested and set up a nice meal for them all.

It was a pleasant night, but Che still wasn't certain they were really in an alternate Xanth. He suspected that the others had similar doubts.

A traveler passed by. She was Sarah, on her way to visit her grandmother. She seemed defenseless.

"But aren't you afraid of monsters or bad people?" Che asked her.

"Oh, no," Sarah said. "I can't be harmed by physical things. Only by words."

The peeve spied her. "How you doing, frowzy?"

Sarah flinched.

"That's the pet peeve," Che explained quickly. "It insults everyone. There's really nothing personal about it."

"Thank you," Sarah said. But she hastened away.

Che considered saying something to the peeve, but realized it would be useless. The bird was incorrigible.

In the morning, refreshed, they resumed travel. This time they made it without undue event. There was the Golem house.

And there, as they watched from a distance, was Surprise, holding her baby. This *was* another reality.

Suddenly Surprise was reticent. "She looks so satisfied," she said. "How can I take her baby from her?"

Now was the time for firmness. "You and I must talk to her," Che said. "And Stymy must smell the baby. We have to know." He didn't say that the other Surprise was just as appealing to him as the one he was with. Curse that elixir!

"Yes," she breathed, looking attractively weak-kneed.

"But she is bound to be confused, at first. So perhaps it would be better if you conceal yourself somewhat, until the time is right."

Surprise blinked, and abruptly her face was unfamiliar. "Like this?"

"That will do nicely," he agreed. She looked like a different young woman though her figure was unchanged. He still wanted to hold her, because he knew her identity. The elixir had oriented him on her, not her appearance. He was learning a distressing amount about love elixir.

They advanced on the house. The other Surprise spied them, and her mouth dropped open with amazement. "Che!" she exclaimed. "But who can your companions be?"

"I have to make a rather strange statement," Che said. "I hope you will trust me to be telling you the truth."

"You always tell the truth, Che. But I thought you were busy with some special project, and that it would be Cynthia who came to see my new baby boy." She held up the baby. "He was delivered just yesterday and I haven't named him yet. He was such a surprise, if I may use that term."

"Yes," Che said. "First, I am not the Che you know."

"Not? You certainly look and sound like him. Are you some demon emulating him?"

"I am Che, but not the one you have encountered before. I am from another reality."

Surprise Two was taken aback. "I don't think I understand."

"That is natural. It is a highly confusing situation. There are many Xanths, each with similar people, plants, and monsters. This one is so similar to the one I came from that I couldn't be sure it wasn't mine, until I saw you. Now I know it is different."

"Are you sure you didn't brush the edge of a forget whorl and get confused?"

"Yes. You see, one of my companions is—you. From the other reality."

Surprise Two laughed. "Your friend is not me, Che, though she does have a similar outfit and hairstyle."

"She used her talent to mask herself, so as not to startle you unduly." He glanced at Surprise One. "Please show her."

Surprise One reverted to her natural aspect. "Hello, me," she said.

Surprise Two stared. "You do look like me now! But how can there be two of me?"

"One from each Xanth," Che said. "Ordinarily you would never meet, but we crossed into your reality for this purpose. Do you wish to verify your other self's nature?"

"I should think so," Surprise Two said. "If she's me, she can do similar magic. Match this." She snapped her fingers, and yellow sparks flew out.

Surprise One snapped her fingers, making similar green sparks.

Surprise Two floated knee high off the ground. Surprise One did the same, a little higher. Surprise Two coughed, and a blue snake flew out of her mouth, dropped to the ground, and slithered away. Surprise One coughed, producing a red snake.

"You *are* me," Surprise Two said. "No one else could demonstrate more than one talent, and even I could not do exactly the same ones again."

"That's why I varied them," Surprise One said. "I did the ones you could have done next."

"I suppose I have to believe you," Surprise Two said. "But whatever possessed you to come here?"

"I—" Surprise One stalled, and looked appealingly at Che.

All four of Che's knees weakened. How could he ever resist her appeal? "We have no wish to bring you any grief," he said to Surprise Two. "But it is possible that we will."

Surprise Two shook her head. "I know that no other me would wish anyone harm, especially not another me. What grief could you bring me, without wishing it?"

"Your baby," Che said.

"My baby!" Surprise Two shrank back, holding her sleeping son closer.

Che couldn't stand to hurt this Surprise either, so he delayed their business. "Please tell us how he was delivered. Was there anything unusual about it?"

"No, it was a regular stork delivery, brought by—" Surprise paused. "A stork like that."

"There may have been an error."

"No error! We signaled in good faith, and—" Again she paused. "Oh, no!"

"There was something?"

"We signaled six months ago. We weren't expecting the delivery yet, but evidently the storks have become more efficient since I was delivered. I was five years late; now they're running early. Aren't they?"

"I am afraid not."

"We were so glad to have our son that we never questioned it. Are you saying there was a mistake?" Tears were forming, brightening her pretty eyes.

That tore Che up. "Did the stork question your age?"

"No, it knew better. I am eighteen. Umlaut went to the Stork Works and insisted that they correct the record, so they wouldn't think I was underage. So there was no problem on that score."

"There was with me," Surprise One said. "We signaled nine months ago, but the stork thought I was thirteen, and refused to deliver my baby."

"And brought him instead to me, here?" Now the tears were flowing in earnest. "This is your son, not mine?"

"It may be so," Che said. "That is what we have come to ascertain."

Surprise Two held out the baby. "I can't keep your baby," she said, her tears dripping off her sweet chin.

"I can't do this," Surprise One said, turning away, weeping.

"We have to know the truth," Che said. "We brought the stork who almost delivered in our Xanth. He can tell the baby he brought by the smell. If you will allow—"

Surprise Two held the baby toward Stymy.

Stymy stepped forward and sniffed. "That is not the one."

The other three looked at him with mixed expressions. "Not?" Che asked.

"Definitely not."

"I can keep my baby?" Surprise Two asked, amazed.

"Yes," Che said.

"Oh, I'm glad," Surprise One said. "You are truly me, and without fault. I couldn't do that to you."

"I couldn't have done it to you, either," Surprise Two said. Then, in sudden tearful generosity: "Would you like to hold him?"

Surprise One paused only a third of a moment. "Yes."

Two gave the baby to One, who held him like an infinitely precious thing.

"But how can he not be yours?" Two asked. "If the stork went from you to me?"

"There are many realities," Che explained. "We are checking the ones where the stork crossed between two to deliver the baby. Yours must have come from another reality, not ours. As far as we are concerned, he is yours to keep. We will check another reality for ours."

"I'm so relieved," Surprise Two said. "It's selfish, I know, but I love my baby."

"He's lovable," Surprise One agreed. "Please take him back now, before I fall in love with him myself. Thank you so much for letting me hold him." She gave the baby boy back.

"You must make the storks correct your record," Surprise Two said, holding her son.

"We have done so," Che said. "But the baby was already gone."

"It must be awful."

"Yes," One said.

"But I am so glad to have met you," Two said. "I knew nothing of all this."

"Neither did I, yesterday," One said.

"We must go," Che said. "We must check the other realities."

"Good-bye," the two Surprises said together, hugging each other, the baby nestled between them. Che wished he could hug them both; they were unutterably lovely in their mutual emotion and generosity.

They started to walk back toward the others of their party, when something appeared in the sky. It was a bug, no a bird, no a dragon—no, a flying centaur. "Cynthia!" Surprise exclaimed.

The centaur mare glided grandly down to land in the field near the Golem house. Che, knowing it wasn't *his* Cynthia, tried to move on toward the forest, to get clear before she saw him.

He was way too late. "Che!" Cynthia called. "What are you doing here? I wondered when I saw you from the sky. I thought you had important business with the Good Magician."

"You can't avoid her," Surprise murmured. "You'll have to explain, as you did so well with my other self."

That seemed to be the case. He turned to face Cynthia as she trotted up. He had always liked the way she trotted, especially when viewed from the front. "Hello," he said somewhat lamely.

"Oh, you can do better than that," she said, stepping up and kissing him firmly but intimately on the mouth.

This was delightful but distinctly awkward. "Cynthia, there's something I need to explain."

"By all means, Che," she said, clasping him so that her large bare breasts pressed firmly against his chest. He had always liked that, too. "Now that we're together, maybe we can get alone and have that phenomenal mating session that got postponed."

That was wickedly tempting. The elixir had oriented him on Surprise, but that did not mean he had lost his feeling for Cynthia. She was a wonderful match for him. But this was treacherous terrain. "I fear I must demur."

"Your time is squeezed? In that case it can be very quick, but still satisfying. Come into the shelter of the forest—or

do you prefer to do it in the air, out of sight of the house?
That's a nice challenge."

"It's not that," he said. "I would love to do it. But I must
not."

Now she was concerned. "Che, is there a problem?"

"I am not the one you take me for," he said bluntly, unable
to finesse the issue further.

"You certainly are fooling me. If you're not Che, who are
you?"

"I *am* Che. But not *your* Che. I'm from another reality."

She was a centaur. She caught on rapidly. "There are other
realities? I don't believe we have discussed this before."

"I didn't know, before. I learned it from the Good Magician. I am here on special business."

Understanding did not necessarily bring belief. "It is not
that I doubt you in anything Che, but perhaps I require more
substantial evidence."

Nicely put. "We have the Surprise Golem from my reality
here also."

Cynthia glanced around, seeing Surprise One. "That's
odd; I thought I saw her standing by the house."

"She is." He gestured to Surprise One. "We need to show
her."

Surprise understood. She walked back to join Surprise
Two. The two women stood side by side.

Cynthia gazed at them for a moment, then nodded. "Point
made. Just what is this special business you are on?"

"In my reality, the stork brought Surprise's baby, but declined to deliver it, citing her age. He thought she was thirteen, counting from her date of delivery. He took her baby to
another reality for delivery where there was not a question
about her age. We are trying to recover it for her."

She nodded. "And this is the one? I know her delivery was
early."

"No, this turns out not to be the one. So we shall continue
our search."

"That's nice. This Surprise is certainly worthy, and it
would be a shame to deprive her of her baby."

"So now we must go," Che said. "I apologize for deceiving you, however inadvertently."

She considered half a moment. "How are you traveling?"

"By foot. We have several other members of our party, too many for me to safely carry alone."

"Suppose I join you, and carry some?"

Che needed only a quarter of a moment to consider. "That would be a generous offer."

"It is an expedient one, as I would like to learn more of this matter, and will not otherwise have a chance."

Che knew Cynthia; she had something else on her mind. What was it? He couldn't always fathom her moods. But there was no point in challenging her. "If you are satisfied to perform this chore, it will be appreciated."

"Let me make amends to Surprise; then I will join you."

"I will explain to my companions."

They separated for the moment, then rejoined when the amenities were accomplished. Che introduced Pyra to Cynthia. No other introductions were needed, as Cynthia and the children knew each other, and all understood the distinction between realities. Cynthia took the three children, while Che carried Pyra and Surprise.

"That is one savvy filly," Pyra remarked. "She has her eye on you, Che."

Surprise was interested. "Well, they are mated, in their own realities. Such interest is natural."

"This goes beyond that," Pyra said. "Didn't you notice?"

"There is something," Surprise agreed.

"I do not understand," Che said.

"Naturally not," Pyra said. "You're male." Both women laughed.

Che knew better than to dismiss her notion; Pyra had proved to be accurately perceptive in his own case. "Please explain it to me."

"There are differences between the realities," Pyra said. "I have seen it endlessly when comparing them via the Mask. Some are of little consequence; others are subtly significant. Such as whether the storks know your age, Surprise."

"Yes, that made all the difference," Surprise agreed. "The other couple also signaled the stork only six months ago. So what seems the same at present has a slightly different history. But the relationship of Che and Cynthia seems the same."

"Perhaps. But let's try this for a conjecture: in Reality Two, the centaur couple is not as close. They may even be considering separation."

"Never!" Che said. "I love Cynthia." It was true, if no longer the whole truth.

"Of course," Pyra said smoothly. "Couples, once formed, seldom if ever separate, in our reality. All marriages and matings are happy and permanent. But suppose that this is not the case in Reality Two? That couples can tire and separate, as they do in Mundania, where half of all marriages founder."

"Xanth isn't Mundania," Che said.

"To be sure. And Reality Two is not Reality One. Assume my conjecture is correct: what would Cynthia do if her relationship was weakening?"

"She would try harder to interest Che," Surprise said. "As she did, before learning he wasn't the same stallion."

She had indeed, Che realized, feeling guilty for being tempted.

"And when she learned he was a different stallion," Pyra continued inexorably, "why did her interest not abate?"

"Because she recognized him as a new prospect," Surprise said. "With all the qualities she liked in her own mate."

"So she followed up," Pyra continued. "Finding a way to accompany him further. Perhaps to ascertain whether there were additional qualities her own mate lacks."

It made entirely too much sense, Che realized. This was doubly treacherous terrain. "I am not interested in any such dalliance," he protested.

"You were not moved when she broached you?" Pyra asked.

Bleep her perception! "She strongly resembles my Cynthia."

"Precisely. So maybe you should take her up on her interest, at least for a night."

"That's outrageous," Surprise protested. "Centaurs aren't like that."

Che felt guilty again. Surprise in her innocence had no notion of his longing for just such a liaison with her.

"Perhaps, in our reality," Pyra said. "But in other realities, perhaps not."

Now Che realized what the woman was doing. She was probing Surprise's attitude on such a liaison, knowing of Che's passion. Fortunately Surprise was having none of it.

Yet he wished that was not the case.

They reached the Stork Works and landed. The speed of flight had made the trip much faster and prevented the obstacles of the terrain, such as weed whackers. "I thank you for you kind assistance, Cynthia," he said as the women and children dismounted.

She led him aside a moment. "Perhaps we could camp for the night. There is a private place within easy range by air."

He tackled the issue directly. "In my reality, matings are permanent. There are no outside dalliances."

She shrugged regretfully. "And does Surprise Golem agree?"

"Of course."

She smiled obscurely. "Really?"

He gazed at her, appalled. *She knew*. She had fathomed his illicit passion, just as Pyra had.

"We—waded through a lake of love elixir. It affected me more than I anticipated. I shall not act on it."

"At such time as you may reconsider, return to this reality. I am of your species, and well acquainted with you. There would be no need of elixir." Then she spread her wings and took off.

He watched her graceful ascent, hating the fact that he wished he could follow her.

6

CROSSOVERS

Surprise watched Cynthia Two fly away. It had been almost as weird interacting with the alternate centaur mare as with her alternate self. The folk of Reality Two were just like those of Reality One, almost. What complicated it was her own surge of jealousy as the two winged centaurs talked privately. Surprise wanted to be the one to get private with Che. Darn that lake of love elixir! When Cynthia Two hugged and kissed Che One Surprise had felt like screaming, though she knew that it was perfectly natural for Cynthia Two to mistake Che for her own mate.

"This has been an adventure of a somewhat different nature than I anticipated," Che said.

Surprise hesitated to agree too emphatically. "It was nice of her to carry the children, so that we could fly."

"She's a nice person." He glanced unobtrusively around, verifying that the children and Pyra were for the moment out of earshot. "She made me an offer. I regret that I was tempted."

She stifled a shock of envy. "Well, she's your mate. Attraction between you is natural, even across realities."

"I am glad you understand. I fear others would not."

She understood far better than she cared to. But she lacked the pretexts of matching species or honest confusion; she could not simply fling her arms around his human section and kiss him. Yet she wished there could be a pretext. She had expressed outrage at the idea of any love dalliance of convenience, but she had been only half sincere. It was his tryst with Cynthia Two she objected to, rather than the notion of any liaison. If Surprise herself could have the chance for a night of love with Che, that no one else would ever know about, she feared she would take it. She loved her husband Umlaut, but this was a special passion that it seemed could be gotten beyond only by indulgence.

Fortunately Che was a centaur, and immune to such notions. It was her guilty human weakness that gave her such an awful secret desire. She would never soil their friendship by revealing it.

They entered the Stork Works chamber, where Pyra had left the Reality Mask. They would of course have to try again. Surprise hoped that this time she found her own baby, and that the other Surprise would in some way be undeserving so she wouldn't have to feel horribly guilty for taking it. Already she had learned that this quest was far less simple, physically and emotionally, than she had supposed. Had the Good Magician known it would be? Probably so, because he knew everything. He had tried to warn her.

Pyra eliminated the first little picture. Now there were five. "Shall we try the next in order?" she asked.

Che glanced at Surprise, sending a minor illicit thrill through her. "Yes," she said. "We can't tell which one is correct, so might as well be methodical."

"This one," Pyra told the stork attendant.

"Exit," the stork said.

They drew aside the heavy curtain and departed the Stork Works again. "Do we have to go through all this dull stuff again?" Ted demanded.

"You insisted on coming," Surprise reminded him.

"You didn't say how dull it would be," Monica said.

"It occurs to me that my usefulness ends when separated from the Mask," Pyra said. "All you really need along is Stymy Stork, to sniff the baby. Why don't I babysit here, so the three of you can fly efficiently and accomplish your mission rapidly?"

Fly essentially alone with Che? What a dream! But she dared not show eagerness. "Are you sure? Keeping these little demons under control can be a daunting task."

"I can show them different pictures on the Mask."

"What pictures?" Ted demanded truculently.

"Huge messy battles in other realities, between goblins and harpies, with horrendous sound effects, for example."

"Great!"

"Not," Monica said. "Who wants to see blood and feathers fly?"

"Also pictures of costume dances in alternate Castle Roognas, with great music and some illicit kissing."

"OoOoo!" Monica agreed enthusiastically.

Ted grimaced. "Ugh!"

"Split pictures," Pyra said. "One for Ted, one for Monica." She glanced at little Woe Betide. "And a third showing a matchless garden of magic matches."

The waif smiled and clapped her little hands ineffectively together.

"What about me?" the peeve grouched.

"A fourth picture, showing the annual Carnivals of Insults, where all the foulest mouths get to get together and mouth off at each other. It usually devolves into a brawl."

"How come I never heard of it?"

"It's not in our Xanth. I found it when exploring alternates. Some of those insults are choice."

"Okay, flame-head," the peeve agreed.

It seemed Pyra had the bases covered. "We owe you one," Surprise said.

The woman shot her a briefly burning glance. "Or two," she murmured. "Be sure to get your business done."

Surprise was shocked. What was she suggesting?

"We shall locate the baby," Che agreed.

Oh, of course. How could she have forgotten, even for a moment? "Thank you so much," Surprise said.

She mounted Che, who spread his wings and took off. Surprise looked back and saw Pyra herding the children back into the dome, shooting out little warning jets of fire when the demons wandered too far afield. She did seem competent, considering she had no children of her own.

"Pyra has more sides to her personality than I had seen at first," Che remarked as they followed the stork across fields and streams.

"She does," Surprise agreed. "I really appreciate the way she is helping. We'll finish much faster this way."

"Yet she came with us because she desired personal adventure. Why should she sacrifice that?"

"Oh, I wouldn't believe for a moment that she has any bad motive."

"Not by her definition."

"Am I missing something?"

"Surprise, she is putting us alone together, as it were. Does that seem odd to you?"

Did Pyra suspect how Surprise felt about Che? She must, because she knew of the love elixir. "Are you suggesting that she believes there is something between us?"

"I do not wish to offend you, but she did suggest something of the kind to me."

"Apart from our elevated centaury love?" What a hypocrite she was!

"Surprise, honesty is my nature. I fear I am not being completely honest with you, and it is weighing increasingly heavily on my conscience, especially after the approach Cynthia Two made to me. I wish to speak frankly at the risk of giving offense."

"By all means, Che. If I have disappointed you or become a burden, I wish to know it."

"No, by no means no! You are excellent. It is that the elixir has had greater effect than I judged at first."

"Me too," she said faintly.

"It instilled in me the desire to be physically passionate with you. Your reversion to your own form did not alleviate this."

"Me too," she repeated. She had never expected to have this dialogue, and felt guilty having it, yet also relieved.

"Pyra suggested that the standard way to abate such passion is to indulge it. It seems that after a fairly intense session it passes and has little further effect."

"As is commonly seen when animals meet at love springs," she agreed. Her heart was racing.

"It seems we have a choice: to suffer as it seems we both are doing, or to yield to the passion in the hope that it will rapidly pass, leaving us otherwise unchanged."

"Yes." She was glad that he was accurately expressive, as centaurs were.

"Yet there are considerations. We are both committed elsewhere, and such a dalliance might be taken as a betrayal of the other parties and damage the relationships, however understanding of the situation the others might be."

"Yes."

"We would of course have to inform them."

"Yes." Then she reconsidered. "Or would it be kinder not to inform them?"

"Kinder, yes. Honest, no."

"We would have to tell them," she agreed. "They would be tolerant but hurt."

"We need to come to a swift decision," he said. "Shall we vote?"

She laughed. "Public or secret?"

"Openly, in turn, as we must come to an agreement. What is your decision?"

"No," she said. "I can't—"

"I agree. We will not indulge it. It will be difficult, but at least we are not at cross purposes."

"Yes," she agreed faintly. Actually she had meant to say that she could not decide first; she needed to know his preference before judging whether she had the willpower to carry through. He had taken it as no to the indulgence, and she lacked the gumption to disagree. So they had decided, half by accident. They would be loyal to their own, and suffer. It was probably best.

The stork descended. There was the Golem house, similar though not identical to the others. They landed in the nearby field. "The prior approach seemed effective," Che said. "Shall we employ it again?"

"Yes." Surprise half-dreaded encountering her alternate self again, maybe taking her baby, but Che's cautious introduction would smooth the way.

She dismounted and walked beside him to the house, changing her hairstyle as she went. Hair could make an enormous difference, when it was supposed to. The door opened as they approached, and Surprise Three emerged, holding a swaddled bundle.

"Why hello, Che," Surprise Three said. "Back so soon?" She walked to him, reached out with her free hand, drew his head down, and kissed him solidly on the mouth.

Surprise One tried to soften her stare of astonishment. Was this the way friends greeted friends in this reality?

Che seemed similarly surprised. "There is something I need to explain."

Surprise Three laughed. "That your passion for me brought you back from your mission early? I can live with that." She kissed him again, he being evidently too stunned to resist. "Come on inside, beloved, and we'll tackle our second stork in style. What form would you like me to take this time?" Then she paused. "Oh, where are my manners? You haven't introduced your friends. Perhaps the lady will hold our foal while we indulge."

This time Surprise One's stare burst out unrestrained. "Your foal?" she asked numbly.

"What else?" Surprise Three handed her the bundle. There inside was a tiny winged centaur foal.

The numbness extended from her voice down to her arms, locking them in place so that they didn't drop the bundle. Che and Surprise Three had mated!

"This I fear is complicated," Che said awkwardly.

"Come on inside and you can explain it while we mate. Oh, Che, it's so good to have you back already!" Surprise Three took him by the hand and hauled him into the house.

He looked helplessly back at Surprise One. "I will try to explain," he said. Then the door closed behind them.

Surprise One stood with the foal in her arms. Stymy approached and sniffed. "That is not the one I delivered."

She had to laugh, out of a mixture of relief and hysteria. "I had gathered as much. Can they be married, in this reality?"

"Evidently they can be. She takes Che for her stallion, reasonably enough."

And Che's passion for Surprise One would extend to Surprise Three, because she was really the same person. That was why he had been vulnerable to her kisses, and unable to hang back. Would he be able to resist her charms long enough to explain his true identity? Could Surprise One herself resist, if faced with an equivalent challenge?

A form was coming in to land; she had not noticed, in her distraction of foal and concept. "Surprise!" he called. It was Che Three, looking and sounding exactly like Che One.

"I will let you handle this yourself," Stymy said, fading back. "I don't think my input would be helpful."

"Hello, Che," she said faintly. "I have to tell you—"

"How you have missed me? I returned as rapidly as I could, eager to see my love and my foal again." He approached, reached down, put his strong hands on her elbows, lifted her up, and kissed her firmly on the lips. "Congratulations on your new hairstyle. I like it."

He thought she was his wife, and there she was holding his foal. "But I'm not—"

"Not sorry? Oh, my love, even a day away from you is too much, and right at this time, too." He set her down and took the foal-bundle from her arms. "But now we are together again. I must possess you immediately. Choose a form."

Dizzy from the kiss and realization, she was unable to speak intelligibly. She changed into a winged girl.

"Ah, in the sky," he said. "Delightful." He spread his wings and leaped into the air, carrying the foal.

What could she do? She flapped her wings and followed him.

They circled over a small lake. "Actually, that form is not ideal for this," he said. "We can't get close enough together. Try a hippogriff."

"I have to explain," she blurted. "I'm not your wife."

A handsome furrow crossed his brow. "Has the past year been a dream?"

"No, it's not that. I'm from a different reality."

He was a centaur; he caught on quickly. "You're a reality traveler? Then what are you doing at my house with my foal?"

"Your wife is—it's an awkward story."

Now he was quite serious. "She is all right?"

She decided not to start with who was in the house and why. "All right," she agreed. "I am Surprise Golem, from a reality where I married Umlaut."

"Umlaut!" He was astonished.

"And nine months ago we signaled the stork, and it delivered yesterday—but balked because it thought I was only thirteen."

"Ah, that confusion of ages, because of your own late delivery. You did not go to the Stork Works to make a correction in their record?"

"It was stupid of me, I know. I just didn't think of it. I somehow thought they would know. After all, my signal was accepted."

"True. They should have rejected the signal. That makes them culpable. Once they accepted it, they should have delivered."

"Then the stork took my baby to another reality. I was horrified."

"Understandable," he said.

"So I came here to try to get my baby back. Only it's not mine."

"And we are not mated in your reality."

"Yes. Only—"

"Surprise, I know you, even if you are not *my* Surprise," he said. "There is love in your kiss and in your eyes. You have a passion for me, as I do for you."

"I confess I do," she said. "Because Che—the one in my reality—and I waded through love elixir. Now we long for each other, but don't want to hurt our spouses. It—it's difficult."

"Who is my spouse, in your reality?"

"Cynthia Centaur."

"The one converted from human? She is a fine person, and would surely understand. You should do the sensible thing and take a few hours off to abate that passion the direct way. Then it would no longer bother you, and you could return to your respective mates."

"We—agreed not to."

"Because you want to be neither unkind nor deceiving with your significant others?"

"Yes, exactly. You understand marvelously."

"It is because I love you, wherever you may come from. Where is my Surprise?"

"In with my—my reality's Che. He's trying to explain, also."

"While she's trying to seduce him."

"I—I fear so."

He laughed. "Evidently your reality is stricter about such things. I suspect she recognized him as a foreign entity and decided to have some fun with him. She's a marvelous tease."

"Fun?"

"She is a creature of fun. Are you not the same?"

That took her aback. "I was, before I lost my baby."

"Which accounts for the odd underpinning of grief I also detect in you. Surprise, I believe I understand your position, and will not try again to seduce you, now that I fathom your identity, though I admit I would like to. Perhaps it would help if you met the other couple."

"Other couple?"

"This way. This should not take long, and your understanding should increase, and with it your ability to settle your own case." He changed direction and flew swiftly across the landscape.

She followed, bemused. Here was a Che who knew her and loved her, or an edition of her, and who had the honor to treat her with the respect due one in her awkward situation. So for slightly different reason they did not indulge their passion, just as she had not with Che One. And for slightly different reason, she wished they could. Would doing it with this Che abate her passion for Che One? But then where would that leave him, emotionally?

They landed before a well-constructed stall. "Hey folk, cease your romancing a moment," Che called. "You have company."

Two figures came out: a man and a winged centaur mare. "Umlaut! Cynthia!" Surprise exclaimed. These two were married in this reality?

"Hello, Che and Surprise," Umlaut said. He looked and sounded exactly like her husband. "You brought your foal."

"And you restyled your hair," Cynthia said. "It looks nice. Che surely likes it."

"I do," Che agreed. "However, there is a matter of somewhat serious import to discuss, and perhaps you can help us come to better terms with it."

"We'll be glad to," Umlaut said. He kissed Cynthia. "We can spare two moments from our romancing."

Surprise almost freaked out at the sight of them kissing, but reminded herself forcefully that this was not her Umlaut. Somehow the matchings had occurred differently in this reality.

"This is Surprise Golem, from another reality, with adapted wings for the moment," Che said. "She lost her baby, and is seeking it here. In her reality she is married to you, Umlaut. He is the father of her baby."

Now it was Umlaut who was astonished. "How did that happen?"

Surprise had to smile. "It seemed natural at the time. How

did you get together with Cynthia? In my reality she is mated with Che."

"I was stranded beyond a bog," Umlaut said. "Cynthia volunteered to carry me across. I admired her form—"

"You couldn't take your eyes off my breasts," Cynthia said.

"Well, they're good breasts. I was not at that point very familiar with centaurs. One thing led to another."

"He emulates so nicely," Cynthia said. "I liked that."

"Here is a complication," Che said. "Surprise waded through love elixir with my alternate self, but both being married elsewhere they chose not to indulge their mutual passion. So they are suffering. I thought the two of you might have some input. How would you feel if for example you were married respectively to Surprise and me, and the two of us were caught by the elixir?"

"I can hardly imagine being married to any other creature," Umlaut said.

"Make the effort," Cynthia suggested. "Kiss her."

"But—" Surprise protested feebly.

"What is your objection?" Che asked her.

"Umlaut—he—in my reality he is my husband. I love him."

"Precisely. This should be an easy coupling to imagine."

"I admit to being curious," Umlaut said. "Provided Cynthia understands."

"I do. I'll even kiss Che," Cynthia said. She stepped up and did so. Then she stepped back. "Oh, my. He's quite a stallion."

"Stop teasing," Umlaut said. He advanced on Surprise, and she was unable to formulate any further objection.

He kissed her, and she felt the familiar rush of delight and desire. She kissed him back, passionately.

"Oh, my," he said also, taken aback.

"I apologize," she said quickly. "In my reality I love you. I can't help responding."

"She loves you," Cynthia said. "And I could see how I

could love Che, had I kissed him before Umlaut. So now we must address the question: how would we feel about Che and Surprise abating a temporary passion born of elixir?"

"They should just do it and be done with it," Umlaut said. "After all, they are married in this reality."

"You're thinking because their—our—whatever—relationship is valid here, it would be all right to cheat on our partners there," Surprise said, annoyed. "That's not good logic, is it?"

"She's right," Cynthia said. "What's right here is one thing. What counts is what's right there. They should not do it."

"Though their passion then lingers, interfering with their mission?" Che asked her.

She considered. "Maybe if they brought their partners in to watch?"

"And really *really* upset them?" Surprise asked in turn.

Umlaut was doubtful. "Would it really, if their partners agreed to it?"

Surprise made a sudden, possibly dangerous decision. "Let's find out. Here are your partners Che and Cynthia. See how they react to the two of us doing it." She advanced on him.

"That seems fair," Umlaut agreed uncertainly.

She took hold of him and kissed him, knowing exactly what he liked. She stroked him in the places that turned him on, and whispered the nothings that delighted him. If there was one thing she really knew, it was how to make love to Umlaut, regardless of the reality.

He responded, as he had to. He kissed her back, and stroked her back, only in neither case was it really her back. It was her front. Soon their clothes were coming off and they were both breathing hard.

"Stop!" Cynthia cried. "I can't stand it!"

"Nor can I," Che said.

They stepped in, and Cynthia was kissing Umlaut, and Che was kissing Surprise. Then he paused, with a visible effort. "But you are not my mate," he said. "You only seem to be."

"You made your point," Cynthia said. "Don't have that illicit affair." She turned to Umlaut. "As for you, you responded too readily. Couldn't you have managed some decent modicum of resistance?"

"Don't blame him," Surprise said. "I know how to push his buttons, even when wearing wings."

Cynthia nodded. "Teach me those buttons."

"Gladly." There followed a spot education session.

Then Surprise and Che took off for "home." "That was intelligent of you," Che said. "You made a fair demonstration that proved your case. I almost believed you were serious."

"I got that way," she said. "It's hard to do a good act without really getting into it. Thanks for rescuing me."

"You looked like my mate making love with my friend," he said. "My tolerance turned out to be less than I supposed."

"It is easy to make sensible decisions when it's not your own rump getting gored. I needed to know how they *felt,* not how they reasoned."

"You were effective in evoking an honest emotional response." He paused thirty-three percent of a moment, centaurs being precise creatures. "May we accelerate?"

"I'm not sure I understand."

"I have learned things about my mate in the course of my association with you. I love you—her. I want to get home to her rapidly."

Oh. "Of course. I'll fly as fast as I can."

They flew at top velocity, and soon returned to the Golem house. Surprise Three and Che One were outside awaiting them. "I think they will have figured things out, as we have," Che said as they glided down for a landing. "I suggest we part quickly and amicably."

"Agreed." He was evidently desperate to romance his wife, and the elixir made her understand all too perfectly.

They landed. Che Three swept Surprise Three into his embrace as she took the foal, and they hurried into the house. Che One glanced at Surprise, noted her wings, and spread his own wings.

"Stymy!" she called. "We are returning."

The stork appeared and joined them in flight. "I trust everything has been resolved?"

"To a degree," she said.

"Well spoken," Che agreed. Then, as they gained elevation: "Shall we compare notes?"

"Did she succeed in seducing you?"

"She came uncomfortably close. She knew exactly which, shall we say, buttons to push."

"She would," Surprise agreed, remembering how she had used her knowledge to do the same with Umlaut Three. There was nothing like marriage to thoroughly acquaint one person with another.

"Only when she had me ready to, um, perform, did she confess that she knew I was not her husband. She had been teasing me throughout, rather more effectively than I thought possible."

"Che Three said she was a tease."

"It is surely an ability you also possess, when you choose to exercise it."

"Perhaps," she said, preferring to retain some secrets. "Che Three returned, and naturally assumed I was his wife, with his foal. He was eager to, well, you know, before I explained. Then we visited Umlaut and Cynthia Centaur."

"The complementary couple," he agreed. "Your spouse and mine, in our own reality."

"The surprising thing was that they made a good couple. They plainly love each other. It—well, it broadened my perspective."

"I understand." She knew he was not being merely polite.

"It seems that there is no single boy for a single girl," she said. "Umlaut was dazed by Cynthia's bare breasts, when they interacted, and she liked his emulations, and now they're married. It must have been similar with Che Three and Surprise Three."

"It was. They were introduced by mutual friends, who I now divine must have been Cynthia and Umlaut. She had always been a fancier of equines, as some girls are, and he much admired her assorted talents."

"I always liked equines," Surprise said. "Even Mundane horses. I suppose that's not coincidence."

"And I have admired your several talents since I learned of them."

"So one thing led to another," she said. "It does seem to be a valid match."

He made an almost humanlike sigh. "Surprise, I fear we are avoiding an issue."

She understood all too well, but she tried to demur. "I thought we had settled it."

"That was before we encountered the revelations of Reality Three."

"Where you and I are married," she agreed.

"We shall take as given that neither of us wishes to change our state in our own reality, or to hurt our partners in any avoidable way."

"Given." He was right: what they had discovered had changed their perspective.

"Yet when Surprise Three addressed me—"

"When Che Three kissed me—"

"There would seem to be more between us than elixir."

"Have you changed your mind?" She did not need to say what about.

"I may have, depending on your perspective."

She thought for barely a tenth of a moment. "I may have also."

"In fact, after Surprise Three—"

"You are not merely willing, but in a manner eager." As, it seemed, was she, guilty though she felt about it.

He blushed. She had not seen that before. "True, though I would never have imagined such a thing prior to the elixir."

"Nor would I, prior to Che Three."

"We have suffered what the Mundanes would call a one-two punch. We can no longer deny its impact."

"I think we should kiss," she said. "To see whether what our alternates can do to us is true for us directly."

"And if it is?"

"I wonder whether what would be forbidden in our reality is proper here."

"That is a pertinent thought. We are in a reality where our love is proper. That suggests that if we are ever to do what we contemplate, this would be the place. It might even be said that we are not the same people here as we are there. What occurs here need not be repeated there."

He had endorsed the rationale she had not quite been able to formulate on her own. They could emulate their selves of Reality Three, and thereafter feel no need of anything further. They could abate the effect of the elixir. "Stymy!" she called to the stork flying ahead. "Please go on without us. Tell Pyra that we'll be there soon. She will understand." All too well, she suspected. Could the fire woman be trusted to keep her mouth shut at home?

"As you wish," the stork said, flying on. Did he, too, understand? He was after all in the business of delivering the results of such signals.

Surprise shut off that thought. "Let's go below. I do not wish to be observed, even though we may be legitimate, here."

"I comprehend perfectly, and agree. Legitimacy can have alternate interpretations."

Indeed it could. She had a mental picture of dangerously roiling waters, yet could not help herself. Her desire was driving her on like the breath of a pursuing dragon.

They circled down, locating a pleasant glade. Of course the most innocent glades could be treacherous; they would have to check it carefully, lest there be a real dragon, or tangle tree, or some other threat. But this one seemed especially appealing.

Che landed first, and his bow appeared in his hands, an arrow nocked. He turned in place, scanning the verge of the forest. She admired his alertness.

She landed beside him, ready with her own magic. "I see nothing."

"That could be because it saw us first," he said with a third of a smile. "But certainly there are no monsters here."

"Just winged monsters," she agreed. It was humor; all magical creatures bearing wings were by definition winged monsters, though some were beautiful.

He turned to her. "If you will, for the kiss—assume your normal form."

That made sense. If she kissed him in the form of a winged monster it would not be a fair test, because the wings would add appeal. They had to know whether they were naturally attracted to each other in their separate natural forms. She banished the wings.

They approached each other. He stood significantly higher than she did. "Maybe you should pick me up, as Che Three did."

He nodded. "Oh, Surprise, I fear I already know how this will end. Once we are certain—"

"Then I will assume a more compatible form for you, as Surprise Three does for Che Three." Form did make a difference, when it came to certain types of interactions. There was no need to specify what. She stood before him.

"Exactly." He reached down, took firm hold of her girlish hips, and lifted her to his upper level.

She reached around his human torso, drawing herself close. Their faces came together. They kissed.

Little hearts exploded outward and formed a dancing cloud around them. She felt as if she were floating, and not just because he was lifting her.

The kiss ended, but they remained embraced. "Oh, Che, it is true," she said. "Now I know what is meant by a kiss that half-summons the stork. I am very much afraid I love you."

"Again, I comprehend more perfectly than seems proper," he said. "I desire—"

His words were cut off by her second kiss. She knew exactly what he desired, as she felt the same. Love elixir normally rendered the participants quickly and thoroughly physical.

He stiffened, and not in a romantic sense. She broke the kiss and looked around.

A man was moving erratically toward them. He looked harmless, but wasn't watching where he was going.

Che quickly set her down, and she retreated behind him, letting him deal with the intruder. Che spun about to face the man, but the man wandered left, then right, and crashed into Surprise before she could avoid him. She in turn crashed into Che, and both she and the man wound up in a heap entangling the centaur's front legs.

Che reached down and lifted the man up by his collar, holding him suspended in air. "What is this?" he asked.

The man looked at him. "Oh, hello, centaur. I didn't see you."

"You crashed into us," Che said.

"Of course. That is my nature. I am Com. Com Plication. I crash into things, and then they crash too. Pewter wasn't right for a week after crashing."

So there was a Com Pewter here in Xanth Three. "You're dangerous," Surprise said.

"Only to things that can't handle crashes," Plication said. "For the others I am merely inconvenient."

"True," Che said, setting the man down, facing away from them. He meandered on across the glade.

"I believe we were in the process of discovering something," she said. "If you concur, I will change my shape. Do you have a preference?"

"Any form will do, as long as it is you. I—" He broke off, spying something else.

She looked. There was another man approaching. He was roughly human, but so fat as to be globular, and covered with what looked like bits of food.

This time Surprise took the initiative. She stepped out to intercept the man. "Hello. I am Surprise Golem."

He stopped walking. "I am Pete. Pete Za."

"What may we do for you, Pete?"

He shook his head. "It is what I can do for you. I felt your hunger, so came immediately."

She did not quite like the sound of this. "My—hunger?"

"I feed hungry folk. What flavor do you prefer?"

Che caught on. "Pizza. You make Pizza."

"Magically good," Pete agreed. "Choose your type."

It seemed that the only way to get rid of Pete was to accept what he offered. "Mushroom," Surprise said.

Pete put two fingers to his collar, jerked outward, and peeled off his front section. There it was: a mushroom pizza, steamingly hot. He handed it to her and glanced at Che.

"Cheese," Che said. The man ripped off another section and gave him a big cheesy disk. Then he went cheerily on his way, having done a favor, he supposed.

"I suspect he misinterpreted the hunger he felt in us," Che remarked. "But this will do for the moment." He bit into his pizza.

"Yes." She was glad for the confusion, for she would not have wanted the kind of hunger she felt to be peeled off a strange man's front. She bit into her pizza. It was very good. She was hungry in that manner also, as it turned out.

They finished eating, and faced each other again. "Now about forms," she said.

"Another," he murmured grimly. "Two, in fact."

She turned. A girl was approaching from one direction, and a boy from the other.

Surprise addressed the girl, concealing her irritation at the interruption. "Hello. I am Surprise Golem."

"I am Celest. My talent is to summon falling stars." She glanced upward. "Like this."

There was a brief whistle and thunk as something plunged from the sky into the ground, gouging out a smoking pit. Celest walked across to the pit and dug into it with her dainty shoe, kicking out a five pointed silver star.

Che intercepted the boy. "I am Che Centaur."

"I am Aaron. My talent is to place wings on objects, like watches. That makes time fly."

Celest approached him, kicking the hot little star ahead of her. "What about stars?"

"Sure." A little set of wings appeared on the star. They flapped, and it flew into the air, circled, and departed.

"That's great," Celest said. "How about a date?"

"Sure," Aaron agreed. He put his arm about her waist and they walked out of the glade together.

"That was convenient," Surprise said.

"They canceled out," Che agreed. "I think a nice form for you to assume would be—" He stopped.

Another person was entering the glade. This was a curvaceous girl with honey-brown hair to the middle of her back, with a bit of a curl. Her skin was peach porcelain so that she almost seemed to glow. She carried a short-haired silver and brown cat with a striped tail. But she looked sad.

Surprise suppressed a hidden sigh. Suddenly this glade had become a major crossroads! "Hello. I am—"

"I am Nikki. I can see folks' natures." Nikki looked directly at her with amber-brown pupils fading to clear muted gemstone green irises rimmed with blue-gray. "Yours is— that's weird! You're nice, but you're not from anywhere close to here. In fact—"

"You're very perceptive," Surprise said quickly. "But why are you here?"

"I need to find a boy who loves cats as I do, and who can get along with Clarabelle." She stroked the cat.

Meanwhile a young man had entered the glade. "Hi! I'm Dave," he called. "I can look at things from different angles." He caught sight of Nikki. "What a lovely cat!"

Nikki turned her marvelous eyes on him. "You're Mundane!"

"I was," Dave agreed. "I liked to cycle and glide. But now that I am encountering folk like you, I believe I prefer Xanth."

"Do you believe in true love?"

"I do." They linked arms and departed.

Che and Surprise faced each other again. "Now that we're alone," Che said, and paused as if concerned that there would be another interruption.

There was. An old man appeared. "It's good to see you young folk getting together, here in Promenade Glade. That's what it's for."

Che and Surprise exchanged half a glance. "This is a meeting place?" she asked.

"Of course. It helps reduce the randomness of such

things. Compatible folk tend to be attracted here, just as the two of you surely were."

They exchanged the other half of the glance. They *had* been attracted to this glade. Which was fine for others, but not for them, as they had not needed to meet each other. The one thing this place would not provide was privacy.

"Thank you for informing us," Che said. "I am Che Centaur, and this is Surprise Golem."

"I am Billy Applegate. I always liked hearts, so made a place for hearts to meet."

"It certainly seems to be effective," Surprise said. "I see another one coming."

It was a woman. She had curly brown hair and blue eyes. "Hello. I am Philomena, but call me Mena."

"Welcome, Mena," Billy said. "I'm sure there'll be a young man along soon, who will find you worthwhile."

"Surely," Mena agreed, smiling.

Surprise took Che's hand. "Let's give them room," she murmured.

He nodded. They had no chance to do what they had in mind here. He lifted her onto his back and trotted into the center of the glade. "Thank you, Billy," he called as he spread his wings and took off. Billy waved cheerfully.

When they were alone in the air, Surprise spoke. "Do you think that this was accidental?"

"I believe in magic, not fate," Che said. "Yet it does seem that we are not fated to have the privacy we seek. I believe we must postpone what we had in mind. I am severely disappointed, yet also relieved."

"So am I," she agreed fervently. "Part of me really wants it, but another part of me will never forgive myself. I think we shall have to endure as we are."

They issued a mutual sigh.

7

DEMON BET

Pyra knew the moment she saw Che flying in, carrying Surprise, that they had not made it together. The elixir-inspired tension between them remained. Too bad. That was not the game, but it was a stage of it. When Stymy Stork returned alone she had hoped it was done.

Meanwhile it had been a job watching the children, who were partly or wholly demon and rambunctious. There was only so much even the Mask could do to keep them diverted. So did she want to have children herself? Maybe, if she was able to keep a firm discipline in the house. If she had the right husband.

There, of course, was the essence. If she accomplished her assignment correctly, she would have the right male. That was why she had agreed to undertake this treacherous mission. There was no other way to nab him.

They landed, and trotted to the garden where Pyra and the others waited. "Wrong reality," Che said as Surprise dismounted.

They surely knew, but she asked anyway: "Are you sure?"

"The baby is a winged foal," Surprise said.

Pyra acted surprised. "How could that be?"

"In this reality, I am married to Che."

So this was one of those. Pyra had seen different matchups in the Mask, but hadn't known whether this was one of them. So now they knew that there was nothing sacred about Surprise being with Umlaut, or Che being with Cynthia. "That is remarkable," she said, knowing it wasn't.

Che angled a glance down at her, in the handsome way he had. "You saw it in the Mask."

"I have seen realities where different couples formed," Pyra agreed. "But there are so many, it is difficult to know which ones we are visiting." Which was true.

"Let's get on to the next," Surprise said a trifle grimly. "My baby is waiting."

Pyra nodded. "I need the Mask," she announced.

"Awww," the three children and pet peeve said together. But it wasn't a strong awww, so they were about sated. They trooped inside the transition chamber.

She restored the array of realities and selected the next picture. "I can watch the children again."

"No, we want to go along this time," Ted said.

"To see the sights," Monica agreed.

That did not suit Pyra's purpose. She wanted Che and Surprise to be alone together, knowing that they were on the verge of working things out. Because they both believed that such an interaction would be wrong, it would be a stage in their corruption. "It is more efficient if they go alone."

To her surprise, Surprise demurred. "Efficiency isn't everything. They might as well come along."

Pyra couldn't argue the case without giving away her motive. "In that case, we will need additional transport."

Surprise became a winged horse. "There you are," Che said. "I'll lift you to her back."

"Naw, we want to ride you this time," Ted said.

"So we can talk to you," Monica said.

Che exchanged a full glance with Surprise. Pyra saw that

they were getting good at that. Then he lifted the children one by one up onto his own back. The peeve joined them, evidently preferring to ride this time rather than fly on its own. It was a curious bird.

Meanwhile Pyra got onto Surprise's back. She had talked directly with Che, advising him of the nature of the elixir; now she could do the same with Surprise, perhaps to better effect. Of course Surprise couldn't answer in this form, but that wasn't strictly necessary.

They trooped outside. The stork took off, leading the way, and Che followed. Then Surprise spread her wings and launched into the air.

Once they were fairly on their way, Pyra spoke. "I know the effect of the love elixir can be abated only one way. I advised Che of that."

"He told me," Surprise said.

Pyra was startled. "You can talk!"

"I assumed the form of a talking winged horse. There are many variants."

Pyra laughed. "I should have realized. That makes it easier."

"Makes what easier?"

"Persuading you to abate it."

"Why should you care what we do?"

"I want to see you accomplish your mission, of course. You can do that more efficiently if you abolish significant distractions."

"This occurred to us," Surprise agreed. "But it didn't work out. Maybe that is just as well."

"Just as well?"

"I don't want to be unfaithful to Umlaut, and Che doesn't want to be unfaithful to Cynthia, even with an alternate Cynthia."

"Yet in the last reality, you said you were married to Che."

"In that reality," Surprise agreed. "Not in our own."

Pyra saw that it was useless to argue the case further. "I suppose that does make a difference."

"It does. Yet we were prepared to do it, had we been able to achieve sufficient privacy."

Oho. So it had not been a straight intellectual decision. "Then maybe there will be another chance, in another reality."

"Or maybe we will complete our missions and return without doing any such thing."

The woman was not very corruptible. That was not good. "Maybe," she agreed. "But I doubt I would have the restraint. I think I would prefer simply to expiate the passion and be forever done with it."

"What is your interest in this?" Surprise asked sharply.

Of course Pyra had to lie. She didn't like doing it, because lies tended to have tag ends that could unravel them, but she had no choice. "Once I walked down to the swamp and dipped my toe, curious to know whether it was really what it was said to be. Unfortunately, it was. The first male I saw thereafter was a passing faun. Naturally he pursued me, and naturally I fled. But the passion flared up and controlled me, and soon I turned around and clasped him, celebrating in the manner of a nymph. In the next hour I fairly wore him out. Then we separated, our desire faded, and I returned to the castle alone. Fortunately the storks tend to ignore the signals of fauns and nymphs, so there was no delivery. I never tested the elixir again. But I know its power, and want to save you the struggle you otherwise face. It's not your fault that you were exposed to it."

"We knew its nature," Surprise said. "We waded through it anyway."

"Because you had no alternative, other than to give up hope of recovering your baby. That preempts everything, of course."

"I doubt that makes me blameless."

"You had a difficult choice. Sometimes blame is relative." There was a key concept she wanted Surprise to mull over.

"Relative blame," the horse repeated, irony in her tone.

"You would do anything to recover your baby, wouldn't you?"

Surprise hesitated. "I'm not sure. I didn't want to take Surprise Two's baby from her."

Darn that conscience! Pyra let it drop, having done what

she could. This mission was far from complete; there was ample chance for Surprise to change her mind.

They were coming to the Golem house. Che descended to land behind a copse out of sight of the house, and Surprise followed.

Pyra slid off. "I'll watch the children," she said.

"Aw—" Ted began.

Pyra flared, the fire almost touching his nose. He got the message and did not complete his complaint.

"Should I change?" Surprise asked Che.

"I see no need, unless the baby turns out to be yours, in which case you will need your hands."

Well, now, Pyra thought. That winged horse form would be ideal for her to complete a liaison with the centaur. That was to be encouraged. "And you can fly folk back," Pyra said.

"That, too," Surprise agreed. Just so.

Pyra took charge of the three children and peevish bird, while Che, Surprise, and Stymy approached the house. They watched from the cover of the copse.

"You're up to something, flame-brain," the peeve said.

For half an instant Pyra froze, which was not comfortable for her fiery nature. Then she bluffed it out. "What's the word, bird?"

"You don't like us much, hutch."

The peeve was on the wrong track. She was relieved. "We could get this business done faster and easier without the four of you along."

"Too bad, tad."

She let that pass. They peered through the brush as the trio reached the house. Would this be the right baby?

The door opened. A walking skeleton stood there.

"Moldy goldy!" Ted exclaimed. "It's Picka Bone!"

"From the skeletal family," Monica agreed.

"Marrow's son," Woe added. Woe, though perpetually five years old, had been around for centuries. "He's nineteen now."

"And handsome," Monica said. "Though thin."

And the baby would be a cross between human and skeleton. That was not the one.

The party left the house. Pyra remained amazed. In three alternate realities, Surprise was married to Umlaut, Che, and Picka Bone. That girl certainly got around.

"Wrong baby," Surprise announced as they reached the copse.

"We saw," Pyra said. "Too bad."

"I admit to being astonished by the differences in unions," Che said.

"Who would have thought I—she—would ever get together with Picka," Surprise said, seeming dazed. "But they told how they met in the gourd, where she was visiting and he was taking temporary work, and one thing led to another. He is certainly a decent person."

"But thin," Monica repeated, and she and Ted giggled.

The children piled back on Che, leaving the horse for Pyra again. Too bad, Pyra thought, that there wasn't a way for Che and Surprise to travel alone together again. Nothing would happen in the presence of the children, and not just because of the Adult Conspiracy to Keep Interesting Things from Children. But maybe when night came and the children slept there could be something.

They flew back to the Stork Works. This time they didn't talk, so Pyra's thoughts were her own.

She reviewed how she had gotten into this business. It had not started, as the others thought, with the stork's balk on the delivery of Surprise's baby. That was merely the official start of the action.

No, it had started with a Demon bet between Xanth and Fornax. Pyra didn't know the stakes, but suspected that Counter Xanth had something to do with it. Xanth had won that from Fornax, and it was slowly being colonized by Xanthians who liked its reversals. Demoness Fornax wanted to win it back. Or maybe it had something to do with Demon status, always important; they were perpetually vying for that. They did it by means of bets on deviously stupid things, such as whether a given mortal would do something or not do it.

This bet related to Surprise: could she be corrupted? If she could be, Fornax won; if not, Xanth won. So they set her up with something she desperately wanted, her baby, and were watching to see how far she would go to recover it. It was a cruel game, for it was one Surprise could not really win. If she refused to be corrupted to get her baby, she would not get the baby. So Xanth would win, but not Surprise, really. If she was corrupted, and got her baby, Fornax would win, but Surprise would always know it had cost her her honor.

This bet differed from most in that the two Demons were actively participating. Each had an agent in the field, as it were, to encourage a positive decision. Xanth's agent was Stymy Stork, who would be rewarded with a promotion to Head Stork. Fornax's agent was Pyra, who would be rewarded by marriage to Che Centaur. That was why she wanted Che to have the affair with Surprise: not only would it start the process of her corruption, with luck leading to the victory of Fornax; it would encourage Che to realize that there was nothing sacred about his marriage to Cynthia. That would set him up for marriage to Pyra, which the love elixir would confirm.

She remembered how she had fixed on Che. Her story to Surprise had had a single element of truth: she had dipped her toe in the lake. She had been alone, seeing no faun or other male, as the island was normally uninhabited except for the guardian monsters. She had avoided the monsters by using a secret entrance. Then, thinking herself secure, she had used the Mask, as she often did in the lonely evenings. And the first image on the screen was that of Che Centaur.

Oops. She loved him from that moment, but could do nothing about it. Until Demoness Fornax contacted her.

What could she do but agree to be the Demoness's agent? She knew it was the only way to get Che, who would otherwise be true to Cynthia Centaur. Pyra had nothing against Cynthia, and wished her well in finding another mate. It was simply that she had to have Che. When she told Surprise that she knew the elixir's power, she was speaking literally.

So here she was, working to help corrupt a girl to whom she had no animus. Surprise was a nice young woman. But that was the point: was she nice enough to be beyond corruption? Demon Xanth had bet that she was. Pyra had to help Demoness Fornax prove she wasn't. It was ironic that Pyra had to encourage Surprise to indulge her temporary passion for Che. Pyra would gladly have taken her place in that respect, but of course he had to clear his own temporary passion for Surprise first. Love was complicated.

There was one other thing: if any of the other participants—Che, Surprise, the three children, or the pet peeve—realized that this was a setup, a Demon bet, then the bet was off and nothing counted. They would revert everything to just before things started, and set up a new bet elsewhere with other participants. The stork would lose his chance, and Pyra would lose hers. Indeed, they would hardly know what they had missed, though some faint memories of the erased event might linger. So though they were on opposite sides, Stymy and Pyra had a common interest in seeing that no one caught on. That meant that they could not be too obvious in pushing their cases.

The danger was the tyke, Woe Betide. She was an aspect of Demoness Metria, who had once been Fornax's agent in the past. If the waif had any real memory of that, she might indeed catch on. That would ruin everything. So she had to be treated very carefully. Both Pyra and Stymy Stork were well aware of that. So completion of the bet was by no means assured, let alone the reward Pyra craved so ardently.

Actually, she knew she would be good for Che. In the course of this adventure he was learning that he did not have to be married to another centaur. He could be with a straight human woman, as was the case in the third reality. It wasn't necessary for her to change forms, either, or to use an accommodation spell. There were ways and ways, and what she wanted mostly was to ride him across the Land of Xanth and see all the sights. He would soon love her, and if not, a mere sprinkle of the elixir of the swamp would fix it. If its effect faded, she would sprinkle him again, and again, making sure he would not revert. Her own passion for him, un-abated, had become set; she wanted him in the same state.

Now, blissfully unaware, Che and Surprise were approaching the Stork Works. Pyra had to control her emotion in Che's presence, lest she give herself away. She had to treat him like merely a member of the party. Until the bet was decided.

Surprise was businesslike. "On to the next reality. I must recover my baby."

Pyra obligingly selected the next reality, and they trooped out to it. "I can watch the children again," she said. She needed to get Che and Surprise alone together again, until they abated their passion.

But immediately the children set up a joint scream. "We want to see the action!" Ted cried.

"And there's no action here," Monica said. "Boring."

Surprise, bound by her annoying niceness, yielded. "Come along, then," she agreed.

Immediately the children clambered onto her back, and the peeve perched on her head. They had chosen to ride with her this time.

That left Pyra to ride Che. That mixed her emotions. She wanted to ride him, but she wanted him to be hers. The one interfered with the achievement of the other.

There was no help for it. There would be other chances. The important thing was the bet. She mounted Che.

They flew across the landscape, as before. The way was becoming familiar, as the general geography was the same. Dull, even. If only she could have the kind of dialogue with Che she wanted!

"You seem pensive, Pyra."

She jumped, startled, then immediately controlled herself. "I suppose I am. I came along on this mission mainly for the excitement, but so far it's dull."

"So much of life consists of interstices. They do get dull."

He was smart and feeling, as centaurs could be. She would have liked that even without the effect of the elixir. "Interstices," she agreed.

"That is why we have the capacity to tune out much of the routine. It leaves our minds free for more interesting things."

"Such as what?" As if she didn't know.

"Intellectual riddles. Feelings. Plans."

Oh. "Yes, of course. Exercising the mind." Though that was not really what she wanted to exercise now.

"Though I find I am wasting that opportunity, dwelling on my problem with Surprise, as you know."

"The elixir," she agreed.

"I know the effect is artificial, but that does not dissipate it. I never thought I could be made to feel that way about a straight human woman."

And not the last one, if she had her way. "One misjudges the potency of the elixir at one's peril." As she herself had.

"Precisely. Perhaps I was made vulnerable by my knowledge that Cynthia is a transformed centaur, originally human. I love her, and so know I can love a human. But I had thought she was the only one."

"The other realities show that any two creatures can love each other."

"Any two?" he asked. "Even a Sphinx and a nickelpede?"

She smiled at what she knew was a deliberately exaggerated example. "Yes, though that would require an extremely potent accommodation spell. You could and would love any woman you shared the elixir with."

"Unfortunately yes. But I am sorry that it is Surprise. She is a wonderful person, with a family, in no way deserving of such a complication."

"You mean you would rather have waded the swamp with me?" She was tempting fate, risking revelation of the larger situation, but couldn't help it; she yearned to do exactly that, turning him on to her as she had been turned on to him. What utter joy she could have of him then!

He considered. "Yes, actually. You have no marriage to complicate, and no baby to rescue. That would ease half the guilt."

A wicked notion came to her, surely delivered by a rogue night mare. "I wonder whether if you waded with me, and we then abated it in the normal manner, that would erase your passion for Surprise, leaving you free?"

"Now that is a truly intriguing thought. But there are two cautions."

She dreaded his logic, but had to ask. "Two?"

"First, that as far as I know, love elixir does not erase prior passion. I retain mine for Cynthia. So it would more likely simply add a third passion. Abating that would merely leave me with the prior two, solving nothing. Second, even if it worked, overriding its prior effect, that would not eliminate the passion Surprise has for me. So it would be only half a solution."

"You are surely correct," she agreed regretfully. "Yet if it should happen to work for you, it should also work for her, and she could wipe out her passion for you with some other male."

He laughed. "Which would be more complicated than necessary. The two of us could more readily abate it with each other without burdening others. Which is surely a relief to you, even in theory."

"Surely," she agreed sadly. This also made her realize that getting him into the elixir with her would not be sufficient, and getting him to abate things with Surprise would not be either. He would not be hers regardless as long as he loved Cynthia. Only if Cynthia died would he be free. That was chilling; was that how Demoness Fornax planned to pay off on her promise? Suddenly Pyra wasn't certain she wanted this. Oh, she loved him and wanted him—but death had never been part of her ambition. She hadn't thought it all the way through.

But what could she do? She had made the deal, and would surely suffer much more grievously if she did anything to interfere with the Demon bet. She had to follow through.

"I apologize for saddening you with such a discussion," Che said. "I meant no disrespect to you. I hope you find your own man with no such complication."

And there might be her answer: wade with Che, abate

their mutual temporary passion, then arrange to share elixir with some other worthy male. Leave Che to rejoin Cynthia, and Surprise to rejoin Umlaut. She would do it if she could, without ever telling him her real reason.

Now she felt better. "I hope so too," she said.

They landed, and the three went to the Golem house. This time Surprise turned out to be married to the twenty-two-year-old Brusque Brassy, who in Xanth One was Becka Dragongirl's man. It was amazing how Surprise circulated in the other realities. So it was another wrong baby.

This time the children elected to ride again with Che, so Pyra rode Surprise, who remained in winged horse form. Since the girl could not do the same magic twice, she was sparing in its use, and did not readily throw away a useful form. That was sensible of her.

"You appear to be able to capture any man you want," Pyra remarked as they flew.

"Unless I took whatever offered," the horse responded. "I am beginning to see that my association with Umlaut was by no means unique. He was just the one I encountered when I was ready."

"That does seem to be the way of it." Just as Che was what Pyra encountered via the Mask when she was primed by the elixir. Did sheer chance govern supposedly unique relationships?

"But I do love Umlaut, regardless."

"And Che Centaur?"

"*Darn* that elixir!"

"I regret being the cause of that."

"It wasn't your fault. We had to reach you. We thought we could handle it."

Just as Pyra had thought she could handle a toe-dip. Education came hard. Now she realized that there was a reason Surprise could have any man she chose, and it wasn't merely her magic or her appearance. She was a genuinely nice girl, as Che had pointed out, who treated others with sincerity and compassion. Pyra was coming to respect that, and didn't want to hurt her either. Yet her mission was to see Surprise corrupted, or suffer the wrath of the Demoness. *Darn*, as Surprise had gently put it, that Demon bet.

She had to say something, and not the truth. "As you know, I believe you should simply get together with Che and abate the elixir-spawned passion. Then you both will be free to pursue your mission without distraction."

"We tried, but couldn't get sufficient privacy. I'm not sure it was a good idea anyway."

"We all get into situations where there seems to be no perfect way out. We do what we have to do." She hoped Surprise would take that as empty reassurance.

"Nevertheless, we will muddle through as we can. The one thing I really must have is my baby."

And there would be the instrument of her corruption. Pyra did not know precisely what the demons had set up, but was sure there would be a hefty price. Surprise would be corrupted, or would lose her baby. It was that simple. That brutal. Pyra felt ill.

This time the geography was slightly different. The Golem house was at the edge of some kind of development. It seemed harmless, so they landed beside it. Pyra took over the children again, and Che, Surprise, and Stymy walked to the house for their key interview.

"Hey, is that an amusement park?" Ted exclaimed, looking at the development.

"OoOoo!" little Woe Betide ooOooed.

"Set up like a comic strip," Monica said. "Let's go!"

"More fun," the peeve bird said maliciously.

"No!" Pyra cried. But she was too late; the mischief was already under way. One had to be on top of it before it started, and that was almost impossible with this bunch. All she could do was chase after them, hoping to corral them before things got too bad.

At the fringe of the suspicious region was a statue of a donkey made from black road paving. Ted leaped up, trying to ride its back, but didn't make it. A fissure opened at the statue's rear under its tail and hot gas hissed out.

"It's a pun!" Ted said, delighted.

"A gassy donkey," Monica agreed, her brow furrowing. "I don't get it."

"Ass Fault," the peeve said.

Both children fell over laughing. Fortunately the waif Woe just stood there looking blank. The statue faded out, its challenge surmounted.

"Time to return," Pyra said, making herding motions with her hands. But now they were surrounded by a small field within a circle of trees, where grass grew with quite sharp edges. They couldn't step through it without getting cut.

"Another pun," Ted said.

"Cutting grass," Monica said. But the grass did not fade. She had not gotten the right pun.

"We'll find some other way out," Pyra said. But she wasn't sure where. They were all pretty much caught in place.

A young woman came to the field. "Who are you?" Ted demanded rudely.

"I am Chasta," the woman said, smiling at him. She was pretty when she smiled, as many women were.

Ted fell back, abashed, as he tended to do when faced with something he was not yet quite able to appreciate fully.

Pyra kept silent, realizing that the appearance of the woman could be a clue to the nature of the pun that would free them.

"What are you here for?" Monica asked, a trifle less rudely.

"I need to shave my legs," Chasta said. "So I can freak out my boyfriend."

"I thought only panties did that," Monica said, eager to learn.

"Smooth legs help." Chasta kneeled at the edge of the sharp grass, took careful hold of a blade, and severed it with a deft twist. She sat back with her knees lifted, brought it to her calf and stroked it across her skin. Her leg was very smooth where the little blade passed.

Ted's eyes began to glaze, but he wasn't old enough to

freak out. Pyra opened her mouth, knowing she had to break this up before the boy saw Too Much. All it took was long legs and a short skirt.

"It's a Razor Glade," the peeve said.

The glade, grass, and woman faded out. That was the pun. "Thank you, peeve," Pyra said halfway sincerely. The bird generally meant ill, but did sometimes have its uses.

Several hoofed animals approached. They seemed harmless, but crowded in so closely that it was impossible to get anywhere. They were trapped by another pun.

The children went at it with gusto. They had not gotten old enough to hate puns. "Can I pet you?" Monica asked.

"Yes," the animals chorused.

All three children set about some heavy petting, as the animals were softly furry and happy for the attention.

"Now you've been petted," Pyra said. "Please let us pass."

"Yes," the animals agreed. But they didn't move.

"Zoo files," the peeve said. But for once it was wrong; that wasn't the pun, and the animals didn't budge. They merely chorused "Yes."

Then a bulb flashed over Pyra's head. "Yes Deer!"

The herd of amicable deer faded. She had gotten it.

Now there was a big nut lying before them. Ted picked it up and put it to his mouth before Pyra could prevent him. He bit on it, but it was too hard for his teeth. "That's one tough nut," he said ruefully.

"You can't crack it that way, dummy," Monica said. "Let me try." She picked up a rock and smashed it down on the nut. But it resisted her effort.

Pyra took it and heated a spot fire around it. The nut scorched but resisted. It was fireproof too.

Then the peeve got it. "The Gordian Nut! Really tough to crack." And it faded.

Pyra pounced on the opportunity between puns. "Now we must get back." As she spoke the peeve came to light on her shoulder. Evidently it had finally had enough of puns.

But a demon was blocking their way. It appeared to be

male, but wore a skirt, and had a big letter S on its jersey. "Who am I?" it demanded.

"Get out of our way, you cross-dressing freak!" the peeve said, using Pyra's voice.

The demon swelled up to 1.33 times normal size. "You have a big mouth, hot chick. How would you like a mouthful of knuckles?" It pushed at her shoulder.

The demon's hand sizzled and smoked as Pyra heated, literally. "Awk!" the peeve exclaimed, sailing off her burning shoulder.

"I have it," Monica said. "You are Demon S—a male demoness."

"O, phoo," the demon said, fading.

"Move. Now," Pyra said. For once the children obeyed; they had evidently had enough of puns for the moment. They trooped to the edge of the amusement park.

Not quite in time. A mountain appeared before them, surmounted by a huge eye. It peered grandly down at them. It was too massive and steep to pass. It had to be another pun.

"What a massive fraud," the peeve said, returning to Pyra's shoulder and using her voice again. "What are you, a molehill with the bloat?"

The mountain rumbled with rage. The eye squinted at Pyra, who of course seemed to be the one talking. She could really get to dislike the bird, if she tried. What was the pun?

"You look sort of peaked," her voice said. "Got rocks in your head?"

The mountain shook as if about to erupt, though it was not a volcano. The eye stared malignantly at them. But another bulb flashed over Pyra's head, triggered by the peeve's word. "Mountain Peeks!" she cried.

The mountain faded. This time the children needed no urging; they grouped around her and ran across the spot the mountain had been, getting out of the comic strip. This time they made it.

Che, Surprise, and Stymy were just returning. "Oh, were

you visiting the park?" Stymy asked. "That looks like fun."
He stepped toward it.

"No!" Pyra and the children cried. As usual, too late.

A whirlwind formed around him. Feathers started pulling
themselves out of his wings and body. He tried to retreat, but
a cone of wind held him in place. "Help!" he cried. "I'm being stripped!"

"Stork Naked," the peeve said. "Serves you right, lame-
brain. Don't you know a strip mall when you see it?"

"We've got to help him," Pyra said. She dived into the
windy park. The children followed, which wasn't what she
had intended; she had misspoken.

The whirling winds caught them all, tearing at their clothing. All three children screamed, not really with horror. This
was legitimate naughtiness, because they weren't doing it
deliberately.

Clutching at her loosening dress, Pyra managed a fleeting
thought: why hadn't the effect stopped when the peeve identified it as a strip mall? She concluded that it was because it
wasn't an original pun; such malls existed in Xanth, lurking
for unwary shoppers. They would have to find another pun
to stop it.

She looked desperately around. There had to be a pun
handy; that was the nature of comic strips, whether real or
emulation. All she saw was a table with several glass bottles,
untouched by the wind. They were labeled FRENCH, ITAL-
IAN, BLEU, THOUSAND ISLAND, RUSSIAN and others. If there
was a pun there she was too frazzled to get it. But maybe she
could fake it.

She picked up the first bottle and dumped it on herself.
Immediately she became clothed with an ornate Parisian
costume. Good enough. She took the second bottle and
sprinkled it on Ted. He developed a Roman toga. She took
the third and flung it at the beleaguered stork. He became
clothed in moldy cheese. She put the fourth on Monica. She
got covered with a dress so patchy it seemed to be in a thousand little islands. The next one she poured on little Woe Be-

tide, who was looking truly woeful as her dress ripped apart. She became a little costumed Cossack girl.

Then she got it. "Dressing!" she cried. "Salad dressing. These are dressings—dressing us."

The wind died. They were left standing in their assorted costumes. They hustled back out of the park before anything else could manifest. As they did, their clothing reverted to normal, and the stork recovered his feathers.

"That was quick thinking," Che said. "Good for you," Pyra."

She basked for half a moment in his praise. Then she snapped back to business. "I should never have let the children get into that park."

"It would have been impossible to keep them out," Surprise said. "They're irrepressible."

And this decent girl was the one she had to help corrupt. She was coming to hate her mission.

She rode back on Che. "Who was she married to this time?" For Surprise still had no baby; it was another false lead.

"Lacuna's younger son Jot. He's twenty-three now."

"Jot? I don't place him."

"We were children when Lacuna suffered her change of life. She got married retroactively, and suddenly she had a husband, a son Ryver, and twin children Jot and Tittle. Few are aware that her history had changed."

"History can change—in the past?"

"It is a difficult concept, I know. It seems that history can be changed, at least with respect to certain individuals. The-oretically I am destined to change the history of Xanth; I have never known precisely what that means. It may be that my tutoring of the Simurgh's chick Sim accounts for it. I am not sure."

"You will change the history of Xanth," she repeated, impressed. "I wonder whether traveling in realities could have anything to do with it? They all seem to have different recent histories, if Surprise's varying marriages are any indication."

"That is possible," he agreed. "We simply don't know. Certainly the Simurgh is involved. I believe she is trapped in the same reality as Surprise's baby."

"So once you locate the baby, you'll know in what reality she is," Pyra said.

"That is our hope." Repeating it seemed to comfort them both.

"We had six realities to check. We have visited five of them. The next one must be the one."

"By elimination," he agreed. "If that is not the one, we shall have some serious reconsideration to do."

"It is the one," she said. "The Mask can't be wrong."

"But there has been a good deal that the Mask has not informed us in advance."

"It could have, had we taken the time to explore each reality more thoroughly. It seemed more efficient just to go and see for ourselves. Who would even have thought that Surprise would have several different husbands?"

"Including me," he agreed. "We assumed that she would have the same husband throughout, so that it would be difficult to ascertain which baby was correct. Unquestioned assumptions are treacherous; I should have realized."

"Unquestioned assumptions must be the autopilot of the mind. Tuning out. We need them to function efficiently."

He turned his head to look back at her as he flew. It was a graceful maneuver, the twist starting in his back and progressing through his neck. "You seem smart for a human."

She realized that this was a considerable compliment from a centaur. That thrilled her. She was getting his attention. She took a breath, hoping it would attract his unconscious attention to her upper torso. "Thank you. I have had time to ponder, living alone as I do." And of course she was tired of living alone. But what was the use, playing up to him, when she had decided to let him go? She was just confusing herself.

"Perhaps, when this quest is done, we can be friends."

"I would like that." A monstrous understatement.

By the time they reached the Stork Works, the day was

waning. They agreed to rest in the Stork Works chamber for the night, and tackle the final reality in the morning. They all knew that had to be the one.

Che and Surprise chose not to be together, so she supervised the children while he slept in the garden. Pyra wrestled with her better judgment and lost. "Do you mind company?" she asked him.

"Yours is welcome," he said generously.

He lay down, his lovely wings folded. She lay by his front legs, her head using a soft wing as a pillow. Divine!

She slept, and dreamed she was taking his handsome head in her hands and kissing him as *he* slept. She knew it was only a dream, but wondered whether he could have any similar dream. No, he would dream of kissing Surprise or Cynthia. Sigh; even in her dreams she could not really have him.

8

HORRORS

They got organized early, as Surprise was eager to finally find her baby. She knew this was the right reality; there were no others that qualified. She would have her baby at last.

Or would she? She had already had some significant surprises, no pun on her name, and feared that more were coming. Her baby had been lost for two days now, and might be that much harder to recover. After all, how would she react if she got her baby delivered, then had someone show up on her doorstep demanding that she give it back? That was a quite relevant question, because it would be herself on the other side, reacting exactly as she would. This was bound to be difficult in both the practical and emotional sense.

She retained her winged horse form, though she suspected she would abandon it the moment she got her baby. The children elected to ride with Che Centaur again, and she allowed them to come in part because she wanted some sort of support, thin and uncertain as it might be. So Pyra rode her, and the peeve joined her too.

"Peeve," she said carefully. "I am in a strained femalish mood today, and if you start tormenting me with insults I won't be responsible for my reaction."

"Let me tell you something," the bird said in her own voice. "Your folks gave me a good home when no one else would. If I lose that, I'll be out on my tail and stuck homeless for a long time. I am not about to risk that, for solid economic reason. I am peevish, not stupid."

Pyra chuckled. "If I didn't know better, I'd suspect you of getting softhearted, peeve."

"You can keep your burned-out opinions to yourself, hotbox," the bird snapped.

Surprise would have smiled, had her horse-mouth enabled it. The peeve had not changed its nature. Its insults were as aptly targeted as ever. That was ironically reassuring.

"If Surprise Seven is as much like you as she surely is," Pyra said, "it will not be easy to take the baby."

"That's one reason I'm tense," Surprise agreed. "I don't know how I'll deal with it."

"You'd be better off if you could cuss," the peeve said.

"That's not her nature," Pyra said. "She's far too nice."

"Fortunately you're not so nice, burn-bottom," the peeve said in her own voice. "Maybe you could steal the baby and give it to her, sparing her the heartache."

"Well—"

"No!" Surprise cried. "None of that! I will have my baby honestly, or not at all."

"Of course," Pyra agreed, sounding regretful.

"Got it, horse-face," the peeve said, subdued.

All too soon they arrived at the Golem residence, which looked much the same. They landed a suitable distance from it, as before.

Pyra jumped off. "I'll watch the children. No comic strip this time."

The peeve stayed. "Let me come, and I'll keep my beak appropriately shut."

"Of course." Surprise suspected that Pyra was right: the

irritable bird had a little bit of heart, though it would never admit it. The bird hopped to her shoulder.

They trooped to the house: Surprise, Che, and Stymy. Surprise took several steps, then resigned herself and reverted to her natural form. She couldn't hold her baby in equine form.

This time the door did not open before they arrived. She had to knock. Evidently visitors weren't expected. That was mildly curious.

Now the door opened. Surprise Seven stood there. Behind her came the sound of a baby crying. Why wasn't she holding it? "Yes?" The voice was sharp.

"I am Surprise Golem, from another reality. I believe you have my baby."

Seven's lip curled. That was an expression Surprise had never tried to manage. "Prove it."

"I have brought along the stork who delivered it. He knows the smell. Let him sniff it."

"Like bleep I will. Go away." The door slammed in her face.

Che exchanged a significant glance with her. "Something here is odd. She does not mirror your nature."

"Maybe she doesn't want to lose her—the baby."

"There's something else," the peeve said. "I can't quite place it, but it's not good."

There was definitely something, Surprise thought. The other Surprises had all been nice girls, very feeling and understanding. This one wasn't. How could that be?

"Let me try," Che said. He stepped forward and knocked on the door.

After a pause that was slightly too long, it opened. Umlaut stood there. The sound of the baby crying in the background returned. "Get out of here, centaur. We don't need your kind in these parts." He tried to close the door, but Che's hoof was in the way.

"We need to check the baby," Che said firmly.

"You need to get your tail the bleep back where it came from." Umlaut kicked at the hoof, trying to dislodge it.

"Let me try," the peeve murmured in Surprise's ear. When she did not object, the bird turned its head aside.

"Dear, come here," Surprise's voice called from a slightly muffled distance.

"What the bleep do you want?" Umlaut snapped, turning and taking a step away from the door.

"What do you mean, what do I want? When I call, you snap to attention, laggard, if you know what's good for you."

"Oh, yeah? We'll see about that." Umlaut forged back toward the voice.

"Get on in there," the peeve said. "The door's open."

Che paused only half a moment. "That was you!" he said. "Imitating Seven's voice, you naughty bird."

"Told you I'd try," the peeve said with Che's voice.

Surprise's mouth fell open. That was why it had sounded muffled: to conceal the true origin of the voice. What a dirty trick. She couldn't praise it, of course; she wasn't like that. But she turned and kissed the bird's beak.

"Ugh!" the peeve said, turning a deeper green. That counted for a blush.

Meanwhile Che was urging her forward, into the house, followed by Stymy. They came to the main room, where Surprise Seven and Umlaut Seven were having a heated argument about who had called whom, and who was deaf. It was evident that they didn't like each other much.

The baby was in a dirty crib, a naked little girl, crying desperately. *Her* baby! Surprise's bosom swelled with grief and love. In barely an instant she was there, picking up the baby, cuddling her. The crying stopped.

The stork put his beak close to the baby, sniffing. He nodded affirmatively. This was the one.

"Hey!" Umlaut cried. "Unhand that brat!"

"Brat!" Surprise repeated, shocked. "My baby!"

Surprise Seven turned to face her. "The bleep it is. It's mine."

"You don't even want her!" Surprise said, appalled. "You let her cry."

"Oh, I want her," Seven said. "I just don't love her."

Surprise tried to speak, but was too amazed and horrified to formulate any words.

Che stepped into the breach. "This is her baby. We have verified it. We intend to take her home to our reality."

"She was delivered here," Umlaut said. "That gives us possession. She's ours."

"She was misdelivered here," Che said evenly. "We have come to correct the mistake."

"You centaurs are supposed to be logical and ethical," Umlaut said. "You know you can't just steal a baby like that."

Surprise saw Che nod, reluctantly. "We must negotiate a fair compromise."

"No compromise," Surprise Seven said. "That brat is mine. I got delivery."

Surprise hadn't known what to expect, but this was far outside any parameters she might have considered. Mean-talking, indifferent parents? She and Umlaut had never been like that. What was the matter with this couple?

The baby girl opened her eyes. She saw the peeve on Surprise's shoulder. She smiled. "Coo!"

The peeve almost fell off. "She likes me!" it said.

Surprise had to smile, faintly. "She's only three days old. She doesn't know any better."

"Compromise is necessary," Che said. "You know this baby is stolen property."

"So?" Surprise Seven demanded.

But Umlaut, gazing at Surprise, abruptly became reasonable. "Let me talk to her."

The two Sevens exchanged some sort of glance. It fairly dripped with mutual detestation and malign understanding. "Do it, charmer," Surprise Seven said. "Take her in the bedroom."

"Put down the br—the baby and come with me," Umlaut said.

Surprise did not want to do either, but realized that she had to try valiantly to be reasonable. There were conflicting rights, however awful the situation.

"I'll watch her," the peeve murmured, jumping to the top bar of the crib.

That would have to do. Surprise set the baby into the crib. She started to cry, but the peeve spread its wings, attracting her attention, and she lay back, watching it. She did like the bird, or at least was intrigued by it. That was remarkable for so young a child, but clearly possible. The peeve was also clearly delighted to have that adoration. It was probably the first time anyone had actually liked it at first glance. The peeve was normally a challengingly acquired taste.

Surprise followed Umlaut into the bedroom. It was the same one she and Umlaut One used, while they prepared to get their own house. That made her uncomfortable.

Umlaut shut the door. "You're a hot-looking babe."

He looked exactly like her husband, but his words were worlds—realities—away from anything Umlaut One would ever say. He was definitely not the man she loved.

"And I'm hot for you," Umlaut continued. "So I'll make you a deal."

She did not trust this at all. "All I want is my baby."

"I will put in a word for you with Surprise—my Surprise. I'm sure she'll agree to give you the baby. After you let me have my way with you."

"You're not my husband!"

"That's what makes it so delicious. There is no joy like stolen joy."

She was disgruntled and confused. Something was nagging her, but she couldn't quite place it. "If that's what you want, you can have it with your own wife, can't you? In fact you must have signaled the stork with her, to become eligible for this delivery."

"I did, but it was a chore. She's not nice like you."

"She *is* me, in this reality! How can she not be like me?"

He smiled. "You saw her. *Is* she like you?"

He had her there. "No. But I don't understand why."

"It hardly matters. Realities differ, that's all."

Then her nagging thought exploded into the foreground of her attention. "How do you know so much about realities?

You weren't even surprised when I announced that I was
from a different one."

"Oh, we were expecting you," he said easily. "We knew
you'd be after the baby."

"*My* baby!"

"That you want to recover." He advanced on her. "Will
you take off your clothes, or do you prefer me to do it for
you?"

She shied away. "Don't touch me! I came here only to
talk."

He shook his head. "Odd. I was under the impression you
wanted to recover your baby."

"I do!"

"You don't even need to pretend to like it. Just let me do
it, you luscious creature."

The weird thing was that he looked so much like the Umlaut she loved, and with whom she had made love many
times. It would be easy to, as he put it, just let him do it. If
that was what it took to get her baby back.

Frozen in indecision, she stood still as he slowly came at
her. He unbuttoned her blouse, and she didn't move. He
tugged it off, and she did not resist. Did it count if she made
no motion of participation? She simply didn't know.

He wrapped his arms about her and kissed her. His lips
felt very much like her husband's. But not exactly.

Suddenly she was struggling free of his embrace. "You
have no soul!" she exclaimed.

"Well, I had a soul emulation," he said. "But that wore
out." He tried to recapture her body.

"But you had half of mine—hers. When the Demons
didn't want mine."

He paused to look at her face. "They gave your soul back,
in your reality?"

"Oh, my! They didn't in yours! You and she—no souls?"

"No souls," he agreed. "Why would they give yours back,
having made the deal?"

"Because the half-souls gave them consciences. That was
inconvenient. They didn't like it. So they put them into the—

the two of us. And left them there, though they didn't have to. So we have a normal existence, together."

"Interesting," he said, uninterested. "It will be intriguing to make it with a souled version of you. Where were we?"

But Surprise was having second and possibly even third thoughts about sitting still for his illicit attentions. He had no soul, and neither did Surprise Seven. That meant no consciences, and no capacity to love. That explained why they obviously didn't like each other much, and cared nothing for the baby. It didn't explain why they even wanted the baby. There was more she needed to know before she could make a decision on anything, especially about yielding to his purely physical urge.

In fact, how could she trust him to do what he promised, after? Soulless folk wouldn't hesitate to lie, to get what they wanted. He might tell Surprise Seven to keep the baby. So her reluctant effort might be wasted anyway. Still, there might be ways to manage the soulless folk, as they cared about only the immediate advantages of a situation, rather than the longer term consequences.

"We were considering exactly how to be sure your Surprise will give me the baby. I think it would be more convenient if she turned her over first."

"How can she do that when you're with me?"

"Che could take her, and I could rejoin him. After."

He studied her cannily, which wasn't an expression she had seen in her real husband. "You souled folk keep your given words, don't you."

"We do. But I haven't given mine. We're still negotiating." She wished there were some other way to get her baby, but she feared there wasn't.

"Surprise gives the centaur Prize, and you give me your nice little body." He eyed the exposed upper portion of that body, making her feel halfway unclean.

"Prize?"

"The brat's name. Didn't you know?"

"I never got possession of the—of my baby! I never learned her name."

"It was going to be Sir Prize for a boy, because he'd be a leader. Just Prize for a girl, because she's a possession, of course."

Surprise choked back a clog of gall at the reasoning. She had to control her girlish emotions if she was to prevail. "Clever," she agreed.

He reached for her again. "Now that that's decided, we can have some fun."

She drew away again. "It's *not* decided. I want to see Prize safely out of this house, after I hear Surprise agree to let her go." Actually she was not at all sure she could do what he wanted even then, because it was wrong. It was bad enough having a passion for Che Centaur, who was a fully decent souled creature, but this soulless version of her husband was too much. She was really looking for some other way to rescue Prize. She liked the name, despite its nasty interpretation he had given. To her, the baby girl was a perfect prize, and possession had nothing to do with it.

"Maybe some other deal," he suggested.

"Maybe." That was what she wanted, but she didn't trust this. He surely had something devious in mind.

"Something we could give you, to make you go away."

"Without my baby? No way."

"Why are you so het up about a squalling baby, anyway? All she'll do is take up all your time."

Surprise refused to be baited. "That's my problem. I will be happy to take her off your hands. Why do *you* want her so much, anyway?"

He evaded the issue. "We have a collection of items of interest. Maybe you would like one of them instead of the brat."

"I doubt it." She was understating the case. What was he up to?

He reached down to haul a chest from under the bed. He opened it with a whispered spell. It was filled with slugs and snails and puppy-dogs' tails, as well as sugar and spice and all things nice. Evidently the Umlaut and Surprise of this reality shared it for oddments of interest. What could she possibly want from such a collection, in lieu of her baby?

Then she realized that to a soulless person, everything was negotiable. If he wanted a baby, but was offered something he wanted more, he would trade the baby for it. He expected her to react similarly. Those without souls could never truly appreciate their nature. That was why the Demons had been so dismayed in the instant they got halves of her soul that they had immediately rejected them.

He lifted out a shoe. Not a pair of shoes, just a single one, with a rather nutty surface. In fact it looked as if it had been fashioned from a large nut. "How about this Cash Shoe?" he asked. "Wear it, and it leaves cash behind."

She had to laugh at the incongruity of it. "That's a pun: cashew. Who needs cash in Xanth?"

"But with enough cash you'll be rich."

"The riches of Xanth are not in money. You have it confused with Mundania."

He didn't argue. He set the shoe aside and brought out another item. "Here is a Tooth Brush."

"That's a brush made out of teeth!" she exclaimed. "Another pun. What good would that do anyone?"

"Well, it bites bad children. It's a good way to keep them under control."

For a fleeting half instant she imagined using that to subdue the rambunctious half-demon children. Then her niceness reasserted itself, banishing the wisp of nastiness as if it had never been. "I wouldn't use anything like that! Children need to be raised with understanding and love."

He shook his head. "Weird." He delved into the chest again. "How about this?" He held up a small white ball.

Despite her aversion to this whole scene, she was curious. "What is it?"

"A Goof Ball. Play with it and you will goof things up."

"What use is that?"

"Give it to the children. They will soon be in no condition to oppose you."

What did he know about the children? Bringing them had been mostly a matter of accident. He knew entirely too much about her, for one supposedly surprised by her visit. "No."

He brought out a small rag doll with a long pin through its hair. "This should really help manage children, even part demons. It's a VooDoo doll."

Again, curiosity overcame revulsion. "I don't understand."

"Merely orient the doll on a person with a spot verbal spell. Thereafter whenever you stick the pin in it, the person feels the same stick, though nothing shows. It is a marvelously safe yet effective way of delivering pain." He withdrew the pin from the doll's hair and oriented on the doll's belly.

"No!" Surprise cried, almost feeling a stab through her own belly. "Put it back!"

"You are difficult to satisfy." Somehow he conveyed a nuance that had a sexual connection.

"Don't you have anything that doesn't hurt people?"

He fished around. "This, maybe." He held up a compact squarish construction. "A Soap Box."

"Isn't that a box for soap?"

"It is a box made out of soap stone. Stand on it and vent your opinions, however obnoxious they may be. It washes you clean of them, leaving a foul taste."

Surprise had a vision of the pet peeve perching on the box and opening its beak—and choking on the taste of soap. But again she rallied. "No."

He studied her, evidently perplexed. "Is there no greed or meanness in your body?"

"None," she said, hoping it was true.

"Let's see." He brought out a bottle of pills. "This should interest you."

"Pills? Why?"

"These are magic pills, compressed from the dust near the Magic Dust Village. They have very strong magic, enough to enable a person to perform some magic in Mundania, or to greatly enhance individual talents. Whatever you do, you could do with greater effect, swallowing one of these. Pop! Twice the power. Make your talents truly effective."

That was interesting. She could use each talent only once, and if once wasn't enough, she could not call it back for another try. Greater power of talents could be very nice. "I don't know."

"Ha! You waver."

That stiffened her softening backbone. "No! I'll never be a pill-popper."

He tossed the bottle aside and brought out a hank of shiny gray yarn. "Steel Wool, shorn from metallic sheep. It will make very fine protective garments that still readily flex and look nice." He held it up, measuring it against her body with his eye. "You would look spectacular in a close-fitting gown woven of this."

He was getting closer. A truly flexible but impervious cloth that enhanced her figure. But not at the expense of her baby. "No."

"Won't you at least try it on?" He shook the yarn, and it dropped down into a slinky garment. "It would be a shame to waste it on a figure inferior to yours."

She fought hard and won. "No."

"Surprise wears it when we go out. She looks great."

That did not have the effect he intended. He was referring to the soulless creature of this reality. Surprise did not want any dress that had touched that flesh to touch her own. "Forget it."

He considered a disturbing moment. She didn't like it when he thought, knowing his thoughts were not healthy for her mission. Then he brought out a packet of something. "Rows Seeds."

"Roses?"

"Rows. Plant these seeds and their flowers will grow only in neat rows. Excellent for decorating walks and around houses; nothing grows out of line."

Surprise thought of that around the Golem house, whose surrounding plants were somewhat sloppily arranged. But again, it was hardly enough to sacrifice her baby for. "No."

"Then what about this?" He grasped one of the dog's tails projecting from the chest and hauled it out. The entire dog came out: a Mundane German Shepherd and Samoyed mix, white and light tan with a white nose, white brows, and freckles. "This is Spunky, looking for a good home."

The dog blinked. "He's alive!" she exclaimed, astonished. "And you had him buried in the chest?"

As she spoke, Spunky cocked his head to look at her. His left ear flopped over. Her knees dissolved. She loved animals, and knew that Mundane pets were in special need of homes, as it took them time to get used to the magic and monsters of Xanth.

But instead of her baby? She couldn't. "No," she whispered, heartbroken.

"Wrong dog?" Umlaut pulled on another tail, bringing out another Mundane crossbreed dog, a combination of black lab and American bull, with long silky hair, black with a white flame pattern on his chest. "This is Hercules. He saved a girl from a rattlesnake, but he's very gentle. You couldn't have a better guard dog."

The dog gazed soulfully at her, in sharp contrast to the gaze of the man.

Surprise struggled. The soulless Umlaut must have done it deliberately, plying her with minor inanimate things before suddenly springing the warm live creatures on her. If the price had been anything other than her baby—

"No. Stop with these things. I don't want any of them." At least, not considering his asking price.

Umlaut shrugged. He jammed the unprotesting dogs back into the chest, slammed shut the lid, and shoved it under the bed. Surprise winced to think of the poor dogs trapped in there, but there had to be some sort of spell to keep them alive. "Then it is time to return to our tryst. You never said whether you preferred to undress yourself or have me do it for you. At least you're halfway there." He eyeballed her bare top again.

"Why should I express a preference?" she asked, flustered.

"So I can have the pleasure of ignoring it."

"I don't trust you. I told you, I need to see my baby— Prize—taken out of this house with Che Centaur." She grabbed her loose shirt and put it back on. Fortunately she didn't need an undergarment.

"That is not convenient at the moment."

There was some additional nuance of annoyance. "At the *moment*?"

"See." He touched the bedroom door, and it became a glassy window showing the other room.

She looked through the pane. There was Che with Surprise Seven. He was standing on the floor. She was standing on the chair, naked, and plastered to his front, kissing him avidly as her hands stroked his back. There was no sign of Stymy Stork; he must have gone outside.

Surprise hauled her slack jaw up. "What is going on?"

"We call it seduction. Maybe it has another name in your reality."

"But he has no interest in her!"

"That seems to be in question. I agree, however, that he does not seem to be responding. Yet."

"How can you watch your wife do that with another male?"

"Oh, it turns me on. Assuming it does the same for you, shall we proceed with our own liaison?"

"No!" But her eyes remained fastened to the awful scene. Every time she thought she had the measure of the horror of this situation, some new ugly twist developed. How could Che tolerate the efforts of that soulless creature?

Unfortunately, she had an answer. In Reality Three Che was married to Surprise Three, so obviously they were compatible. In Reality One the two of them had waded through the love elixir and suffered greater effect than anticipated. Here was Surprise Seven, looking exactly like her, catering to that passion. How could he resist?

Yet resist he did. His arms did not enclose her, and his lips did not respond to her ardent kisses. He merely stood there despite maneuvers that should have driven him to distraction.

At last Seven gave it up. "Bleep! You win."

Che did not respond to that either.

"I should have tortured the baby. Just a few pinches would have made her scream."

Now the peeve spoke. "You agreed not to, shrew, provided he allowed you to exercise your dubious wiles on him. Face it: you gambled and lost."

So that was it! The witch had threatened the baby, and Che had acted to prevent that. He had been noble rather than dissolute. She owed him for his loyalty.

But why had Seven wanted to tempt Che? There, too, she might have an answer: she was turned on by him, and her soulless condition allowed her to do whatever suited her whim of the moment. So she had chosen to pass the time in her own unscrupulous fashion.

Umlaut's questing hand touched her hip. She shook it off. "We're done here," she said sharply. Part of her mind wondered why he was being so careful to obtain her consent before acting; surely he would try to force her if he thought he could get away with it. Of course if he tried force she would smite him with her magic; maybe that was the reason. But she suspected there was something else. She had not yet fathomed the complete depths of this ugly situation.

She pushed open the door and entered the other room. She was ready to kill someone, even if it was her other self. "You want to torture my baby?" she demanded dangerously.

Seven, naked, shrugged. "Why not? She's a pain to take care of."

That had to be deliberate baiting. Did Seven want to fight her? What would it be like, to struggle magically against one who could match any talent, once? "What's going on?"

"You are trying to take our baby, that's what's going on," Seven said arrogantly. "Why don't you simply get your pushy little butt out of here and leave us alone?"

"Because you have *my* baby," she retorted. "And you are mistreating her. She can't remain with you."

"She can and will," Seven said. "What are you going to do about it?" She remained naked, the view compelling Che's unwilling attention. In fact she was flaunting her body to distract the centaur, making aspects move or jiggle. Surprise had to admit it was a good body, well managed.

It was definitely a challenge, to both of them, with different facets. Surprise had never been a violent person, but she had been driven to the verge of her limit. "I'm going to—"

"Surprise," the peeve said from its perch on the crib.

That made her pause. The peeve never called her by name, only by some insult, though they understood each other and got along well enough, considering. "What?"

"I have something to tell you that you need to know."

"Stay out of it, bird-dropping!" Seven snapped.

The peeve did not respond with another insult, oddly. It focused only on Surprise. "That woman is dangerous. She is not what she seems."

"I'm going to fry you for dinner, if you don't shut your lying beak," Seven said fiercely.

That, too, was odd. The peeve could lie with the best of them, but had never done so to Surprise or her family. What did it want to tell her, and why was Seven so dead set against it? "I already know she has no soul."

"Not exactly," the peeve said.

Seven strode toward the bird. Surprise conjured a pane of hard plastic to bar her way, knowing Seven would immediately dissolve it with another spell, but not thinking of anything better on the spur of the moment. She didn't like spurs; they were likely to get her into trouble.

But Seven did not. She batted at the barrier with her fists, uttering words Surprise hardly knew and would never use herself. Odd, odd; why didn't she use her magic?

Surprise put her head down to listen to the peeve. "What is it?"

"That's not really Surprise," the peeve said. "That's a souled entity, but no better for it."

"I don't understand." Indeed she did not.

"I recognize her because I have run afoul of her before. She is Morgan le Fey, a Sorceress from ancient Mundania. She's looking for a body to take over, in the manner of the

Sea Hag, and evidently Surprise Seven is it. Beware of her; she is utterly unscrupulous."

"Morgan le Fey!" Surprise exclaimed, amazed. "Why would she want my baby?"

"Because that's my future host and entry to Xanth proper," Seven/Morgan said. "You might as well know, since the bleepity bird blabbed anyway." She had finally abolished the plastic pane.

"Somebody had to, bitch-butt," the peeve retorted.

Surprise fumbled for emotional or intellectual anchorage. "But you're tormenting her! Why ruin the one you want to use?"

"I am taking good care of her body. It's her mind that is of no value to me, as I will banish that when I take over."

It made such dreadful sense that for the moment Surprise was speechless.

Che filled in the dialogue. "How did you get the stork to deliver the baby to you, since you are obviously unqualified?"

"It was a sacrifice," Umlaut said. "We had to leave our marriages and pretend to be a couple, and actually signal the stork, nine months ago, fooling the system. What a chore!"

"You liked it at the time, lout-brain," Morgan snapped.

"I liked her body, not your mind, you arrogant fairy," he retorted. "You sneered all the way through."

"Naturally, dullard. Who in her right mind would want to signal with *you*?"

"My wife would!"

"Big deal! Your wife's made of metal."

Surprise exchanged a fleeting glance with Che. This was fascinating in its ugliness.

"And your husband's an ogre," he said.

"Exactly who are the two of you married to, in this reality?" Che asked.

"The crossbreed twins delivered to Esk Ogre and Bria Brassie," Umlaut said. "Epoxy Ogre and Benzine Brassie."

"But they're only fifteen years old!" Che said.

Both Umlaut and Morgan looked at him. "What's your point, horse-nose?" she asked.

"The Adult Conspiracy forbids underage stork summoning."

"Not here it doesn't," Umlaut said. "There is no Adult Conspiracy in this reality. Children can and do attempt stork summoning, if they're minded to."

"And some succeed," Morgan said. She smiled, not nicely. "Epoxy is satisfactory, when I choose to have him so; his talent is to make things hard and fast. But the lout here has a problem: Benzine's talent is to make things soft and loose."

"Haw haw haw!" the peeve laughed. "No wonder Um Lout is so hot to make it with other girls!"

Umlaut looked ready to kill. Surprise would have been shocked, had she had a few more of her wits about her. What filthy laundry was being aired here!

"That does not explain why you attempted to seduce me," Che said to Morgan.

"Apart from the fact that you're a handsome equine specimen?"

"That can hardly be your prime motive."

"To distract you from the lout's effort with Surprise," Morgan said. "What counts is that she agree to give up her claim and leave the baby here. We need that release, or there could be complications."

Umlaut had attempted to seduce her in exchange for giving her the baby. Now Surprise realized that the other facet of that deal was that she would agree to give up her baby if she didn't want to be seduced. The spines on this mace struck every which way.

"Complications. Because Prize is really Surprise's baby, not yours," Che agreed. "But that doesn't explain how she was delivered here. How did you arrange the fissure between realities? You couldn't have managed a feat like that on your own."

The naked Sorceress eyed the centaur speculatively. She took another breath, deeper than it strictly needed to be. She evidently had not really given up on him. Any ordinary man would have freaked out by now. "You are observant. I like that. Yes, that required Demon magic. Fornax did it."

"But Demoness Fornax can't interfere with Xanth. Demon Xanth wouldn't allow it."

"Demon Xanth has no authority to prevent it. As a tag end of a prior Demon agreement, Demoness Fornax has half of Surprise's soul, and Demon Jupiter has the other half. That gives them a certain tacit claim on the bodies. Fornax may use this body as a legitimate entry to the Land of Xanth, after I am done with it. That's her business. I am maintaining the body for her in the interim."

Surprise could only marvel at the dastardliness of the deal. None of the participants cared half a whit whom they hurt. The Good Magician must have suspected this; that was why he had tried to dissuade her from coming after her baby. Yet what a ghastly fate awaited innocent little Prize if Surprise did not rescue her!

"I think we have heard enough," Che said grimly. "You folk have no legitimate claim on this baby. We'll take Prize now, regardless."

"I think not," Morgan said.

"You have a way to stop us, knowing that your Sorceress magic cannot match Surprise's abilities in this limited venue?"

Because it seemed that Morgan could not use Surprise's talents, which were attached to her soul. Only if at least part of that soul were returned to the body would her talents return. Morgan surely had powers of her own, but she was at a disadvantage here. Che was tacitly reminding Surprise of that.

"I have tried to be reasonable," Morgan said, facing Surprise. "But since you will not have it, it's no more Miss Nice Sorceress. You must make a more difficult choice: the baby or the children."

"The children!" Surprise said, appalled. "You would threaten them?"

"Of course I would, you ninny. While we dickered here I sent an apparition to separate them from their naïve baby sitter. Now they are lost, and will surely come to grief, and it will be your fault. Unless, of course, you elect to yield your claim on the brat. Then I will indicate the location of the children."

Surprise was frozen with painful indecision. She couldn't desert her baby—but neither could she sacrifice the children. What a terrible pass!

Che rescued her again. "You pretend that it is an either/or choice, malign Sorceress. That is not so. We shall search and locate the children, then take the baby to her rightful home."

Morgan took another deep breath, as she made a high-silhouette quarter turn toward him. "Lots of luck, stallion."

The centaur ignored the naked taunt. "Come, Surprise, peeve. We have work to do." He led the way out of the house.

Stymy Stork was there. "Did you get the—?" He broke off, seeing that she hadn't. "I'm sorry. I could not face that thing in your body."

"Not your fault," Surprise said. "But now we can use your help, if you are willing to lend it."

"Whatever you ask," he agreed. "I'm sure Pyra will too."

"So will I," the peeve said. "I like Prize and hate Morgan le Fey."

"Thank you," Surprise said tearfully.

They walked out to where they knew the children would not be. Pyra was running toward them, alone, with news they already knew.

9

STYMIED STORK

Stymy was chagrined as they left the house and came to meet the distraught Pyra. It seemed that not only had Surprise not recovered her baby, the children had been lost, because of the mischief of the Sorceress Morgan le Fey who now occupied Surprise Seven's body. He had not anticipated this bypath.

He knew that his exit from the house made him appear cowardly, and that Surprise and Che could have used his help inside. But the moment he recognized Morgan he knew he had to retreat, because she could when she chose read minds to a certain extent. If she discovered that there was a Demon bet, and that he was the agent of Demon Xanth, she would either use the knowledge to force Surprise to yield the baby, or blab it to them all. That would abrogate the bet, and everything would revert to the starting point. If it was determined that Stymy had given away the truth, then Demon Xanth would forfeit the bet. He couldn't risk that. So he had gotten away from her as rapidly as feasible and waited outside.

He did want Demon Xanth to win, and not just because of

the promised promotion to Head Stork. He liked Surprise
Golem and wanted her to prove herself. And it would be horrible to leave the innocent baby with the mean-spirited Morgan. So if there was any way for Surprise to win back her
baby without being corrupted, he had to help her find it. The
alternative was too ugly to contemplate.

Pyra was the agent of the Demoness Fornax. She was his
opponent, yet they had a common interest in seeing the challenge proceed, and in keeping the secret of the bet. Pyra
seemed like a decent woman; he was sure she would not deliberately have lost the children. The bet concerned the corruption of Surprise, not the children. Morgan's foul play was
no part of Pyra's effort, though Demoness Fornax was evidently using her to force the issue. Fornax was taking advantage of a loophole involving her possession of half of
Surprise's soul in this reality, bargaining with Morgan to put
pressure on Surprise. Demon Xanth must have gone along
with it, for the sake of the bet. Stymy had assumed the corruption would be merely a matter of temptation, such as her
having an affair with Che Centaur. Now he saw that it was
uglier than that, with Surprise being forced to choose between evils. He did not like that, but had no control over that
aspect. All he could do was encourage Surprise to be true to
her decent nature and do the right thing, hoping she was
strong enough.

They came together with the tearful Pyra. "I was watching
the children, honest I was," she said. "Then suddenly, puff!
and they were gone. The three of them were illusion. I went
back and followed their footprints. They diverged from the
way I had gone. I had followed illusion children, being led
astray. But the footprints disappear in hard ground and do not
resume. I don't know what happened to them. I'm so sorry!"
Her tears burst into little flames as they struck the ground.

"It's not your fault," Surprise told her, as she had told
Stymy. She had such a generous personality! "But we can
use your help finding them."

"Anything!" Pyra said. "I should never have been fooled.
I just never thought—"

"None of us did," Che said. "What we encountered in that house was beyond our worst expectations." He efficiently summarized the situation; as a centaur he was good at that. "So as I see it, we shall have to split up and search in every direction. You and Surprise can search the close land; we flying creatures will search in circles farther out. The children can't have gotten far. Doubtless they were deceived by illusion too, thinking you were with them. Then when they were fairly lost, your image disappeared and they were stuck. If they have any reasonable sense, they will either follow their own tracks back, or wait where they are in the hope of being found soon. With luck, one of us will accomplish that."

They worked out five quadrants: two semicircles starting at the place the children's footsteps ended, for Surprise and Pyra to search, and three larger sections beyond for the winged creatures. They agreed to return to the starting point before dark, unless unable, to compare notes. It seemed perfectly sensible.

But Stymy knew it would not turn out sensibly. The Sorceress Morgan le Fey would not hide the children where they could be readily found. She would have some more devious angle. She wanted to force Surprise to give up her baby in exchange for the children. They were all likely to come up empty winged. Still, all they could do was search diligently, hoping to foil the fell plot.

Because if Surprise had to choose between baby and children, she would be corrupted, as it was not a choice that could have any clean outcome. Demon Xanth would lose, and Stymy would remain a hopelessly fouled-up low-echelon stork. Pyra would have her reward, but probably not have any real joy of it, as she meant no harm to either the children or the baby. The innocent test of character had become a guilty grind.

The three took wing, flying to their agreed sections. Stymy's was to the south, a nondescript region inhabited by the usual dragons, nickelpedes, and stray human and crossbreed folk. The children surely knew to stay clear of the dangerous ones, and actually they could defend themselves reasonably well, being part or full demon.

Maybe they had had the wit to set up a signal to attract the attention of a rescuer. Stymy flew back and forth, peering down. No recognizable signal.

A nasty thought occurred to him: suppose they did not know they were lost? If the phantom Pyra remained with them they might not realize they were going astray. She could lead them into a cave, hiding them, entertaining them with balls of fire or flashes of lightning. Did Morgan have an evil accomplice? The air might be no place to look for them.

Stymy glided down to the ground, looking for traces. He found none. There was only a man walking by.

Well, there should be no harm in asking. Stymy approached the man. "Hello. I am Stymy Stork, looking for lost children."

"I am Nine. I can stitch any two things together, such as a person and a tangle tree. Would you like a demonstration?"

Stymy thought about being stitched to a hungry (hungry was the only way they came) tangle tree. "Thank you no. Have you seen three children pass this way?"

"No children," Nine said cheerfully. "How about getting stitched to a thyme plant? A stitch in thyme saves Nine."

This man was evidently talented, but was being of little help. "Thank you no." Stymy spread his wings and took off.

He landed not far away, in a glade with a spotty object in the center. "I'm spotting you!" the thing cried, flinging out spots. Several stuck to Stymy, soiling his white feathers. He had been spotted. He struggled to wipe them off, but they clung like coagulating glue. Ugh!

He found a puddle of water and with its help managed to soak and pry the spots off. He had lost valuable time. He was about to take off again, when another stork landed. "Beware the spots!" he called.

But the spotter did not fling out any more spots; evidently it had used up its stock and was recovering. The stork approached him. It was female, and he rather liked her look. But not her look, paradoxically: she was glaring prettily at him.

"Did you deliver an unlicensed baby here?" she demanded.

"Yes, actually, to the Golem residence. But—"

"You beast!" she cried, attacking him with her beak.

"But I couldn't help it," he protested, trying to protect himself. "I had to—"

She caught a wing feather in her beak and yanked it out. That hurt. "This is my delivery territory! You had no right!"

"I couldn't deliver to the original girl, because—"

She caught a tail feather and yanked it out. "You brute! You utter birdbrain!"

"She was underage," he continued desperately. "At least, I thought she was, according to my records."

She yanked out a head feather. "How *could* you!"

Her determined effort was denuding him! But how could he oppose such a pretty lady? "It wasn't my fault. The record was wrong."

She yanked out more. "Ridiculous. Babies are sent out only when ripe. They can't be underage."

That set him back, until he realized her misunderstanding. "The mother. She was listed as thirteen, instead of eighteen. I'm already on probation; I didn't dare make a wrong delivery."

"So you delivered it here, and got *me* in trouble!" She plucked out several more feathers. "They think I delivered an illegitimate baby. I could get fired. All because of you." Another feather.

The pain and humiliation overwhelmed him. "It's not my doing. It's a Demon bet!"

She went quite still, staring at him.

"Oh, bleepity bleep!" he swore. "I shouldn't have said that."

"Now you had better say more," she said.

"Please, please, forget what I said. Everything's at stake."

"Well, it would be."

"But if any of the participants learn or catch on, it's all off, and my side loses if it's my fault." He shrank into himself. "And it is. I shouldn't have blabbed."

"How does it end, if it ends?"

"If the bet is voided, everything reverts to what it was before the bet got in motion. But if I am responsible, Demon Xanth will lose the bet, and it must be something important. I can't stand to be responsible."

"Tell me all, and I'll decide whether to keep my beak shut."

"How can I trust you? You just defeathered me. I'm stork naked."

She considered. "True. I was mad. I thought you did it on purpose, or out of stupidity. Now I see you are a helpless creature of fate, as I am. I apologize."

"That doesn't restore my feathers. I can't even fly until they grow back."

"There's a healing spring not far from here. This way." She walked away from him.

What could he do? He followed her, ashamed of his nakedness.

"There," she said, pointing with a wingtip.

It looked like a mud puddle, but he took her word and walked into it. The pain stopped and new feathers sprouted wherever the mud touched. He got down and rolled in it, getting all of his skin and feathers restored. He was whole again. No wonder he hadn't known about this spring, if it existed in his own reality; who would have guessed?

"Congratulations, mudball," she said. "You're re-feathered."

And completely black with mud. He would not be able to fly with that fouling his feathers. "Is there a clear water spring or river or lake nearby?"

"I'll take you there while you tell me the whole story."

What did he have to lose, at this point? "Maybe we should start with an introduction. I am Stymy Stork."

"You can't be. That's *my* name."

"Your name?"

"Stymie Stork."

"Oh, now I see. I'm the male variant, with a Y."

"I'm IE."

"I am glad to meet you, Stymie Stork."

"Likewise, I think, Stymy."

"We have the same territory. We're equivalent."

"Almost," she agreed, glancing modestly aside.

"Except for gender," he agreed. "And you're lovely. Pardon my candor."

"You aren't lovely." But she seemed flattered.

He climbed out of the mud and they walked to the clear water she knew of. He told her the whole story of the bet and the challenge to Surprise Golem to recover her baby without being corrupted.

"But that's a rigged case," she protested. "If she sacrifices the children to get her baby, she's corrupted. If she sacrifices the baby to save the children, she's corrupted. Your side loses either way."

"That's why we have to find the children," he said. "So she doesn't have to make that choice."

"I see." She considered a moment. "I know Surprise Golem. She lost her soul four years ago, and hasn't been decent since. She faked a marriage to Umlaut and even signaled the stork with him nine months ago, but of course we refused to honor the order. She doesn't deserve a baby."

"Not as she is in this reality," he agreed. "I didn't know that when I delivered. I can't think why I wasn't suspicious."

"Because Morgan le Fey enchanted you to not be," she said. "Now that you've explained about the way she took over Surprise, things are clarifying. You were a victim of circumstance, as was I."

"Yes."

They walked in silence to the clear river she knew of. Stymy waded gladly in. In two and a half moments he was clean and white again. He emerged and shook himself off.

"I will keep your secret," Stymie said. "I'm not one of the participants, so if I don't tell, there's no harm done."

"Thank you!" he said, vastly relieved. "I could kiss you." Storks did not kiss in the sloppy way humans did, of course; it was more a matter of clicking beaks together. But the sentiment was similar.

"Not if I kiss you first," she said, and clicked his beak. "I'm sorry I pulled your feathers. I didn't understand."

"That's all right," he said, stunned in much the way a human man would have been by the gesture.

"I have been in trouble much as you have," she confided. "I'm on probation too. One more bad mistake and I'm out on my tail. That's why I was so angry. I searched for you—for whoever made that wrong delivery—and, well, I have a temper."

"I noticed," he agreed.

"I didn't understand. I wish I could make it up to you."

"You have done that, by restoring my feathers and agreeing to keep silent about the Demon bet."

"You're very nice." She clicked his beak again.

"Don't do that! You'll get me all excited."

"That had occurred to me," she confessed.

"I can't be distracted. I have to search for the lost children."

"I'll help you search, to make up for your lost time."

"I haven't lost a lot of time yet. But I need to resume the search."

"And I need to make it up to you, for my misunderstanding. And because I understand about fouling up and being on probation. That's my case too."

"We are much alike," he agreed.

"Describe the children we are searching for."

Stymy was glad to oblige. "The boy is Demon Ted, age ten, half demon, sort of surly in expression. He is constantly rebellious and getting himself and others into trouble."

"Absolutely typical male human child. I have delivered many who grew into such children."

"The girl is DeMonica, also ten, half demon, and looks like Ted's twin, but she's actually no relation. She's cute, with hair that changes without notice, and she's looking ahead to when she can fascinate boys with her panties."

"Typical human girl. But what's this about panties? Don't all girls wear them?"

"Yes, but boys aren't supposed to see them. They freak boys out."

"They do? How odd."

Then Stymy remembered something. "There's no Adult Conspiracy here!"

"Conspiracy to do what?" she asked blankly.

"In my reality, it is known in full as the Adult Conspiracy to Keep Interesting Things from Children. Such as cuss words, and how to summon us storks to deliver babies."

"How quaint. Why should this information be concealed?"

"To prevent children from doing it too soon. There needs to be a certain maturity to be responsible for babies, who need good care."

"That is a point," she agreed. "Xanth is really no better than Mundania in that respect."

"It is in my reality. Children don't learn the secret until they are eighteen, or have a special need to learn it sooner. So they have mature, lasting relationships, and marriages never break up."

"That *is* a change! Here couples have external affairs and marriages break up half the time, and children suffer."

"That explains a lot," Stymy said. "We were amazed to learn that Surprise and Umlaut are married to Epoxy Ogre and Benzine Brassie in this reality. They faked being with each other, and even sent out a summons together. That would never happen in our reality."

"I think I am getting to like your reality. I wish I could deliver there instead of here. I would feel much better about the future of my deliveries."

The idea of having her in his reality thrilled him. But of course that was irresponsible. So he focused on the subject. "The third child is about age five, Woe Betide. She's actually the—"

"The child aspect of the Demoness Metria," she said.

"Metria is here?"

"Metria is everywhere, I think. That demoness really gets around. She fits right in with our culture."

"I can imagine," Stymy said, thinking of the way Metria tried endlessly to seduce any male of any species she encountered, not from any real passion but simply to make mischief.

There was a swirl of smoke. "Did I hear my nomenclature?"

"Your what?" Stymy asked.

"Character, denomination, appellation, designation, luminary, celebrity—"

"Name?"

"Whatsoever," the smoke agreed crossly, forming into the most luscious imaginable human torso, with the head of a stork. "What are you odd birds up to?"

Was there any harm in telling her? "We're looking for three lost children."

"Ha! Does one of them look like this?" The demoness fuzzed into mist and reformed as little Woe Betide.

"Yes!" Stymy said. "Have you seen her?"

The grown demoness reformed, this time as a stork's body with a human head. "Naturally not. She's my child aspect."

"She's from a different reality. Not this one. So you can probably coexist."

"Now that promises to be interesting. I can fission into halfway crazy D. Mentia and me, and we can interact, but Woe is too young to know how. I'd like to contest her."

Stymy knew he shouldn't, but his beak was already opening. "To what her?"

"Confront, encounter, congregate, converge, adjoin, animal flesh—"

That would be meat. Or—"Meet?"

"Whatsoever! I'll help you look for her."

Why not? She certainly had an interest in rescuing her other reality child self. "We think the Sorceress Morgan le Fey led them astray and is holding them hostage. We must find them to stop that."

"Morgan! Even I dislike her, and that's hard to score."

"Hard to what?"

"Accomplish," Stymie said impatiently.

"Whatsoever," the demoness agreed as crossly as ever.

"We'll fly low across the land, and descend to investigate any prospect," Stymy said. "Oh—Metria, one of the children is your son Demon Ted."

"I have a son?"

"In my reality you married a mortal man, got half a soul

and conscience, and after sending about fifteen hundred signals managed to get a stork to pay attention."

"My alternate did that? I'm sure I could have done it faster. She can't be very cogent."

"Very what?"

"Sound, solid, satisfactory, telling, convincing—"

"Persuasive?"

"Whatsoever," she agreed crossly. "Though it is true you storks have a canned ear for demon signals."

"A tin ear?" Stymie asked.

"Whatso—hey, you skipped my litany."

"Sorry about that," Stymie said without apparent regret. "I just want to get on with the search."

"For suitable prospects," Stymy reminded her.

Metria became a full stork, a sexy one. "I'm a prospect. Investigate me."

"Are you here to help or hinder?" Stymie demanded sharply.

"One or the other." The demoness spread her wings and took off.

"She annoys me," Stymie muttered.

"Understandable," Stymy said, privately pleased by her interest. He didn't care to admit that Metria in saucy stork form was quite interesting. It helped him understand why human men tended to have eyes for more women than they ever hoped to accommodate.

They flew to the next glade. There was a group of several pink vaguely storklike birds. "You check farther ahead," Stymy called. "I'll ask these if they have seen the children."

He descended. The birds were not only pink, their beaks were spoons. They were roseate spoonbills.

He landed and approached them. "Hello. I am Stymy Stork." Introductions were always better, first.

"We're sposeate roonbills," the nearest one replied. "We panstrose sinitial ounds."

Stymy digested that. After a long moment and a short instant he figured it out: they were transposing initial sounds. That was their talent, or curse. "So I gather."

"We dish we widn't," another spoonbill said.

Stymy remembered now: such switches were called spoonerisms. Naturally the spoon-beaked birds practiced them.

Still, maybe they could help. "Have you seen three lost children?"

The spoonbills considered. "Yes, we taw swo," one said. "In the fext nield."

Two? Maybe the third wasn't in sight at the moment. "Yank thew!" Stymy called as he took off. Oops.

The next field did have two children. But not the right ones. Unless the Sorceress had somehow changed their appearance. One was an athletic looking girl of about almost fourteen, holding the other, a boy of about almost one and a half.

He landed before them and got right to business. "Hello. I am Stymy Stork. Who are you?"

"A talking stork!" the girl said, amazed. The little boy clung to her more closely.

"Yes, storks can talk, when we need to. I'm looking for two ten-year-old children and a five-year-old girl. Their names are Ted, Monica, and Woe Betide."

The girl shook her head. "I am Sophia Isadora, an acrobat from—from—"

"Mundania," Stymy said, catching on. Sometimes folk came to Xanth involuntarily, and it was best not to inquire the details.

"Mundania," she agreed uncertainly. "This is Devin Mc-Clane Kowalick, also from there. We're hopelessly lost."

Stymy had to do something to help them, but had no time to spare. "Go to the next field. The spoonbills are nice birds; they will surely help you find your way to a human village. They talk oddly, but they mean well."

"Thank you," Sophia said politely. She took Devin's hand and led him toward the next field.

Stymy spread his wings and took off. He hoped there was a suitable human village nearby. It usually took involuntary visitors a while to get their bearings. But in time they would come to like Xanth, and even develop magic talents of their own.

They landed in the next glade, spying two figures there. But these were not the children. One was a lovely young woman with almost transparent skin. In fact she was translucent throughout, her body an appealing pink. Beside her was a similarly translucent man, gray throughout, looking surly.

"Hello, people," Stymy said. "I am Stymy Stork, and this is Stymie. We're looking for three lost children."

"You lost your deliveries!" the woman said sympathetically. "You poor things."

"No no," Stymy said quickly. "These are three older children, ages ten, ten, and five. Have you seen them?"

"Not at all, I'm sorry to say," the woman said. "I am Rose Quartz. My talent is to soothe troubled hearts. I can't help you find your children, but I can ease your heartache about the loss. All I need to do is embrace you."

"The bleep you will," the man said hotly. "You're entirely too friendly with strangers."

"It's my nature," Rose said. Then, to the storks: "This is my boyfriend Smoky Quartz. He's constantly heated up about something. That's *his* nature."

The third stork fuzzed into smoke, then reformed as a luscious translucent blue human woman. She approached Smoky. "Well hello, hot, hard, and handsome. I'm Crystalline Quarts, and—"

"Crystalline what?" Smoky asked.

"Milky, Brown, Yellow, Citrine, Amethyst—"

"Quartz," Rose said, her color deepening almost to red.

"Whatever," the demoness agreed crossly. "Let's go and make beautiful inclusions together, Smoky."

"Do that, and I'll bash you into rock crystal," Rose said, not at all soothing at the moment.

"Now don't get fractured, Quartzite," Smoky said, backing away from the demoness. He had evidently caught on to what was real and what wasn't. The two translucents moved away.

"If that's the way you're going to help us search, we don't need it," Stymie said severely.

Crystalline morphed back into stork form. "I just couldn't resist. It's my nature. When I saw how hot and smoky he was I just had to have a piece of him."

Another cloud of smoke appeared. "A peace of what?" it demanded.

What was this? Stymy knew it couldn't be Metria, because here she was in stork form. "How do you spell that?" he asked the cloud.

"T H A T, of course," the cloud responded.

"I mean the other word you used."

"W H A T," the cloud replied.

"Could it be PIECE?" Stymie asked.

"Whatsoever," the cloud agreed irritably as it formed into a fourth stork. That stork eyed Stymy speculatively, fluffing out her wings in an appealing manner.

"What are you doing here, Mentia?" Metria asked.

"Something interesting was happening, so naturally I came to sea what was up."

"To do what?" Stymy asked before he thought.

"See," Stymie said impatiently.

"Whatsoever," the Demoness Mentia agreed irritably.

"This is the Demoness Mentia, my altar ego," Metria said.

"Your what ego?" Stymy asked.

"Mound, platform, structure, edifice, sacrificial stand—"

"Alter, as in change," Stymie snapped, her beak clicking sharply. "And we are Stymy and Stymie Stork, searching for lost children."

"So pleased to meat you," Mentia said, stepping closer to Stymy.

"To what me?" Stymy asked, unable to curb his tongue in time. "I mean, how is that M-word spelled?"

"Spelled M E E T," Stymie said.

"Whatsoever," Mentia agreed irritably.

"Now that's interesting," Stymy said. "In my reality, Mentia is a little crazy, but doesn't garble words."

"Some folk call her synonym and me homonym," Mentia said. She now stood quite close to Stymy.

"We both garble words," Metria agreed, stepping closer herself. "Only in slightly different ways."

"But if you are alter egos, how can you exist apart?" Stymy asked.

"We fusion," Metria said.

"You mean fishing," Mentia said.

"Fission," Stymie said crossly and irritably. "Why don't you two egos get back together and help us find those children?"

"Maybe we should," Mentia agreed.

The two storks marched toward each other, collided, and fused into one stork. "Now I am hole," she said. "I mean holo."

"Whole," Stymie said. "But still half-reared."

The stork exploded into smoke, which swirled around and formed back into two storks. "We fragment," one said.

"We're too internally conflicted," the other agreed.

Stymy realized that two additional searchers were probably better than one. "Let's look for the children."

They took wing again. Two things occurred to Stymy: one was that if they checked only the glades, they could miss children lost in the forest sections. The other was that Stymie had reacted much as Rose had, when a demoness came too winsomely close to him. Was she jealous of the attention other females paid him? He hoped so.

"It occurs to me that we need to check the forest too," he said. "The children could be caught there."

"What a grate idea," Mentia said. "I'll go into the deep dark forest with you."

Once again he couldn't stop his tongue in time, despite knowing he was playing her game. "What kind of idea?"

"G R E A T," Stymie called. "Great."

"I'm glad you agree," Mentia said smugly. "Stymy and I will check the forest."

Stymie looked as if she had swallowed a stinkworm. But she had inadvertently agreed, so had to let them do it.

They flew down into a thinnet, which was of course a

thinned thicket. "I had better stay quite close to you," Mentia said, "to protect you from the frights of the forest." She suited action to word, her silky left wing touching his right wing.

Did she really want to help find the children? She was probably just as mischievous as Metria, being of the same substance, as it were. "No need," he said gruffly. "I can take care of myself."

"Really?"

What was with her? "Really."

She stepped in front of him, spread her wings and enfolded him before he could react. "Stay still as a steak."

Stymy froze, mainly because he had no idea what else to do. He had never before encountered romantic aggression like this. It was not entirely objectionable; she was a very soft and pretty stork, even if he knew she was really a demoness. "As a what? Spelled how?"

"It's a big stiff pole," she said, keeping him closely clasped. Her embrace was so tight that his feet were off the ground. In fact he was floating.

"S T A K E," he spelled uneasily. "Now if you will kindly let me go—"

"Not yet," she murmured. "We're not threw yet."

That was what he was afraid of. But he seemed to have no fair way out. "Not what-spelling yet?"

"Finished. Done. Ended." She let him go and stepped back.

"T H R O U G H," he spelled as her feet landed back on the ground. Then he looked around, surprised. "What did you do?"

"What did I dew?"

"D O! We aren't where we were."

"Oh, that. I moved you to safety before the B's could sting you to death."

"B apostrophe S?" That didn't make sense, what else was there? She must have used the correct word.

"That weigh," she said, pointing with a wing.

"W A Y," he agreed, looking. "But that's a monstrous hive in the shape of a ship! It must have thousands of B's."

"Exactly. You were about to walk into it. That would have annoyed the scholars something awful. I had to get you away from it before they noticed."

"Scholars?" He couldn't think of a homonym, but it didn't seem to make sense as it stood.

"That's an Ark-hive," she explained patiently. "Where scholarly B's research new types of honey and sting-venom. One of several arks. They don't like to be disturbed."

Stymy thought about blundering into such an ark. Indeed, he would have gotten badly stung. But Mentia had intercepted him and floated him to safety before the B's noticed. "You're right," he admitted. "I do need your protection."

"I garble words, not dangers," she said, satisfied.

They resumed their search, avoiding the hives. Only to be intercepted by several green toothy reptiles in vests. They looked like allegories or allegations or worse. "We'd better flee," he whispered.

"Flea? There are no fleas on me."

She had trouble both ways with homonyms. "F L E E," he said urgently. "Before those monsters chomp us."

"Oh, those aren't dangerous," she said. "They're invest-i-gators. All we have to do is answer their questions."

The lead gator approached. "Inspector Al here," he said, flashing a badge. "What's this about a blundering bird being stung to death?"

"I caught him before he struck the ark," Mentia said. "So he escaped."

The gator made a note on a pad. "Very good, citizen. We don't like a ruckus." The gators departed.

Soon they encountered another young woman. "Do you birds need a memory repressed?" she inquired. "I am Summer; my talent is to repress a single memory in someone."

"No thank you," Stymy said. "We are looking for three lost children."

"Sorry; I haven't seen them," Summer said, and went on.

Belatedly, he wondered whether Summer's talent ever bounced back at her. Could she have seen the children and repressed the memory? Probably not, he hoped.

"I don't want to be negative," Mentia said. "But I don't think the children are in this area. No one has seen them."

"Let's ask one more person," Stymy said, suspecting she was right.

They saw a man resting by a tree. Stymy introduced himself, and asked.

The man shook his head. "I've been here all day, and not seen them. I'm Scott; I can dematerialize atoms. But then they get upset and fuss, and revert the moment I stop concentrating. It's a nuisance. I'd trade for your problem."

Stymy tried to think of some way Scott's talent could help them find the children, but couldn't. "Thank you."

"Let's keep looking," Mentia said encouragingly.

They quested through the forest, but found no children. "We had better rejoin the others," Stymy said.

They found an avenue to the sky and flew up. In two and a half moments they found the others.

"And what did you accomplish down there?" Metria inquired with a wry twist to her beak.

"We flu around, but found no children," Mentia said. "We saw a gate or ark, nothing else."

"F L E W," Stymy spelled. "G A T O R."

Neither Metria nor Stymie seemed to believe that, but didn't make an issue.

The day was fading. "No children here," Metria concluded. "We'd better be on our ponderosity."

"Your what?" Stymy asked.

"Way," Mentia said, getting the wrong word almost right.

The two storks did not fly away. They simply dissolved into smoke. "So how long did it take to seduce him?" one asked the other.

"No thyme at awl," the other responded. They faded out, leaving nothing behind but Stymie's glare.

What could he say that she would believe?

But she rescued him. "Those demonesses never tell the truth, they just make mischief. So I know she didn't get anywhere with you."

"Nowhere," he agreed, relieved.

"Let's make a bower."

He stared at her. "But we hardly know each other."

"I think we do. Well enough." She clicked his beak again. "Soon you will depart and I'll never see you again. So anything we do together must be done now."

Stymy was beyond resistance. No real female had ever liked him, let alone offered to make a bower with him. She had offered to help him search for the children, so that the lost time would be made up, and had done so. She had shown real interest in him. She understood what it was like to be a virtual outcast among storks. He liked her more than he would have imagined before this day. How could he refuse?

"I suppose we do have time, this one time," he said, wishing that this didn't have to be the end of it.

"And I will keep your secret mission secret forever," she reminded him. "I hope your side wins. I wish I could have helped more."

"You helped a great deal. I'm sorry the demonesses got in the way."

"It's their nature." They laughed together, understanding perfectly.

They made a bower together. Then they entered it and sent the signal that Summoned the Man.

10

PEEVED DREAMS

The peeve flew to its sector, determined to find the children if they were there. It wasn't that it really liked the children; it didn't like anyone or anything. But they got along well enough, with their shared propensity for mischief. Mainly it was that Grundy and Rapunzel Golem provided the peeve a good home, which was a considerable improvement on its residence in Hell, as it had told Surprise, and it didn't want that messed up. So it would do its best.

And the baby Prize liked the peeve. That infused the peeve with a weirdly unfamiliar and sloppy emotion that for want of a better explanation suggested that the peeve liked the baby back. Nothing like that had ever happened before. No emotion other than irritation had ever motivated the peeve before. Oh, there was the guarded mutual respect it shared with a few, such as the Gorgon, Hannah Barbarian, and Grundy Golem, but this wasn't the same. It would take some getting used to, but there it was. If Surprise lost the baby, there would be nothing. Now that the peeve had discovered that tiny bit of like, it didn't want to lose it.

The peeve flew down to the edge of its search territory. It expected to do an efficient job, crisscrossing the land in a lattice pattern so that nothing would escape its notice. If the children were here, the peeve would find them.

Almost immediately it spied a doll-like girl walking nervously along a forest trail. She wasn't one of the children, but maybe she had seen them. "Hey, dollface, have you seen three children around here?"

The girl paused in place, standing in her own tracks, which was what folk normally did. She was extremely well formed, as dolls could be, with a large bosom, small waist, and long legs. "A talking bird!"

"A talking doll!" the peeve mimicked. "Are you too stupid to answer my question?"

For some reason the girl frowned. "You've got a foul beak on you, bird."

"Thank you. You've got an overstuffed shirt on you, and not enough stuffing in your skull. Now are you going to answer, or is that beyond your meager powers of focus?"

She frowned worse. "Who are you, bird?"

"I am a pet peeve. Couldn't you tell?"

She burst out laughing. "A pun! What a stinker."

"Thank you." The peeve always thanked folk for true observations, mainly because that tended to annoy them.

"I am Barbie Que," the girl said. "My talent is to cook raw food instantly by touch. It's another pun."

"Ha," the peeve said sourly. "Ha. Ha. There: I have laughed. It was an effort. Now can you compress the air in your head enough to answer my question?"

"No, I haven't seen any children. Only an awful ram or wolf with ten tongues who I fear wants to devour me."

The peeve's sympathy was limited. But she had finally answered its question, so it dallied a moment and a half more. "Come on, sister: is it a ram or a wolf? The one won't eat you; the other will."

"I think it's a crossbreed. It has big horns and huge sharp teeth. I don't want to get gored or chomped."

"Idiot, you have no need to be afraid of it," the peeve said. "It should be afraid of you."

"I don't understand."

"Of course you don't, doll-brain. Here it is: consider it raw food, and touch it. That will cook its goose."

Barbie's pretty mouth fell open. "I never thought of that! You're right." Her cute little chin firmed. "I'll tell it to be-gone if it doesn't want to be roasted."

"No time like the present, D-cup. There he is."

Barbie's manicured hair swirled as she spun around. "Oh!" she cried with maidenly distress.

"Hey, dog-snoot!" the peeve called, using Barbie's voice. "I dare you to try to devour me!"

The crossbreed monster was taken aback. He curled several of his tongues around to form words. "I don't want to eat you. I want to be your friend. I was hoping you are as lonely as I am."

"My friend!" Barbie exclaimed with maidenly shock. "But what big teeth you have, wolf!"

"Wolfram Tungsten," he said. "Two names for the same element. So I'm part wolf, part ram, and have tongues ten. It's a burden."

"You're a pun too!" Barbie exclaimed.

"Yes. Half the folk I meet don't get it, and half sneer at it. That doesn't leave many to befriend. I thought maybe a creature like you would understand."

"Oh, I do!" she exclaimed, thrilled. "Now that I know your nature." She kissed the wolf on a ram horn. "You really don't want to ram me or wolf me down?"

"Not as a meal," the peeve said, picking up a couple of marvelously naughty unintended interpretations. "Ha-ha-ha!"

Both maiden and monster glared at it. "Let's leave this birdbrain," Wolfram said.

"Delighted," Barbie agreed. The two newfound friends departed together.

Well, it had been fun while it lasted. The peeve had gotten off a couple of decent insults and a snide observation before the subjects caught on. It resumed the search.

Soon the peeve located something not by sight but by smell. It was a boy hiding invisibly in a gnarly crevice of an old beer-barrel tree. "What are you up to, twerp?"

"Oh, you found me," the boy said, disappointed.

"Of course I found you, brat. I'm sniffing out children."

"But I'm Hidey. I can hide from anything."

"Visually maybe. Not from a good nose."

"Oh, I forgot!" Then Hidey faded out, losing his smell.

"Did you see any other children, gamin?" the peeve called.

"None, hummingbird!" the boy's voice replied from midair. He really was good at hiding, and he had gotten off a good insult: the peeve was small, but not that small. That had to be respected.

There was yet another irrelevant person, this time a lonely-looking young woman sitting on a stone. The peeve perched on a low branch before her. "What's bothering you, airhead?"

She looked up. "My name's Lydia, not Airhead."

She had missed most of the insult. That was annoying. "You didn't answer my question."

Lydia sighed. "I have a good talent, I'm sure of it. But no one is interested. I can interpret dreams, but most folk can't even remember their dreams. I wish I could find somewhere where dreams are remembered. But I have traveled all around Xanth, and there's nothing."

The peeve was about to launch another cutting insult. But then Lydia looked at it and spoke again. "Oh, one of your pretty green feathers is ruffled. Let me straighten it." She reached out and set the feather in order. For some reason that stifled the insult.

"Maybe I can come up with something," the peeve said, hating the sudden foolish irrational wish to be helpful. "I'll ponder it."

"Oh thank you, lovely creature!" she exclaimed.

The peeve returned to the quest. There really was nothing significant. Just ordinary stupid pedestrians who hadn't seen any children, and routine monsters like tangle trees and nickelpedes. Certainly no lost children.

Then the peeve spied a vine bearing a gourd. It was a large one, and yes, it was a hypno-gourd, an entry to the dream realm. Could the children have gotten into that? There were no bodies lying with their eyes glued to the peepholes, but they could be hidden by a spell by the Sorceress Morgan le Fey. That would be a fine way to hide the children for an indefinite period. Their bodies would be absolutely still and silent, while their minds were locked into the horrors of the dream realm. They could be anywhere in there.

Well, there was one way to find them: by their minds. If they were in the dream realm, they'd be happily making mischief in the bad dream sets, not invisible at all. The disruption should be considerable. They shouldn't be hard to locate.

But it wouldn't do to look into the peephole and freeze the way others did, because there was no easy way to escape the trance. The peeve knew it needed to be in full control. Well, for a bird who had had experience with Hell, there was a way. The peeve flew toward the gourd, closed its wings, and plunged through the peephole. It had entered physically.

It found itself in the standard opening setting: a creepy haunted house in a scary forest. Everything was in thick shadow, and there was a faint background of eerie music. Ideal for giving innocent folk the queasies.

But this was not a social visit. The peeve flew rapidly around to the side and into a broken upstairs window, bypassing the ghosts and pitfalls of the main drag. It found itself in a bedroom with a creaky bed festooned with cobwebs. A skeleton lay under the covers, awaiting the approach of a frightened victim. Then it would groan and stir—the peeve wasn't sure how fleshless skeletons could groan, but they did when they needed to—and with luck frighten the victim into jumping right out the window in mid-scream.

But this was no time for fun. The peeve flew to the bed

and perched on the bare skull. "Wake up, hollow-head. Have you seen any children here?"

The skeleton jumped, startled in the manner normally reserved for human victims. "Whooo?" it asked, dazed.

"Ted and Monica Demon, and Woe Betide. Ages ten, ten, and five."

The skeleton began to get organized. "I meant, whoo are you?"

"I asked first, bonehead. Answer before I poop on your pate."

The skeleton grabbed with bone fingers, but the peeve was already in the air and hovering. It had had decades of experience avoiding angry folk. It dropped a small blip on the skull's polished pate. "That's just a warning, vacuum-head. Next one will be poop du jour."

The skeleton had very little wit in its hollow head, but that was enough for it to know when it was overmatched. "No children here."

"Thanks for nothing." The peeve flew to the closed door and scrambled under the sill.

Now it was in the upstairs hall. A female ghost was lurking, facing the stairway, expecting a victim to ascend.

"Take off, empty skirt," the peeve said loudly right behind her.

The ghost did. She sailed up and passed halfway through the ceiling before recovering. She drew herself back and floated down, looking nervously around. She was accustomed to being the spooker, not the spookee.

"Good thing you don't have anything to see down here," the peeve remarked from under her full bell-shaped dress.

"EEeee!" she screamed, capitalizing the first two e's in her dismay as she sailed up again, pulling her skirt close about her invisible ankles.

"You might at least have the courtesy to wear ghost-white panties," the bird peeved.

"Get out of here, you dirty little snoop!" she cried angrily. "You're messing up the set." She huffed up her top section like a forbidding matron.

"Just tell me whether you have seen three children here, balloon-bra."

The ghost pulled her décolletage tight as her face went grimly white. "No children, you nasty little beak."

"Thank you, paleface."

The peeve flew on down the stairs, passing an empty pair of walking shoes that were tramping down the steps, making a clattering calculated to freak out any visitor already shaken by the apparitions downstairs. Accordingly, it dropped a small smelly offering in one shoe as it passed. "Courtesy of the trade, footfalls."

Both shoes froze for fully half an instant, then leaped up and turned over to dump out the dottle. Naturally it stuck in place. The shoes knocked their heels together, finally dislodging the gooey gob. They made violent kicking motions. The peeve nodded, satisfied; one might almost get the impression they were annoyed.

There were no children in the house, and no evidence of the disruption of their passage. But they could have entered the dream realm via another site, especially if they had visited it before; it generally held the place of each visitor, so no one could avoid anything by waking and returning another time. All settings would have to be checked, until the children were found. That was apt to be a big job, but easier if any of the denizens of the dream realm had news of them.

The peeve flew out the back, rapidly checking the zombie graves; the children wouldn't be underground, being alive. It reached the edge of the horror set, which was a wall painted realistically with further gloomy trees, graves, and suggestions of dark monsters going bump in the night.

There was room to scramble under the wall where the ground dipped. The peeve scrambled, and emerged in the next set: a halfway pleasant scene with a village in a valley, not far below a massive cracked dam that looked about to burst asunder. Beyond it loomed deep dark storm clouds threatening torrential rain. This stage would be to craft dreams for folk concerned about flash flooding; it was probably quite a sight when that dam let go.

The peeve flew through the village, searching for signs of mischievous children. There were none. In fact the village seemed unoccupied. This was either the off season, or there was no current call for a bad flood dream.

It came to a slope beset with caves; those could hide a lot, if they were extensive.

A dull-looking man sat before one cave. The peeve approached. "Hey, dullard—any children here?"

"Who wants to know?"

"I, the pet peeve."

"I'm Dennis. This here's the cave complex of Denver, where all the denizens live when they're not working on sets."

That would be the spot dream sets, which required a lot of design, manufacture and assembly before they could be used in bad dreams. "Children work on the sets?"

"Sure, many. Which ones you want?"

Uh-oh. That could mean multiple dream children. "Live human ones, part demon or even full demon. Ages ten, ten, and five."

"Live children?" Dennis asked. "None of that kind here, just dream children. I thought that's what you meant."

So much for that. The peeve flew on, looking for the edge of the scene. It didn't want to fly into a realistically painted wall.

There was a swirl of smoke that paced it. "What are you up to, bitty bird?"

"What wants to know, smoke-face?"

The smoke formed into a human head, neck, and part of a splendid set of breasts seemingly molded from stone. "I'm a buffet."

"You're a what?"

"Slap, smack, cuff, box, spank—"

"Bust?"

"Whatsoever," the head agreed crossly. "The top section of a statue."

"You expect me to call you statuesque."

"Certainly. Do it." More stone flowed to fill out the burgeoning bosom.

The peeve refrained. "What are you doing here, Metria?"

"Finding out what you're doing on this course, birdie."

"I'm looking for three lost children."

"How long have they been lost?"

"Centuries!" the peeve said sarcastically, losing what little patience it possessed.

"That long ago? Maybe they're at Buick."

"Where?"

"The colony they founded at Buick Rock."

"Where?" the peeve repeated peevishly.

"Chevy, Chrysler, Jeep, Ford, Volks—"

Ah. Mundane crates. "Plymouth?"

"Wherever," she agreed crossly.

"Is there a Plymouth Rock here in the dream realm?"

"No."

"Then get out of here, you infernal tease!"

"I can't. I'm not through with my dream."

"Demons can't dream, you twit."

She looked dismayed. "Oh, that's right! Anyway, I'm currently busy elsewhere. I can't be here." She faded out, leaving only a wisp of smoke in the form of the heaving outline of her overstuffed halter.

The peeve flew on. Demons were usually a pain in the tail, and this one more so. It found the boundary wall and scrambled under.

There was a sound, a sustained note. The peeve went toward it, and found several large lakes or small seas. Each was at a different level. The notes were coming from them, each an octave apart. "What's this?" it asked itself.

The demoness reappeared, head, shoulders, bosom trailing into a fuzz of smoke. "The C's," she explained. "High C, middle C, low C."

"Get out of here, smoke-tail!"

"Spoilsport." She vanished.

The peeve flew on across the C's. The dream realm was big, and this wasn't accomplishing much. There needed to be a way to check all of it at once. How could that be accomplished?

At the edge of the lowest C a man of middle age was standing. Maybe he could help.

"Say, grizzlepuss—have you seen three children around here?"

"Call me the Mariner," the man said affably. "I work with water." He dipped his hand in the C, splashing the water into an arc. The water remained in the air, and the Mariner put his boots on it and climbed it like a ridge.

The peeve was impressed despite its cynicism. This was useful magic. "What are you doing here?"

"My sole motivation is to find rare and peaceful fishing spots," the Mariner said. "I always get pulled into some adventure that diverts me. I have an enchanted fishing rod and spear to catch huge catfish, if I ever find the right water."

"The dream fish that got away?"

The question was meant to be annoying, but the Mariner merely smiled and agreed. Couldn't win them all.

A big whiskered fish poked its head out of the C. "Meow," it said.

"There's one now," the Mariner said, whipping his fishing rod around. But in his distraction he forgot his spell on the floating splash of water, and it dropped him into the C with a great splash. The catfish, of course, was gone.

Then the peeve caught on. Fishy business. "Metria."

The demoness appeared beside him, shifting from catfish to luscious human woman form. "I couldn't resist," she confessed.

It occurred to the peeve that the bothersome demoness could be useful after all. "How would you like to really mess up the dream realm, prune-bosom?"

"Those are overripe melons, not dried plums," she said, glancing down at her swelling front. "You didn't notice, muck-tail?" She was handling the insult distressingly well. "How can I mess up big time?"

"Form into a super megaphone and let me use you to blast out my announcement about the children across the entire spectrum."

Metria considered. "That's too much like doing you a favor, pigeon-brain. I can't risk it." She faded out.

The peeve hardly cared to admit it, but the demoness was annoying it almost as much as it hoped it was annoying her.

It found the next boundary wall and scrambled under. The next scene was a jungle filled with tigers, crocodiles, mean men with big knives, and other Mundanian brutes, all of them slavering. A lovely young woman in revealingly tattered clothing was fleeing everything, staying barely ahead of the pursuit. This was of course a standard bad dream, probably for delivery to some naughty Mundane maiden. The peeve understood that the export trade was very good; Mundanes were constantly in need of punitive dreams.

Naturally the peeve approached the girl. "Hey, tear-skirt—have you seen three children around here?"

She ignored him, continuing her panting progress up the slope as the monsters gained on her. She panted quite well; human males would be staring.

The peeve landed on her tousled tresses. She had long red hair that flew fetchingly out behind her head. "I said, HAVE YOU SEEN ANY CHILDREN, straggle-locks?"

She tried to brush it off her head, but the peeve fluttered up, avoiding her swing, and landed again when her hand was safely past. "Answer, or I'll poop."

That got her attention. "Get out of here, you stupid little bird, before you mess up the shot."

"You were warned." The peeve let loose a foul poop that splattered on her glorious hair.

"Ugh!" she cried, trying desperately to brush off the stinky stuff. But her effort only got her dainty hand gooked too. "Yuckety yuckety yuck!" she cursed.

"Cut!" someone yelled loudly. The monsters paused in place. A stout man in a visor appeared, carrying a megaphone. "That's not in the script, Diana. You know you're not supposed to use foul language. What's the matter with you?"

The luscious redhead became a small blonde woman wearing glasses. "This awful bird just soiled my hair!"

"What bird?" the man demanded. For of course the peeve had vacated the moment the action paused. It was inspecting the megaphone from cover. It also noticed that there was a crew with a fancy camera, and a number of other hangers-on. This was a full-fledged filming. Could this dream be intended for a Mundane movie starlet?

"An obnoxious little green talking bird," Diana said. "Look at what it did to my hair! Director, you've got to do something." She showed her poopy head. "I didn't escape to fantasy to endure an outrage like this."

The director snapped his fingers. Immediately two plain women appeared with water, soap, sponges and other apparatus and got to work on the soiled hair and hand. In one and a half moments they had her clean and shining again.

"Action!" the director said, the megaphone amplifying his voice. Diana resumed her vibrant full-breasted red-haired persona and her panting fleeing, and the monsters their slavering pursuit.

A shape appeared on the slope above. It had four legs below, two in the middle, two arms above, a head in front and another at the top, and glinted somberly. The monsters held back, wary of this apparition. "Avast, varlet!" it cried.

The maiden paused. "A knight!" she exclaimed. "My rescue is at hand!"

The knight lifted his visor to peer down at her. "A damsel in distress."

"Verily!" she exclaimed gladly, her bosom heavily active. Her décolletage had slipped somewhat, revealing additional rondure. "Swoop me up in your mighty arms and take me away from all this."

But the knight did not swoop her up. He peered down inside her fragmented halter as if there was something interesting there. "A point of observation, damsel. Do I bestride a horse?"

"No," she said, surprised. "It is a great black bull."

"Does my armor shine?"

She looked more carefully. "No, it glints darkly."

"And what does that signal to your limited intellect?"

She clapped the back of her hand to her forehead. "You don't serve the light."

"I am a dark and stormy knight," he agreed. "I serve the Dark Power. I certainly have a use for a creature of the light as lusciously exposive as you are, but I would not term this 'rescue.' Acquisition is more like it. Now yield thee to my dubious mercy forthwith and I will not throw you to the monsters after I and my virile steed are done with you. You will serve as a scullery maid betweentimes."

"Never!" she cried despairingly, evidently having some inkling of his sinister intent.

"Too bad, slut." His visor snapped back into place, and a long dark lance appeared in his hands. "I will simply run you through in another fashion." His armored bull snorted and charged, steam blowing from its nostrils.

"eeeEE!" she cried, in her distraction capitalizing the last two e's. She dodged to the side, so that the point of his lance missed by a medium hair breadth. He was unable to stop his charge quickly, as it was downhill, so he moved on down, skewering bystanding monsters galore. The monsters were hardly pleased.

Meanwhile the maiden, having dodged the bull-et, re- sumed her plunge up the hill, panting anew.

The peeve flew back into the scene. "You were about to tell me about the children, Diana," it said.

She flinched, but couldn't answer without violating the script. She forged on up the slope.

"So it's like that," the peeve said, landing back on her head. "Are you sure you don't want to answer? It would be such a shame to poop such lovely fresh-washed hair again."

Now the fleeing maiden came to the brink of a horrendous cliff. Vultures circled above the abyss below, eying her hun- grily. The monsters behind closed in, knowing they had her trapped. "Get lost, you little turd," she hissed. The air shim- mered around the dirty word, and the hint of a foul smell wafted out.

"So be it, wastrel." The peeve readied a phenomenal poop.

Diana leaped into the void, avoiding the valiant effort, and also, incidentally, the charging monsters. She sailed down- ward in a swan dive, her lovely hair spreading like a parachute. The peeve was annoyed; she had caused it to waste a significant deposit. After all, quality poop didn't grow on trees.

Well, she wasn't going to escape that way. The peeve folded its wings and dived after her.

A Mundane helicopter zoomed across, its enormous whirling propeller almost chopping through the peeve. The peeve had to take immediate evasive action to avoid losing some tail-feathers. "Bleep!" it swore.

The helicopter dropped a dangling ladder right before the diving maiden. She caught the bottom rung with both hands and swung like a pendulum below the machine, hair and skirt flaring appealingly. "Saved!" she cried.

A large man with a complexion reminiscent of a warthog leaned out of the copter. "Ha!" he exulted. "Now you are in my power, you luscious wench!"

The maiden looked up. Panic spread across her face and down her neck to her bosom, almost obliterating a heave. "Oh, no! Black Repete!"

"Your ancient nemesis," Repete exulted. "Come on up, my lovely, so I may have my ill way with you repeatedly before I throw you to the monsters."

"Never!" Diana cried plaintively.

"That's what you think, you tempting tidbit. If you won't come up, I'll come down." Repete swung himself onto the ladder, showing heavily muscled arms. "I'll ravish you in midair. I always wanted to do that."

"Eeeeek!" the maiden cried despairingly.

But now the peeve caught up. It perched again on her hair. "*Now* will you tell me about the children?"

"You unmitigated—" she started.

"Thank you," Black Repete said. He hadn't seen the peeve.

"One more chance," the peeve said, lifting its tail.

"Oh! You're awful!" she cried in the very depths of disgust.

"I am indeed," Repete agreed. He was almost down to where she clung.

Then the maiden let go of the rung.

"Cut!" the director bawled through his megaphone.

"That's not in the script!" He and the monsters were standing at the brink of the cliff, above.

"Bleep the script!" Repete growled. "What happened?"

The maiden dropped below camera range, bounced on the safety net, and sailed up almost as far as she had dropped. "That bleeping bird was going to poop on me again!" she said furiously.

"What bird?" Repete demanded.

By this time the peeve had reached the director's megaphone. It put its beak to it and let forth its loudest voice, suitably amplified. "**THIS** BIRD, MORON!"

Several startled assistants and a monster or two almost fell off the cliff. The director lifted up the megaphone, but the peeve clung to it. "WHERE ARE THE CHILDREN?" its voice reverberated.

"What children?" the director asked, trying to shake the bird off.

"THE LOST CHILDREN, IMBECILE."

"You've ruined the whole scene," the director complained. "We'll have to shoot it over from the beginning."

"Not before you tell me about the children, dimwit," the peeve said, finally shaken loose from the megaphone.

"I don't know anything about children!" the director said. "This is an adult-rated dream. No children here."

"What about in the rest of the dream realm, jerk?"

"How should I know? I'm just doing my own scene. Now get out of here, you speck of dirt, before I call the law."

"What law? I'll poop on your head." The peeve flew up over the director.

Then the entire scene froze. The director and monsters were unmoving, the helicopter blades became visible and still, and Diana hovered in mid-bounce, part of an eyeball-freaking panty showing under the floating skirt.

The great Night Stallion stood in mid air. "This law," he said without moving his mouth. "We can't have our sets disrupted by intruders."

"Too bad, horse-face. I won't leave until I get what I came for."

"You will leave when I hurl you out, bird."

That made the peeve nervous, but he bluffed it out. "Try it and I'll poop on your mane, founder-foot."

The air wavered around the Stallion. A tremendous force coalesced, focusing on the peeve. The entire realm of dreams seemed to turn inside out.

When it cleared, the peeve remained where it was. It had not been ejected. "What's the matter, numbskull? Lose your power?"

"You're not of this reality," the Stallion said, surprised. "I lack power over your dreams."

"Tough spit, cow-eye. So you'd better just tell me what I need to know."

The Stallion steamed slightly, but his voice was even. "What is that?"

"Where are the three lost children? Ted, Monica, Woe Betide?"

"That would be complicated. I would have to inventory all our children, to ascertain whether those three are among them."

"Get busy, laggard. Do you think I have all day?"

The Stallion blinked, and the scene vanished. Now they were in a somber hall, just the two of them. An independent observer might somehow have gotten the impression that the horse of another color was angry. "Tell me about these children. Are they of this reality?"

"No. They're visitors, like me."

"What are you doing here?"

"As if you don't know, fleabag."

"I do not know the affairs of other realities," the Stallion said evenly. Wisps of acrid vapor drifted in minor air currents. "In fact I was unaware that individuals could travel between them. How did you manage that?"

"The Stork works, dullard. That connects with all the realities. You didn't know?"

"I did not know the storks allowed children and birds to utilize their facilities."

"It's a special case, hoofer."

The Stallion nodded gravely. "So it seems. I suspect there is something larger here than meets the eye."

"You do have bigger orbs than I do, horse-head. If you can't see it, why should I?"

The equine body glowed dangerously. "I may not be able to eject you from my realm, alien bird, but I can put you into dreams that will make you wish you had departed."

"Listen, rump-rot, I've lived in Hell. What do you have that can match that?"

The Stallion considered. "You strike me as a creature almost without conscience. What interest do you have in finding children?"

"What business is it of yours, puke-tail?"

"If you want me to locate them for you, that becomes my business."

The peeve searched for a way to refute that, but could not. "The Sorceress Morgan le Fey is holding the children hostage so as to force Surprise Golem to give up her baby for Morgan to use. We have to find those children so Surprise can keep her baby."

"Surprise surely cares. Why do you?"

The peeve squirmed uncomfortably. "Is this relevant?"

"Motive is relevant. Before I help you, I need to be sure you are not planning to harm her or the children."

"I wouldn't do that!"

"A creature without conscience would sell out anyone for personal benefit. Convince me you would not."

The peeve saw no alternative but the truth. "The Golems gave me a good home. The baby likes me. I don't want to mess that up."

"Suppose the Sorceress Morgan offers you a mountain of divine birdseed?" The Stallion flickered, and the mountain appeared, formed of every kind of seed, common, rare, and exotic. There were even the seeds of Doubt, Dissension, and War, which were guaranteed to give a bellyful in short order.

The peeve licked its beak, but held firm. "The harpy can eat it herself for all I care."

"And if she offers you the Big Book of Insults for All Oc-

casions?" The huge tome appeared, bound by two hefty
leather straps, with wisps of smoke leaking out from between the pages.

The peeve hesitated half a flicker. "Including the filthiest
ones?"

"Including ones that scorch foliage and make maidens
swallow their teeth."

But the peeve remembered nice Surprise Golem. How
could her welfare be traded for a pot of puke? "No."

"What about a perch over an abyss filled with beseeching
faces?" The abyss appeared below them, filled with the features of humans, monsters, and crossbreeds of every fantastic description, all staring up pleadingly.

The notion was dizzying. All those faces to poop on!
"Well—"

"Or the combination," the Stallion continued persua-
sively. "Birdseed to stoke your poop-tract, insults galore,
and the faces of everyone who ever disliked you?" The three
scenes superimposed in an artistic dream.

Even Hell had not offered such opportunity! There had
been a time—a long time—when that would have been irre-
sistible. But as of the past year the peeve had begun to experience life with a loving family, and as of the past hour had
been the recipient of a single unfeigned smile. It would be
ludicrous to trade seeds, insults, and faces for such pittances,
yet the Golem family, including the new baby, had somehow
lassoed the peeve's wizened heart and would not let go.
"No," it whispered regretfully.

"That is not a purely rational decision. How can any puny
trace of emotion be allowed to interfere with unadulterated
self-interest?"

"I know," the peeve agreed, ashamed. "I'm just not the
bird I was."

"I will help you," the Stallion said abruptly. The Temptation scene retreated to the background, restoring the somber
hall. A monstrous megaphone appeared. "Now hear ye," the
horse said, his voice amplified beyond all reason by the in-

strument. "All children are to report to headquarters this moment for tallying. Any child hanging back will be denied candy for a week."

There was an immediate scramble, and the hall filled with children. There were humans, elves, goblins, trolls, ogrets, skeletons, demons, cubs, little dragons, small ghosts, puppy cats, kitty dogs, and more alien youngsters.

"Which are yours?" the Stallion asked.

The peeve eyed every child. "None of these," it said sadly.

"Then they are not in the dream realm."

"Then my job here is done. I wasn't able to help Surprise."

"You have helped her by eliminating one sector," the Stallion said. "That is the most you can do."

"I wanted to do more."

"That is the penalty of developing your soul, conscience, and empathy."

"Now he tells me," the peeve muttered. Then it remembered something. "There's a nice girl named Lydia who is looking for work. She can interpret dreams, but few folk remember them long enough. I wonder—"

"We can use her," the Stallion said. "Next time she sleeps we will bring her here and present her with our uninterpreted dreams. We like to understand them perfectly before using them, so they can't go wrong, but some are awkward."

"Tell her the pretty green bird arranged it."

"I will."

Meanwhile the children had discovered the objects in the background. "Seeds!" one exclaimed, and several dived into the mountain, throwing seeds at each other. "Insults!" another cried, trying to unfasten the containing straps. "Poopdeck faces!" a third said, looking down into the abyss.

"I had better get out of your way," the peeve said.

The Stallion glanced back. The seeds became candy, the book a giant *Fairy & Elf Tales* volume, and the faces became a mural on the floor. "Awww," the children groaned, disappointed.

"Just fly through the bull's-eye."

The peeve found itself back in the cliffhanger horror sequence, which was being rerun. The Dark and Stormy Knight was charging the Desperate Maiden, who was dodging aside. Now it was evident that this event was carefully choreographed; the knight was not really trying to impale her, but to make it look like a very close call. The dreamer who received that bad dream would not know that, of course.

The bull was snorting, its armored eye glaring. The peeve flew right at the eye, passing between the slats of the armor and diving into the angry pupil.

It emerged from the gourd whose peephole it had entered. The standard dull Xanth scenery remained. It was good, in its fashion, to be back.

The peeve resumed its search of the remaining sector, but was sure the children weren't there. Maybe someone else would find them. At least it had done what it could.

And learned something about itself. Indeed, it was not the bird it had been.

Piquant Sea

The Centaur flew across his sector, searching for traces of the children. His gaze was keen and so was his hearing; he was confident he could spot them if they were here. They tended to be noisy little rascals, always up to some mischief; that made them easier to spot.

He came to a large lake or small sea, half shrouded by fog. He realized he was thirsty, so he glided down for a drink. He landed on the bank, brought a cup from his arrow quiver, and dipped out some sparkling water.

Then he paused. Things were not the same in this reality as in his own. He was not necessarily married to Cynthia Centaur here, for one thing. What looked like good lake water could be a huge love elixir pond. He already had trouble enough with his illicit passion for Surprise Golem; he did not want any further complication.

A creature emerged from the fog. It looked like a small human woman, or a large elf, but not exactly. It was female, with cat ears and tail, and wings. A crossbreed of some sort.

The creature saw Che. "Well hail, centaur! What are you doing in this neck of the woods?"

"I am Che Centaur. I thought I would take a drink of this water, but I am uncertain of its nature."

"And I am Chaska, half human, half demoness, and half whatever," she replied, changing form to small winged centaur. "My talent is seeing through fog. Have no fear of this water. This is the Vitamin Sea, very healthy."

This surprised Che. "How can you have a talent in addition to shape-shifting?"

"Why shouldn't I?"

"Folk are normally limited to one magic talent. Mine is flying. Any others I have to develop by serious practice, such as accurate archery."

She glanced sidelong at him. "You're not from around here, are you?"

"I am from far away, yes."

"So you don't know that there is no limit on magic talents in Xanth. Not that I have more than one; it's my demon ancestry that enables me to shape-shift." She became a fully human bare girl with wings.

"I did not know that," Che agreed. "Thank you for your information about this water." He lifted his cup and drank.

The water was dizzyingly healthy. He felt wonderful. And alarmed. Had she told him the truth? Suppose it was after all love elixir? She had for the moment assumed bare human form, which in that species was considered seductive. After his experience with Surprise Seven, who had tempted him far more than he cared to admit, he did not trust anything about this reality.

"You are welcome," Chaska said. She walked back into the fog, and disappeared.

Che felt no passion for her. So she had not tricked him; the water was merely full of healthy vitamins. He was relieved.

Chaska reappeared. "I just thought: might you be looking for other winged centaurs?"

"Actually I was looking for three lost part-demon children. But I wouldn't mind meeting others of my kind."

"I know where they are, through the fog. Catch my tail and follow me." She returned to small winged centaur form and switched her tail toward him.

Was this wise? Yet winged centaurs might be willing to help him search for the children, or know where they might be. It seemed a fair thing to risk.

He caught the tip of her tail. She spread her wings and leaped into the air. He followed. She plunged into the bank of fog, and he followed. In a quarter of a moment he was lost in the thickness of it, having no idea where he was with respect to land or sea. He had to trust Chaska's direction and motive.

They popped back into clear air. There below was an open stall such as flying centaurs used. "I believe they are home now," Chaska said. "Have a good visit." She twitched her tail from his grasp and disappeared into the fog.

"Thank you," he called after her.

He glided down to the stall. As he landed, two winged centaurs emerged, one male, the other female. "Hello," he said. "I am Che Centaur. I am looking for three lost children."

The male approached to shake hands. He had flame colored wings and a fiery coat. "I am Challenge Centaur, with the talent of the production of fire."

The female approached. Her coat was brown with lightning streaks. "I am Chellony Were-Centaur, with the talent of the production and control of lightning."

"Pardon my ignorance," Che said. "Did you say were-centaur?"

"Yes. I have five forms. This one, straight centaur—" her wings disappeared. "Straight human, winged human—" She assumed those forms, the human woman sprouting wings. "And winged horse." The horse appeared.

"I am amazed," Che said. "I am from far away, where our only magic talent is flying."

"As for the lost children—ours are not lost, as you see." Chellony glanced back into the stall, and three small winged centaurs emerged.

"They are part-demon children," Che said.

"Like Chaska!" one of the young centaurs exclaimed.

Chaska reappeared. "Are you ready to play in the fog?"

"Be back by nightfall," Chellony called as the three leaped into the air to join Chaska.

"We will," a child called back as they disappeared into the fog.

"We have not seen any part-demon children recently," Challenge said. "Other than Filly Buster and De Flate."

"Those are not the names, unless they somehow got changed," Che said. "What are those children like?"

Chellony smiled. "Filly Buster is a cute girl, but she will talk your ear off. We find ears lying on the ground where she has been."

"The only one who can shut her up is her friend De Flate," Challenge said.

"The children I seek are named Demon Ted, DeMonica, and Woe Betide," Che said. "They lack those talents. So I think you have not seen them. Has there been anything else?"

"Just a large lost bird," Chellony said.

Something about the way she said it alerted Che. "Would that bird be telepathic?"

"Indeed. And from very far away."

"Another reality," Challenge said.

"The Simurgh!"

"So you know of her," Chellony said.

"Yes. I tutor her chick, Sim."

Both centaurs paused with surprise. "That is indeed another reality," Challenge said. "In this one, the Simurgh is male, and has no chick."

"Many things are different," Che agreed. "I find it confusing at times."

"I am femalishly curious," Chellony said. "You must have to know a great deal, to tutor one as smart as that chick must be. Has Sim ever asked a question you were unable to answer?"

"Many times," Che agreed ruefully. "Then I have to research. For example, when I mentioned that the Demon Tallyho assigns talents to babies, Sim asked who assigned talents for adults who developed them later. I haven't yet learned the answer to that one."

"I can appreciate why," Challenge said. "I would never have thought of the question, let alone the answer."

"Maybe you should make up a name, such as the Demoness Jessica," Chellony suggested. "So as not to appear ignorant."

Che was horrified. "I would never—"

Both centaurs burst out laughing. They were teasing him. No centaur would pretend knowledge he lacked.

"I believe the Simurgh has been waiting for you," Chellony said. "She has not wished to interfere in the events of this reality, so has kept to herself. She contacted us only to be certain we did not object to her presence."

"I must talk to her," Che said.

"If she wishes."

Che smiled. "I understand your meaning. No one can contact the Simurgh without her agreement. But I believe she will talk with me." He sent out a thought. *Simurgh—Che Centaur is in this reality with friends.*

Welcome, good centaur.

The two other centaurs nodded together. "She knows you," Challenge said. "Go to her."

"Thank you." Che spread his wings and took off in the direction indicated by the Simurgh's powerful mind-signal. He was no longer concerned about the fog, knowing she would not mislead him.

He landed in a small crater. There was the Simurgh in a huge nest she had fashioned. "I am so glad to have found you," he said. "Though at the moment I was looking for the children."

It is a trying time, she agreed. *Though it has allowed me opportunity for thought.*

"You think?" he blurted before *he* thought. "I mean—"

I know what you mean, good centaur, she thought, amused. *As it happens I know a great deal, but there are aspects of understanding that I lack. For example, there is the question of the soldiers Magician Trent brought with him when he returned to Xanth and became king. They were Mundanes, but in time Mundanes can develop magic talents, as the magic of Xanth slowly infuses them. The question is why this was not observed.*

Chex was surprised. "I never thought of that."

You were busy with other matters, such as tutoring my chick. Now I believe I have made sense of that matter: the soldiers did develop talents, but they were so minor as to be unnoticed. Such as the ability of a man to change his eyes from one shade of blue to another, or altering the color of his nails, or the ability to speak to basilisks.

"But the sight of a basilisk will turn a person to stone!"

The Simurgh smiled mentally. *Therefore there was never occasion to invoke that particular talent.*

"I see that you keep yourself busy regardless of your situation."

Another mental smile. *Unfortunately I never found the lazy bone.*

"What kind of bone?"

It is the cure for the WORK Ethic curse.

Oh. She was having a bit of fun with him. "How is it you are caught here?" He had a fair notion, but wanted to be sure.

The fissure between realities defined its two connections, she thought. *When it terminated, they were no longer defined. I could leave this reality via the Stork Works, but not be sure of returning to the one I left without that definition. There are an infinite number of very similar realities.*

"What about the one where you are missing?"

There are an infinite number of those, also. I have a foolish preference to return to my own, rather than a similar one.

"But if you can't be sure of the correct reality, how can we?"

You cannot, she thought. *You will have to discover a way to identify the correct one.*

"But we lack expertise!"

True. It is a challenge. We depend on you.

A fluorescent bulb flickered over his head. "Does this have anything to do with my destiny?"

Everything, good centaur. You are destined to change the history of Xanth. You must endeavor to change it as little as possible.

"By locating the closest reality," he said, awed. "Lest the land I know be rendered moot."

True.

He moved on to the more immediate problem. "Surprise. Baby. Stork. Morgan le Fey. Children." Each word he said oriented his mind so that the Simurgh could instantly pick up all that was relevant. In five instants she had it all.

I will help you to the extent I can. The three children are not in this sector as such. But if they were transformed, there is a chance. There are three blips I am unable to fathom fully.

"But you know everything in the universe," Che protested.

In my reality. This is not that. The blips are very small, while my thoughts are large. We do not relate. But they do seem to be from a different reality.

"That could be the three children," Che agreed. "How to I locate them?"

The blips are deep inside an anthill. You must enter it and verify them personally.

"I am too big to enter an anthill," he said with a certain brief humor.

As it happens, another anthill owes me a favor. They have a drone who got touched by a forget whorl and lost his mind. You can take over that body. That should suffice. The Simurgh sent him a detailed thought, clarifying the situation. Now Che understood.

It took a bit of practice for Che to get used to walking on six legs and communicating via antennae, but these things were natural to the host body and soon he had them down. He also learned to use the special sense the Simurgh bestowed on him: awareness of the direction and nearness of the alien presences. These might not be easy to verify; the pique ants never brought them out into the open. There was definitely a mystery there.

The hill was near a pond that was the size of a sea in ant terms: the agreeably pungent and pleasant Piquant Sea. It was somewhat higher than the water level, so was unlikely ever to flood. In fact the ants probably had to delve deep to reach the water level, if they wanted to be sure of plenty to drink. Overall, it seemed like a very nice site, but somewhat exposed; didn't ant-eating creatures regard it as an easy meal? Evidently not.

He spied some tasty-looking berries. Each one was larger than he was, in this form, but he was hungry. He went to puncture one to get some of its juice.

Do not, good centaur, the Simurgh's thought came. *That is the notorious diary/diarrhea berry, unique I suspect to this reality. If a person eats one, he spews out his secrets in the manner of a diary. If he eats two, he has severe digestive difficulty. At your present size, one sip could inflict both curses on you together.*

Che decided he wasn't that hungry after all. He moved on, in a new direction.

You are losing your way, the Simurgh's warning came.

How had he done that? Che turned about and resumed the path toward the anthill.

He was distracted by a bug traveling the other way. The bug had feelers, so Che touched them. "Who are you?" he asked.

"I am a beetle from Mundania," the bug replied. "I thought coming here would solve my problem, but it only modified it."

"What is your problem?"

"I am manic/depressive. I cycle through episodes of joy and misery. I would gladly dispense with the one in order to avoid the other. But here in Xanth I cycle through episodes of magic and repression."

"Can you clarify?" Che asked, interested.

"I am entering my magic phase now. But it manifests erratically." The bug looked at a nearby blade of grass. It burst into flame. "Next time it may become a drop of water," the bug said. "I wish I could control my effect."

"I agree: you have exchanged one curse for another," Che said sympathetically.

"I will move on now, before some effect harms you."

"Thank you."

Resume your mission, the Simurgh thought firmly.

He had done it again. This time he focused determinedly and completed his trek to the anthill.

He approached the main entrance to the hill. A guard challenged him immediately, recognizing him as a foreign ant. The communication was electronic, but his mind interpreted it as verbal dialogue.

"Halt, intruder drone! You are not from this hill. I can tell by your smell."

"I am Ambassador Che of Pique Ant Hill 53. Here is my credit." He sent the authorizing signal.

"We don't have relations with Hill 53."

"You do now. You must accept a proffered Pique Ant ambassador, as you are pique ants too. By antly protocol you are obliged to grant me the hospitality of the hill for a day and night."

"This is highly irregular."

"Nevertheless legitimate. I'll take your best guest room, with room service and an early audience with the queen."

"This is preposterous. No one gets treatment like that."

Che affected lordly sarcasm. "Oh, are you an authority on protocol?"

The guard had to give way, not being equipped to respond to higher intellectual challenges. "I'll check with my supervisor."

"Do that, officer."

The guard checked, and the supervisor reluctantly yielded to the requirement. It was indeed protocol, though seldom implemented. Most anthills, pique and otherwise, simply minded their own business. Che soon found himself in a comfortable chamber just off the main drag, with a docile worker ant serving as servant and intermediary. He was, after all, a drone: one of the few full males in the ant kingdom. Ordinary workers were stunted females, constrained to serve and feed their betters. This worker was Anona Ant, completely unassuming and undistinguished.

Che touched her antennae with his own. Her whole meek, subservient personality came through with that touch. "I hunger," he informed her.

She waited. After most of a moment he caught on: she was literal minded. He had informed her of his state, but had not told her what to do about it. "Bring me an appropriate meal."

She departed immediately. He knew that the chef-ant would know what was appropriate and provide her with it.

Soon she returned with a glob of royal jelly. Che had never encountered that before, but his ant host body reacted: this was princely fare.

He took it and started eating. Anona retreated to a crevice area and waited.

He signaled her with a glance, and she approached for an antenna touch. "Are you hungry?" he inquired.

"Yes, lord."

"Would you like to have some of this?"

She was thrown into a crisis of indecision. Her mandibles quivered. "I don't know."

He caught on. She was not one to have likes or dislikes; her station was beneath preferences. "Common ants are not supposed to eat royal jelly?"

"Yes."

"But you are also supposed to do what I tell you."

"Yes."

"I want you well and vigorous, to better help me in my mission here. Take a small part of this glob. A globule."

That direct instruction resolved her doubt. Anona took a globule and delicately ate it, while he consumed the rest.

The effect was swift and remarkable. Che felt invigorated

and princely, while Anona's appearance shifted in subtle but effective ways. She was becoming more female. She was a neuter ant, a repressed female. It was diet that did it: one fed on royal jelly became a queen; those denied it remained physically like juveniles. He had committed a breach of antly protocol by having her eat it.

Well, too late to do anything about it. He wouldn't do it again. Meanwhile, it could get her in serious trouble. He knew that ant queens normally beheaded competition. "Do not reveal that I gave you royal jelly," he cautioned her.

"I will not tell," she agreed obediently.

He knew where he needed to go, but was not sure he would be given free access. So he approached the matter cautiously. "I wish to tour the hill."

Anona waited.

Oh. "Take me on a tour of the hill."

She took him through the hive: the workers' quarters, the guards' barracks, the fungus farm, the mess hall, the deep water well region, the high ridge where sharp-eyed ants watched for possible approaching threats, and past but not into the sacrosanct queen's apartment. And not to the one section he needed to visit: where the three alien visitors resided. His awareness informed him where it was, but she never went there.

Back in his chamber, he cautiously broached the matter. "You did not show me everything, Anona."

Her return impulse was perplexed. "I showed you all I know, lord."

"There is another region. Perhaps it is secret."

She struggled with the notion of secrecy, something normally foreign to her open nature. Then she made a connection. "You gave me royal jelly. I must not tell. That is a secret."

"Yes. But that is not the secret I meant."

She struggled further, and managed to make another connection. "I am now becoming female. You are male. You want me to—" She broke off, not conversant with the process. The ants did not need any Adult Conspiracy to mask the process of reproduction; workers simply lacked the capacity. But now, like a child on the verge of adult interest, she was struggling with it.

"No, no," he said quickly. "That's not it."

"You are rejecting me," she said, her antennae wilting.

Now she was becoming emotional, like a non-centaur woman. He was coming to appreciate why royal jelly was limited to royal ants. "No, not at all! I just—" But how could he explain?

"I am not adequate," she wailed electronically. He felt her utter devastation. She had no experience with the female state, so tended to overreact.

"You are fine, just the way you are," he said quickly, and felt her mood swing positive. "I just did not have this in mind when I came here."

"I'm sure I can please you, if you show me how," she said eagerly.

Che had three problems with this. First, he did not want to take unfair advantage of a truly innocent ant girl. Second, he did not want to further complicate his emotional life, which already had an illicit passion for Surprise Golem. Third, he had no idea how ants signaled the stork, if that was what they did. He might figure it out in time by trial and error, but that was bound to be awkward.

Then he had an idea he hoped was unworthy of him. He could ask her to take him to a truly private place. She might not know about the alien presences, but think that the place they were kept was deserted. Thus she might after all lead him to where he needed to go.

However, being an ethical centaur, he rejected that unworthy ploy. "This is not the place or the time," he said. "I must first accomplish my mission."

"Another place, another time," she agreed, pathetically ardent. "What is your mission?" She now had more initiative, too, no longer waiting for direct commands.

And of course he couldn't tell her that. For one thing, his true mission was secret; for another, he was not at all sure this chamber was as private as it seemed. The pique ants had been a mite too obliging in providing it, and might be watching him in ways that didn't show.

"To ascertain whether this hill is suitable for my hill to establish formal diplomatic relations with," he said. That was true; it was part of the deal they had made with Hill 53. But it was hardly the whole truth.

"Oh, I'm sure it is," she said. "We're a wonderful hill, with many fine qualities and good workers. Not long ago we raided another colony and took some slaves, and now they are loyal workers. Except—" She broke off, perplexed.

He was interested in whatever mystery this hill had. "What is it?"

"Some were odd. I don't know what happened to them."

Well, now. "Were there three of them?"

"Yes, I think so. They looked regular, for their variety. Like ordinary vari ants. But they weren't the same as the others."

Like three transformed children, he thought. So they had been hidden away, per a directive from the Sorceress. "Could they be ench ants?"

"Yes! Ench ants."

"I would like to see those ench ants."

She rippled her antennae in a shrug. "They're gone. I never saw them, and heard no more of them after the raid."

Che had a fair idea where they would be. But he still needed a pretext to go there, and had to find a way to get into a section that was surely well guarded. Maybe he could go alone at night, when the hill was quiet, and explore.

"Well, let's relax for now."

Anona was glad to cooperate. "Anything you wish, lord."

He folded six legs, settling to the floor. She settled next to him. Now she had a musky female scent that stirred his awareness. How far was her transformation likely to go?

A guard ant appeared at the entrance. Che got up and went to touch antennae, as it was the only way to know what brought the brute here.

"You are looking for ench ants?" the guard demanded.

Was this trouble? How did they know of his private dialogue with Anona? Straightforward seemed to be best. "I am."

The guard moved aside and a regular worker ant came forward. Che touched antennae. "I am Conspir Ant. Some of us seek to overthrow the queen and establish a new order. To do that we need to gain control over the ench ants. Are you with us, foreign drone?"

Che distrusted this. "I have no interest in revolution. I merely want to see the ench ants."

"Then we shall have to kill you, for you know too much."

"This is ridiculous!"

But already the guard ant was pushing into the chamber. Its forelegs had huge sharp pincers suitable for snipping off legs or head. It came at Che with those weapons raised. He retreated; as a drone he was stronger than worker ants, but wasn't equipped to resist a warrior ant.

The guard quickly backed him against a wall. He could not retreat farther. The two pincers came at him with terrible efficiency.

Then the guard halted, its antennae waving. Something had charged it from the side, and had hold of one leg just below the pincer. It was Anona!

Che leaped forward, grabbed the captive pincer, and bent it back. After a moment the leg snapped off right beyond where Anona was holding it.

The guard seemed not to know its loss. Its other pincer shot toward Che's neck.

But now he knew how to fight this thing. He dodged aside, grabbed the leg behind the pincer, and bent it as hard as he could. It too snapped, rendering the guard helpless.

Conspir Ant was retreating. "Stop him!" Che cried, but he lacked antenna contact so his cry was silent. Instead, he charged the other ant and used his mandibles to chomp one of its hind legs. Loyal Anona chomped another.

Then the hall beyond was filled with guard ants. There were way too many to overcome. They were done for.

Che managed to touch antennae with Anona. "Stop fighting! We can't handle these."

She stopped immediately. They retreated back into the chamber as the guards crowded in menacingly.

"You did well," Che told Anona, and felt her electric thrill of responsive joy. Then they waited for the end. Actually it would be the end only for her, because he would merely revert to his centaur form. Yet his mission would be incomplete.

But the guards did not attack. One approached Che to touch antennae. "Come with us, drone."

Surely to be formally executed. "Leave Anona," Che said. "She is no part of this."

But that was not to be. The guards marched both of them to the queen's apartment and shoved them in together.

Suddenly they were in the presence of the Pique Ant Queen. Anona prostrated herself abjectly. Che, uncertain what to do, merely bowed his head.

The queen approached. She was a splendid specimen of her kind, twice Che's size and devastatingly female. She clearly had no doubt of her command of the situation, and neither did he. She touched antennae briefly with Anona, then with Che. To describe her touch as electrifying would have been a severe understatement. "Tell all."

Such was the power of her command that he did not hesitate. There was no confusion or holding back; the truth poured out. "I am Che Centaur, occupying an ant body so as to investigate three inhabitants of your hill. They may be three human or demon children transformed to ant form by an evil Sorceress. If so, we must rescue them."

"They are not," the queen said. She disengaged, wiggled an antenna at a servant skulking in the background, and touched antennae briefly with the servant. Then she returned to Che. "I have summoned them here so you can verify this."

"But if you captured them in a slave raid, how can you be sure of their nature? They seem to be from another reality." He hoped she understood that concept.

"They are from another reality," she agreed. "But they are not transformed human or demon children. They are enchanted ants. We do not know their ultimate origin, but it seems they were not welcome there, and were put among workers subject to raiding. They had passed through several hills by the time we got them and recognized their worth."

"Those other ant hills wanted to lose them?"

"So it seems. Before I clarify their nature, it seems best that you meet them. Then you will understand."

Soon the three ench ants arrived. They were all suppressed females, exactly like other workers. Che lost interest in them immediately.

"Do you wish to interview them directly?" the queen asked.

Che realized with a start that he had not completed his mission. "I suppose I should." But he didn't.

"Try again," the queen advised.

Why hadn't he already done so? It wasn't like him to be so forgetful. He took a step toward the three, then was distracted by Anona, still humbly prostrated before the queen. "About her," he said. "I gave her royal jelly, unthinkingly. She tried to protest, but I didn't understand. She did not willfully disobey the protocol."

"Have no concern," the queen said. "Anona is my loyal servant, reporting everything to me. That is how I knew about your refusal to betray me to another hill."

"But she never left me! She defended me at the risk of her own life."

"Because that was her directive. I was curious about your nature and motive, so assigned her to you. This is not conscious on her part; I am partially telepathic, and she is partially so also, so I am able to receive the communications she receives and sends. More specifically, my talent is to read minds only when others are thinking bad or evil thoughts. Since it is by definition evil to oppose my rule, I learn what I need. But I can't be in all places at all times, so Anona serves as my surrogate, evoking those thoughts if they exist. Be assured that no harm will come to her as long as I govern; she is far too valuable in ferreting out plots such as the one you encountered."

"I wondered whether I was under observation, but I didn't know how."

"You have forgotten your mission again."

This brought him up short. He advanced on the three,

amazed that he had been distracted so often; it wasn't like him. In fact he was normally quite focused. He remembered a time when—"

"Try again," the queen advised.

Now he was really confused. "What is happening?"

"The three ench ants have the talent of aversion. They can escape notice, or be forgotten, or even repulse active interest. Each seems to have one variant; together they are virtually impregnable. This can be overridden, but the moment concentration lapses, they are lost to the attention of the other party. We use them to repel hostile raids; aggressive hills don't even know why they never get around to raiding ours. They are our prime defense."

That explained why the hill could afford to be on an exposed location. Anything interested in attacking or eating ants would be repelled. That also explained why he had had such trouble approaching the anthill: the generalized aversion had been working on him. This was a rare and highly effective defense. "But why didn't the other hills they were at appreciate their value?"

"Because the three did not wish to be recognized. They were looking for a more compatible situation. We offered them that, completely exempt from other duty, well fed and housed, and they are satisfied."

"You did not mention appreciation. Don't they crave that?"

"Centaur," the queen said kindly. "They are *ants*. All they want is to be allowed to do their job without interference. Their job is protecting the hill."

Che struggled with his duty. "Queen, I do not wish to question your information, yet I should verify the identity of these three directly. Can their aversion magic be turned off?"

The queen crooked an antenna at the three. They seemed to shimmer, and now he saw them more clearly. He went to them, and did not get distracted. He touched antennae with the nearest.

"What is your real identity, and how did you come here?"

"We are from a far reality," the ench ant responded. It was a neuter worker, quite ordinary except for its aversion magic and its limited initiative. "Where we hatched, all ants are like us. But we wandered too far afield, and got on the back of a snoozing stork. Before we knew it, we were caught high in the air, and then at the Stork Works. By the time we were able to dismount safely, we were in a different reality, where no ants had our abilities. We felt lonely, so searched for ants that had at least some mind abilities."

"The queen! She is telepathic."

"Yes. That is not the same, but we concluded that it is close enough. She understands mind powers, and treats us well. We will remain here."

The antenna communication did not allow for deceit. Che had no doubt that these were ants, not transformed children. "Thank you."

"Your Simurgh must be fascinating," the ant said. "Her mind is overwhelmingly strong. She is a very powerful queen."

The ant had picked that up from his mind, interpreting it in ant terms. He could not conceal the truth either. "Yes." He broke contact.

The three ench ants faded out, either gone or forgotten. Anona was gone. Che was now alone with the queen. "Before you depart," she said.

"Yes?"

"I trust you appreciate my cooperation. It allowed you to accomplish your mission, even though the result was negative."

"That is true. I do appreciate it. Is there some return service I can do for you?"

"There is. I have not had relations with a drone in some time. I have been busy. I believe I will take a small refreshing break."

Suddenly he caught her meaning, which she had not signaled before. The worker ants were incapable of deception, but now he understood that the queen could communicate exactly what she chose, keeping the rest of her mind private. She was looking for a spot liaison, which by the rules of this reality and her species was legitimate. "But I am not really an ant," he protested. "This is merely the body of a mindless drone."

"But you provide that mind, centaur, and an apt mind it is. No ant has the intellect you do. I appreciate a male with a formidable mind."

This, unfortunately, was typical of females, just as appreciation of physical qualities was typical of males. "I am not at all sure—"

"My time is limited," the queen said.

"But—"

Then she became the most magnificently alluring female creature he had ever encountered. It was not mere appearance or manner; there were magic pheromones galore. There was no gainsaying her. All his concerns about his mate Cythia Centaur, or Surprise Golem, or any other relationships became abruptly moot. There was only the queen of the pique ants.

He stepped toward her, overwhelmed by her phenomenal sex appeal. There was no longer any doubt about the ant mating process. He was sure he would be aghast hereafter, but right now he had no choice.

He blinked. He was standing a short distance from the anthill, which had shrunk to diminutive size. No, it was normal; he was back in his natural centaur body. He spread his wings and took off.

"Thank you, Simurgh," he said to the air around him.

Welcome. I concluded that your mission was done, and that you wished to depart your ant host.

"I did," he agreed. "It's not that the queen ant was not worthy or appealing, but I have emotional complications that interfere with such a dalliance."

It will take her a while to realize you are gone, as the drone body remains.

"Bleep!" The cuss word came through verbally, though it was telepathically projected.

Or maybe not, the Simurgh concluded.

Che felt guilty. The queen had helped him, and was entitled to a return favor. He had reneged.

You wish to return for a limited time?

That brought him back to reality. "No."

I will try to find some other intelligent male to occupy that body for the occasion she desires.

That made him feel better. However, the day was late. "I need to return to report my finding," he said. "But what of you, Simurgh?"

First recover Surprise Golem's baby. Then calculate the correct home reality. I will be in mental touch, now that we have connected. When we are ready to return, I will carry the flightless member of your party, and we will pass the Stork Works and select our destination. All should end well.

Che hoped that would truly be the case. Somehow he lacked the confidence the Simurgh projected. After all, as far as he knew, they had not yet found the children.

12

HELL & SLIMEBALLS

Pyra walked through her sector, almost certain she would not find the children. It was evident that Demoness Fornax had enlisted more than one ally, contrary to the Demon deal, and was using the Sorceress Morgan le Fey to force the issue with Surprise Golem. Pyra had never met the Sorceress, but couldn't stand her; she made the contest unfair. But it was not her place to do anything about that.

In her role as a helpful acquaintance of Surprise it was now her job to locate and rescue the three lost children if she could. She would play that role completely. She no longer wanted to corrupt Surprise, but would have to do her best in that respect too. The difference was that now it wouldn't bother her much to lose. She knew she didn't deserve Che, and she didn't want to hurt him by taking him away from Cynthia Centaur. She had to find someone else. If only she could somehow override the love elixir and do it naturally.

She came to an arch. It was formed of translucent stone

wedges with pearly surfaces that glowed faintly. "Moonstone!" she exclaimed, recognizing the type.

The scene beyond the arch was different from what was around it, and she realized that this was magic, leading to some other realm. It must be someone's secret access to a special playground or vacation spot, for the other region looked fabulously entertaining.

Could the children have gone through it? What she could see was surely appealing to little imaginations. There was even a candy stand in sight.

Pyra was not one to enter anything she did not properly understand. She brought out the Reality Mask and oriented on the arch. It showed pictures of several arches, and within each was a different scene. Some were parks, some forests, and some quite alien landscapes.

Then she caught on. "Moonstone! This is a shortcut to the moons of Princess Ida!" For there seemed to be an infinite number of ever-smaller moons, each a world in itself. This could be a route to one of them.

But who would have put such an edifice out here in nowhere? That would have required real magic, and what use was it?

Who but the Sorceress Morgan le Fey, with the considerable help of the Demoness Fornax! This was an attractive nuisance that would virtually suck the children in. Morgan would not need to do anything more; the children would be gone.

Still, there was a problem. Folk could not go to the moons of Ida physically. They had to leave their bodies behind, because the moons were too small. So the bodies slept, somewhat in the manner of those who entered the dream realm via the peephole of a gourd. If the children had entered here, where were their bodies?

Pyra walked around the arch, instead of through it. She saw that it did not lead directly to the other world; it was in the wall of a stout stone building that looked like a mausoleum. A tomb big enough to hold a number of bodies. That explained that: the bodies were stored there, and reanimated when they emerged. *If* they emerged.

Pyra felt a chill. Had the Sorceress disposed of the children permanently? No, because then she would not be able to bargain with them as hostages to trade for Surprise's baby. They had to be recoverable, or the deal would be no good, and Surprise would be uncorrupted. So this had to be a two-way arch. Like the piper who piped the children into the mountain, not hurting the children but teaching the cheating villagers a terrible lesson. Pyra had always rather admired that piper; he knew what was what.

She walked all the way around the building, finding no entrance other than the arch. So she couldn't go in and look for unconscious children in crypts or whatever. In any event she would not be able to wake them, without their souls. She had to find the souls first, and bring them back; then the bodies would reanimate.

Pyra nerved herself, then walked through the arch. She experienced a momentary delirium; then she was in the other world. She was now a compacted soul, vastly smaller than her physical body, but looking and feeling much the same. Even her weight; gravity was the same, though this world should be way too small to match that of Mundania and Xanth. These moons were indeed remarkable.

She was on a pleasant pebbled path. She walked along it, and came to a fancy gate with a sign: WELCOME TO ALWAYS-ALWAYS LAND. Beyond it were innumerable fancy entertainments ranging from roller coasters to candy-cane houses. This was definitely a lure for children. Indeed, children were everywhere, running and screaming in childish glee while their parents looked somewhat harried.

She entered and looked around. Where would *her* (so to speak) children be? It would take forever—perhaps literally—to check every one of the distractions. She needed to locate the children in the next two hours or so, or to be certain that they were not here. She needed help.

Who would help her, and why? She was an attractive

woman, apart from her fire; she could probably entice a man to do it. But he would want payment of a certain sort, and might tell her anything to get it, then be off like a ghost the moment he had it. Men were like that; she had seen it often in the Mask. A woman would be a better bet, but what did Pyra have to entice a woman? This was a problem.

She studied the assorted booths in sight. One had a man who passed his hands across the limbs and necks of the children who put them out. What was he doing? She walked close enough to observe more closely.

The sign on the booth said JASON'S BASIN—A HAIR RAISING EXPERIENCE. The proprietor—Jason, surely—stroked his fingers across flesh and left a train of shaven skin. One boy had a hairy arm; it was hairless after the stroke. Another boy put his head in, and Jason neatly shaved the hair off the back of his neck. One girl verging on teenhood sat on the counter and swung her legs inside for stroking and shaving, before her shocked mother hauled her out. Pyra smiled; teens were notorious for testing the limits of the Adult Conspiracy. Of course there wasn't any in this particular reality. Still, parents obviously tried to protect their children.

Another booth's banner said FANNIE'S FANS and had a picture of a folding fan. Children were getting ordinary-looking fans that turned out to be anything but ordinary. One labeled FANCY made sullen folk suddenly like others, becoming their fans, as it were. A FANDANGO made its users dance exuberantly three times as fast as normal, snapping their fingers sharply. A FANTASTIC made folk feel so great that they practically floated. The FANATICAL made them extremely enthusiastic. One who picked up a FANFARE suddenly spoke in trumpet tones. The children plainly enjoyed such shenanigans.

Another booth was labeled POX & BUGS. This was extremely popular with children. The pox was in the form of a big red hen that would dab children unmercifully with red pox marks unless someone made such a fierce display that it scared the chicken off. It was a chicken pox. The bugs were in the form of lice that made people lie uncontrollably. Children were running around telling the tallest stories they could imagine. Probably this wasn't allowed at home, but here they had a pretext.

Still another was labeled JAMES' SUN BEAMS. The man in this booth put on a dizzying display of beams, focusing them without a lens, directing them into dark corners to light them up, making them turn corners. Then the sun went behind a cloud, and his act was halted.

All this was fine, but it wasn't accomplishing her purpose. Shaving fingers, fans, cowardly fowl, and bending sunbeams would not find the children for her.

She looked some more. There was a stall saying LLIANE & LLIANA—ILLUSIONS GAL-LORE. They were making a thing of all the L's, but if the children had been masked by illusion, this could be relevant.

She approached. Fortunately this booth was not busy at the moment. "Hello. I am Pyra. I am looking for three lost children."

Blonde Lliane—her name was on her cap—smiled. "Maybe you could check with the Llost & Ffound office. Children get mislaid all the time."

"Thank you; I will do that. Can you direct me there?"

"Walk down the center aisle," the other woman, brunette Lliana, said. "Turn right. You can't miss it; it's at the end of that aisle."

"Thank you." But this didn't seem enough. "I am not a child, but I am curious about your show."

"My talent is to make illusions real," Lliane said. "My sister's talent is to make real things illusion. We complement each other, which is why we prefer to work together. Would you like a demonstration?"

"Yes, please." Illusions were cheap magic, but could be very effective.

"Here is a real thing," Lliana said, picking up a red ball from a basket with several balls of different colors. "Take it, feel it, verify its reality."

Pyra did so. The ball was quite solid.

Lliana took it back, then held it back out to Pyra. "Now try it."

Pyra reached for the ball—and her hand passed through it. It had become illusory! "That's impressive."

Lliane reached out to touch it. "Now try it," she said.

Pyra touched it, and it was solid again. "That is impressive," she said. "Can you do it to living things too?"

"No, only objects," Lliana said. "If there's an illusion of a person, my sister can make a statue of it, but not a living creature."

"And living things don't stand still long enough for her to make them illusion," Lliane said.

So they couldn't have done it to the children. That was a relief. "Thank you," Pyra said. "Here is my talent: fire." She heated herself so that the flames danced along her body.

"Too bad," Lliana said. "This carnival already has a fire-eater."

"Oh, I'm not looking for work here. Just for the children. Now I'll check that Lost and Found office."

Pyra followed their instruction, and soon found it: LLOST & FFOUND—Jean Poole, proprietor. She paused, assessing it: gene pool? Surely a stage name.

"May I help you?" Jean inquired. She was young, hardly more than a girl.

"I am Pyra, looking for three lost children, ages ten, ten, and five. Have they—"

"No lost children have been turned in here today," Jean said. "When did you last see them? They may be at a game booth, such as the Fairy Tails."

"Stories?"

"Yes. The fairies' tails go to the Fairy Tail Tree, and children pick them for stories."

Pyra considered. "Are the stories suitable for children?"

"Oh yes, of course."

"These ones wouldn't be interested, then. They're naughty children."

Jean laughed. "Sorry I couldn't help you."

"Thanks anyway. I can't even be sure they're on this world."

"Oh, you're a worlds-traveling tourist?"

"Not exactly." Pyra didn't want to talk about herself, so asked the girl about herself. "Is your name a pun?"

"Only partly. My talent is to have all the talents in my ancestry. The trouble is I don't know them all, so can't use them unless I happen to discover them by accident. My father is Whurl Poole, whose talent is making whirlpools. His parents were an anonymous woman and a forget whorl that met in a love spring. My mother is Blue Jean whose talent is making pants; her father was Denim, who could turn cotton into a hard substance, and her mother Jean could sew without using her hands. My parents met after running into the same forget whorl that was one of Whurl's parents, so they may have forgotten more than they ever knew. It's a problem, because I want so much to know about my past. My magic depends on it."

"I appreciate your problem," Pyra said.

"I work here so I can meet many people," Jean said. "Some of them may have known my parents, and known more about them than I do. Darn that forget whorl, even if it is my grandfather."

"I hope that works," Pyra said sympathetically. She was discovering that actually talking with folk and getting to know them was far more evocative than merely seeing them on the pictures of the Reality Mask.

She walked back toward the main aisle. She passed a booth whose banner said DON'T BE A LITERALIST. She paused, curious despite her need to get on with her search.

"Have some milk," the man in the booth said. "It's the cream of the crop." He proffered a glass.

Pyra accepted it and sipped it. It was indeed cream. "You're the literalist," she said, catching on.

"Yes, any figure of speech I use becomes literal," he agreed. "So I am being careful not to say that you look good enough to eat."

"Thank you for not saying that," Pyra said, smiling. She moved on.

Then she saw a nearby stall containing a handsome but clearly disconsolate man. The sign said FINN THE AMAZING FIRE-EATER. So why wasn't he eating fire? She had a certain interest in the subject.

She approached the booth. "Finn?" she inquired.

The man looked up. He had flame-colored eyes and appealingly scorched skin around his mouth. She liked his look. "No show today," he mumbled, and returned his head to his hands.

"I know something about fire. What happened?"

He looked up again, sadly. "You really want to know? It's a dull story."

She flashed him a fetching smile, exerting the female aspect of her nature. "I really want to know."

He reacted as he had to, becoming more accommodating. "I eat and breathe fire. That's how I earn my keep. But I'm a fraud."

"How could you do it, if you're a fraud?"

"My magic is really to breathe combustible fumes. I have a magic sparker to ignite them. Then I can do clever things with the flames. But my sparker is used up, and I don't know where to find another. I'm finished. I dread telling the boss; I'll get fired. Ha-ha." But he wasn't laughing.

This continued to be interesting. "Maybe I can help."

"Do you have a sparker?"

"In a manner of speaking. Blow some fumes."

He pursed his lips and blew out a small jet of gas. Pyra passed one hand near, and the jet ignited. Suddenly it was a column of fire.

"You did it!" Finn exclaimed, the flames playing around his teeth. "You lighted my fire!" His reassessing glance at her body hinted that there was more than one interpretation of his statement. Neither interpretation bothered her at all. She liked to verify that she could still fascinate the male eye when she chose. There was a certain pride of power in being female.

"I'll make you a deal. I'll light your fire if you will help me search for three lost children."

Finn shut his mouth and the fire went out. "But you can't stay here forever. When you go, I'll be quenched again."

She saw his point. But she had an answer. "You can look for another sparker while I look for the children." Of course he could look without her company, so that wasn't much of an offer.

He considered. She smiled encouragingly and took a deeper breath. Men could be illogically influenced by such irrelevant things. She hadn't promised him anything, but the mere whiff of the hope of such a promise could work occasional miracles.

It did. His eyes connected to her chest and turned off his mind. "Agreed. How can I help you search?"

"What is the most likely distraction half-demon children would go for?"

He smiled, and his face became handsomer. "The Hell & Slimeballs Express. It's notorious. Children love it."

That did sound apt. "Take me there."

He lifted the counter of his booth out of the way and stepped out. "This way, Miss—?"

"Pyra."

"Pyra," he agreed. "Of course."

He brought her to a little station marked HELL & SLIME-BALLS EXPRESS. A miniature train with several cars was rapidly filling with children. A man in an engineer costume sat on the little engine.

Then Pyra noticed another sign: ADMITTANCE—A PIECE OF SOUL. That set her back. "I don't want to lose any of my soul!" For that would make her smaller, as her body here was composed of soul stuff, and she would be missing it when she returned to Xanth.

"Readily solved," Finn said. He went to the admittance booth. "Pyra and I will serve as guards."

"Great!" the man said. He gave Finn two tickets.

Finn took Pyra's hand and led her to a front seat. The two of them barely fit; it was sized for children. In fact it was really two seats along the sides with their knees colliding in the center. "I happened to know they are short of guards.

There have been a couple of accidents and folk aren't eager
to serve. Don't let the children know."

"It's dangerous?"

"Not normally. It's probably just an aberration. But until
they're sure things are clear, they try to put a guard or two on
every train."

Pyra looked at her ticket. It said GUARD—FRIENDLY COUR-
TEOUS SAFE. Then something occurred to her. "The ones I'm
looking for aren't on this train. How can I check the others?"

"The trains pass each other along the way. You can look
across to see whether your children are there."

Pyra nodded. "That seems feasible."

The last car filled and the engineer started the train moving. It chugged along, emitting cute balls of smoke from its
little stack. The children screamed with anticipation. The occasional parents along looked resigned.

"Fasten your seat belts, kids," Finn called. "It gets steep."

"Awww!" they chorused in protest. But the parents insisted, and most of them did belt up. Pyra and Finn tried to
set an example by fastening their own.

The track climbed a steep hill. The train handled it, rising
at a daunting angle. The children screamed again, loving it.
Some might have fallen out, without the seat belts. As it was,
a number were leaning out over the edges of the cars, daring
each other.

The train made it to the top of the hill. Now Pyra saw that
this was actually a tall wooden structure, the height of a
roller coaster. The train crested the ridge and accelerated
down the other side. It was scary and the children screamed
with due appreciation.

At the foot of the hill, when the train was going at break-
neck speed, another set of tracks swerved close and another
train passed, going the opposite way. Pyra nearly popped her
eyeballs checking the children on it. None of them were Ted,
Monica, or Woe Betide. She wasn't sure whether to be disappointed or relieved.

Now the train made a dangerously sharp turn and ran beside a meandering river. Huge sea monsters popped their

heads from the water and plunged ugly toothy heads toward the train. The children screamed again, this time with more authority. But the gaping jaws snapped closed just shy of the train; no children were gobbled.

"The tracks are enchanted," Finn explained conversationally. "The monsters are real, but they never seem to learn that they can't get at the morsels. It makes a fine show."

"Except for accidents?" she asked.

He looked somber. "Best not to speak of those too loudly. We're pretty sure the enchantment remains tight."

"*Pretty* sure?"

"Well, until we find out exactly what has gone wrong, we can't rule anything out. But the spell has tested perfect every time."

Yet there was some sort of mischief they weren't openly talking about. Pyra didn't like that. Suppose the demon children got caught in an "accident"?

The train turned and chugged into a thick forest. Now the monsters of the woods came out, looking vaguely like dinosaurs, with wetly glinting teeth. They made horrendous passes at the occupants of the train, but couldn't touch them. The children, encouraged, started making faces and calling "nyaa, nyaa!"

They came to a mountain, but this time did not climb it. The train plunged into a tunnel, and darkness closed in like a massive fist. Then the monsters of the subterranean realm appeared, with hugely glowing eyes and questing long noses. They couldn't get close either.

Light appeared: the glow of heated rock. Rivers of lava coursed along beside the tracks, and there was a sinister rumbling. The children had been getting cocky; now they held on a bit nervously. Where were they going?

"This is one good show," Pyra murmured.

"It gets better."

It did. Suddenly there was a jump in the tracks, and the train zoomed downward into a seeming abyss. The monsters could be seen in the high distance, looking balefully down; they didn't dare go into this dread depth. Weird shapes coiled around the tracks, forming a menacing kind of tunnel, but the train rushed heedlessly on. Pyra found herself hoping that this wasn't where any accidents were occurring.

The train slowed, and demons with pitchforks menaced the children, again with no success. Several buxom demonesses turned, hoisted their skirts, and made as if to flash their panties, but somehow something always got in the way so they were never quite visible. "This is an Adult Conspiracy–Approved tour," Finn said.

"I thought there wasn't an Adult Conspiracy here."

"Oh, are you from one of the Non-Conspiracy worlds? Here at Always Always Land we try to honor it, because many of our tourists are from Xanths where it counts."

That was just as well, because several of the slightly older boys were watching rather too eagerly, prime candidates for freaking out. One of the crazy things about boys—and men—was that they never seemed to learn the danger of panties, and so got freaked out again and again. Or maybe that was more properly Always-Always.

"My home reality honors it," she said.

"We draw from many realities, and many moons. We pride ourselves on being a major tourist attraction for children. Folk come here from most of the moons."

A subway train station formed around them, with regular lights and platform. The train glided to a stop. They were at a banner saying WELCOME TO HELL.

"Rest stop," the engineer called. "The station is safe, but don't go beyond it."

The children piled out onto the platform. There were machines with every flavor of—slimeballs. They seemed to be big gooey globs of spun sugar. The children quickly grabbed all the balls they could hold and returned to the train, where they soon got into a slimeball-throwing contest.

The train resumed its course. In a moment another train passed it, and Pyra flexed her eyeballs again trying to check every child in it. None of the three she sought were there.

Now the train was climbing. Hell, it seemed, was deep underground. It forged to the base of a mighty chasm, passed into a tunnel on the opposite side, turned, crossed the canyon at a higher level, entered another tunnel, and came to a screeching halt.

"Trestle's unsafe," the engineer said. "Lucky I saw it in time."

"This is our call," Finn said grimly, getting out.

Pyra followed him. They emerged from the tunnel and saw the trestle. It was a network of wooden timbers braced in triangles supporting the tracks. A section had been knocked out. The tracks were unbroken, but the weight of the train with its passengers would surely bear it down and dump them all into the abyss. The engineer had been right to call a halt.

"What do we do now?" Pyra asked worriedly.

"We fix it."

She gazed nervously at the destruction. "That's our job?"

"Someone has to do it. You can return to the train if you wish. I'm going after fresh timbers."

That shamed her. "No, I'll help, if I can."

"Let's see what we'll need." He walked to the track above the gap and peered down. "Tooth marks," he said.

"Something bit through the trestles?"

"Something big."

She saw the marks, and the damp ripped edges. Saliva? "I thought the spell protected the tracks."

"The tracks, yes. Evidently it doesn't extend to the base of the trestles. The monsters must be getting smarter. They bit where they could reach, before the train got here."

"A smart monster," she said, chilled.

"Something you should know," he said grimly. "We'll have to go down far enough to replace the fractured planks."

"Yes, of course. We can rope ourselves to the tracks so we won't fall, and swing across."

He nodded. "Good idea. You're smarter than the average tourist."

"Thank you," she said, flattered.

"But that wasn't my point. Where do you think the monster is?"

Now she got it with a vengeance. "Lurking. Waiting for us to get within its reach."

"Exactly. So maybe you had better return to the train after all."

"So you can get chomped alone? That won't get the job done."

He gazed at her, his eyes narrowing in assessment. "This is serious. I can't afford to have an uncertain assistant. If you have any doubts at all, go back now."

She was shamed again, though she knew he wasn't trying to. He naturally assumed she was a weak woman. She had been able to intrigue him before with her womanly charms, but now he was serious about his manly nature. "I can take care of myself. I can't lift heavy planks, but I can fend off the monster."

"Can you?"

She let her fire show. "Yes. I can burn anything. You handle the repairs; I'll keep the monster clear."

He nodded. "So you're not a fraud, like me. You really have magic fire."

"You're not a fraud! You just don't have a magic spark." As she spoke she realized it was true. When the need came, this man was proving to be brave and capable. He had character rather than magic.

Finn shrugged. "I will fetch planks. They are stored nearby near the tunnel. You reassure the children and be ready to use your fire when I get to work below the tracks."

She did that. "There is a break in the trestle," she explained to the children and parents. "We are repairing it. Stay with the train until the job is done."

The engineer got up. "You'll need help."

"You know the nature of the work," she said, keeping her voice calm. She was warning him.

"Yes."

Several parents stood: a daddy and three mommies. "We'll help too."

"I don't think—" Pyra started, taken aback.

A mother gave her a direct look. "You can protect us, fire woman?"

She understood, and had caught on to Pyra's talent. "Yes, I think so. But it may be uncomfortable." She flared her body, radiating heat. "If I have to burn—something."

"We'll risk it," the woman said.

"In that case, the men could use another man to carry and hammer. I could use some good eyes to spot danger early."

"You'll have them."

Soon there was a pile of fresh planks and several coils of rope. Then men anchored themselves to the tracks and swung down to use crowbars and hammers to remove bad planks. When they had the region clear, the women tied ropes around planks and carefully lowered them down to the hanging men. They were all sensible folk, and the work was proceeding far more rapidly than it would have with only one or two.

They swung the first plank into place and hammered it to the base of the tracks. They placed the second, forming a triangle. At this rate it would not take long to shore up the trestle.

There was a horrendous roar. "Monster ahoy!" a lookout woman called.

"Stay well clear of it," Pyra said. "I may have to use a lot of power."

The three men had no time to climb to the tracks. They hung in place, looking grim. They feared they were about to die. Strictly speaking they couldn't die; they would merely lose their soul bodies and return to their larger or smaller soul bodies on their home moons. But that would be an un-pleasant and inconvenient process, and death seemed rather real.   •

The monster appeared: a dinosaur so big that it walked along the bottom of the chasm, its head reaching almost to the tracks. It had to have been the one that had bitten off the trestle. It opened its mouth below the three men, big enough to take them all in, in one gulp.

Pyra pumped up her heat. She focused on the monster's head, and projected her fire there. A glowing sheet formed at the toothy nose, and its surface scales crackled as if being roasted.

It rocked back, howling. The men applauded; they knew good magic when they saw it. Then they got back to work on the timbers.

"It's reconsidering," the lookout woman said.

So it was. A sore was developing on the monster's nose, but that was a tiny wound on such a large surface. The creature was coming in again, this time more cautiously.

Pyra projected another panel of fire, but the monster ducked beneath it, came up beyond it, turned about, and gaped its giant jaws toward the men.

Pyra sent out another panel of flame. This one singed the surfaces of the bared teeth and bored in toward the nerves. The dinosaur snapped its mouth closed and ducked down. "Mmmmm!" it groaned as its roasting teeth continued to hurt.

The men placed another plank. Soon they would be done.

"Coming back," the woman said.

The thing was determined! Pyra readied another panel of fire. She could keep this up as long as it could.

This time the monster pursed its lips and blew directly at Pyra. The gust of wind caught her skirt and boosted her off the tracks. She fell—

Directly into the monster's waiting mouth. The thing had fathomed the nature of its opposition and outsmarted her!

But it had also outsmarted itself. She landed on its tongue—and the flesh scorched as she heated incandescently. The tortured tongue flipped her up and out.

But as she sailed through the air she knew that she would fall far from the trestles, and not be able to defend the men anymore. They might be doomed.

"Finn!" she called as she sailed by. "Spark!" She sent ignition as he opened his mouth.

Then she was falling, falling, and had to take care of herself. She heated the air around her so that it expanded explosively, generating cracks of thunder. That hot air cushioned her landing as she came to the floor of the canyon. She was safe.

She walked toward the trestles, hoping to climb back up to the track. That wasn't her concern. What about the men? Could Finn do enough with his flaming breath?

The monster, satisfied that it had eliminated the pesky opposition, opened its mouth and readied a mighty chomp that would take in all three men and the new planks they had installed.

Finn breathed out a devastating column of flame. It shot into the monster's mouth and down its throat. "HOOOOO!" it cried, truly in pain. In a big, in fact a monster moment, it turned tail and ran, surely for the nearest underground lake for quenching.

The women applauded again. Finn had saved the day.

By the time Pyra climbed to the tracks, the men had finished their job. The trestle had been repaired and was ready for the train. She walked toward the train, brushing herself off. She was hopelessly mussed.

"Pyra!" Finn cried, spying her. "I owe it all to you. You gave me fire. You're wonderful."

"Well, I wanted to see the job finished," she said gruffly. She realized that sounded ungracious, but she wasn't sure how to correct it. She wasn't used to being complimented, especially when mussed.

"I think I love you."

That stalled whatever else might have been on her mind. She stood there, having no idea what to say. The very notion was ludicrous. She couldn't possibly return the feeling.

Then he kissed her.

Her knees melted, but she didn't collapse because he was holding her. Tiny burning hearts formed and orbited their heads. They set fire to the notion "ludicrous" and destroyed it like an ugly monster.

"Is that how they signal the stork?" a child's voice asked. Pyra realized belatedly that the trainful of children was watching.

"Hush, child," the mother cautioned. "She hasn't even shown him her panties."

Indeed she hadn't, Pyra realized, blushing at the suggestion. What had she so suddenly gotten into?

"I shouldn't have done that," Finn said apologetically as he led her to the train. "I thought the monster was going to chomp us. Then you gave me the spark, and made me look like a hero. You're such a wonderful woman in every way."

"I'm nothing of the kind! I'm a hot-tempered scheming hussy!" Of course now the parents and children were listening to their dialogue as the train started, but she no longer cared.

"Are you? Then you would do well at Always-Always Planet. Why don't you stay here with me? I won't need a spark if you are here."

"I can't. I have other things to do."

"You have to find the children, of course. But after that?"

The most astonishing thing was that she found herself tempted. Finn had proved to be a brave and capable man, and he did need her. She could do worse, much worse. Of course there was that elixir-inspired fixation she had on Che Centaur, but she had already concluded that was no good. This was a worthy alternative.

But there were complications. "I am not of this world."

"None of us are," he said. "We're all workers or tourists. Children come from all the Worlds of Ida to be entertained here."

"I'm from Xanth."

He stared, and the children and parents murmured in awe. "You're a real person? Not a might-have-been?"

"I'm real," she agreed. "My body lies in a vault while I search here."

Finn sighed. "I should have known you were too good to be true. Of course you won't give up your real existence for a might-be life."

Now that he was seeing reality, she found herself warming to unreality. "Is this really what you want to do with your life? Put on fire-eating shows?"

He smiled ruefully. "No. It's just what I can do. Or could do, when I had the spark. My real passion is to be a sculptor and work with colored stone."

"Oh, are you good at that?"

"No, I have no sculpting talent at all. It's just my foolish dream."

"To the left," the engineer announced as the train pulled out of the canyon, "is the famed Ogre Orchard." Pyra looked and saw the shaggy huge ogres tending stony fruit trees. "Those fruits are pummelgranites, good for practice fracturing stone."

She had dreamed foolishly of snatching a centaur from his loving mate. Finn's dream was better than hers. He was not daunted by her fire; he liked it. "Suppose you were on an island in a swamp with nothing much to do all day, and only me for company?"

"With you for company there would never be nothing much to do," he said gallantly.

The children laughed. They were finding this far more entertaining than the sights the train tour was showing. "He really likes her," one said. "She likes him too," another said. "Maybe if we're real quiet they'll forget we're here and will signal the stork," a third said. "Yeah!" they all said, while the parents were suitably horrified.

Pyra forged back to the subject. "I meant the sculpting. Would you be satisfied to do that all the time?"

"Between kisses?"

She had to laugh. "Yes."

"Would you give me all I wanted?"

She pretended to misunderstand. "All the colored stone?"

He pretended to believe that. "And all the kisses."

Decision was coming upon her. "Yes."

"Then there would not be time for sculpting."

The children laughed gleefully, carrying the parents along. Pyra knew she should be embarrassed, but the idea of being with a man that hungry for her kisses appealed.

"There are ways for might-be folk to come to Xanth," she said. "I have a friend who knows how to form empty bodies from organic material. Then the soul from the moon comes and animates it. Xanth was repopulated with dragons that way not long ago. You could do it too, if you wanted to."

There was a murmur of awe through the train. All of the parents and children longed for exactly such an avenue. But it had to be carefully arranged, so most of them would never make it. That was their tragedy.

"I want to," he said without hesitation.

"Then consider it a date." She kissed him, and the children and parents applauded. This time the fiery orbiting hearts were twice their prior size and intensity.

The train completed its round. The engineer talked with his supervisor as the children unloaded. "These guards saved the train. A smart monster chomped out a trestle, but they organized repairs and used fire to drive it away. They're heroes."

"Then they have a job here," the supervisor said.

"No, she's real, and she's taking him with her."

The supervisor turned on them a look of unadulterated envy. "Good for them." Then he peered more closely at Pyra. "You're right; she's real. We don't get many of those here."

But they had not yet found the children. Pyra approached the supervisor. "Have you seen three demon or half-demon children here in the past two hours, ages ten, ten and five?"

"Multitudes. But I take it you mean from Xanth."

"Yes. They are real children, though perhaps ensorceled."

"Ensorcellments don't work here. Their souls would form their real selves. There have been none from Xanth."

She was satisfied with his verdict. "Thank you."

"Any time you want to serve as guard again, you'll have a free ticket."

She laughed. "I earned it!"

"You did. We'll put guards with flamethrowers on the trestle bridge. We don't want to lose any more children."

She could appreciate why.

She returned to Finn and joined him in his fire booth for a few more kisses and half a smooch, so he wouldn't forget their agreement. "Remember, check every so often for a body that looks approximately like you. When you find it, animate it. It will then assume your perfect likeness, and I will take you away to my island." She paused. "It's not really an island, it's a circular mesa in a swamp. We'll have to wade through the swamp to get there. The swamp is made from love elixir."

"It won't have any effect," he assured her. He was probably right: he was already smitten. So was she.

She walked toward the exit. It was time to recover her body and report that the children were not in her sector. She was almost relieved; she had done her best, without having to make any difficult ethical decision with respect to the children. Instead she had perhaps found a solution to her social dilemma.

13

GUILT TRIP

Surprise Golem conjured herself to the edge of her segment and started searching. She really appreciated the way the others were pitching in, including even the stork and the peeve; it made the search so much more competent. She suspected that they needed all the competence they could garner, and more, because the Sorceress Morgan le Fey was not about to make it easy for them.

And if they failed to find the children, what would Surprise do? What *could* she do, except make the awful bargain the Sorceress demanded? Either way, something invaluable would be lost. She couldn't stand to sacrifice either the children or her baby. Yet she might have to choose between them. She did not know which way she would go.

She could fly if she chose, but concluded that walking was better; she wouldn't overlook anything on the ground. The children might be anywhere, in any form; only a tediously careful search could be sure of locating them. So she walked, and used her magic to make X-ray vision so she could see through trees and rocks, covering a wider swath.

This section of Xanth seemed to be deserted. She encountered no people, animals, or unusual plants; this was a purely routine quiet forest. That itself might be suspicious; why were the usual monsters and pun formations absent? Had the Sorceress somehow cleaned out the region? Why?

She saw something she could readily have missed: a crevice in the ground. It was only a finger-width wide, but quite deep, and it extended in a zigzag manner as far as she could see to left and right. She peered down it with her X-ray eyes, but saw only the parallel walls extending down. She picked up a thin stick and poked it into the opening, and it did not touch the bottom. How could it be so long and deep, yet so narrow?

She knew of only one crevice of that nature: the Gap Chasm. That was not very far from the Golem residence; she had often visited it in her own reality. This must be an off-shoot, maybe one that didn't exist in her own frame. Was the difference significant? She could not afford to assume that it wasn't.

She followed the crack north, toward the main chasm. Sure enough, it soon widened, like a river wending its way down toward the sea. It became wide enough for a person to fit in, and still too deep to fathom. Could the children have wandered here, and fallen in? That didn't seem likely; they were active and often obnoxious, but not foolish. Also, as full or part demons they had some demon powers, and could float when they put their minds to it. Still, they were insatiably curious, especially about significant natural features. They might have followed it, and entered it where they had opportunity.

And if they followed it far enough, they could wind up in the Gap Chasm itself. Of course they knew Stanley Steamer, the Gap Dragon; he was no threat to them. Or was he?

She paused in place. In this reality she was married to Epoxy Ogre and had no soul. Umlaut was married to Ben-

zine Brassie, and had no soul either. Why should the Gap
Dragon be any child's friend in such a reality?

But Ted, Monica, and Woe Betide didn't know of the ill
nature of Surprise Seven. They might think this reality was
more similar to their own than it was. They could run gladly
up to the Gap Dragon to play—

She shuddered. She needed to check more swiftly. She
doused the X-ray vision and made herself float, using a variant spell she hadn't used before. She floated rapidly over and
along the widening crack. Her best bet might be to locate the
Gap Dragon and ascertain first whether the children were
near him, and second whether he was dangerous to them. If
neither was the case, she could move back and search the
Gap offshoot crevices more carefully.

The crevice widened into a canyon. Now the bottom was
visible, a thin line way down. She cruised along and the
walls retreated on either side. Then the canyon debouched
into the main valley that was the Gap Chasm.

Now the walls were far apart. There were trees here, and
rivulets, and grazing animals. It was a peaceful scene, part
of a land isolated by the fantastically high cliffs that
bounded it. There was only one predator here: the Gap
Dragon. If it appeared, the grazers would take evasive action, though there was nowhere they could really escape.
They might even be resigned, and simply let the dragon take
whichever ones he selected.

That was not her concern. Her business here was only the
children. If she could be sure they were not here, she would
depart. She wished she could orient on their identities, but in
this different reality she lacked a way to fix on them. She
needed to tune in, in their presence.

She saw a puff of steam ahead. That should be the dread
Gap Dragon, a terror to all except his friends. She floated
toward the steam.

She was correct: there was the Gap Dragon, a low-slung
serpentine six-legged monster with a big toothy head and
small wings. He had to have been descended from a variety
of flying dragon, but he couldn't fly. Instead he whomped,

making vertical wriggles, one set of feet lifting and landing at a time. He was a steamer, considered by some to be a lesser threat than a fire-breather that could roast an animal where it stood, or a smoker that could stifle it in a roiling cloud. But steam, when used well, was just about as dangerous. Steamers had been known to stifle the other kinds, dousing their fires and dissipating their smoke.

She floated before him. "Stanley Steamer," she said. "I am Surprise Golem. I know you; do you know me?"

The dragon shot a fierce column of steam directly at her. She barely had time to conjure a protective shield. The steam bounced off it and formed a frustrated cloud.

But when she conjured the shield, she stopped floating. She could exercise only one talent at a time. She landed on her feet with a jolt.

The dragon whomped forward, ramming into the shield. Surprise had to levitate hastily to avoid getting flattened by the falling barrier. Which of course faded out.

The dragon aimed his snoot upwards and fired another fierce jet of steam that would have cooked her in place had it scored. She summoned a gust of wind that blew it away— and dropped to the ground, her levitation gone.

The dragon pounced on her. She became a tar baby that caught and held the crunching teeth. "Stop this attack, Stanley," she said. "I'm trying to talk to you. I know you can understand me."

The dragon blew out a waft of steam that melted the tar baby, freeing his teeth. She countered by becoming a fire woman, not solid like Pyra, but made entirely of fire, her flames unaffected by the teeth. "I don't want to hurt you, I just want to talk to you."

The dragon snapped repeatedly at the flames, getting nowhere. Then he got smart and inhaled, sucking the flame woman into himself.

Surprise became an iron-spine cactus, impossible to swallow. "I'm warning you: desist."

Stanley steamed the cactus, melting the spines. Surprise converted to a diamond girl, her sparkling flesh invulnerable to both steam and teeth. "You crazy beast, quit!"

The dragon picked up a stone in his mouth and made ready to smash the diamond body to diamond dust.

That did it. Surprise became a device, a form of demon adept at crushing things: Demon Vise. She caught the dragon's head in her square jaws and squeezed, slowly. He struggled, whomping his green body around, but was unable to break the powerful grip. "Give up?" she asked grimly.

Instead, Stanley blew out so much steam that the ground below the vise melted and caused it to sink. Rather than get mired in forming lava, Surprise changed form again, releasing the head. This time she became a small cloud of smoke, demon-fashion, while she considered her next approach.

"Okay, no more Miss Nice Girl," she said. "I'm going to make you pay attention."

Stanley charged the cloud, revving up a new head of steam. Surprise transformed into a female gap dragon, with six legs and long eyelashes. "What are you up to, steam-for-brains?" she inquired in steam pulses.

This did get his attention. "Who are you?" he demanded in the same language.

"I am Surprise Golem, as I said. You don't remember me?"

"If I had encountered you before, I would have steamed and eaten you. You're a shape-changer?"

"Not exactly. My magic is to have any talent once. When I studied the matter, I discovered that I actually borrow each talent from someone else, but thereafter that person resists losing the talent again, so I can't take it twice. Eventually I might be able to, but it doesn't matter, because there are so many talents that I can simply take a similar one next time. Did you notice that I never repeated?"

"No. What I noticed was that you didn't know my name."

"It's not Stanley?"

"It is Stefan Steamer. So I knew you were an impostor."

Surprise took stock. No wonder the dragon had been determined to steam her! "I apologize. In my reality you are Stanley."

"Your what?"

"I come from a different reality. It's hard to explain.

Things are like this, only not quite. Like your name being different. Like myself being different. The Surprise Golem of this reality is a soulless creature who doesn't care whom she hurts."

"What do you want with me? I doubt it was to smooch."

"I am looking for three lost children. I need to know if you have seen them. I hope you didn't eat them."

"If I had seen them I would have eaten them," Stefan agreed. "But I didn't. Are they bouncy delectable sweet-tasting children?"

"No, they're part demons."

Stefan blew out a discolored wad of steam. "Yuck!"

So demons didn't taste good. "That's all I needed to know," she said. "I must find those children."

"Hold up two moments, Golem. You're really from a different reality?"

"Yes, where you are named Stanley and are friends with Princess Ivy."

"Ivy?"

"Evidently not the case here. She has three daughters, triplets, who like to play with you."

"They wouldn't last longer than the time to steam them."

"They are Sorceresses."

He considered. "That would make a difference. Queen Ivy does not have triplets here. I would know."

"Queen Ivy?"

"Queen of the Naga folk, because her husband Naldo Naga is their king. He and I get along. Therefore I tolerate Ivy; Naldo would be annoyed if I steamed her."

"Then who governs the human folk of Xanth?"

"King Dolph, of course. And his wife Nada Naga. I get along with her too."

Surprise realized that this was another marital realignment. In her reality, Dolph had loved Nada but married Electra, and they now had twin daughters. So what had happened to Electra, here? She decided not to inquire. "In this reality I am married to a different person than I am in my own. I can't say I like the person I am here."

"As it happens, I do know of that Surprise. I understand she's talentless."

That might explain why Surprise Seven was so ready to make an ugly deal with the Sorceress, and even signal the stork with a man she detested. Surprise's talent was attached to her soul. When the Demons took her soul, that deprived her of it. Fortunately in her own reality they had returned her soul, or enough of it so that her body regenerated the rest. "That should establish my foreign nature."

"Yes. I thought that the Sorceress was with you. But she couldn't do what you're doing now."

"I certainly hope she couldn't. She has my baby. I must recover my baby girl."

Stefan evidently made a decision. "I will summon Nada."

"I'm not sure I want to meet her in this reality, unless she has information on the lost children."

"She may. She can find out, if she chooses."

There was something skew about this. "If she chooses?"

"She has a problem. Maybe you can help her with it."

"She would want to bargain?" Surprise asked distaste-fully. "Over the lives of children?"

"Isn't that what you humans do? Make deals?"

"Sometimes," she agreed grudgingly.

The dragon lifted a foreleg. On it was a thin golden chain supporting a ring in the form of a snake biting its own tail. Stefan gently steamed the ring, and it seemed to wriggle. It was surely an amulet.

There was a sound beyond the rim of the great canyon. A huge bird appeared, flying swiftly toward them. It was a roc.

Surprise looked for cover. "Even you can't handle a roc," she warned the dragon. Rocs ate dragons, and anything else they chose.

"That's King Dolph in bird form. He's carrying Nada."

Now she saw that the monstrous bird carried a large snake in its talons. That would be Nada Naga in her serpent form. She could move rapidly in that form, but not nearly as swiftly as a roc bird could.

The roc came in for a landing, shaking the ground. The

snake dropped down just before that, slithering out of the way. It became a serpent with a human head: a naga. The naga slithered up to the dragon and they touched noses with no harsh steam issued.

Then Nada Naga faced Surprise. "You are human?"

Surprise changed back to her natural form. "I am Surprise Golem, daughter of Grundy Golem and Rapunzel Elf. I am from another reality."

Nada became lushly human, in the form of the serpent woman Surprise knew in her own reality. She lacked clothing, but in a moment the roc became the man Dolph, who brought her a royal robe. She donned it, and then a small gold crown. "I am Queen Nada Naga, now Nada Human. What is your business here?"

Surprise tried to condense it. "I have to recover my lost baby from my alternate self here. The Sorceress Morgan le Fey hid the children who accompanied me and wants to make me give up my baby to recover them. So now I need to find them."

"Why not just let the Sorceress have your baby?"

"I couldn't!" Surprise said in anguish.

"Why not?"

"She's my baby! I'm her mother. I can't give her up."

"Then why not let the children go?"

Did the queen truly not understand? "My conscience won't let me. One of them is your daughter, in my reality."

Nada turned to the dragon. "Thank you, Stefan. You were right to summon me." She turned back to Surprise. "Come with us."

"Will you help me search for the children?"

"We may. First we must talk."

"I have hardly two hours. I can't take time off."

"You don't have a choice. Dolph will carry us back to Castle Rockbound."

"I can't go there," Surprise said, appalled by the woman's indifference. "I realize that you don't have the same children here, but I can't leave them to whatever fate the Sorceress has in mind. I must do my utmost to rescue them."

"Pick her up," Nada said to Dolph.

The man became the roc. One giant claw reached to enclose Surprise.

She changed to roc form herself. "No!" she squawked in bird talk.

Nada nodded. "You do have a conscience."

"Of course I have a conscience!" she snapped in squawk talk. "Don't you?"

"Yes. But you are going to have to trust me. You must accompany us to the castle. We will help you if we can."

That seemed to be the best she could hope for. Surprise returned to her natural form.

The roc enclosed them both in the talons without squeezing; the foot formed a kind of barred cage. Then the big bird took off.

"Here is the situation," Nada said as they traveled. "The Surprise of this reality is without soul or conscience. She can't be trusted. Any deal you may have with her is suspect. I had to be sure of your status."

"Because I look just like her," Surprise said, realizing. "I *am* her—only with my soul."

"And with your full talent, near Sorceress caliber. You could be dangerous."

"I'm not trying to threaten you or anyone in this reality. I realize that things are not the same here, with different marriages and different kings and queens. I accept that. I just have to do what I came to do: save the children in my care, and recover my baby."

"And if the Sorceress offers you all of that, if you help her overthrow the present king so she can be installed as the new ruler?"

Surprise stared at her with horror. Could that be what Morgan le Fey had in mind? No wonder Nada was nervous!

She tried to answer honestly: "I don't know. I don't want to have to choose between the children and the baby. I would hate even more to have to choose between all of them together and what I know is right."

"It is fairly easy to choose between right and wrong, when

you know which is which," Nada said. "It is harder to choose between wrong and wrong, or between mixed situations."

"Yes!"

The roc squawked. "Yes, dear," Nada called. "That's a good point; I'll tell her." She focused again on Surprise. "He reminds me that knowing which is which can be difficult, because what is right to one person may be wrong to another. So we wonder at times whether there is any such thing as inherent right and wrong."

"Yes," Surprise agreed again. It was clear that the king and queen had really thought about this. "Just as there may be no such thing as a natural order of things in Xanth. I have seen several realities, and what one rejects, another accepts. Like the Adult Conspiracy."

"The what?" Nada asked blankly.

"Never mind; it would be complicated to explain, and maybe irrelevant. It is a particular convention in my reality that applies mainly to children."

"At any rate," Nada continued, "Dolph and I have a problem, and you may be able to help us handle it. I realize that you don't want to take time off from your search for the children, or to make any unethical bargains, but perhaps you will consider this as a convenient package: we will put the resources of the kingdom into a swift search for the children, and hope that you will help us while we await the result. Both can be accomplished within the two-hour period you require. Does this seem fair?"

"Yes," Surprise agreed, relieved.

They arrived at Castle Rockbound, which seemed much the same as the one she knew at home, Castle Roogna. Dolph landed and reverted to human form, and they walked through the orchard.

"We had better pick some fresh pies," Nada said. "So we won't have to delay for a separate meal."

Surprise picked a sweetie pie and a milkweed pod; that was the extent of her appetite at the moment.

The moat monster lifted its head, eying Surprise, plainly knowing who was new here. It was not one he recognized.

"It's all right, Sourdough," Nada called. "This isn't who she looks like."

The monster shook his head.

Nada turned to Surprise. "He thinks you're soulless. Would you mind showing your talent briefly?"

Surprise conjured a junior porcupine, which looked like a cross between a pig and a pine tree, except that it was covered with quilts.

"What is that?" Nada asked, startled.

"A real porcupine from Mundania is covered with sharp quills, which it slaps into the nose of whatever tries to bite it. This variety is child safe because the quilts are soft."

"Quill to quilt," Nada agreed. "So small a shift." Then she faced the moat monster. "Could the soulless Surprise do that? The talent attaches to the soul."

The monster agreed that Surprise was different. Meanwhile the porcupine wandered toward the zombie graveyard. It would surely find a welcome there, as the zombies liked soft covers.

"Dear, tell the staff to organize a search for three children," Nada told Dolph. "Use magic. We need them within two hours."

Surprise gave the descriptions of the children, and the king departed on his errand. "He's such a dear," Nada remarked.

"It's hard to believe he is the king of Xanth. He acts like your servant."

"It's love. He's loved me since he was eight years old, and I have loved him since I was about twenty, when I took love elixir. He is really quite kingly when not with me. We also have a fine son, Donald."

Surprise realized that the name derived from DOlph and NADA or her brother NALDo. "A son instead of two daughters."

"He can change his own and others' forms, temporarily," Nada said proudly.

Soon Dolph rejoined them and they went to a private chamber and closed the door. "No one will disturb us here," Nada said. "Now as we finish eating, Dolph and I will explain our situation." She went and kissed him. "Are you up to it, dear?"

"Yes, if there's a chance of fixing it."

Nada nodded. "You see, we have a spell we received as a wedding gift, that could really do us some good, but we lack the ability to invoke it completely. We think you may be able to do it for us."

"I'm not sure I could do better than you could. Doesn't a spell work for whoever invokes it?"

"To a degree. You see, this is a Guilt Trip."

"A guilt trip? I don't understand."

"The spell conjures a path you can take that leads to your greatest guilt. At the end is a stone you can tap to alleviate guilt. But a person can't alleviate her own guilt, only that of someone else. That's because the stone is a Punk Rock, with a very bad attitude. So Dolph and I have tried to take that trip together, and abate each other's guilt. But we have not been able to make it to the end. Our guilts cripple us, and we have to turn back. You, in contrast, seem to have little to feel guilty about; you should be able to reach the stone and ask it to ease our guilts."

"But couldn't anyone here do that?"

Dolph grimaced. "We prefer that others not know our guilt. You are from elsewhere, where things are different; you won't be spreading it about as gossip."

"I wouldn't do that!" Surprise protested.

"We trust your discretion," Nada said. "And hope that you can do this for us, and we can find the children for you."

"Yes, of course. It's a fair bargain." Surprise hesitated. "I hope you aren't guilty of murder or something. I don't know how that could be absolved."

"Not murder," Dolph said. "Not exactly."

"Now dear," Nada said. "You know it wasn't that."

"My conscience doesn't," he said uncomfortably.

"In any event, the Rock does not absolve the guilt as such," Nada said. "It corrects it, allowing you to change it, so you have no further cause for guilt. It's a very strong spell."

Surprise nodded, appreciating that. The Rock seemed to

offer some kind of absolution, though she still wasn't sure exactly how it worked. "I'll try. Please tell me what your guilt is, so I can tell the stone."

Nada shook her head. "We don't care to speak it here in the castle. The walls have ears." She turned suddenly and smacked an ear that had quietly sprouted from the wall behind her. It reddened and shrank.

"And eyes," Dolph said, flicking a bit of grit into an eye just opening in the wall beside him. The eye blinked and watered, but couldn't dislodge the grit and had to fade out.

"But the Guilt Trip Path is private," Nada said, bringing out a small bottle. "Are we ready?"

"I am, I think," Surprise said, marginally bemused.

Nada opened the bottle. "Guilt, we invoke you," she intoned. "Take us on the Trip."

Vapor issued from the bottle. It curled up, spreading. It formed a pattern against the wall that had recently sported the ear and eye. Now that wall had a nose. The nose sniffed the vapor, sneezed, and blew itself back into the wall.

The pattern shaped into a picture drawn on the wall. It showed a path meandering through a pleasant meadow. It looked almost real; flowers were scattered across it, and several puffy clouds floated above it. The vapor was a good artist.

"I'll lead," Dolph said. He stepped into the wall—and through it, following the path.

"Do you care to go next?" Nada asked Surprise.

Surprise hauled her lower jaw back up into place. "Yes." She stepped into the wall where Dolph had, bracing herself for a crash.

There was none. She found herself on the path in the meadow. Now she smelled the flowers.

She looked back. There was a square outline behind her, where the wall had been, and inside it stood Nada Naga-Human. She waved, smiling. Taken aback, Surprise returned the wave. The vapor had really made a portal to another scene. Magic could still surprise (no pun) her on occasion.

Nada stepped forward, joining them on this side of the

frame. Then she turned, reached up, and drew down a curtain across it. The curtain showed the meadow scene on the near side, and surely the wall on the other side, concealing the access. Such a bottle of vapor would be very very nice for folk shut up indoors, offering a private escape.

But where was the guilt?

"You will see," Dolph said. "The Guilt Trip does not let you walk silently. You have to reveal your greatest guilt." He walked on.

Surprise followed, wondering. Why should anyone volunteer to talk about what he was ashamed of?

"You will see," Nada repeated, answering her thought.

The path wound through the meadow and around a low hill. There was a nice brook chuckling along. "I always loved Nada Naga," Dolph said. "Ever since I met her as a child. I was required to betroth her, for the sake of a human/naga alliance, but she quickly won my heart, even before she blossomed into the most beautiful woman in Xanth."

Surprise found nothing odd or guilty here. Nada *was* the loveliest creature in human female form in Xanth. How could he fail to love her? Men were notorious for being swayed by appearances. Women, fortunately, had more sense; that was why they ran things, while letting the men believe that males governed. Why ruin a good thing?

"But I also got betrothed by the girl from the past, Electra," Dolph continued. "She was under an enchantment, and had to marry me by the time she turned eighteen, or die. She loved me, but I didn't love her. She was plain, and not a princess, and her magic talent was modest. She could not compare to Nada the Naga princess."

"No one could," Surprise said.

"Oh, any demoness could, if she chose," Nada said.

"But demons lack souls," Surprise said. "So they aren't suitable. It's *all* appearance, with them."

"Not necessarily." But Nada did not clarify.

"And so when it came time for me to marry," Dolph said, "I had to choose between the two: the one I loved, or the one who loved me. I was selfish and chose the lovely princess. Thus Nada is my queen, and I still love her and find no fault in her."

"That seems reasonable," Surprise said.

"But I find fault in *me*," he continued inexorably. "Because she did not love me, and I knew that; she had to take the love elixir. I was fifteen, she twenty; she would not ordinarily have loved or married a younger man. A boy, really. I knew nothing of stork-signaling; she taught me that. She guided me in governance too; I have been a better king because of her."

Surprise was perplexed. "Then where is the guilt?"

"Two things: I took her against her will. She had to agree, to safeguard the liaison between our species, which the naga folk desperately needed. So she took the elixir, but I shouldn't have made her do it."

"Yet if she is happy now—"

"But she might be happier without me," he said. "She has benefited me, but I have not necessarily benefited her. If I had it to do over, I would steel myself to let her go. After all, I could have taken the love elixir with another woman, and been satisfied."

Surprise glanced back at Nada, but the naga princess was silent, her face impassive. "What is the other thing?"

The king winced. "Electra loved me and would gladly have married me without the elixir. She was enchanted to love me at the outset, when I woke her from her long sleep, but that was replaced in time by real love as she came to know me. She also was cursed to die if she did not marry me by her eighteenth birthday. I thought that was at least partly psychological, and that she would survive and find a life elsewhere. When I chose to marry Nada, Electra made no complaint. She said she was happy that I was happy and had a good wife. Then she died."

Dolph stopped speaking abruptly. He stood shaking with the force of his manifest guilt. Nada stepped forward and put her arms about him comfortingly. "You didn't know, dear. It wasn't really your fault."

"I should have married her!" he said. "I should have been unselfish. It would have worked out some way. It would have been better for both of you."

Surprise did not comment. In her reality Dolph had married Electra, and it had worked out very well. She had become the first Xanth princess in blue jeans, and her plainness had somehow blossomed into a certain competent appeal. She had been friendly with everyone, and was widely admired. They had two bright, attractive, Sorceress daughters, Dawn and Eve. So Surprise could not say that Dolph had not made a mistake in this reality. His choice had cost a worthy girl's life. He did have guilt.

Nada moved ahead. "I too have two aspects of guilt," she said. "First, that I deceived Prince Dolph by pretending to be eight years old when he was nine, when I was really fourteen. By the time he learned the truth, he loved me. I should never have done that."

"You were required to," Dolph said. "Your family made you do it, because they needed you to marry a human prince."

"It was still wrong. Maybe if I had let you know my real age, and you handled it and loved me, then it would have been all right. But I should never have deceived you for political reason."

"It was a shock when I learned," Dolph said. "But I did accept it, and loved you ever since. So it was no continuing deception, and you never deceived me since."

"Still it was wrong, and I bear the guilt." Nada paused, evidently marshaling her courage, then continued. "But the larger guilt is elsewhere. There was a demon who was interested in me, D. Vore. He was eligible, being a prince; I could have married him and had an alliance for my people with the demons. That would have accomplished my parents' purpose. But I was fixed on the human connection, and thought it would be more advantageous to marry a human prince. In fact—" she paused again, flushing slightly. "I thought that it would be easier for me to control a young human than a mature demon. I liked the notion of queenly power. So I chose the human, knowing he would choose me if I did not dissuade him. It was my decision."

"Yet it worked out," Surprise said. "You have been a good and supportive wife to him."

"Demon Vore's passion for me was greater than I judged," she continued as inexorably as Dolph had before. The guilt path was driving her. "When he saw that he had lost me, he swelled into a huge mushroom-shaped cloud and faded into the wind. He had returned to the earth that spawned him. In fact he was dead." She stopped, verbally and physically, as Dolph had before, in tears. "I killed him with my indifference."

"You couldn't know," Dolph said comfortingly.

"Yet if I had it to do over, knowing what I know now, that you could have made it with Electra and I with Vore, I would marry him. That would save two lives."

Surprise could see her point. Each had done the selfish thing, and bore the continuing guilt of it. They had a good life together, yet were haunted by what might have been.

"And that is our respective guilt," Dolph said.

Surprise was perplexed. "You have expressed it well. Isn't that all you need to do to complete the guilt trip?"

Both shook their heads. "We have not expressed the last vestige of our guilts," Nada said. "We have been unable to make ourselves reveal our final secrets. So we are unable to complete the trip. But you seem to have little if any guilt, as I noted before. You can achieve the end, and touch the guilt stone for us."

"Maybe I can," Surprise agreed. "But I remain confused about a detail. Just what does the stone do? Does it simply make you feel better?"

"No," Dolph said. "It fixes the guilt."

Nada had said something of the sort before. Surprise still couldn't make much sense of it. "But if the other people are dead, how can it ever be fixed?"

"It is retroactive," Nada said. "It changes spot history. It leaves nothing to be guilty about."

Surprise was amazed. "Retroactive! That is powerful magic! Are you sure it is wise?"

"We can't live with our continuing guilt," Dolph said. "We regret changing history for others besides ourselves, but the main folk affected are the two who will have their lives restored. We believe that is best."

Surprise had to agree, especially because she knew how well both marriages had worked out in her own reality. Yet she had one more question. "You love each other and are good for each other. Won't this break you up?"

"Yes," Dolph agreed. "I hate that."

"I fear for his welfare without my guidance," Nada said.

"I love you, dear," Dolph said.

"I love you, dear," Nada echoed.

They embraced and kissed. They made a truly lovely couple, the handsome king and the lovely queen.

Surprise remained uncertain. "Are you sure you want to do this?"

"Yes," both said together.

"Our love is suspect," Nada expained. "We harmed others to achieve it."

"We don't deserve it," Dolph said.

They kissed again. Little hearts circled them.

Surprise shrugged. They were in evident agreement, so it was not her place to argue further. "Then I will try."

She forged ahead along the guilt path. But now her own guilts beset her, and she had to speak them aloud; the path compelled it. "I was imperious as a child, thinking I could do anything. I flaunted my talents, embarrassing other children. I was hard to handle; they had to bring in a gargoyle to tutor me. When I discovered that I could use each talent only once, I was crestfallen, and for a time I was afraid to use any talent. I should have realized that character counts more than magic, and for that willful ignorance I still bear guilt."

"But didn't you mature, in character?" Nada asked.

"Yes, and I hope I am a better person now for that effort. But the early guilt remains."

"I intend no offense," King Dolph said. "But as guilt goes, that's trifling. Every child is imperious, and has to learn better. I did. You were normal, apart from your remarkable talent."

Surprise forged on along the path, talking compulsively as she did. "Then I forgot to get my record at the Stork Works corrected, so the stork thought I was only thirteen, and took my baby elsewhere. Now I am here in this reality, complicating things, trying to correct that mistake. In the process I waded through love elixir with Che Centaur, and now we have an illicit passion for each other."

"Why not enjoy it?" Nada asked. "Such artificial passion doesn't last long when indulged freely, unless the person wants it to, as I did with Dolph."

"That isn't proper, in my reality," Surprise said uncomfortably.

"But if you don't use it up, it will last forever," Dolph said. "If you really don't want it, the sensible thing to do is to have a wild affair, for the brief time it lasts."

"Have you done that?" Surprise demanded.

Nada laughed. "Of course he has. We both have. Once I slipped some love elixir into his water when he was setting out on a tour of the kingdom, and made a pretext to stay behind. It was hilarious."

Surprise did not trust herself to speak. She kept being surprised by the differences between realities.

"When I drank that water," Dolph said, "the first female I saw was an old ogress of the classic description: her face looked like a bowl of overcooked mush that someone had sat on. But there was no help for it. I assumed the form of an uglier ogre and had at her. She bashed me in the snoot a few times, but I would not be denied. And do you know, she was the best lover I ever encountered. She said so was I; that's the way ogres do it, you know."

"I nearly passed out, laughing, when he told me about it," Nada said.

"But I got Nada back," Dolph said. "I put elixir in her drink when she went to negotiate with a goblin chief for a new boundary between the naga and goblin territories. The naga hate the goblins, you know. That messed it up awfully, because they were able to set no boundaries."

"We still hate goblins," Nada said. "But sometimes I arrange a tryst with that one chief, by that fuzzy line, for old times' sake. He's a wonderful brute, and he can't keep his hands or anything else off me. A woman likes to be appreciated."

Surprise spoke very carefully to mask her utter shock. "We don't do it that way in my reality."

"Just one partner?" Dolph asked doubtfully.

"It must be dull," Nada said sympathetically.

"Just one," Surprise agreed grimly. "So my passion for Che Centaur is illicit and inspires guilt."

Dolph and Nada exchanged a glance, as of how to handle a person with a truly unreasonable fixation. "Of course, dear," Nada said. "That's the way it is, for you."

"Even if no one died," Dolph agreed.

Surprise forged on, her feelings mixed. She had revealed her greatest current guilt, and learned that it was not even a blip on the screen in this reality. She wasn't sure whether to be embarrassed.

She came to the end of the path. There was the great Punk Rock, in the shape of a punkin. She looked back and saw that neither Dolph nor Nada had been able to make it to the end. Their remaining unexpressed guilt held them back.

Surprise stood beside the stone. Now what?

"Invoke it!" Dolph called.

"Tap it with a finger," Nada added. "And name us both."

Surprise reached for the Rock. It made a nerve-jangling sound, warning her off. It did indeed have a bad attitude. But she nerved herself and tapped it. "King Dolph Human. Queen Nada Naga-Human."

Something like a spark jumped to her finger and coursed up her arm all the way to her mouth. Awful sour music sounded, making her body twitch with distaste. The Punk Rock was possessing her, exploring her body and mind, verifying that she had indeed come to it properly, having revealed her own guilts. Grudgingly, it told her what to do next.

She faced the two, who remained back, pain showing on their faces. Royal pain. "Dolph, come forward," she called. "Reveal your final guilt."

"I can't," he said.

The nastiness of the Rock pushed her. "You *will*." She pointed to the path behind him. It caught fire, scorching the foliage on either side. Surprise wasn't sure whether this was magic from the stone, or her own that it required her to employ. The fire advanced, forcing the king to come toward the stone lest he be burned.

As he advanced, he spoke. "When I remember Electra, and how she was, I think she might have been a better wife for me than Nada." He was flushing with shame for his betrayal of his wife as he reached the stone at last.

"Oh Dolph, you could have told me," Nada said. "I would have forgiven you. I know I'm not perfect."

Surprise kept a straight face. That was his most secret shame? That he had some bit of doubt about his wife? Surprise knew that there were many men who might have been better for her in one way or another than Umlaut, but it didn't bother her. She had married him, and was loyal to him; what might have been didn't matter. It was physical unfaithfulness that mattered.

She spoke again, her voice coarsely musical. *That* was the effect of the Punk Rock. "Nada, come forward. Reveal your final guilt."

Nada tried, but her feet didn't seem to want to move. Surprise pointed to the path behind her, and a wisp of smoke curled up. Was she using a different spell this time, per her limit? Nada hastily moved.

"Demon Vore was older than I am, by thousands of years," she said. "When I remember him, I think I could have had an older man, instead of a boy." She blushed furiously.

"Of course I was a boy," Dolph said. "You made a man of me. I bless you for it."

Nada made it the rest of the way to the stone. "Oh Dolph, we've done it," she said. "We have spoken our betrayals of each other. Now at last we can clear our guilts."

"Now at last," Dolph agreed. "I love you, Nada. I think I always will."

"We can still have trysts," she said.

"That will be great." They kissed.

Again, Surprise withheld her reaction. These two people, so completely in love, expected to break up their marriage retroactively, so that it never happened, so they could do right by the two who had loved them and died. Yet they also expected to have a kind of continuing romantic association that would be illicit in Surprise's reality but was reasonable in this one. She was beginning to get her scruples realigned, recognizing that she could not judge the folk of this reality by the standards of hers. What they were doing seemed to make sense for them.

All she said was "What now?"

"Now we go back," Nada said. "Thank you so much for your help."

"We couldn't have done it without you," Dolph said.

Surprise turned to the brooding stone. "Thank you, Punk Rock."

There was a flare of discordant melody. The Rock was not pleased to have served.

They walked back along the path. There was no resistance. Dolph and Nada held hands and paused frequently to kiss. They seemed sorry about having to part, yet also glad to be doing it. Surprise suspected she would never completely understand.

They reached the covered panel. Dolph lifted up the curtain, revealing the exit to the castle, and they stepped through. Nothing seemed to have changed. The portal faded out behind them; this guilt trip was done.

"Oh, Dolph, we've done it!" Nada said.

"No one else will remember except Surprise," he said.

"I won't tell," Surprise said, realizing this was expected.

Dolph and Nada embraced and kissed once more, lingeringly. "Until the tryst," Nada murmured fondly.

"But secret, lest it reveal the change," he said.

"Of course. Now let's see what the search for the children has turned up."

They left the room and went to the main chamber of the castle. There were several people there. One of them was Electra, much like the one Surprise knew, in blue jeans and crown. She came to hug Dolph. "Are you finished, dear?"

He hesitated barely an instant. "I think so, yes."

There was a swirl of smoke and Demon Vore appeared. "And what were you doing with the human king, you luscious reptile?" he inquired cheerfully as he swept Nada into his arms.

"You have no idea, smoke-head," Nada said affectionately.

Surprise recognized these as the spouses Dolph and Nada had in her own reality. This reality was now a step closer to that one.

"What about the search?" Dolph asked.

Two attractive teen girls appeared at the entrance and ran bouncily up to him. Surprise recognized them as Dawn and Eve, the one fair as the morning sun, the other sultry as dusk. "I checked the whole area, and nothing alive knew anything about any lost children," Dawn said.

"I checked every nonliving thing, and they didn't know either," Eve said.

They had gotten the suddenly restored daughters to search, Surprise realized. The daughters who had not existed in this reality before the Guilt Trip, but didn't know that they had only recently been retroactively generated. Her mind threatened to spin out of control.

It got worse. Ten-year-old DeMonica appeared and joined her mother, Nada. "I asked Magician Humbolt about it," the girl said. "He says the children were transformed."

"Thank you, DoMinica," Nada said. A flicker of pain crossed her face, quickly suppressed.

Oh—this was not DeMonica One, but DoMinica Seven. But why the pained expression? Then Surprise realized that this meant that Dolph and Nada's son Donald must have disappeared along with their marriage. That was the penalty for clearing their guilt. But surely Donald remained on Ptero, the moon where all folk who ever existed or might exist dwelt. He simply had lost his entry to reality.

"And how were they transformed?" Vore asked.

"Not physically, exactly," DoMinica said. "They—they just don't relate well, now, Humbolt says."

The demon blew two jets of smoke from his ears. "The Good Magician is ever the one for obscurity."

That much hadn't changed, Surprise thought.

"Did he say how to relate to them?" Nada asked her daughter.

"You just have to go there and look the right way. They're there, if you look right."

Nada faced Dolph. "Dear—I mean, oh dear, that means our search is not over."

"We will have to mount a search party and go to the appropriate region," King Dolph said. "And try to look the right way."

"Thank you," Surprise said. "That will surely help."

"How come we're doing this, anyway?" DoMinica asked. "Why are we helping the humans?"

"I have no idea," Nada said with a smile.

"I caught that!" DoMinica said. "That's an Obscure Smile, mom. You know something you're not telling."

Nada shrugged. "Maybe I do. Leave me my little secrets, child. When you come of age you'll have secrets of your own."

"I sure hope so."

Fortunately only Surprise saw the similarly obscure smile King Dolph made. He had not forgotten either. The two had changed from love and marriage to love without marriage, at least not to each other. Would they retain the kind of illicit passion Surprise had for Che Centaur, that would have been fine in another reality? Fortunately for them, in this reality they could have trysts, as they put it. Surprise envied them that much.

As they organized for the search, Surprise reflected on the similarities and differences between her reality and this one. Two couples had been brought into alignment, but Dolph was not king in her reality. A portion of the history of this reality had been significantly changed, but most of its residents were unaware of that. Serious guilt had been abated, but only those who had felt that guilt remembered it. And Surprise remembered too, of course, but she would not tell. Others would not readily understand.

At least they had made progress on the search for the children. If only they could figure out how to look.

14

CHILD'S PLAY

"Come, children," Pyra said cheerfully, her body flashing with its inherent flames. "There is a patch of candy canes growing close by, and jelly beans."

Naturally Demon Ted and DeMonica followed her eagerly, and Woe Betide was satisfied to tag along. It was fun to get sick on candy canes and jelly beans. They followed a little path through the tangled brush. Sure enough, there was the patch, with the stripy canes standing tall and the bean plants twining around them. It was what adults called compatible gardening.

Ted and Monica plunged ahead, eager to get started on getting sick before Surprise returned and Knew Better. Woe, smaller and slower, lagged. Thus it was that she saw what happened. She saw Pyra contemplating—well, that was too big a word for her small vocabulary, but it meant looking at—the children. The woman nodded as if satisfied with something. Then she faded out.

Woe Betide wondered what had happened. One moment Pyra was with them, and the next she wasn't. She had simply disappeared. So Woe went to inspect the spot where the fiery woman had stood hardly a moment before. There was nothing except the faint aroma of magic.

"Ted!" she called. "Monica!"

"There's enough for you too, brat," Ted called back. He liked calling her that, knowing that she couldn't dissolve her form and re-form as his mother.

"Not that. Pyra's gone."

Both Ted and Monica looked. "Where'd she go?" Ted asked.

"She just faded."

"But she's supposed to be watching us," Monica said. "She knows she can't even blink without us getting into mischief."

"She blinked out," Woe said.

"She must be hiding," Ted decided. "To make us think we're alone, so she can catch us getting into trouble."

They looked all around, but found no sign of Pyra. They tried making horrible faces and calling her nasty names, but the woman did not reappear. Finally they concluded that she really was gone.

"Maybe we'd better get back," Monica said uneasily. "Just in case." She tended to be the most responsible child, being the older girl.

They collected armfuls of canes and stuffed beans in their pockets, then sought the path they had come on.

There was no path.

Now they began to get alarmed. This was more than just chance; that path had been there before.

"She did it on purpose," Ted said, voicing the dark suspicion they had held back on.

But Woe, being full demon instead of half demon, had more perception than they did. "She was never here. She was illusion."

"Illusion!" Monica repeated. "Why?"

"To get us away from the real Pyra," DeMonica said with belated insight. "To lose us. Someone wants us lost."

Woe Betide clouded up. "We're lost!"

Monica gave her a quick hug to stabilize her, acting motherly. "We won't stay lost, dear."

"Who wants us lost?" Ted demanded belligerently.

Monica considered. "Maybe that other Surprise who's got the baby."

"Why'd she care? We're going back to our own reality soon anyway."

"Unless she wants us to stay here, to keep the baby company. So we're lost until the real Surprise and Che and all go home."

"Lost!" Woe repeated piteously.

"Oh shut up, brat," Ted snapped.

Woe felt a surge of righteous rage. "You wouldn't say that, if I could change back into your mother."

"Tough beans, brat. Now make yourself useful: light a match and wish us unlost."

A match! Of course. Woe opened her matchbox and brought out a magic match. She struck it and it flared brightly. And doused itself.

"What happened?" Ted asked.

"Nothing happened," Monica said. "That's the problem."

"What did you wish for, brat?" Ted demanded.

"The matches don't grant wishes, dum-dum," Monica said. "They grant folk their heart's desire."

"Same thing, harebrain."

"No it isn't, crazy-face. A person can make a wish, but can't change her real heart's desire."

"So what's her real heart's desire?"

"To change to Metria and spank your insolent butt," Woe said boldly. "But Humfrey's stasis spell balked it."

"Why you little bleep!" Ted grabbed for Woe's little arm, but his hand passed through her flesh as if it were mist. She was a child, but she was also a full demon, and could dematerialize at will. He couldn't touch her, literally.

"Ted!" Monica said. "You said 'bleep'!"

"And I'll say it again," he said nastily.

Then both paused. Woe saw the problem: how could Ted

have violated the Adult Conspiracy and said a bad word? How had Monica been able to repeat it?

Then a little bulb flashed over Monica's head. "This is a different reality. No Adult Conspiracy here!"

"Oh, wow!" Ted said, delighted. "Bleep, bleep, BLEEP!"

"Just because you can, doesn't mean you have to," Monica reproved him. "Anyway, all you have is one word."

"Well, I haven't had time to learn any more," he said defensively.

"We're still lost."

"Because the brat's heart's desire isn't what it should be," he retorted.

"That's readily solved. She can light a match for one of us."

"Me first," Ted said. "Do it, brat, or I'll really cuss you out."

Cowed by the threat, Woe took out another match, struck it, and held it before him. This one was not stifled; it flared brilliantly.

"$$$$! ####! ****!!" Ted exclaimed zestfully. The air shimmered and the grass around his feet wilted.

"Ted!" Monica cried, covering her ears.

"Well, I got my heart's desire," he said. "To be adult enough to handle really bad words."

"You were supposed to want to be unlost."

"&&&& it," he said unrepentantly.

Monica gave up on him. "Woe, please light a match for me. Maybe my heart's desire is what it should be."

Woe lit a third match. It flared.

Monica changed. Her hair grew longer and her lips turned bright red. Her eyes became huge and dark, and her hips developed a certain subtle sway.

"You sick all a sudden?" Ted asked.

"No, I have become alluring, in the manner of a big girl, with the power to daze men with a single glance and half a smile. I didn't realize that was my fondest heart's desire; I thought it was, oh, maybe third or fourth on the list."

"Alluring! You?! What a laugh!"

Monica batted her long eyelashes at him and let out a

quarter-smile. Ted's laugh stalled as he stumbled back, dazed. Woe realized that the match had indeed granted her desire, and this reality's lack of the Adult Conspiracy had allowed it to be granted. That was dangerous.

Monica turned away, and Ted slowly recovered. "Just be thankful I didn't flash my panties at you," she said.

"Aw, I'm too young to freak."

She casually lifted a section of her skirt, giving him a half-reared glimpse of panty. He fell to the ground, totally freaked out, and lay there staring at the sky. "You forget: no Adult Conspiracy here. If you can cuss, you can freak."

Woe nodded. Indeed he could; Monica had proved it. Their age of ten was no longer any barrier to adult behavior. That was doubly dangerous. The two half-demons often acted like brother and sister, but they were unrelated. If Woe could change back to being Ted's mother, she would nearly freak out with dismay at the potential for mischief. As it was, she was merely concerned about a situation she did not understand.

That made her realize something: there might be no Adult Conspiracy in this reality, but she remained bound by it. Apparently the Good Magician's stasis spell had locked her into the nature as well as the substance of childhood. The older children might revel in breaking the Conspiracy rules, but Woe herself was unable to. She was forever locked into her innocence.

But that was the lesser problem at the moment. "How are we going to get unlost?" Woe asked plaintively as Ted recovered from his freak-out.

Now the two older children turned serious. "That's right," Ted said. "All the cusswords and all the glances in Xanth won't be any good if there's no one to use them on."

"And we don't want to be stranded here when the others go home," Monica said. "So we'd better focus on finding where we are and how to get back to rejoin the others."

Ted looked around. "This looks pretty much like regular Xanth."

"Then maybe if we just walk, we'll get somewhere."

They walked. Soon they found a path and followed it. But Woe was nervous about it. She looked back, and saw no path. "Monica!" she cried. "Look!"

Monica turned. "Oh, no! It's a one-way path. Just tangled brambles behind."

"One way," Ted said. "That explains why we couldn't go back before. We were on it all along."

"Led by a fake Pyra," Monica agreed. "It didn't take much to lose us."

"Well, we're children. But we'll be smarter next time."

Woe hoped his confidence was justified. There was certainly something strange going on. If someone had wanted to be rid of them, why hadn't they been led into the clutches of a hungry tangle tree? Why go to the trouble of putting them on a one-way path? Where did it lead?

"Maybe we'd better get smarter sooner," Monica said uneasily. "If we follow this path, we're going right where someone wants us to go."

"Right," Ted agreed. "Might as well make some trouble for him." He looked to the sides. "It's pretty thick and brambly."

"To keep us on the path," Monica said.

"I'll forge through and make a new path." Ted stepped off, into the foliage.

But immediately he fell back, looking ill. "Oooh," he groaned.

"What happened?" Monica asked, steadying him.

"I think I'm gonna—" He shut his mouth.

"You are going to what?" Monica asked, concerned.

The boy's mouth reluctantly opened. His belly heaved. Half-digested candy cane and jelly beans flowed out and spattered on the ground. "Puke," he said belatedly.

"But you didn't eat enough candy to get sick," Monica protested.

"I was fine until just now. But when I touched those leaves—"

Woe inspected the leaves. She raided the stored memories of her adult self; those that did not relate to Conspiracy matters were open to her. "Sick Leaves!" she said.

"No wonder," Monica said. "Those always make you sick when you get near them."

Ted seemed recovered, but a bit wan. "Let's not cut across the brush."

"We'll follow the path," Monica agreed.

Woe saw no way to avoid it, but she didn't like it. They had been put on this path by an illusion, and it did not let them go back; the sick leaves were filling in behind as they progressed. The trap was still springing. She doubted they would like where this path led.

They came to an intersection. Their path joined a larger path at right angles. The new one was two-way; they could go in either direction. They consulted, and decided to explore both ways. Ted went left and Monica went right. The path they had been on faded out; now there was only the two-way track.

"But what about me?" Woe asked woefully. "I'm tired." Actually demons did not get tired the way fleshly creatures did, but it was appropriate for her age.

"You sit there, brat," Ted said. "We'll come back for you after we find the best route." He paused. "If we don't forget."

Woe burst into tears.

Monica hurried to console her, and to reprove him. "Do that again, Demon Ted, and I'll freak you out so bad you'll still be lying here by nightfall," she said fiercely.

"Aw, I'm real scared," he said derisively.

She put her hand to her skirt.

"Okay, okay. I'm on my way." He hurried along the path.

"He was just teasing, honey," Monica said. "We won't forget you. I promise."

"Okay," Woe said bravely. "I'll wait."

Monica went to the right, and soon disappeared around a curve. Woe remained alone, nervously reminding herself that it was just for a little while.

She looked around, and saw something lying near where the one-way path had been. She picked it up. It was an eating utensil, a small fork with five dull tines. Someone must have dropped it and not missed it. There wasn't much use for it here, where pies and fruits could be best eaten by hand. But it was well made, with little runes along its sides. She decided to keep it.

Ted appeared on the right. Then Monica arrived from the left. But they had gone the opposite ways. Woe found this confusing.

The two older children spied each other. "What are you doing here, bimbo?" Ted demanded.

"I'm following my path, pith-head," she retorted.

"You couldn't have gotten ahead of me."

"I didn't try to."

"Ahem," Woe said.

Both children saw her now. "Cheese and crackers!" Ted swore. "We're back where we started!"

"But that's impossible," Monica said. "I never turned."

"Neither did I. It must be a circle."

"Then we should have passed each other on the opposite side," she said. "We didn't."

"This is weird."

"Really weird."

"So it's a magic circle," Ted said. "How the bleep do we get off it?"

"Maybe this is the trap we were sent into," Monica said. "To get on the circle and never get off."

Ted looked around. "Sick leaves everywhere."

"There must be a way," Monica said. "Woe, what do you think?"

"Would this help?" Woe asked, holding up the little utensil.

"A fork!" Ted exclaimed. "That's what we need. Gimme." He snatched it out of Woe's hand.

"Ted!" Monica said warningly.

This time he ignored her. He held up the fork. "Fork, I invoke you," he said.

A fork in the path appeared before him. The fork in his hand disappeared.

"You figured it out!" Monica said, kissing him on the ear. "You're a genius."

"Well, smart, anyway," he agreed, obviously pleased as his ear turned pink.

Woe's feelings were mixed. She was glad that they had found a way off the circle, but sorry she had lost her nice fork, and irritated that Monica had changed emotions so readily. She should have punished Ted for his meanness to Woe. But of course Monica was a child. In that corner of her mind where Metria lurked, Woe Betide knew that allowances had to be made for children.

They were about to follow the new path when there was a galloping sound. A blue-eyed blonde centaur/unicorn filly galloped up, her bouncing bare front causing Ted's eyeballs to bulge dangerously. Woe was seeing increasing reason for the Adult Conspiracy; in their own reality Ted would hardly have noticed such a detail, or at least not taken it seriously. Bareness made children snigger, not pant.

"Hello," the filly said. "You must be the new arrivals. We had a report someone was on the circle drive."

Ted remained transfixed by the centaur's breathing, of all things, and Monica was fidgeting jealously as she studied the crossbreed filly's silver hooves and horn, so it was up to Woe to explain their situation. "We're lost," she said.

"Yes, of course. I am Elysia Centaur, of centaur and unicorn descent. I was sent here to pick you up."

"You can pick me up any time," Ted said breathlessly.

Monica spoke, suppressing her evident disgust with Ted. "I am DeMonica, of demon and naga stock. This is Demon Ted, half demon, half human. And the child is Woe Betide, demon."

Good; Monica had not revealed Woe's full identity. Woe did not trust this situation, despite the seeming friendliness of the filly. Why had she been sent to pick them up?

"We just want to go home," Monica said. She, at least, wasn't fascinated by bare fronts. "Somehow we got on a one-way path and couldn't get off."

"Of course," Elysia said. "The Sorceress did it."

All three children stared. "Sorceress?" Monica asked.

"Morgan le Fey, from Mundania. She's notorious. Anyone who gets in her way gets sent here to the other realm. We know of no escape. So we'll bring you to the castle and show you the ropes, and you'll surely do as well as the rest of us."

"We know of no Sorceress," Ted said, finally getting some of his attention back.

"Few do. She hides in the body of Surprise Golem, and has some nefarious scheme going. We don't know what it is, but she must have been afraid we would interfere, and got rid of us."

"The baby!" Monica said. "She's messing up Surprise so she can't get the baby."

"You misunderstand," Elysia said. "Surprise is involved with the Sorceress, lending her her body."

"No," Monica said. "We are from another reality, and so is our Surprise Golem. She came to fetch her baby, who we think was misdelivered here."

Elysia nodded. "That would certainly make you a threat to the Sorceress. We did not know about the baby. We're somewhat out of touch here, having no access to news of Xanth except what is provided by refugees such as yourselves."

"Now can we go home?" Monica asked.

"I am sorry, but no. We would all like to return to Xanth, but we can't. We know of no way back."

No way back. That made Woe freeze with dread. But this still didn't quite make sense. "Why the path?" she asked.

"To fetch you in before the bloodhounds came for you," the filly said. "They come out at night, seeking blood. The only safe place is the Prime Monister's castle."

"The what?" Ted asked.

"The Prime Monister. The ruler of the land-bound monsters. He is a horror, but he takes care of those who serve him. It is not a nice life, but it is better than the alternative. Now we must take you there."

"We?" Monica asked.

"My friends Cassy and Caitlin Centaur are coming. We will carry you."

"We don't want to go to a monster's lair," Monica said nervously.

"None of us do, dear. But it's not as bad as the bloodhounds." Woe thought of hounds seeking blood, and shuddered.

"Maybe we better go there, for tonight," Ted said reluctantly.

The two centaurs arrived. Cassy was red-haired and Caitlin was brown-haired; both were bare-chested, of course. Cassy lifted Woe onto her back, Caitlin lifted Monica, and Elysia picked up Ted, to his evident delight. Centaurs were of course used to the way human men and boys reacted to them.

The Monister's castle was spectacular. It was huge, covering much of a mountain, with turrets rising high above it. Its outer wall was solid stone, with metallic spikes poking out. No creature would care to come up against that rampart.

"The bloodhounds are that bad?" Woe asked.

"Yes," Cassy said. "They smell all the blood inside, and charge the castle, but the only blood they get is their own as they hit the spikes. We are safe from them, inside."

"What about the Prime Monister?"

Cassy shuddered. "Try to stay beneath his notice. He's not much interested in children."

That did not sound good. "What is he interested in?"

"Workers, mostly. Cooks, scullery workers, cleaning maids, stable hands—it's a big castle, and requires a considerable staff."

Woe felt a certain hesitation. "What else?"

"Maidens," Cassy said reluctantly. "Of all species. We don't know what he does with them; they never tell. But we dread it."

It certainly seemed bad. There were things in the prohibited dusky recesses of her mind that hinted at what a male monster—monister—would do with young females. They would need to get away from this castle as soon as possible.

They trotted up to the front gate. The guards evidently recognized the centaurs and waved them on by. The massive portcullis slammed down behind, shutting them in. For ill or worse, they were here for the night.

They did not stop at a chamber. Instead the three centaurs trotted through the castle to a giant central courtyard. "The castle is built on an old volcano," Cassy explained. "Mount Pinatuba's saucer once rested here."

Woe knew very little about volcanoes, but this was odd. "Saucer?"

"In Mundania, we understand, volcanoes sit on tectonic plates. Pinatuba sits on a tectonic saucer."

This was way beyond Woe's very limited understanding. "Okay," she said.

"Normally volcanoes and other mountains don't like to move much," Cassy continued blithely. "Plates just aren't very mobile, except extremely slowly. But saucers move all the time. I understand someone found a mustard seed's amount of faith and moved the mountain from north of the Gap Chasm to south of it. They were lucky 'Tuba didn't blow its top right then, and cool Xanth another degree."

"Okay," Woe repeated blankly.

"So this is the old depression where the volcano once rested," Cassy concluded. "The mountain that rings it is what is left after Pinatuba departed. It's an ideal spot for the castle, because the walls are already made, as it were."

"Okay."

Cassy turned her front section around and lifted Woe off her back and to the ground. "You won't like it here, but you will have plenty of companionship."

Meanwhile Caitlin and Elysia were similarly lifting down Monica and Ted. Elysia kissed Ted on the forehead as he passed her face, and his expression turned to mush. The Match had given him far too much maleness for his age.

"Snap out of it, doughboy!" Monica snapped jealously. And she had become too female.

"Now we'll introduce you to some guides," Caitlin said. "Then we'll be off, because we have to round up any more refugees out there. The Prime Monister is very strict."

"How come nice folk like you serve a monster?" Monica asked.

Caitlin smiled wistfully. "We are land monsters too. We

don't have much choice." She looked around. "Akimbo! Extricate! New arrivals."

Two of the folk clustered in the courtyard came over: a boy and a girl of about ten. "Aw, what's the point?" the boy demanded in a surly manner.

"This is Akimbo," Caitlin said. "His talent is to cause tangles of any size or complexity. He's not bad once you get to know him."

"I am too!" Akimbo retorted. "I'm real bad! I'll tangle your tail something awful, filly."

Caitlin picked him up and kissed him on the cheek. He turned to mush just as Ted had. The filly centaurs clearly knew how to handle boys. There was just something about a bare-bosomed kiss. "You'll get along fine with Demon Ted," she said as she set the boy down. She addressed the girl. "This is Extricate, Kate for short, whose talent is sorting out tangles. Kate, meet DeMonica, who I just brought in from the endless traffic circle. You'll show her around, won't you?"

"Sure," Kate said amicably. "Are you really part demon, DeMonica?"

"Half demon," Monica said proudly. "Half human."

Caitlin looked around again. "Teddy!" she called.

A little boy of about five came. He looked mischievous. That was a good sign. "This is Teddy Bare," the centaur said. "His talent is to make people naked. We try to discourage that, though it doesn't affect us centaurs. Teddy, this is Monica; she's a demon."

"Yeah?" Teddy asked. He looked at Woe. Her dress fuzzed and faded, making her bare.

She instantly reformed her dress, as it was from her demon substance. "Stop that, or else."

"Or else what?" he demanded.

"Or else I might do this." She stepped into him and kissed him hard on the mouth.

"Oooh, ugh!" he cried, trying to rub the flesh off his lips. The other children tittered. Woe had recently learned something about making unruly boys behave.

"You'll get along fine," Caitlin said, smiling. Then she, Cassy, and Elysia trotted off.

"Do we gotta show these new twerps around?" Akimbo demanded, his natural surliness returning.

"We may be new, but we're not twerps," Monica informed him.

"Yeah? Well I think you—"

Monica smiled at him in the new sultry way she had since the incident of the Match, and lifted her skirt half a whit so that the edge of her panty almost showed.

"Are no twerp," Akimbo concluded weakly. "I'll get my friend Arlis to help." He turned and called. "Hey, Arly! C'mere!"

Another boy walked toward them, this one about twelve. "Hi, Kimbo. Who's your pretty friend?"

"DeMonica. She's half demon and—" Akimbo leaned close to whisper. "She's got panties!"

"Wow! Can I see them?"

"No!" Monica snapped.

"They're probably immature anyway."

Monica didn't rise to the bait. Age twelve was interesting, and he had called her pretty, but there were limits. "We don't plan to stay here long. Tomorrow we're going home."

Arlis, Akimbo, Extricate, and Teddy laughed, though there was more than a tinge of ruefulness in it. "We all want to go home," Arlis said. "C'mon, I'll show you around."

They had become a group of seven. Arlis led the way across the courtyard, which Woe now saw was quite varied. There were assorted trees growing in it, some forming thickets and thinnets, and a number of tents and ramshackle small buildings. This was evidently where most of the captives lived.

"Hi Notty!" Arlis called to an older boy.

"Hi, Buttnose," the other replied.

"Buttnose?" Monica asked.

"That's my talent," Arlis said with resignation. "Always to be called by a nickname, never my real name. I'm stuck with it. Notty's talent is Nots: tying things up in Nots, like trees, rocks, and such."

"Nots? Don't you mean knots? And how do you tie a tree or rock in knots?"

"Like this," Notty said. He touched a small tree, and suddenly its trunk was not. The base and foliage remained, just not the trunk. "And this." He touched a rock, and it became a pile of sand. The rock was not.

"Ah, there's my girlfriend," Arlis said, approaching a pretty girl in light blue with hair like a floating cloud. "Hi, Skyla! You look airy today."

"Are you calling me an airhead, Goatface?"

"No, I think you are lovely." Arlis turned to the others. "She's going to be mistress of the sky when she grows up."

Skyla kissed him. "And I'll be your mistress when you grow up, Barley."

"I can hardly wait. Maybe your friend Miranda can teach me how sooner."

"She better not, Smartis!"

Arlis glanced back again. "Miranda can teach anyone anything, except new tricks to her dog, Old."

"And here is Tish," Arlis said. "Her talent is making folk freak out."

"Without panties?" Monica asked.

"Without anything. She could go naked and folk would still freak out."

"Hello, Smartis," Tish said. "Have you found a way out of here yet?"

"Don't I wish." They moved on, but Woe was thoughtful. A talent of freaking out anything could be useful in an escape attempt.

"And here's Sonya, whose talent is figuring things out," Arlis said.

"Hi, Tuna." Apparently the nicknames did not have to be even close to the real name.

"Can she figure out how to get out of here?" Ted asked.

"No, just puns and challenges," Sonya said. "Things with answers. There's no way out of here."

The introductions continued, but Woe lost track of them. There were just too many people here, and all they had met so far were the children.

"Better make a place to spend the night," Akimbo recommended. "There's a pillow-bush, and the trees provide pretty good shelter. Pie-plants are plentiful. I'll introduce you to Stephanie; she can summon tsoda pop for you to drink. You can be wherever you like."

"Thank you," Monica said. "We'll do that." But Woe knew that look: Monica had no intention of settling down. They had been trapped in the Punderground before, and made every effort to escape; this was similar but worse, so they would have to try harder. Monica was assuming the Lead Female role, since there was no adult in their party to do it.

Indeed, Monica exchanged a glance with Woe, acquiring her support. Woe was glad to give it.

There was a despairing scream. "What's that?" Ted asked, alarmed.

Arlis looked pale. "That's Cadence. I know her voice."

"Why did she scream?"

He looked grim. "Maybe I'm wrong."

"I doubt it," Sonya said. "There's only one thing that would affect her like that."

"Still, we'd better ask."

They went in the direction of the scream, and soon came to a winged centaur filly. No, her body was that of a white tiger instead of a horse. Woe had not seen that species before. "She's a centiger," Arlis explained. "Maybe she'll tell you her story." He waved. "Hi, Cadence!"

The centiger cleared the fading horror from her face. She had short spiky dark blonde hair, gray-green eyes, and dark gray wings. She was adult, fully developed, and lovely for her type; Woe would have known by Ted's staring, if it hadn't already been obvious. "Hello, Ozzie."

"These are new arrivals Ted, Monica, and Woe Betide," Arlis said. "We heard your scream. Are you all right?"

"The messenger just left. The Prime Monister has summoned me for tonight."

There was a silence.

Monica approached. "You must want to get out of here pretty much."

"So much I'm ready to fly over the wall and wait for the bloodhounds."

No one laughed. They knew she wasn't joking.

"Can we talk alone?" Monica asked.

Cadence shrugged, causing Ted's eyeballs to steam. "If you wish." She seemed resigned to her awful fate.

"Come on, kids," Extricate said. "I'll show you where the pies are."

Woe started to go with them, but Monica sent her a look, and she stopped. "Diffuse and check around to make sure no one overhears," Monica murmured. She knew that Woe, as a full demon, could do that.

Woe diffused into a thin mist—she lacked the mass for thick smoke—and suffused the area. She formed a vague face. "No one's snooping," she reported.

"Stay alert, though."

"She's a full demon!" Cadence said. "Can you trust her?"

"Yes. She's Ted's mother, locked into child form. She doesn't want us trapped here."

"There is no escape." Tears dribbled from the centiger's eyes.

"Please tell us your story."

Cadence hesitated. "How would that be relevant?"

"We three children are from another reality where things aren't quite the same. We may not be bound by the same rules that apply here. We may be able to escape, if we can figure out how. Maybe you can help us, and escape with us. Several of the children have special talents that may also help. I'm trying to put it all together."

"You seem smart for your age."

"I'm not. But I'm sensible when I have to be. I try to get the facts and make sense of them. Sometimes they add up."

Cadence nodded. "My grandmother was Hia Harpy. She spied a handsome human male about to drink from a love spring he obviously didn't recognize as such. She thought it would be a good joke to flash him just as he finished, then fly away, endlessly tormenting him. Humans normally despise harpies, so this would get him back for that. But when he saw her and was smitten, he had the wit to splash the water on her, and so she was caught in her own trap and loved him too. They had quite a session before the elixir wore out and she could fly away, disgusted with herself.

"But of course the stork found her, and delivered a big egg from which the winged human girl Lena hatched. She was raised by the harpies and thus had a somewhat fowl mouth. Her magic talent was summoning the nearest Mundane animal. This was frowned on, so she seldom used it. She was curious about her origin, so when she came of age to be independent she flew to the love spring where she had been summoned. She landed and gazed at it, awed by its significance. But for it, she would never have existed. In her distraction she tripped over a stick and fell into the pond. She panicked and accidentally used her talent. The nearest Mundane animal was a white tiger who had recently crossed into Xanth. He saw her and she saw him, and suddenly she understood exactly how it had been with her parents.

"Lena and the tiger went their separate ways after wearing out the elixir, but the stork had taken note, and in due course delivered me. I was raised by my mother, and moved to the Magic Dust Village at the age of five when my mother got caught, toasted, and eaten by a dragon. They needed workers there to process the magic dust, and I worked hard as I grew up. The intensity of the magic in that region must have affected me, because most crossbreeds don't have very strong magic, while mine is very strong. It is not flying; I can do that because I inherited it from my mother and grandmother. Whatever I sing becomes temporarily real in my vicinity. I thought that made me proof against hostile magic, but I was wrong. When I turned fifteen I set out to find adventure. When I inadvertently crossed the Sorceress Morgan le Fey, not knowing her nature, she banished me to this other realm, and I have been stuck here for several months.

"And now the Prime Monister has summoned me. I don't

know what he will do to me, but I'm sure I will never be innocent again. My dreams of finding a handsome man of my kind will be ruined; no one will want me when the Monister is through with me. I am doomed." She wiped away another tear.

"The Monister doesn't kill you and eat you? Others have returned from their nights with him?"

"Yes, but they refuse to talk about it. They seem afraid and ashamed, and withdraw from their friends. I know it's something really horrible."

Woe, listening, knew that somewhere in her sealed-off adult memories was an explanation, but children would never understand it, and certainly she didn't. Somehow the Monister hurt the girls worse emotionally than physically. Cadence was surely correct: she needed to escape right now.

"Can't you sing about escape from the Monister?" Monica asked. "And make it real?"

"No, the Monister damps out any magic that might be used against him. Even if it worked, it would be temporary, and I'd be back in his fell clutches."

"Here is what I am thinking of," Monica said. She was taking hold nicely, and would surely some day be a competent woman. "You carry the three of us to the place where we first were lost, and we'll search for an escape. If we came into this realm, we must be able to pass out of it. We just need to figure out how. Maybe Sonya can give us a clue."

"She can figure only puzzles and things," Cadence said.

"This is a puzzle. Maybe it just needs to be phrased correctly."

"Maybe," the centiger agreed with faint hope.

"Is there anyone who can see into the future?"

"Well, Tu-Morrow can tell a person what he'll encounter next day, once."

"Once?"

"When a person learns what will happen, it seems that knowledge changes it, so his future changes. Tu-Morrow can't tell it after it's been changed."

"Maybe he can help, though. We'd better ask."

"I suppose it can't hurt."

"We don't want others to know what we're trying," Monica said. "Because someone might tell the Monister. We need to plan and act rapidly. Within the hour."

"Within the hour," Cadence agreed.

Woe realized that since the centiger expected to die soon anyway, she had nothing to lose by going along with Monica's plan.

Woe went to locate Tu-Morrow and Sonya. Soon they were there. Tu-Morrow was an older man who had surely seen more yesterdays than tomorrows. Sonya of course was not much older than Monica.

"Here's a puzzle," Monica said to Sonya. "How can I get from one realm to another?"

"You have to look at it a different way," Sonya replied. "That's all I can say."

"You mean like upside down? Backwards?"

"No. More like seeing the spaces."

"What does that mean?"

"I don't know. It doesn't make much sense to me."

"Where do you see me tomorrow?" Monica asked Tu-Morrow.

The man focused and seemed confused. "Somewhere else, yet not elsewhere. That doesn't make sense either."

But it made sense to Woe Betide. Monica would see the escape and use it, and be in the other realm tomorrow. She just had to figure out how to do it.

"Let's get started," Monica said. "Now."

Woe located Ted, who was guzzling tsoda pop in the company of several appreciative girls. He was still expanding into his new sense of masculinity. "We have to go," she whispered in his ear.

"Awww."

"Unless you'd rather stay here while Monica and I fly away with Cadence."

"Cadence!" His eyes widened with the memory of her bare body. Bare evidently trumped the covered bodies of the girls. "Okay."

The three children got on Cadence's back. She spread her wings and took off. In three moments they were flying over the castle wall.

An ogre guard looked up and spied them. "Shee flee!" he bawled. There was an immediate flurry of activity.

"The hounds will be after us," Cadence said grimly. "If we don't find a way through, they'll tear us apart."

"We'll find it," Ted said, though there was a quaver in his voice. "Won't we?"

"We'll find it," Monica agreed. "Somehow."

Soon they came to the endless circle, then to the candy-cane patch where the children had first discovered they were lost. Cadence landed there and settled down on her feline legs so the children could slide safely off.

"Here is where the path was," Monica said. "This has to be the place. All we have to do is see it different."

They tried. Ted looked cross-eyed, but that didn't help. Monica held her head sideways, but that just made her dizzy.

Yet there had to be a way, Woe thought. How could they see it?

There was the sound of baying. "The bloodhounds!" Cadence said, shuddering. "Can we hurry?"

What could be different? Woe racked her little mind. She had to see differently. But what was there was there; she could close her eyes and not see it, or open them and see it the same as it was. There was no difference about it.

The bloodcurdling baying drew rapidly closer. Then a huge hound appeared, blood-red. It spied them and let forth an ear-shattering howl of discovery, telling the others. In a moment and a half there was a ring of them slowly closing in on the four escapees.

"We are about out of time," Cadence said. "Maybe you had better get back on my back. I can avoid them for a while."

Ted looked up. "Bloodhawks!" he said.

Woe looked. He was right: blood-red hawks were clustering in the sky above them, slowly circling. There would be no escape through the air.

"Why are they so slow?" Monica asked.

There was a huge ugly bellowing roar not far away. "Oh!" Cadence said, looking faint. "That's the Prime Monister! They're waiting until he gets here. So he can have his awful way with me after all." Now she looked sick.

"*Do* something!" Monica yelled at Ted.

"*You* do something, smarty-pants!" he yelled back. "It was your idea to come out here instead of having fun with all those nice girls."

There was an ominous glow from behind the trees. The Prime Monister was about to arrive.

"It's too late," Cadence said, her four knees wobbling. "We're doomed."

Woe Betide knew that none of them would figure it out. She was the only one who could, because—because her adult self had once been in a situation that—which suggested that this was actually a Demon b—

The scene wavered. "Eee!" Monica screamed with all the eee's she could manage for her size. She had spied the Monister.

The scream disrupted Woe's thought. She tried to get it back, but it was gone. "Mice!" she swore.

The ground shook with the force of the Monister's tread, and the air flickered with the awful force of his ghastly presence. Ted and Monica stared, transfixed.

"Let the children go," Cadence pleaded tearfully. "They didn't mean anything. I'm the only one who—"

The pleading beauty was drowned out by the bellow of the blast. The huge beast loomed over them. Drops of drool fell to the ground, making the leaves it struck curl and fester.

Woe concentrated with all the limited power of her little mind. Sonya had said they had to look at things a different way. Like seeing the spaces. Woe didn't understand that, so she took it literally. Instead of looking at the prime Monister she looked at the space around him.

And the space was the shape of two big trees and a low-hanging cloud with trailing curlicues of mist. It looked exactly like Xanth proper.

There it was! "I got it!" Woe cried. "Ted! Monica! Get on Cadence with me and close your eyes!"

The others hardly seemed to hear her, but Cadence reached out without looking and lifted the three children to her back. "Close your eyes!" Woe repeated. "You too, Cadence."

They closed their eyes as more drool fell around them, its stench making breathing miserable. Woe focused on the trees and cloud. It was just space between them, in Xanth. That was where they wanted to be.

The burning-garbage breath of the Monister blew down at them, making their noses itch. The thing was cranking open his mottled jaws. But Xanth was just that space framed by trees and cloud. "Jump, Cadence!" Woe cried. "Straight ahead!"

The centiger shuddered and tensed. Then she leaped into the maw of the Monister.

And landed in the space of Xanth. The horrors of the other realm were gone.

"Open your eyes," Woe said.

They did so, cautiously. And stared. "Where are we?" Ted asked.

"Xanth," Woe said proudly. "I found the way."

"But how?" Monica asked, amazed.

"I looked at spaces."

"I don't understand," Cadence said. "I thought I was leaping into a fate arguably worse than death."

"This is better than death," Woe said. "Here in Xanth it's a space. If you look instead at the shape of the space between the trees and cloud, you'll see where we came from."

Cadence looked. "I don't see—" Then she stiffened with horror. "The Monister!"

"Stop looking!" Woe said. "So you won't go back there. Shut your eyes."

Cadence did, and in a moment relaxed. "Yes, I have it now. No more looking at spaces. I can hardly believe we're free."

"Well, the others aren't," Monica said. "We'll have to go to the castle and rescue them before the Monister goes back there."

"Including those nice girls," Ted said. His attitude toward girls had changed considerably since he picked up on the secrets of the Adult Conspiracy.

"Including them," Cadence agreed, spreading her wings.

"You did it, Woe," Monica said. "You understood what we didn't, and saw what we couldn't. You saved us. You're a heroine."

Even Ted was impressed. "I won't call you brat anymore," he said.

That, coming from her rebellious son, was the best reward of all. Woe Betide was quite satisfied.

15

MAGIC VS. MAGIC

S urprise Golem returned to the starting place for the search with a heavy heart. The royal search party would be arriving soon, but she was pretty sure they would not find the children. The local version of the Good Magician said they simply had to look the right way. Wasn't that what all of them had been trying to do all along?

Suddenly she came across a tense tableau. A large cat was crouched facing an old woman and a dog. There was apt to be mayhem soon. The odd thing was that she had the impression that neither side wanted it.

"What is happening here?" Surprise asked.

The woman looked at her. "I'm not sure. Amber and I found ourselves in this odd land, and Amber growled at an odd girl, and the girl disappeared and the cat appeared. We don't want any trouble but we don't know what to do."

"You're from Mundania!" Surprise said. "You and your dog."

"Yes, of course. But we have the feeling we're not in Kansas anymore, so to speak."

"You're in the Land of Xanth," Surprise said. "Where magic is common. I think you have encountered a werecat." She looked at the cat. "I don't think the dog meant to threaten you. She just didn't understand your smell. Will you change back now?"

The cat became a girl. "I don't like being growled at."

"I'm sure the dog is sorry." She looked back at the others. "Let's introduce ourselves. I am Surprise Golem, and I can do magic too." She changed momentarily into a rock bird, and back to her natural form.

"I am Ruth Sutpen," the startled woman said. "And this is Amber." This time the dog wagged her tail.

"I am Raina Werecat," the girl said. "Maybe I overreacted. I'm sorry. How can I make it up?"

"What these good folk really need is guidance to a safe haven, where they can get to know their way around," Surprise said. "Why don't you do that, Raina? I'm sure they would appreciate it."

"Well sure," Raina agreed. "I know a good place nearby. Follow me."

"Follow her," Surprise told Ruth. "The folk of Xanth are friendly and helpful, once you understand them."

"Thank you," Ruth said, evidently relieved. They followed the werecat. Surprise went on to her rendezvous.

The other members of her party arrived back one by one or two by two. There were some new faces. What had happened?

There was a second stork with Stymy. "This is Stymie Stork," Stymy said, introducing his friend. "She has my territory in this reality. She helped me search. She—I—we—"

"We're in love," Stymie said. "We knew we'll probably never see each other again, but we'll get together if we possibly can."

"Congratulations," Surprise said. "I hope it works out." It hadn't occurred to her that storks themselves had romances, but it made sense.

"We searched diligently," Stymy said. "And we had the

help of the demonesses Metria and Mentia. Synonym and homonym. But we didn't find any lost children."

"But how can Metria—"

"The Metria of this reality. She's not locked into her childish aspect. I told her that her son was one of the children. I don't think she has a son in this reality, but she did help search."

"That's what counts," Surprise agreed, slightly unsettled.

The peeve arrived. "I found a gourd and searched the dream realm, in case they went there. The Night Stallion summoned all the children there, but ours weren't among them."

"The Night Stallion helped you search?"

"It seemed he wanted to get rid of me, for some reason."

Surprise had to laugh. "Thank you, peeve."

Che returned. "I did not find the children, but did find the Simurgh. That accomplishes part of my separate mission."

"Part of it?"

"It seems there may be a problem returning to our own reality."

"A problem?" Surprise asked, alarmed.

"There are so many different realities that it is almost impossible to locate a specific one accurately. We may have to settle for one very close to the one we left."

Surprise did not like the idea of that, but Pyra was arriving back and she didn't want to argue at the moment.

"I searched a Moon of Ida called Always-Always Land. I did not find any children," Pyra reported. "I did find a man. I hope to bring him to Xanth in due course, if you will fashion a suitable body for him, Che."

"I shall be happy to," Che agreed. "Give me a description."

Pyra gave it, and Che asked questions, getting it straight. So Pyra had found love too. This quest was having complications Surprise had hardly anticipated. She didn't object, as long as they found the children. But since none of them had, it seemed that they would have to deal with Morgan le Fey on her own terms.

"I'm sorry," Pyra said. There seemed to be more there

than Surprise understood, but maybe she was reading something into it that wasn't warranted. Maybe it was simply that the children had been taken while under Pyra's care. But there really hadn't been anything the fire woman could do about it.

"We have tried," she said. "But we haven't found the children. I shall have to talk again with the Sorceress."

"But you know her price," Che said. "This isn't right."

"I know her price," Surprise said heavily. "But I can't let the children be permanently lost."

The others gazed at her sadly, not arguing.

They went to the Golem residence, which had become a place of horror rather than comfort.

Morgan le Fey was doing something to the front of the house, looking exactly like Surprise. "What's the poop, spook?" the peeve demanded, taking the initiative while Surprise tried to come to a decision. It was perched on Che's head and was using Che's voice. The centaur seemed happy to allow it.

The Sorceress set down her hammer. There was a bassinet and a pile of framed papers beside her. "I'm setting up a board for my pictures, you little piece of excrement."

"You're an artist now, witch?"

"No. These are collected pictures of familiars." She held up a picture of a fierce hawk.

"Haw haw haw! As if a picture can do anything."

Morgan fastened the picture to the board. "Invoke," she said.

The hawk came to life, hopping out of the picture, leaving the paper blank.

"Kill." The Sorceress pointed to the peeve.

The hawk launched into the air, winging powerfully toward the peeve. Then it backpedaled in air, for Che's bow was in his hands, drawn, an arrow nocked and tracking the hawk. No creature gambled that a centaur might miss.

"Return," Morgan said. The hawk flew back to the picture frame, entered it, and became the picture.

"That is interesting magic," Che remarked, putting away his bow.

"I have other pictures. Just be glad I didn't invoke this one." She showed a picture of a mean-looking golem. He was holding two sticks that were linked together by a short chain. "This is Numb Chuck. He fights with his sticks, but has no feeling, so can't be dissuaded by pain or the threat of it."

Che didn't comment, and Surprise knew why: the centaur's unerring arrow would stop the golem regardless, by crippling him even if he couldn't die.

"Or this one," Morgan said, showing a picture of an elf.

"What's so bad about an elf?" the peeve asked with Surprise's voice.

"This is Levi Athan, a crossbreed between an elf and a whale. He looks like an elf but has the mass of a whale."

"Leviathan," Che said, getting the pun. "He would be difficult to stop." But Surprise noted that he hadn't said impossible to stop.

Morgan picked up the baby and turned to Surprise. "Well?"

Surprise struggled. Here was her chance to get her baby back, saving her from the awfulness she otherwise faced in life. Yet how could she sacrifice the children in her care?

What was right? She had to choose between evils, and neither alternative was good, but she had no choice but to choose. On the one hand was a single innocent baby. On the other were three uninnocent children. Three against one. She hated it, but that was the number. She had to go for the benefit to the greater number.

She looked at Che, Stymy, Pyra, and the peeve. None of them gave any indication. They were leaving it to her.

"Free the children," she said brokenly. "Keep my baby."

"*My* baby," the Sorceress said, gloating. She clutched little Prize like the trophy she had been made. The baby cried. So did Pyra, oddly, her fiery tears scorching the ground.

Surprise was too choked up to say anything more. She turned and walked away from the house.

"They're free now," Morgan said.

"I'll check," Che said. He took off.

"Bleep," the peeve muttered as it fluttered across to perch on Surprise's shoulder. It looked toward the baby. "There goes the one person in Xanth who likes me."

"That's not so," Surprise said through her tears. "I like you."

"That's an exaggeration."

"Some," she confessed. "But you're really helping now."

"How touching," Morgan said sarcastically. "Now get your tails out of here, all of you. I have a brat to raise."

Surprise suffered a surge of fury. She opened her mouth.

"Easy, girl," the peeve murmured. "This isn't necessarily over."

Surprise saw Stymy Stork and Pyra exchange a glance. Was there something she didn't know?

There was a speck in the sky. Che was returning with the children. But there was something else: a second flying figure, smaller but too big to be any ordinary bird.

"Bleepity bleep!" Morgan swore.

The two winged creatures came to a landing: Che and some kind of crossbreed centaur female. "Well look at that!" the peeve exclaimed. "I haven't seen one of those since I left Hell."

"What is it?" Surprise asked.

"A centiger. Very rare."

Ted and Monica jumped off the back of the centiger and ran forward.

"This must be stopped," Morgan muttered. She hurled some sort of spell, clearly not bound by the Xanthly limit of one talent to a person. The two children stopped in mid-run. The centiger froze in place.

"This is bad," the peeve said. "It's a stasis spell with a side effect."

"Side effect?" Surprise asked.

"It silences the subjects on whatever topic is specified in the spell. Their minds remain restricted longer than their bodies do. She must have had it ready, just in case."

"What would she want to silence them about, after releasing them?"

"That's what we had better find out. A person can't even use such a Hell-spell without being pretty much damned already. She has to have really bad reason."

And the peeve had lived in Hell, and surely knew what it was talking about.

Only Che moved. "A temporary stasis spell will not avail you, Sorceress," he called. "I am proof against it, to the extent that I can still talk, because I know the truth."

"Triple bleep!" Morgan swore. "The Simurgh's been at him. I didn't count on that. I'll have to bind him to me immediately." She walked toward the centaur.

"Beware, Che!" the peeve called. "She's going to enchant you!"

"Shut your beak, you tiny turd!" Morgan snapped. "Anyway, it's too late. I'll make him love me. He's already soft on this form." She forged on, first divesting herself of all her clothing, then raising her hands to make some sort of gesture, while the others stood aghast at the abusive language. It horrified Surprise worse to hear it from the lips of her own alternate self of this reality. She also wondered what the Sorceress could know of the illicit passion she shared with Che; neither of them had spoken of it.

But she couldn't dwell on that at the moment. "What's she doing now?" Surprise asked.

"That's the windup for a dominance spell," the peeve said. "The victim is locked into the will of the spell caster. It starts with a love-elixir–like session to lock it in, but it's not the same. After the first bout, the victim constantly craves more, which may be dispensed only grudgingly by the spell-caster, as an occasional reward for complete submission to her will. It's one of the worst of the Hell spells. What I don't get is why she wants to make him her love-slave, when she wasn't really interested before."

"Maybe she's mad because he resisted her seduction."

"I don't think so. She was merely playing with him, diverting him while Umlaut Seven did the dirty work with you. This is serious magic."

The more Surprise heard of this, the less she liked it, and she had not been keen on it to begin with. She wanted to stop it, but couldn't think of a spell to invoke that would counter the deadly mischief of the Sorceress. It would have helped if she had known what was happening in more detail.

The Sorceress hurled her spell. It scintillated with evil power as it sailed toward the centaur, who was unable to move. But just before it reached him, a little figure swung around his torso and hovered before him.

"Woe Betide!" Surprise exclaimed.

"She's full demon," the peeve said. "A stasis spell can't properly hold one of those. She was probably shielded from it by Che's upper body anyway."

"But what is she doing!"

"She's intercepting the love-slave spell."

The spell bathed the child and dissipated. Che had been saved, but the child had just been enslaved.

"Curses!" Morgan swore. Her bare body was beautiful, but her attitude was ugly.

Woe ran forward. "I hear and obey your command," she said. She went to the house, sorted through the pile of pictures, selected one, and took it to the board. She checked the tools and found a screw driver and a screw. She used those to fasten the picture to the board.

There it was: a nice portrait of a cat. One of the stored familiars.

They all stared at the picture. How could a dominance or love spell have translated to such an action? What did it mean? Obviously the Sorceress' intent had been foiled.

Then the peeve burst out laughing. "Woe is a child!" it said. "Too young and inexperienced to have been affected by this reality's absence of the Adult Conspiracy. She took the command literally, not understanding its adult significance."

"I don't understand either," Surprise said. "This makes no sense to me."

Then Stymy and Pyra caught on, and laughed together.

For some reason they had both stayed clear of the recent action. "She fetched a screw driver," Stymy said.

"And a cat," Pyra added. Both dissolved back into laughter.

Woe turned to Morgan. "Did I do it right? I screwed your kitty."

The Sorceress turned angrily away without bothering to curse again. For half an instant the child's expression darkened because of the rejection, but in the other half of the instant it brightened into secret satisfaction. The spell had been broken; she was no one's love-slave.

"What am I missing?" Surprise asked, annoyed. "I have no idea what's going on."

The stasis spell broke. Che came trotting over. "Nothing," he said to Surprise. "You are missing nothing you need to know, you sweet person, and are the better for it." Then to the child: "That was very good, Woe. Thank you for intercepting the spell meant for me."

"I had to help," Woe said bashfully. She seemed to have about half of a childish crush on him, perhaps a fading legacy of the dissipated spell.

"You did. You saved me from an extremely awkward enslavement." He glared at Morgan. "Get dressed, you lady canine. You wasted your Hell-spell and can have no further power over me."

"Bleep," the Sorceress muttered with extremely bad grace.

Surprise gave up on the baffling riddle. "Why did she want to stop you? You were only bringing the children back after she agreed to free them."

"To silence me, when she discovered that I had been rendered partly immune to the stasis/silence spell," he said. "Because I bear the news that she did not honor her part of the deal. She did not free the children."

"That was an accident of timing," Morgan said.

He ignored her. "They freed themselves, and Cadence was carrying them here when I intercepted them."

"Cadence?"

"Cadence Centiger." The creature came forward. She had

the body of a white tiger, the forepart of a female centaur, and wings. "The children freed her too," Che explained. "Actually they worked together. They were already free before you talked with Morgan, and I think she knew it."

"Already free?" Surprise repeated blankly.

"Therefore she reneged on her part of the deal. So you aren't bound by yours. You can take your baby."

"I can take Prize?"

"As I understand it, yes." He glanced at the others. "Do you agree?"

Stymy nodded. "I agree."

Pyra considered, then nodded also. "As I understand it, yes."

"Dang tooting!" the peeve said.

"And we can all go home," Che concluded.

"Not yet," Monica said, her tone oddly mature for her age.

Surprise looked at the child. "You aren't ready?"

"We have to free all the others the Sorceress sent to the other realm, now that we know how to do it."

"Of course," Surprise said. "I'll take the baby, and support you in what you have to do."

"I think not," Morgan said from by the house. She picked Prize up from the bassinet. "I am keeping the baby." She stepped quickly into the house and slammed the door behind her.

"Bleep," Che said, uttering a rare imprecation. "She acted too quickly. I should have blocked her."

"She won't hurt the baby physically," Stymy said. "She wants to save that body for herself."

"I'm not completely sure of that," Pyra said. "She might choose to sacrifice the baby rather than lose it."

"Then I must go in and take it from her," Surprise said.

Che shook his head. "She's a Sorceress. She can throw magic at you that you've never seen."

"I've seen it all," the peeve said. "I'll help."

"You will need more," Pyra said. "I'll help."

"So will I," Stymy said. "I will try to find the baby and

take it outside." His beak curved somewhat. "I promise not to take it away from you again."

"In that confined space, more of us might only get in each other's way," Che said. "Suppose I go with the children to free the other captives? Woe Betide knows how to do it."

"Whatever works," Surprise agreed, heading for the house. Most of what she could think of was her baby. She had almost been cheated of her most precious thing!

The peeve settled on her head, and Stymy and Pyra flanked her. They went up and tried the door, but it was locked. "I can burn through it," Pyra said.

"Whatever," Surprise repeated. Her heart was pounding.

Pyra put one hand on the knob. It heated, and the wood around it smoldered. Then it came loose in her hand, together with the lock. She pushed the door with her other hand and it swung open. She hadn't had to burn the whole door, just the lock.

They entered. Surprise didn't know what to expect, and wasn't disappointed: there was nothing. They were in the antechamber.

She was about to go to the main room, but the peeve halted her. "It's a trap," it whispered. "She's hiding behind something, ready to attack you."

"How do you know that?" Stymy whispered.

"It's standard operating procedure, SOP. I learned all about it in Hell, from some of the worst in the business."

"Then I'll spring the trap," Pyra whispered. She walked into the room.

The Sorceress pounced on her from behind something, stabbing downward with a knife. The blade touched Pyra's shoulder—and melted.

"Well, now," Pyra flared, the flames brightening the room.

Morgan hit her with a freeze spell. The flames were snuffed, and ice formed on Pyra's head and shoulders. She dropped to the floor, stunned. It seemed the Sorceress had been ready for her.

Surprise stepped into the room. "I want my baby."

Morgan whirled, another knife appearing in her hand. She stabbed underhanded this time, aiming for the gut. "Knife," the peeve said belatedly.

The knifepoint touched Surprise's stomach—and stuck there. She had made her skin develop a surface of tarry cork. The knife was caught. "I want my baby," she repeated.

"It's mine," Morgan said. She picked up a chair and hammered at Surprise with it.

"Club," the peeve said. "Third weapon will be a rope or net." Meanwhile Pyra was recovering and getting to her feet.

The knife dropped to the floor as Surprise let that talent go and took another. This time her skin became like steel. The chair crashed against it and splintered.

A net appeared in Morgan's hands. She flung it over Surprise. But Surprise's body became like Pyra's, with little flames dancing on its surface. The net puffed into fire and ashes. The peeve's warnings, now coming just before the events, gave Surprise the leeway she needed to prepare counters to the threats.

"Dragon next," the peeve murmured in her ear. "SOP."

"Then try this," Morgan said. A dragon appeared, a steamer, blowing out white vapor that could cook whatever flesh it touched.

Surprise became an ice dragon, whose breath sucked the heat out of everything it touched. It nullified the steamer's heat and sent it running. Then she oriented her nose on Morgan herself, but the Sorceress was already retreating.

Where was the baby? That was all Surprise really wanted. She saw Stymy checking around, searching for it.

"Small monsters," the peeve said.

There was a loud scuttling. Half a slew of nickelpedes appeared, heading for her legs. It would be difficult and distracting for the dragon to freeze them all. So she conjured a local flood of mild acid. It didn't burn her own legs, but stifled the nickelpedes, who could not breathe. They scuttled desperately, mainly out of the house.

"Medium monsters," the peeve said.

They appeared almost but not quite immediately. Huge

mean dogs, blood red including their blazing eyes and glistening teeth. They massed and charged, and Surprise lacked room to evade them.

"Bloodhounds," the peeve said. "Make a lake of blood."

"Thanks, peeve." Surprise conjured the lake, filling the cellar of the house.

The hounds smelled it and dived into it, utterly diverted. They had no further interest in the living folk, who had very little blood in comparison. In hardly more than a moment they disappeared.

"Foiled again," Morgan muttered.

"Take the offense," the peeve advised.

Morgan threw a fireball at it, but the peeve jumped clear so that it passed harmlessly, then settled back on Surprise's shoulder. "Nice try, harridan."

"How?" Surprise asked. She was unable to concentrate properly amidst all this distressing violence.

"Make the house invisible," Stymy suggested. "So you can see only the people—and the baby."

Brilliant! Surprise focused, and the house disappeared, along with the pool of blood. All that was visible were Surprise, Pyra, Stymy, the peeve, Morgan—and the baby, nestled in a little hammock that had been concealed by two items of furniture: an easy chair and a difficult chair.

"Curses!" the Sorceress swore. She ran toward the hammock.

"Blast her!" Pyra urged. "While she's distracted."

It was possible. But Surprise could not bring herself to do such harm to a living person, even an enemy. Instead she conjured the baby to herself. As she did, the house reappeared, as she could not exert two talents at the same time. But now she had the baby in her arms.

"You spared her," Pyra said.

"It was the right thing to do."

"So it was," Pyra agreed, seeming oddly relieved. Surprise didn't have time to wonder why the fire woman should be relieved that Surprise had not done what she urged. Surprise had to get away from the Sorceress before worse happened. She turned and started for the door.

"Not so fast, innocent," Morgan said. "Now choose: protect the baby, or protect yourself."

"Huge monster," the peeve said.

There was a ghastly bellowing roar that shivered the timbers of the house. "What is that?" Stymy asked.

"The Prime Monister," Morgan answered. "Returned from the other realm."

"Oh, poop!" the peeve said. "Conjure yourself away from here. Now."

"And leave you, Stymy, and Pyra? I can't."

"Use your magic to protect the baby," Morgan suggested.

"Don't listen to her," Pyra said. "Save yourself."

Surprise conjured an invulnerable capsule around the baby, proof against heat, cold, or magic. But that left the rest of them vulnerable. She couldn't borrow another talent without losing the one that protected the baby. "Carry this away to safety," she told the stork.

Stymy hooked his beak into the loop on top and lifted the capsule. But before he could depart, the Monister's feet landed on the house, splintering it. Its head crashed through the roof. All they could see was its gaping mouth. Rancid drool rained down around them.

"My turn," Pyra said. "If you die, I lose." She leaped as the jaws snapped shut, her body blocking them so that they could not close on Surprise.

But the teeth did not crunch Pyra. Instead she flared so hotly that they melted. She became a veritable fireball, charring the Monister's tongue, lips, and the roof of its mouth. Then the fireball rolled on into its throat, roasting its flesh along the way.

The Monister screamed in agony and fled, smoke pouring from its nostrils.

"Thank you, Pyra," Surprise said weakly, disturbed by the Monister's pain.

"Oops," Stymy said.

Surprise looked at the capsule. It was empty. "But it can't be!" she exclaimed. "It's proof against magic."

"The witch pulled another fast one," the peeve said. "That

was a mock baby. It disappeared when the capsule cut off the magic."

"But then where is the real baby?" Surprise asked, dismayed.

"Where you'll never find it," Morgan said. "Ha ha ha."

"What can I do?" Surprise asked desperately. "She's too devious for me."

"You can agree to let me keep the brat, and get your nice little behind out of here," Morgan said.

"I can't do that."

"Maybe I can persuade you. Where she is now she will die slowly of exposure, with much crying along the way. If I can't have her, you can't either. At least with me, she'll survive."

"Don't make any deal with the Sorceress," Stymy said. "You can't trust her; you know that."

"But I don't want Prize to suffer."

"The female hound will make her suffer worse, in the long run," Stymy said.

"But still—"

"There's bound to be a trick," the peeve said. "Take time to fathom it before you make any decision."

That seemed to make sense. "I'll wait."

"It's the brat's funeral," Morgan said. "Assuming they ever find the body."

"Cover your ears, Surprise," the peeve said. "I'm going to get rid of her. I don't want you to hear what I'm about to say to her."

Surprise did so. That blocked off the sounds the peeve sent hurtling toward the Sorceress. Even so, Surprise's hair curled and frizzled, the backs of her hands stung, and the few splinters of house timbers that hadn't already burned charred now. It was the verbal torrent from Hell.

The Sorceress retreated before the barrage, and was gone. The peeve went silent, with only a few wisps of smoke drifting from its beak. Cautiously, Surprise uncovered her ears.

"Well spoken," Stymy said, brushing off singed feathers. "That would have done a harpy proud."

"Someone had to say it," the peeve said. "I do have harpy ancestry."

They made their way out of the wreckage of the house. And paused, amazed.

There were children, people, and creatures all across the landscape. King Dolph, with several members of his party. The centiger Cadence, who evidently knew them all, was checking them off a list she had. She saw Surprise emerge, and called to her. "I am making sure no child gets left behind. Then we'll have to see about getting them returned to their families. Ted, Monica, and Woe Betide are with Che Centaur, locating them, bringing them across, and teaching them how to do it so they can never be trapped that way again."

"Trapped where?" Surprise asked.

"In the other realm. It's like Xanth but largely unoccupied. The Prime Monister built a castle there and enslaved all those the Sorceress Morgan le Fey sent across. Now all of us are free, or will be as we liberate them. We owe it all to Ted, Monica, and Woe Betide. I don't know how we can ever thank you."

"I didn't do it," Surprise said. "I'm just trying to recover my baby."

"I saw the Prime Monister come to the house," Cadence said. "I saw him flee, so knew you had somehow bested him. The Sorceress must have brought him and the bloodhounds across. We are so glad to be rid of them! Are you a Sorceress yourself?"

Surprise hesitated. "Not quite. I do have magic, but I'm just a girl who wants to go home with her baby. The Sorceress has hidden her somewhere."

"Suddenly I see how we can thank you," Cadence said. "We shall find your baby. She must be in the other realm."

Surprise realized that was probably true. "I must look there."

Cadence shook her head. "Don't cross over yourself; it requires a special ability to return, and the children do it much better than adults do. We have many children who will be glad to help." She looked around. "Auth! Ticity! We need you!"

A boy and girl detached themselves from the confusion and came across. "Sure, Cade," the boy said.

"Whatcha want?" the girl asked.

"These are Auth 'n' Ticity, brother and sister," Cadence said. "They work together to verify anything's validity. They'll be able to tell if any baby we find is yours."

"But I don't even know where to start to look."

"Maybe the familiar cards will provide a clue."

"They're by the house," the peeve said.

They went to the house and found the pile of pictures, which had not been disturbed. Surprise picked them up and sorted through them, seeing many types of animal. Then suddenly she paused. One of them was a picture of Prize!

Auth and Ticity looked at it. "Yes, that's the one," Auth said.

"But how can she be a familiar?" Surprise asked, appalled.

"Anything can be a familiar," the peeve said. "Morgan just seems to have many."

"She keeps them in the other realm," Cadence said. "And summons them across by invoking their pictures. So now we know where your baby is. Unfortunately, only the Sorceress can use her cards."

Surprise remembered how the hawk had come to life. It had been conjured from that other realm. That was where the sorceress stored her creatures. It did make sense. "How can I get her back?"

"Maybe Iffy can help," Cadence said. She lifted her voice. "Iffy!"

Another child responded. As she came toward them, Cadence explained: "Her talent is to create magical items, though she can't do it perfectly. Since she's been to the other realm, she should be able to orient on it."

Then, as the girl arrived, Cadence held up the picture. "We need to find this baby, quickly. Can you make something to point to her? She's in the other realm."

"Sure," Iffy said. "Maybe."

"Maybe?" Surprise asked, uneasy.

Iffy put her hands before her. A small arrow appeared between them. She held it and pointed it at the picture. It flashed. Then she held it over her head. It turned slowly and oriented in a new direction. "That way."

"In the other realm," Cadence reminded her.

"Sure."

Che Centaur trotted up. "I believe we have freed all the folk who were caught in the other realm," he said to Cadence. "I have arranged for a mess area to feed them."

"You've been doing more than that," the peeve said. "You've been talking privately with some of those children."

The centaur shrugged. "Perhaps."

"It is surely a mess, with all those children," Surprise said with as much of a smile as she could muster in her stress.

"But there remains much to do," Che said.

"We'll do it," Cadence said. "You had better help Surprise now. We have a line on her baby."

"Of course," he agreed immediately. "I will take you wherever you are going." There was something slightly measured about his manner, but of course he was under stress too. This whole business was difficult.

"We have an arrow," the peeve said, perching on Surprise's head.

Iffy passed the arrow up to Surprise, then ran off in the direction of the mess area. Surprise held it, and it pointed like a compass, showing them the way. She realized that she could have made a similar arrow herself, had she thought of it. But she wasn't thinking well right now.

"You will be happy to know that Pyra is all right," Che said. "She burned the Monister until it ran so far away it is unlikely to return at all soon. Now she is making her way back here. I offered to carry her, but she said it would take her time to cool off sufficiently to be carried. I must say she did not look as if she were still burning."

"I think she likes you," Surprise said.

He shrugged. "Perhaps. But she says she found a boyfriend during her search for the children. I helped her make a mass of protoplasm that he could inhabit."

"Then she must be waiting for him to get to it."

The arrow wavered. "Ah, this must be where we have to enter the other realm," Che said. He did not seem particularly surprised. "I have learned how to do this, but I think you should learn too, so that you can never be trapped there."

Surprise was in a hurry to recover her baby, but realized that what he said made sense. So she paid attention to his instruction, and practiced, and soon was able to see the spaces and phase into the other realm. It was much like Xanth, only emptier.

"There are two women who know how to enter this realm," Che said. "Cory and Tessa. They call it sidestepping. But it is better for us to do it for ourselves."

They resumed travel through the other realm. "Is Prize all right?" Surprise asked. "Morgan said she would slowly die of exposure."

"And hunger," Che agreed. "Because she needs her mother. But it has not been long; I'm sure she remains in good condition."

"Where is Morgan?"

"That is my concern. I doubt she will allow you simply to come and take your baby. She has to know you are here. The larger question is why didn't she simply take the baby and flee to somewhere so far away you couldn't find them?"

"She still wants my agreement!" Surprise said, a bulb flickering. "She's been trying to trick or force me to give that all along. So I won't come back some other time to claim Prize, if I lose her now."

"That is surely it," he agreed. "I fear there is some last ploy she has in mind. This may be some kind of trap."

"If I have to spring it to recover my baby, then so be it."

"Spoken like a devoted mother," the peeve said. "No, I'm not being sarcastic. I want you to save her."

"Thank you," Surprise said. "I do appreciate it."

16

No Idea

They came to a shimmering glade. There was the bassinet with the baby. And there, after half a moment, was the Sorceress Morgan le Fey, still looking exactly like Surprise herself. Now she wore identical clothing, too. There was even a second little green bird with her. But there was no mistaking her manner. "Very touching, avian poop, and I am being sarcastic." She faced Surprise. "I have just about exhausted my patience with you, you stubborn innocent. I suggest that you give up this futile quest and yield my property to me."

"You can't have my baby!" Surprise said, sliding off the centaur's back and walking purposefully toward the bassinet.

"Then maybe we'll let the centaur select which one of us gets the prize," Morgan said, stepping forward to intercept her. "Is that agreeable to you, you simpleminded creature?"

"Don't agree!" the peeve said.

But Surprise was confident of Che's loyalty. "Certainly. He brought me here for my baby."

Morgan put her arms around Surprise. "That will do. Now we shall give him the chance to make that choice."

"Let go of me!" Surprise said, struggling. But the other girl was as strong as she was.

"In a moment." The ground dropped out beneath them. They fell, entangled, into a developing pit. They rolled and tumbled, locked together. The peeve squawked but did not let go of her hair.

They came to rest at the bottom, unharmed but disheveled and dirty. "Get away from me," Surprise said, renewing her struggle.

This time the Sorceress let her go. "What was the point in that?" she demanded.

"In what?" Surprise asked as she got to her feet and brushed herself off. .

"In dumping us into this awful pit," Morgan said.

"Me? You did it!"

"Well, it won't work. I'm going to float myself right up out of here." But then the Sorceress looked stricken. "Oh, no! It's a null-magic pit!"

"What are you talking about?" Surprise invoked her own float spell. Nothing happened. She tried a different variant of it. Still nothing. She snapped her fingers to make a spark. Nothing.

It was true: magic was damped out here. They would have to scramble out physically. But the wall of the circular pit was vertical, too hard to get a grip on, and too high to jump past. At the brink sat the bassinet; at least it had not fallen in too.

"Now you've gotten us both stuck," Morgan said. "You evil Sorceress."

Surprise stared at her. "What did you call me?"

"Oh come off it, Fey. Don't try to pretend you're me. You'll never fool the centaur."

"Bleep!" the peeve said.

"I was afraid of this," the peeve said from Morgan's head. "I tried to warn you."

"Shut your beak, you little fake!" the peeve on Surprise's head said.

"What's going on?" Surprise asked it.

"She's trying to fool Che into thinking she's you. She's even got a fake peeve."

"You're the fake, you turdy birdy!" the other peeve said.

A dreadful realization was reluctantly crossing Surprise's awareness, like a rain cloud filled with pus. The Sorceress had set this up to make them fall together, so that Che could not tell them apart by sight. That was why she had clung to Surprise as she opened the pit. She had deliberately mixed them up. The peeve knew who she was, because it had clutched her hair, staying with her—but how could Che ever tell the two Surprises and two peeves apart?

Che looked down into the pit. "What happened?" he asked.

"She opened this magic-nulling pit, and now I'm stuck in it with her," Morgan said. "I can't float or conjure myself out. You'll have to fetch me out."

"She's lying," Surprise said. "That's the Sorceress."

Che peered from one to the other. "You look alike, except for the pattern of smudges."

"We *are* alike," Morgan said. "Physically. It's our minds and souls that are different. Please, don't leave me down here with this witch any longer. I'm afraid she'll attack me."

"What a liar!" the peeve said.

"You're the liar!" the other peeve said.

"I can't tell you apart," Che said, looking baffled.

Surprise paused to take stock. "What were you warning me of?" she asked the peeve. "The pit?"

"No, the agreement. Now if Che chooses her, you've agreed. She can take the baby away."

"But I wasn't agreeing to that!" Morgan said.

"It's a standard device from Hell," the other peeve explained to its companion. "Get a person to make a blank agreement, then invoke it in a different way. It's a cheat, but it's valid. She can take your baby."

"Can that be right?" Surprise asked Che, appalled.

"Technically, yes," he said. "But of course I don't mean to give the baby to the wrong person."

"That's a relief," Morgan said.

"Bleep!" the peeve said. "She's got it down pat."

Surprise realized it was true. Morgan had perfected the part. She had evidently planned for this, as a last ploy to get technical permission for her to take the baby. The peeve had known of the Hell technique, but Surprise of course had not. She had literally walked into it.

Now she had to find some way to persuade Che that she was who she was. But how could she, when the Sorceress was mimicking her nature?

"It seems we have a problem," Che said. "I do not want to make a random choice, because there is a fifty percent likelihood of it being mistaken. So I must question the two of you, and ascertain the truth by logic and analysis."

"Of course, Che," Morgan said, exactly as Surprise had been about to.

All she could do was agree. "I trust you, Che."

"First I must ask you to differentiate yourselves," Che said from above. "So I can keep you distinct without confusion. Please, one of you remove your clothing."

Surprise was appalled. "That is not proper," she protested.

"It's against the Adult Conspiracy," Morgan said.

"I realize that, but we are all adults."

"My baby isn't," Morgan said.

Che picked up the bassinet and moved it away from the brink of the pit. "Now there is no underage child present. Please cooperate. I need to be quite sure who provides which answers, even if you get entangled again."

It did make sense. "Scissors, paper, rock?" Surprise asked the Sorceress.

"Okay."

They threw their hands out together. Surprise had Paper. Morgan had Rock.

Morgan sighed exactly as Surprise would have. "I lost." She did not argue further, as Surprise would not have. She was exactly the good sport expected of the real Surprise. Reluctantly she pulled off her dirty clothing. Soon she stood naked. She had a good figure, of course, slender and full in the proper places.

"Ooo-la-la!" her peeve chortled. "You'll freak him out, with your bare—"

"Quiet!" Surprise snapped. Then wanted to bite her tongue. She was playing right into the scene.

"Thank you," Che said. His eyes did seem to be somewhat sweaty, but his voice was steady. "Now I will address questions to you in turn. Please wait until I address you before answering."

Both of them nodded. He had to do it his way. Surprise hoped that his elixir attraction to her form, now displayed so well by Morgan, did not distort his reasoning capacity.

"Bare Surprise: when we abated our illicit passion so as to be able to return to our respective spouses, who felt the most guilt: you or me?"

Surprise stifled a shocked intake of breath. This was one perceptive trick question! How could Morgan know that they had *not* indulged their passion? This would unmask her.

Alas, not so. "We did not do so in any physical manner," Morgan replied. "Therefore there was no guilt to apportion." Somehow she had learned about that.

"Thank you," Che said. "Clothed Surprise, what is your answer to that question?"

"The same," Surprise said, knowing that it sounded as if she was merely copying the real Surprise. The Sorceress must have picked up on the fact that the two of them still had that passion, so had not abated it.

Che gazed at them both, considering. Nude Morgan was breathing hard. Surprise wondered at that, as they were merely standing still on either side of the pit. Then she realized that it was deliberate: the Sorceress was attracting his attention, inciting him to desire her, so that his judgment would be clouded.

"However," Morgan said, "I would do anything to recover my baby, even that. Take me out of here, give Prize to me, and I will share intense guilt with you."

Surprise was appalled. How could anyone make such an offer? She would never have done so.

Then she reconsidered. Yes, she would, to recover her

baby, rather than allow Prize to suffer in the possession of the Sorceress. But again the Sorceress had beaten her to it, and she was temptingly naked. No wonder she had been such a good sport about losing the clothing contest. Maybe she had lost it deliberately, to gain that advantage.

"You would assume that guilt, to save your baby?" Che asked.

"If that is the way it must be, yes," Morgan answered. "Nothing is worth more than her welfare."

He studied her breathing body, which was now artfully posed. Surprise was both disgusted and fascinated. She had learned some things about fascinating centaurs in the course of this adventure. Obviously the Sorceress knew them too.

Of course Che would never accept it. He was an honorable centaur, and besides, he knew better.

"That is persuasive," Che said. "I believe we have an agreement."

Surprise stared at him, shocked. How *could* he? Everything she knew about him, and everything he knew about her, suggested that this was not at all the way it was done, if it was done at all.

"We do," Morgan said. "Fetch me out of here, gallant centaur."

Che spread his wings, flew slowly into the pit, caught Morgan's upstretched hands with his own, flicked her bare body with the tip of his tail to lighten it, lifted her, and swung her onto his back. He ascended, while Surprise watched incredulously. She wasn't able even to voice a protest. This was just so unbearably sudden, amazing, and awful.

"Let me pick up the bassinet," Che's voice said from beyond the rim. "Then I will fly us to a suitable place for the rendezvous."

"By all means," Morgan's voice agreed.

In little more than a moment, which seemed not only brief but cruelly twisted out of shape, they were gone. Surprise was left alone in the pit.

"What a dirty deal!" the peeve said.

She had forgotten the bird. "How *could* he?" she asked

tearfully. "Couldn't he see that that would not be my way?"
Yet, again, she knew she would have done it, had that been
the price of her baby. And she did retain her passion for Che,
so it would not have been onerous, whatever she might try to
pretend. So she wasn't really innocent, much as it pained her
to confess it to herself.

"He should know," the bird agreed. "But the way she was
flaunting that borrowed body of hers, he must have been half
freaked out. Males are like that; their common sense vacates
when they see a desirable body."

"Yes," she agreed sadly. The disappointment and hurt was
threatening to overwhelm her. "Do you mind if I cry?"

"No. I would cry too, if I could. In fact I think I can. I've
been learning how."

Surprise let the tears flow freely. She knew she was
trapped here, perhaps doomed to perish, but her concern was
for the horror her baby faced. All because she had not been
able to persuade Che she was the real Surprise. She had lost
out to the cynical acting of the Sorceress.

"I met a man once whose talent was conjuring forget
whorls," the peeve said. "His name was Levi. I wish he were
here now, so we could forget."

"I don't *want* to forget," Surprise said. "I'd rather suffer
than ever forget my baby."

"I met another who could change the environment with
her emotions. She was Dina. I think you have some of that
talent; this whole pit is bleak."

"It has reason," she agreed bleakly.

"Did you ever wonder how the night mares deliver bad
dreams to Mundanes despite the lack of magic?"

"No. But now that you mention it—"

"Their horseshoes are made of magic dust."

Surprise manage to smile through her tears. "You're trying to divert me, aren't you, peeve? To make me feel better."

"Less worse, anyway."

"It's not working. But thank you for trying." She kissed
the bird on the beak. The remarkable thing was that the
peeve did not protest.

They settled into joint gloom, waiting for nothing. If they had not quite been friends before, they were friends now.

Some time later there was a voice. "Surprise!" It was Che.

"I am here," she responded, not having the heart to add "of course." Where else would she be?

He fluttered to a landing in the pit. "I am sorry."

"You found out you picked the wrong one!" the peeve said, its voice dripping with disgust.

"I did," Che agreed soberly.

"After you gave the baby to the witch."

"Yes."

"So did she pay off before taking off?"

"No. She was gone the moment she held the baby, satisfied that she finally had the necessary permission."

"Serves you right, moron!"

"Peeve, please, don't," Surprise begged. "He couldn't know."

"You don't blame me?" Che asked.

"I can't blame you, Che. She played me better than I did, and she was, well, nude."

"Yes. She made her body most alluring."

"Surprise wouldn't have done that, idiot," the peeve said. "Couldn't you tell?"

Che nodded. "Yes, I could tell. However—"

"You let her dazzle you with the promise of sex!" the peeve said. "Didn't you know she would renege the moment she got what she wanted?"

"I knew," the centaur agreed.

"You *knew*!" For the moment the peeve ran out of words.

"Yes. It was the verification of what I suspected. Surprise would not have reneged, of course—but neither would she have made that particular deal."

"I would have," Surprise said. "If I had to. But not that way."

"Precisely. So I was pretty sure it was Morgan le Fey I was rescuing."

"And you gave her the baby!"

This time Surprise did not protest the peeve's accusation. "If you knew—how could you—?"

"I gave her a baby."

Something was emerging from the fog of her confusion. "Not *the* baby?"

"The real Prize is now with Stymy Stork. I made an arrangement with some talented children to exchange Prize for the baby Kaylynn, whose talent is to change her appearance to any other. Another girl's talent is to exchange places with anyone else. She is Ronica. When we finally located Prize, I signaled them and they got swiftly to work while Morgan was distracted with Surprise. She exchanged with Prize while carrying Kaylynn, then left Kaylynn and exchanged with another person so as to get well clear."

"So the witch got the wrong baby!" the peeve exclaimed, suddenly well satisfied.

"But didn't that leave another person there, where Morgan's fury would strike?" Surprise asked. "She might return when she discovered she had the wrong baby."

Che smiled. "I'm afraid I was unkind. That other person is Martin, whose talent is to make people really cold. He would have struck the moment Morgan spied him and attempted some ill deed, if she did. As it was she did not. At least not while I was there."

"Cold?" the peeve asked.

"Attempted?" Surprise asked.

"Morgan would have become a block of ice."

The peeve burst out laughing.

Surprise was doubtful. "But wouldn't that kill her?"

"You softhearted fool!" the peeve said. "Who cares?"

"Not that Sorceress," Che said. "It would take her a day or so to thaw. By that time ペン'd be long gone. Ronica will see that baby Kaylynn is returned safely to her friends. She can exchange with a known person even if she doesn't know where that person is. We simply needed the substitute baby long enough to be sure we identified the right mother for Prize. I am satisfied that you are that one."

"Thank you," Surprise said weakly, still not quite assimilating her sudden change of fortune.

"Those rescued children have been eager to help."

"You cunning rogue!" the peeve said. "All the time you were setting up the trap to catch the Sorceress."

"I did need to be sure. I knew she would not let Prize escape readily, and suspected there would be some sort of faceoff to force Surprise to agree to let her baby go. So I prepared. Timing was essential; had she caught on prematurely she would have hidden Prize elsewhere. Fortunately it worked." He faced Surprise. "I am sorry to have had to put you through this trial. But a mistake was unthinkable."

"Oh, Che!" Surprise cried, this time with tears of relief. She fell forward to hug him.

He caught her and lifted her up, kissing her. She kissed him back, passionately, overwhelmed by the emotion of her reprieve. Somehow there seemed to be an awareness, as if something was watching closely. She hardly cared.

Then he drew back his head. "Oh, Surprise, I love you, but we must not."

That restored her to reality. "We must not," she agreed. "It would be—corrupting."

"Too bad," the peeve muttered. The faint foreign awareness faded, almost as if disappointed. Surprise would have wondered about that, had she not had more emotion to control than seemed proper.

"Now we must return to the others, and go home," Che said.

"Yes." She got on his back, and he spread his wings and flew up out of the pit.

Soon enough they were back with Cadence, Stymy, Stymie, the three children, Pyra, and a man Surprise didn't recognize. "This is Finn, from the Always-Always Moon of Ida," Pyra explained. "My betrothed."

Surprise realized that there was much going on that she hadn't kept up with. "Congratulations," she said weakly as she took Prize from the stork and held her close.

"We're hungry," Ted said.

"There were so many children here they ate up all the good things," Monica explained.

Cadence looked around. "Courtney! Corona!" she called. "We need you."

Two girls ran up to join them, obviously twins. "Anything for the folk who freed us," Courtney said.

"Courtney can make anything grow on a tree," Cadence explained. "Corona can convert Xanth trees to Mundane trees, and vice versa. Courtney, the children need to eat before we go on our way."

"Got it," Courtney said. She stepped up to the nearest acorn tree and touched it. Suddenly new buds sprouted, forming into chocolate pies, candy canes, tsoda pop pods, and assorted other childish delights.

Ted and Monica grabbed what they liked and stuffed it into their faces. "Thank you, girls," Surprise said somewhat dryly. She would have preferred healthier foods, but this did not seem to be the occasion to insist. It would only delay their return trip.

Cadence helped them carry Ted, Monica, and Woe Betide to the Stork Works. "We can never thank you enough for rescuing us," she said to them.

"You and the others helped us just as much," Surprise reminded her.

Then Cadence set wing for the rescued children, for there was still much organizing to do. Just as with the Punderground children, they had to be gotten home to their families. The remaining group entered the Stork Works.

There was the giant Simurgh awaiting them. *Now comes the hard part,* she thought to them. *Locating the correct home reality.*

Surprise remembered that Che had found the Simurgh when looking for the children. She had been caught here, and would be returning with them. "But can you fit inside the chamber where we choose realities?" she asked.

Not in this form, the Simurgh agreed. *I shall change.* Then she shrank into the form of a clothed human woman. "Now I am Serenity, with the talent of spreading peace around me. Please do not bruit my alternate identity about elsewhere."

Indeed, Surprise felt her tensions and nervousness fading

in the presence of Serenity. This was exactly what she needed. "We'll never tell," she said, speaking for all of them.

They entered the inner chamber, where Pyra set up the Reality Mask and oriented it on their home reality. Six pictures appeared. "That's odd," she said. "There should be only one."

"Not so, unfortunately," Che said. "It seems it is as tricky to locate our home reality as it was to locate the one with Surprise's baby. This is because there are so many very similar ones, the equipment simply can't focus that finely."

"But what about my misdelivery?" Stymy asked. "I returned to my original reality without a problem."

"That was because of the fissure between realities," Che said. "They were locked together by that special event. The moment you returned, that fissure closed, and the only way to pass between realities was via the Stork Works. That is quite a different matter, because there are an infinite number of realities, and the storks address them all."

"It was the mischief of the Sorceress Morgan le Fey," Serenity said. "I would be annoyed, were it my nature."

"So how do you propose to run down the right reality?" Pyra asked. "Visit them all, as we did before?"

"That probably would not be effective, because we have no one to verify the correct one by sniffing a baby," Che said. "I shall simply have to judge which one is correct, and hope that I get it right. I am fated to change the history of Xanth, and this may be the occasion. I hope to change it as little as possible."

Pyra sent an obscure glance at him; Surprise recognized it because of her recent experience with the Guilt Trip. What was on her mind? But Che was already focusing on the problem. "Let me examine each of these closely. Please magnify the first."

The first picture expanded to fill the screen. "Please focus it on something with which I am familiar, like the throne room of Castle Roogna."

The throne room appeared. There was King Dor, Queen

Irene, and a centaur just being ushered into the royal presence. "That is Charles Centaur," Che said. "I know him; he is sensible, honest, capable, and stalwart."

Surprise laughed. She hadn't done that in a while. "Haven't you just described all centaurs?"

"And not prejudiced against crossbreed centaurs, such as we winged ones," Che added.

"That cuts the list down considerably," Surprise agreed.

"Turn on the sound," Che said.

The sound came on. "We have an awkward problem at Centaur Isle," Charles said, evidently answering the king's query.

"Tough udders, horse-foot!" the floor said. The king's talent was to talk to the inanimate, and have it answer, and it tended to talk too much in areas he frequented. "You uppity centaurs can just go—"

Queen Irene tapped one foot warningly, and the floor was abruptly silent. She was still shapely, with excellent legs despite her age.

Che smiled. "She always did know how to keep the talking inanimate in line. Her Sorceress talent is to grow plants magically swiftly, but any object on the ground knows better than to peer up under her skirt and say half a word about panties."

"Which is just as well," Surprise agreed. "The inanimate tends to be crude, loud, and not very smart."

"Of course we will help in any manner we can," King Dor said. "We value our good relations with Centaur Isle, though as you know, we also maintain them with the winged centaurs."

"Yes, and I for one approve that," Charles said. "This is a rather different matter. We have discovered that a geological fault is causing Centaur Isle to drift away from Xanth."

"Whose fault?" Irene asked.

"This is a Mundane term," Charles said. "It refers to a certain stress and slippage in the ground that can cause the landscape to rearrange somewhat. If this continues, it will in time remove our Isle from Xanth. We do not desire this."

"Maybe our daughter Io can help," Dor said.

"Next," Che said.

"What's wrong with this one?" Pyra asked.

"In our reality, their daughters are Ivy and Ida. There is no Io."

"That's right," Surprise agreed. "You're correct; that can't be ours, though it looks the same."

The second reality expanded. The scene was the same. "But Ivy's talent is Enhancement," Charles said. "We don't want the fault enhanced."

"This may be ours," Surprise said.

"You centaurs will have to face an unpleasant reality," King Dor said. "Only magic will halt this process. Ivy can enhance the magic in the centaurs so that they can oppose the fault."

"Magic in centaurs!" Charles said, shocked. "This is obscene."

Queen Irene smiled. "To us, the open display of certain natural functions is obscene, but we have learned to accept it in centaurs."

"Just as we have accepted magic talents in humans," Charles agreed. "But we don't ask you to violate your sexual scruples, and don't expect you to ask us to violate our magical ones."

King Dor sighed. "Then perhaps we can contact Demon Litho. He should have the ability to solve your problem, if he cares to."

"I remember Demon Litho," Charles said. "His force is Melding, which means combining at the atomic level."

"Atomic?" Irene asked.

"Another Mundane term," Charles explained, "as we lack an equivalent magical concept. He lost a Demon game millennia past and was forced by the Demon Xanth to meld his world with Xanth's world, underneath. That allowed the voles to leave Litho and enter Xanth. His force also affects the formation of magic dust. But how could he save Centaur Isle?"

"He could meld the underlying rock of Xanth with that

of the Isle," King Dor said. "Thus preventing the Isle from departing."

"This seems promising," Charles said.

"This reality seems promising," Surprise said.

"Yes it does," Che agreed.

"I think not," the peeve said.

They turned to the bird. "Not?"

"Why aren't the inanimate things talking?"

The peeve was right: the floor and furniture should be putting in their annoying remarks. "Dor must have another talent," Che said.

They tried the third picture.

"How do we contact the Demon Litho?" the centaur asked.

"This is not an easy thing, Charleton," Kind Dor said.

"Oops," Surprise said.

They tried the fourth picture. "It can be done," King Dor said. "However—"

"Now comes the kicker," the throne said. "Kick the centaur in the—"

"Tail," Irene said warningly, tapping her foot. "Or I'll shrink you into kindling."

"She shrinks things?" Surprise asked. "Instead of growing things?"

They went to the fifth picture. Surprise was becoming tense. Suppose none of the six fitted perfectly? Of course there had to be one, because their reality couldn't have disappeared. Yet she worried.

"So the Demon will want some sort of payment," Charles concluded. "Do you have any idea what that might be?"

"We did have contact with Litho once before," Dor said. "Our impression was that he wanted an outlet to Xanth proper, so as not to be confined perpetually to the depths. We did not feel free to grant that, but perhaps the centaurs will."

"What would this entail?"

"Probably a central plaza he can use as an entry, and when he manifests in his usual giant form, some centaurs should hasten to serve as his guides on the surface. We understand from the Muse of History that his nature is somewhat imperious and violent."

"We should be able to handle that," Charles said.

"There is likely to be a side effect," Dor continued. "That melding will make Centaur Isle closer to Xanth more than physically. It will become more magical. Centaurs who never evinced magic talents may do so now."

Charles stood silent.

"What's the matter, horseradish?" the floor asked. "Smell something bad?"

"Like a rat?" the nearest wall asked.

"In your hat?" the throne inquired snidely.

Queen Irene lifted one foot high enough to deliver a considerable stomp, and the threat silenced the inanimate jokers. In the process her leg showed a fair sight beyond the knee.

Finn's eyes began to sweat. "That's some leg," he murmured.

Pyra elbowed him. "She's sixty-two years old," she snapped.

He pulled his eyes away with a slight sucking sound. "Promise me you'll have legs like that when you're that old."

"I promise," the peeve said with her voice. The children sniggered.

"I think this is our reality," Surprise said.

"We should check the last one also," Che said, recovering his own eyes as the queen set her foot back on the floor. "Just in case."

"I can't wait only longer. I want to get home with Prize. Please, can't we just go now?"

Che looked around at the others. "Any objections?"

There were none. So they summoned the stork attendant. "This one," Che said, indicating the picture.

Then they walked out of the Stork Works. Everything looked familiar. Now that they had chosen, Surprise was having second or third thoughts, averaging two and a half thoughts. *Should* they have checked the sixth reality?

Serenity turned to Che. "I believe your destiny has been

fulfilled. I hope the change in Xanth history is minimal. Thank you for rescuing me."

"You are welcome," he said.

She became the huge Simurgh, spread her wings, and took off. In three quarters of a moment she was gone.

"That's one big bird," the peeve said. It seemed that it was unable to field a good insult for a bird that awesome.

A stork approached Stymy. It was Stifle, who had been officer of the day at the Information Office. "It is good to see you again, Head Stork."

Surprise was astonished. "You are Head Stork? I thought you were just a routine delivery stork with a troubled record."

"It would be complicated to explain," Stymy said. "But I owe it to you. You have my deepest appreciation."

"But I didn't do anything for you," she protested. "You were the one helping me."

"It was what you didn't do," Stymy said mysteriously. "Believe me, you will never have a problem with any future delivery." He turned to Stymie. "And you will be my consort, of course, with authority beyond any other stork. I am truly glad to have found you."

"I am glad too," Stymie said. They clicked beaks.

"What birdbrained mush," the peeve remarked.

"Now if you will excuse me," Stymy said to the others, "I have a business to attend to."

"Of course," Surprise said faintly.

The two storks departed back into the Stork works.

"Do you need transport to Lion Mountain?" Che asked Pyra.

"No, thank you kindly. Finn and I will make our own way there, and wade through the swamp. But—" She hesitated.

"There is something else?"

"After you make your settlement with Surprise, will you come and make it similarly with me? Finn will understand."

Che stared at her. "I don't understand."

But suddenly Surprise did. "The love elixir! When you crossed with him you got splashed!"

"Something like that," Pyra agreed. "I do not wish to interfere in his life, but the effect lingers until abated."

"I can't commit to that," Che said.

"Perhaps not," Pyra agreed sadly. "But you do know where to find me, if there should be occasion." She turned to Surprise. "I'm glad you prevailed. You may never know how important your victory was."

"But all I did was recover my baby."

"That too." Then Pyra and Finn set off by foot on their own.

"I hate it when folk talk in riddles," the peeve said.

"Don't we all," Che agreed.

That left Che, Surprise, and the three children. "Do you wish to assume a flying form?" Che asked.

"I'm afraid to."

"She's afraid to fly!" Ted exclaimed, laughing.

"In a manner," Surprise agreed. Her illicit passion for Che remained, and clearly his remained for her. She dared not assume a feasible form lest they both got carried away. How were they ever going to get rid of that?

"I believe I can carry the four of you," Che said. "If you will hold Woe Betide so she doesn't fall off."

"No need," Woe said. "The mission is done." She fuzzed and became Metria. "Come on, kids. I'll take you domicile."

"Where, Mom?" Ted asked dutifully.

"Lodgings, habitation, house, dwelling, abode—"

"Home?" Monica asked.

"Whatever," she agreed crossly.

The two children laughed. Metria glanced at Surprise. "Thank you for the babysitting."

"Thank you for what Woe Betide did."

Then Metria became a ball of smoke that enfolded them, and all three were gone.

"We're alone," Surprise said nervously.

"Almost," the peeve said.

"Perhaps," Che agreed. He did not need to remind her that the demoness was not necessarily as absent as she seemed. She was surely quite curious about what Pyra had said, and wanted to see what they did when they had the chance.

"Please fly me home."

"Gladly."

She got on his back, he flicked her and Prize to make them light, and took off.

Was there a ghostly sigh of disappointment in the air?

"You know it can't be," Che said.

"I know."

"Yet—"

"I know," she repeated.

The peeve said nothing. It knew there was something, but that an insult would not accomplish anything.

That was all, externally. They flew across the landscape to her house. Che landed and she got off, feeling her weight recovering.

"Will you be all right?" Che asked.

"I hope so. Now go home to Cynthia."

"I am eager to rejoin her."

"As I am to rejoin Umlaut."

"We do love our spouses."

"We do."

He spread his wings and took off, circling upward. She waited a moment, and when she saw him glance back her way, she waved. He waved, then set off straight for his home.

"Some day you will have to tell me what's going on between you two," the peeve said.

"I'll tell you now: we waded through the love elixir together, but never consummated the urge. Don't tell."

"My beak is sealed."

Prize gazed at the peeve and smiled. It was as if the baby were rewarding the bird for its constancy. Prize had become the most important human being in the peeve's life.

Surprise turned and walked toward the house she had left three days before, carrying her baby. All she had done was recover the baby that should have been delivered without a challenge. Yet how much else had happened along the way!

The peeve peered at the house. "That's odd."

As she came to the door, it opened. Umlaut stood there.

"Surprise! You're home! I worried, but the Good Magician said you were on a special mission and would return soon."

"I was, and did," Surprise agreed, kissing him. "This is Prize, our new baby."

"Great! I had this weird dream that the stork got fouled up on your age. I'm glad that wasn't so."

Surprise kissed him again, then saw something odd. The house—it was the one she knew, certainly—but it was facing the opposite direction. That was what the peeve had noticed.

Could they be in a wrong reality after all? One whose present was the same, but whose history and conventions differed slightly? Were illicit trysts feasible here? She shuddered, dismissing the possibility. She must have misremembered about the house.

"Was the mission interesting, dear?"

"You have no idea."

AUTHOR'S NOTE

Sometimes I wonder whether it was a mistake to turn 70. I had been living a reasonably healthy life, eating well—by that I mean, following a healthy vegetarian diet—exercising, and in general keeping my body and mind in good order. But then things started going wrong. I developed a backache, and soon after I passed 70, an X-ray of my spine showed severe degenerative disk disease. I had to have an MRI—Magnetic Resonance Imaging—which is like being electronically sliced into eighty thin slivers, and take physical therapy sessions, where young women instructed me in various leg bending and stretching exercises, and massaged my spine. I had a front tooth replaced by an expensive implant—and in three weeks it fell out, and I had to have a bone graft there to serve as a basis for a replacement tooth implant. That will take months; meanwhile as I type this, I have a nice hole in my face that makes folk avert their gaze, especially when I smile. It turns out that my prostate is also enlarging; that may or may not be mischief. I wonder what sort of physical therapy they have for that?

At this time Florida was also hit by four hurricanes. We have a repulsion spell to keep them away from us, and that has worked well the past fifteen years, but maybe its batteries got weak, because Hurricanes Frances and Jeanne headed determinedly for us and didn't miss by much. Charley and Ivan also took dead aim on us but were diverted. Male eyes do divert more readily than female eyes. The spell did weaken the ladies' power so all we got were gale-force winds, but that was enough to take out our electric power for a week. We sweltered, and had to throw out our once-frozen or refrigerated food. We flushed toilets by dipping buckets of water from the pool, and ate ambient-temperature meals. We visited our daughter to get showers, as it does get ~~stinky~~ tiresome to be grubby for a week.

So much for my deteriorating personal life. Of course this novel remained in stasis, because my notes and text were locked in the computer. I did make penciled notes covering the midsection, though. When the power returned—ah, relief!—I caught up on backlogged correspondence and resumed writing, and did manage to complete the novel on schedule, as can be seen.

Now before you say that I did lose some marbles from my hollow skull, let me explain that yes, I know there is no reference here to the feeding of a newborn baby, and that babies don't smile in the first few days, unless they're having gas pains. They don't go for days without having natural functions that require diapers and cleaning up. Neither do they recognize green birds and say "Coo!" I have to make something clear: this is Fantasy. If a stork brings a baby, instead of the more messy procedure they seem to prefer in Mundania, surely that baby can prosper without having to be fed in a way that might freak out more conservative readers. Okay?

Of course there were one and a half slews (translation: about 175) of reader suggestions, and I did my best to use them up, with certain exceptions. Some fit so well for the next novel, *Air Apparent,* that I reserved them for that. Some related to the children of characters who do not appear in this novel, so I saved them for when they can appear on-stage, as it were. But the rest were used, up through about SapTimber 2004. I regret that some excellent ideas were given short shrift, simply because there are more good ideas than room in the novel. The development of reader-suggested characters into significant ones, such as Azalea and Pyra, was mostly random; they were there when I needed characters.

Here is the list of credits, in the approximate order of use in the novel. The occasional @ symbols denote the email names of contributors, when I lacked their mundane monikers: Title *Stork Naked* from a Looney Tunes cartoon, and story of a forgetful stork—Barbara J. Hagman. Demon Ted and DeMonica as main characters—Jeannette Nelson. Adult Conspiracy started with Ivy—Darryl R. White. Summoning spots on the wall to analyze—Sabbir Muhit. Spoken words become tangible shapes for art—Susan Cormier. Lighthouse—Michael Irelan. Talent of summoning flying rugs, conjuring useful elixirs, showing what's happening to someone in a hologram—Erin McKee. Talent of confusion—Sonja. Liquid of beer-barrel tree cures a blue nose—William Bennett. Talent of granting wishes only for those with wishes for others—Glenn Mundee. Pleasant Tree—Bailey@. Ash Tree—Ashley Leonard. In-fan-tree, with its unusual fans—Rochelle Boku (Chelle Bell). Ann Serr with the answer—Susan K. Holt. Gross Prophet—Jon Conyers. Thesaurus gives Metria words—Max Jenkins. Dyslexicon—Adam Bracken. Unclear missives of Cuba—Dale Smith. Woe Betide as a character, Simurgh missing, Phrases becoming literal—Nickelle Ismert. Woe Betide as match girl with magic matches—Marvin J. Cox. Demon Ted puts reverse wood on stork—Gina Joven and family. Demon Ted part of a hostile takeover of the Stork Works—Ted Ball. Storks summon the Man—Phillip J. Houx. Gold, Silver, Copper, and extinct Ivory Coasts—SMoon Woman. Stork loses baby's name in forget whorl—Roxanne Gill.

Stork-eating monster—Timothy Ferguson. Lazy storks attach talent to body instead of soul, Punapple Pie—Carolyn Bolger. Stork nests in Iberian cathedrals—Crystal Purcell. A kiss that half-summons the stork—Matthew Presley. F-Bomb makes folk explode with profanity—Vincent Champeau. Azalea, raised by flower fairies—Aaron Ellis. Lion Mountain—Al Horton. Pyra—Bailey. Lotus who talks to flowers, Celest summoning falling stars—Laura Munion. Talent of growing plants on animals—Phun Pun. Talent of the validity of numbers—Dawn Queen. Punderground—John a Tolle. Stopwatch—Joey Morris. Square Meal—Terese Couture. Baby Shower—Lars Cook. Werehouse, Hair Die—Dorian Jensen. Iron Knees—Adam Kestle. Eyer—Coleen Fleshman. Kidnapper—Anne Berlioux. Olive Yew—Little Safiétou. Infant Tile, Penned Ants, Juven Isle, Bellied Ants, Adam Ant, buzzard, Rose Quartz—Anna Bryant. Congenial Tea—Dale Brown. Age Spots—Summer Wilson. The faun & nymph game—Rachita Jain. Pun Gents—David J. Barone. Escape Root—Greg Biscoping. The Loch Ness Monster's siblings—Spader Dunno. Twins Kalt and Frosteind—Cooper and Bernadette. Talent of making any drink from any liquid—Zach Brenske. Wade, who wades through any depth of water—Wade Moriarty. Imp Otence—Joe Leather, Leslie Patterson. Weed Whacker—Jessica Davis. Backpack, diskette—Kayla Michelle Swenson. Talent of being harmed by words, not physical things—Sarah Husbands. Com Plication—Joanne Tessier. Pete Za—Gabe Pesek. Aaron placing wings on objects—Curtis White. Nikki and Clarabelle—Carmin Rose. Dave—Bob Seaman. Billy Applegate—Joshua Watson. Philomena "Mena"—Sherylina & Deborah Leonardi. Ass Fault—Wade Svec. Chasta—Barbara Spencer. Razor Glade—Rachel. Gordian Nut—Gary Appenzeller. Demon S cross-dressing—Stephanie Lindlief. Mountain Peeks—Katie Van Brunt. Cash Shoe—Jay Yates. Tooth Brush—Candace Heath. Goof Ball—Breanna Kay. VooDoo talent—Emioprotector967. Soap Box—Bridgette Allen. Magic pills—Brian Cuz. Steel Wool—Del Branham. Rows

Seeds—Arlis. Spunky Dog—Joshua Watson. Hercules Dog—Kristina Haydee Rivera. A stitch in thyme saves Nine—Ryan Robert Richardson. Being spotted—Bobbi Nunn. Spoonerisms in Xanth—Kermit Scheaffer, relayed by Dave Pierce. Roseate spoonbills uttering spoonerisms— Carol Jacob. Sophia Isadora—Laura Stansell. Devin Mc-Clane Kowalick—Rachel Kowalick. Thinnet—David Kaplan. Ark-hives—Nehemiah Lewrel. Invest-i-gators— Stephen English. Talent of repressing a single memory in someone—Summer Lei Shidler. Barbie Que—Elihu Hernandez. Ten-tongued wolf/ram (tungsten)—Mike Bennett. Hidey, who hides—Ethan Suntag. Talent of interpreting dreams—Lydia Nelson. Denizens live in dens—Kevin. Metria's Buick Rock—Stephen and Padraic Kenny. High C, middle C, low C—Damire1249@. The Mariner—Jason Rashid Floyd. Diana—Daphne Johnson. Dark and Stormy Knight—Albert J. Gallant. Chaska, human/demon girl— Brianna & Chris Haining. Vitamin Sea—Michael Ybarra. Challenge and Chellony Centaur—Amanda Howard. Who assigns talents for late adults?—Jessica Lee. Minor talents of Trent's soldiers—Ed Starr. D. Flate neutralizing Filly Buster—Gabe Pesek. Lazy bone cures WORK ethic curse— Robert Pickthall. Diary/diarrhea plant—Christopher Walsh. Magic/Mundane (manic/depressive) cycling—Jim Seawright. Talent of reading minds only when people are thinking bad or evil, talent of switching locations with another person—Monica Marie Ruiz. Fingers that shave off hair— Jason Vasquez. Fannie's Fans—Kelley Huston. Chicken Pox—Timothy Pierce-Tomlin. Lice make a person lie— Yasir. James controlling sunbeams, Scott dematerializing atoms—Tim Jorgenson. Lliane and Lliana making illusions real or real thing illusion—Rebecca Heath. Jean Poole and her ancestry—Robbie Demko. Fairy Tails—Jeff Steinbrugge. Pummelgranites—Timothy Fox. Explanation for Surprise's talents, twin sisters who make anything grow on trees, or switch Xanth and Mundane trees—Courtney Loose. Donald, Dolph and Nada's son—Sam Blanchard. Guilt Trip—Devonia Newsom. Punk Rock with bad attitude—Gary Bushman. Sick Leaves—Colin Virshup. Circle Drive and fork—Elijah Reynold. Blonde centaur/unicorn crossbreed—Eylsia Brenner. Prime Monister—Ryan Bennett. Cassy and Caitlin Centaur—Caitlin Elyssabeth Harris. Mt. Pinatuba on a moving saucer—Jason Kincaid. Mustard seed's amount of faith moved Pinatuba—Steve Fisher. Akimbo who makes tangles, Extricate who sorts out tangles—Ryan "Ogre" Johnson. Teddy Bare, who makes folk naked—Ryan Bennett. Arlis, always called by a nickname—Arlis Monzeglio. Talent of tying things in nots—Susan Gingrich. Skyla—mistress of the sky—Agent Llyr. Miranda and dog Old—Maria Alina Garcia. Talent of making folk freak out—Tish Overall. Talent of figuring things out—Sonya Hylton. Ability to summon tsoda popka—Stephanie Howard. Cadence, winged centiger—Caitlin Grimsley. Tu-Morrow telling of tomorrow—Ana Novo. Ruth Sutpen and Amber—Chris Bymaster. Werecat with any human form—Raina "Tiger" Neal. Numb Chuck with the nunchaku—Ethan. Leviathan with elf form and mass of whale—Levi Morrow. Evil Sorceress stopped by a child beneath the Adult Conspiracy—Breanna Larson. Auth 'n' Ticity verifying things—Bailey. Iffy, creating magical items—Cynthia R. Haynes. Levi who conjures forget whorls—Levi Morrow. Talent of changing the environment with her emotions—Dina Burgess. Night mares have shoes made of magic dust—Stephanie Howard. Baby able to change appearance—Kaylynn Johnsen. Talent of making people really cold—Joseph Martin. Serenity, spreading peace—Serenity Wilson. Centaur Isle drifting out of Xanth, needs magic—Timothy D. Koughan. Explanation for Demon Litho and the voles—Jim Delaney.

That's it, until the next. Harpy reading!

Turn the page
for a sneak preview of the next
Xanth novel

AIR
APPARENT

by Piers Anthony

(0-7653-0410-4)

Available now from Tor

TOR®

www.tor.com

Wira was uneasy. Her husband Hugo had been absent half an hour, and it wasn't like him to stay away longer than he said. Especially not this night.

For tonight, after seventeen years of marriage, Hugo's father Good Magician Humfrey had finally removed the Spell of Hiding that kept the storks from being aware of Wira no matter how ardently she summoned them. She was fifty-five years old chronologically, thirty-three physically, and her thyme was starting to wilt. If they waited much longer, the storks would never deliver to her, regardless of any spell. This time the signal would go out. She knew that Hugo was eager to send that signal, and so was she.

Where was he? He had gone to the cellar to fetch a celebratory bottle of Rhed Whine. That should have taken no more than ten minutes, and he would hardly have dawdled. Something was wrong.

Wira got off the bed, donned a nightrobe and slippers, and made her way out of their chamber. She pattered down the familiar stairs to the ground floor, and thence to the cellar. She knew every crevice of the castle, of course, and made no misstep.

But as she reached the cellar floor, she experienced a faint tinge of uneasiness. Her magic talent was Sensitivity, and though it normally applied to people, plants, and animals, it could sometimes attune to situations. This situation was uncomfortable.

"Hugo?" she called tentatively.

There was no answer.

The tinge became less faint. In fact, it intensified into a wary semblance of dread.

"Hugo, where are you?" she called less tentatively.

There was a definitely untentative silence.

Something was wrong. Not only was Hugo absent, there was something else in the cellar. She smelled its misty essence.

She snapped her fingers. Little magic echoes bounced off the cellar walls and floor, verifying its dimensions. Except for a muffled place on the floor, the vague shape of a man lying down.

Had Hugo fainted? But this wasn't Hugo. The shape was vaguely wrong, and of course the smell.

She squatted and reached forward to touch it. Her fingers encountered a clammy kind of flesh. It was definitely not quite alive.

Wira screamed.

The Gorgon, Humfrey's Designated Wife of the Month, and coincidentally also Hugo's mother, was the first to respond. "Wira, dear," she called from the head of the cellar stairs. "What's the matter? Are you hurt?"

"Oh, Mother Gorgon, there's a dead man here, and I think he's not quite human. And Hugo is gone."

There was half a pause. "This bears investigation. Let me fetch a lamp."

Wira waited by the body while the Gorgon got the lamp.

Wira did not need light, of course, as she was blind. She had always been that way, and really did not mind it as long as she was in familiar territory. But others had some kind of problem with darkness.

She heard the returning footsteps, smelled the curling vapors of the lamp, and felt its slight warmth. There was also the faint sibilance of a small nest of snakes. The Gorgon was back and ready to take charge.

Wira had always gotten along well with the Gorgon. That was partly because the Gorgon's face tended to turn others to stone, but Wira could not see it, so was not at risk. That enabled them to be friends without precautions. The Gorgon was actually a very nice person, but strangers tended to be prejudiced by her magic face, and were nervous about her snake hair. The snakes were normally friendly, and could be good company on a dull day.

"It is definitely a body," the Gorgon said. "It's not breathing and it's cold, so it must be at least halfway dead. But who killed it, and what is it doing here?"

Wira had a horrible thought. "Oh Mother Gorgon, you don't suppose Hugo could have—have—"

"Of course not, dear. Hugo doesn't have a murderous bone in his body. Not even a stiff one, as far as anyone knows. When are you two going to signal the stork?"

"Tonight," Wira said, blushing. Sometimes the Gorgon's language was a trifle serpentine. But she had reason: her sister the Siren was long since a grandmother. She seemed to have forgotten about the stork-hiding spell.

Now the Gorgon had a nasty thought. "You don't suppose he could have gotten cold feet, or whatever?"

"Never," Wira said positively. "He wanted to—to do it. To be a father."

The Gorgon sighed. "He's so young."

"Mother, he's forty-three."

"Exactly."

Wira didn't argue the case. Technically she was a dozen years older than Hugo, but she had been youthened to sweet sixteen to marry him, so seemed a decade younger. Mothers always thought their sons were too young. "He wouldn't have left without word to me. Especially not tonight. Something must have happened to him."

The Gorgon was focusing on the body. "I have another foul thought. Maybe somebody killed this poor man, dumped the body here, and abducted Hugo to frame him for the murder. That would explain everything."

"Except where Hugo is, and who the victim is, and who the real murderer is," Wira agreed.

"Yes, there may be a detail or three to fill out. We'd better get Humfrey in on it."

"But it's night time," Wira protested. "He gets grumpy when disturbed at night."

"He gets grumpy any time," the Gorgon said. "You don't see much of it because you have an ameliorative effect on him. I think if he'd been half a century younger he would have married you himself."

"Mother Gorgon!" Wira exclaimed, horrified.

"Oh come on now, girl. You know he's taken with you."

"Because I'm his daughter-in-law."

"That, too. Anyway, he already has about five wives too many; he certainly doesn't need any more. Now I'm going to get him up, grumpy or not, and bring him down here to fathom the situation. It will give him another pretext to bury himself in the Book of Answers."

"Oh, I hope the Answer is there!" Wira breathed. "I miss Hugo so much!"

"He's been gone only half an hour, dear."

"Yes, and it's awful."

The Gorgon gazed at her. Wira could tell when someone was looking at her; there was a certain subtle mood. "You really do love him, don't you, dear."

"Yes!"

"And that is why *I* am taken with you, Wira. Without you he's pretty much of a rotten-fruited gnome."

"He is not!"

"Of course not, dear," the Gorgon agreed, smiling knowingly. Wira could also tell when a person was smiling; it curled up the corners of the voice. Then the Gorgon went off to roust out the Good Magician.

Wira remained in the cellar, uncertain what else to do. She knew the Gorgon meant well, but the woman sometimes unnerved her. Meanwhile, there was this awful situation to deal with. Could someone really have tried to frame Hugo for the murder? To make it seem that he had committed a terrible crime, and fled the scene? But how could such a thing have been done here, in the Good Magician's Castle? The castle was enchanted to exclude all but the most powerful magic.

Yet something of the sort had happened. That was frightening in itself.

She checked the shelves along the cellar wall, just in case there was some indication that would help resolve the mystery. She knew the stored potions by the shapes of their bottles and faint odors. The first shelf held bottles of pills from pharm-assist plants that a pill pusher had harvested for the Good Magician long ago. The pills lent certain temporary talents to those who swallowed them. There were gra-pills that enabled folk to wrestle well, purr-pills that caused folk to turn reddish blue while feeling very satisfied, and ap-pills that kept doctors away. Also princi-pills for those lacking in ethics, sim-pills for those with too much intellect, and pill-fur coats for those who didn't mind stealing clothing. All was in order, undisturbed.

The next shelf contained assorted gloves or mitts reserved for particular Challenges: an amity, which made a person very friendly, an enmity which had the opposite effect; a hermit, which was a solitary lady's glove; an imitate that enabled a person to copy things; a comity that made the wearer courteous; an emit, that caused a stink; an omit that somehow had been left off the list; a submit that could be used under water; a permit that allowed almost anything; and an admit that added a glove and also let a person into the castle. At the end of the shelf was a vomit that she knew, better than to touch. None had been disturbed. The problem seemed to be confined to the (ugh) body.

"Ludicrous, woman," Humfrey's voice came grumpily from above. "Can't it wait until morning?"

"Do you want poor Wira to stay in the cellar all night?" the Gorgon's voice retorted.

Wira had to smile, wanly. The Gorgon was using her to make Humfrey mind. It was true that the Good Magician liked her, though Wira was sure it was not in the way the Gorgon had implied. Wira was sensitive to his moods, and so could manage him to an extent. And of course she was helpful around the castle. That was important, as the castle needed constant attention. The assorted Wives came and went every month, and Hugo wasn't much for detail work, so that left it mostly up to Wira. Fortunately she liked details.

The Good Magician arrived at the scene. "That's not exactly a dead body," he said immediately.